T. Torrest

DOWN THE SHORE
A rock-and-roll romantic comedy

For My Parents

who took us on countless trips
to the Jersey Shore.

Down the Shore
T. Torrest

Cover design: Hang Le
www.byhangle.com

First Edition 2015
Second Edition 2016

Just a quick note about our characters:
If you read an early version of *Remember When*, you may notice the discrepancy with Jack's name. Originally, he was Jack Danner, but his surname has since been changed to Tanner. No biggie, but I didn't want to confuse anyone. Carry on.

DOWN THE SHORE

CHAPTER 1

(Technically) Friday, May 26, 1995
1:21 AM

Brendan Byrne Arena (backstage)
East Rutherford

I rehook my bra and pull my micro-sized concert tee back over my torso as Rider MacLaine stuffs his dick back into his jeans.

Rider's the lead singer of Dark Forest, the awesome alternative band that opened for Pearl Jam tonight. My friend Tess and I had front row seats, enabling Rider and me to do some serious eye-fucking during the show. About midway through Pearl Jam's set, we received The Message, like I figured we would. A security guy had come over to Tess and me with a couple of backstage passes, and I knew Rider was looking for a little more than just sight sex.

So I blew him. Sue me.

His band was phenomenal and it was the least I could do to say "thank you." Except that I just happened to say it by taking off my shirt and wrapping my lips around his cock. And he said "you're welcome" by pulling out and shooting his wad into his nearby sweat towel.

Kind of gentlemanly, right?

Rider's pretty hot, but I'm not expecting to ever see him again. That's the mistake most girls make: mooning over the posters on their walls, dreaming too hard about the rock star staring back at them. Pinning all their hopes on just that one chance to try and make the guy their own; envisioning a happily ever after with some guy who doesn't even know they exist.

If you happen to be one of those girls, I'll save you a lot of trouble right now and let you in on a little secret:

There's no such thing as happily ever after.

1

"So, listen," he starts in. "We're leaving Jersey tonight. I'd get your number, but…"

"Rider," I laugh out. "You think I'm expecting you to *call* me?" I cross my arms against my stomach, trying to contain my laughter.

That brings a smile to Rider's face. "I guess I just thought you'd expect me to at least *ask*."

The guy is gorgeous, he's an amazing musician, he's got a great big beautiful cock, and now I come to find that he has a conscience. A girl could do worse. But I'm not delusional enough to think that that girl will ever be me. "Don't sweat it, Rider. All I was expecting from you was a little fun and that's what I got. Thanks." My eyebrows rise as I try to contain my smile.

Rider's amused. He puts his shirt back on and says, "You're pretty cool, uh…"

"Livia," I finish for him.

"I knew that."

"Sure you did."

I roll my eyes and we both laugh.

"Hey, listen. Maybe I was just trying to be nice before, but I think you're really cool. I actually *want* to call you next time I'm in town. How 'bout that number?"

I'm flattered by the offer. But this scenario is nothing new; I've been here before. These rockers are probably so sick of girls trying to tame them, trying to lay some sort of claim just because the guy dropped a load in their presence. When a girl like me comes along, a girl who isn't looking for some lifetime commitment, it's a breath of fresh air.

"How 'bout we just plan on maybe seeing each other next time you're playing here. If I'm around, I'll find you."

He gives me a nod, then holds out his fist. "Rock on, Livia."

I fistbump him back. "Rock on, MacLaine."

Rider reclaims his hand and starts to walk off. "Well, I guess I'll see ya. Thanks for the head."

Ugh. The guy is an amazing lyricist, and *that's* his parting line?

I shake my head at his retreating form as the inevitable regret sets in. I have to admit that I don't necessarily have all my shit together. But then again, I'm only twenty-three. No one has their life figured out at twenty-three, am I right? Caught somewhere between my teen years and the rest of my life, I have no idea who I'm supposed to be.

But hot damn, is it so wrong to have a little fun while I try to figure it out?

I brush off my tights, straighten my miniskirt, and head back into the VIP room to check on Tess. She's sitting on a green couch talking up the drummer, Sal, and I know that there's no way she's already taken care of business. Tess has always been a love 'em and leave 'em type of gal, so it's a rare occasion when I see her still making small talk with her latest conquest. She's so flipping gorgeous that most guys come pretty quickly, and she's found that she doesn't have much use for them after that. I swear, the girl's life is a constant search for the guy who can hold out long enough to get her off.

So, either Sal is the magic stud who has somehow breeched that wall, or she hasn't closed the deal with him just yet. Based on their current body language, I'm guessing the former scenario is bloody unlikely. Damn. Now I have to wait on her to get the deed done, and that means we might be here for a while. I'm no slouch, but nine times out of ten, *she's* the one waiting for *me* to finish up, based on that whole Quick Draw McGraw situation I just mentioned. It's already late and I'm tired, but there's no getting around it: I know it's my turn to play backup for my girl.

Payback's a bitch.

I grab a beer from the bar and join them on the couch.

"So, you went to med school?" Tess asks Sal. "That's incredible. Hey Liv, check it out. Not only is he an amazing drummer, but Sal here is also a *doctor*."

Sal laughs. "No, no, no. I never graduated. I said I went to med school. I didn't say I got my degree."

Those two are yukking it up as my eyes scan the room for Rider. I expected to see him back in here, trolling for his next object of prey. Not that the chase would've been a problem for him. Trust me, I wasn't the only girl in that audience who wanted to get him backstage.

3

In my experience, I've found that there are two types of rockstars:

1. Those that nail some random groupie before calling it a night, and
2. Those that nail *numerous* random groupies before calling it a night.

I'm only mildly surprised to find that Rider falls into the first category. Good for him. I really did like the guy, and I don't want my favorable impression of him tarnished.

In any case, that's neither here nor there. I'm more focused on the fact that I now have to rally for the endless evening still ahead of me, and shit. I've got work tomorrow.

"Hey Liv. I'm beat. Ya wanna get out of here?"

Tess's words surprise me, but I'm not about to argue. Sal looks a bit taken aback, but I don't doubt that he'll be able to find a second-string tight end with which to spend his evening. That he's already made his way over to the bar to talk to another girl shows me that he doesn't doubt it either.

Now that it's just the two of us here on this scratchy couch, I ask Tess, "What's going on? You and Sal not getting along?"

Tess plays with the strap of her Coach wristlet. "No, he was really nice. But I'm just not up for it tonight. We can stay and just hang out though, if you want."

No, thank you. I've already made my kill for the evening. There's really no reason to hang around. "No. I'm actually tired, too. Let's bolt."

Tess and I are normally partners-in-crime for this sort of thing. She's a music lover like me, so we typically spend our weekends checking out the local bands at the nearby clubs. But when an actual band like Pearl Jam comes to town? Tess and me are all over that shit.

Tess is a bit of a rock slut like me.

That circumstance is only due to the fact that I am a born-and-bred, unapologetic lover of all things musical. Always have been, always will be.

I'm a bit obsessed with rock and roll, but that doesn't stop me from digging *all* music, even the bad stuff. Rap. Country. Pop. There's a time and place for everything. I truly get that.

And regarding the good stuff, how could I possibly dig rock without tossing a nod to the masterminds who were responsible for it? Jazzy greats like Django Reinhardt. Louis Armstrong. Miles Davis. Bluesy tunes like "The Thrill is Gone" or "Georgia on My Mind" always make me melt, and a voice like Billie Holiday's goes down like warm maple syrup on a piping hot pancake. It's comfort food for my ears.

Going back even further, you've got your masters, the guys who started the whole music revolution in the first place. Bach and Beethoven. Tchaikovsky and Chopin. And the big daddy of them all, the guy who was so cool, Eddie Van Halen named his kid after him: Wolfgang Amadeus Motherfucking Mozart. The dude kicked some serious ass.

So, truly, I can appreciate all of it.

Even with that said, Tess and I are pretty much rock-and-roll chicks above all else. And when we find ourselves confronted with a band full of hot guys who just happen to be super-talented to boot? Well, it doesn't take much more than that to get us wrapped around their little fingers.

Or other body parts.

Just to be clear: If the band sucks... we don't.

Normally, we'll call dibs early on during the show, and most times, we manage to weasel our way backstage to meet our prospective partners for the evening. Tess is hot and she's always been the type of girl to get noticed, so having her in my camp makes that possibility a little easier to invoke.

Once we get backstage, the story is always the same. We get invited into the VIP room where our sweaty, exhausted rock stars are already whooping it up and drinking their faces off with all the other hopeful girls like us.

The key is to get their attention early. Separate yourself from the crowd.

While the rest of the girls are hanging all over the guys and trying to get them to leave the room, Tess and I tend to use a

5

different tact. We'll normally grab a bottle of champagne and make a big production of opening it, laughing our heads off as we try to get it uncorked, bending and twisting and "fighting" over which one of us is going to get the honors. It's a performance we've played out a million times. With all the commotion, we'll manage to draw a bit of attention, and by the time the cork pops, all eyes are on us. Works every time.

I mean, if we actually went through the trouble to get our asses backstage, the guys have just presumably played an amazing show. They're not looking to leave the room yet; they're looking to *celebrate*. So, Tess and I try to make it pretty clear that we're there to just hang out and party, toast their success, help them blow off a little steam.

They appreciate that.

After a little while, once I've got my target winnowed out and he's got a few drinks in him, it doesn't take long for him to make his move. *That's* when I know he's ready to leave for a more, ah... *private* party.

And I never disappoint. I'm not one of those cock-teases, crushing on some rock star from afar, pouting when our first kiss doesn't have him falling madly in love and proposing to me right there on the spot. Hell, sometimes we don't even *have* a first kiss before the guy is unbuttoning his fly.

And I am totally cool with that.

I already have a boyfriend anyway.

Well, sort of. I've been dating this guy Mitch for a while. Only like three months or so, and it's *well* established that we're not exclusive.

"So, how'd it go with Rider?" Tess asks once we're outside.

"Okay, I guess. He was really nice."

"Was his *dick* nice?"

That makes me laugh. "Yeah. We became pretty close friends almost immediately."

"Details."

"Blowjob."

"Rock on."

6

And that's really all I need to tell her about the encounter. I could go into the whole story, but it's not like Tess needs to live vicariously through me. She's had plenty of encounters of her own.

Just not tonight. Oh well.

We get into the car and Tess immediately blasts the radio. We'd listened to Pearl Jam the whole way here, but since we're new fans of Dark Forest, we change out the CD for the one we bought at the concession stand at the arena.

It really was a good night.

As I hear the rumbling strains of "Turning Point" blaring out of the speakers, I hold up my palm to my friend. She smacks it for a high five and then we head home.

CHAPTER 2

Friday, May 26, 1995
8:42 PM

Our Car
Garden State Parkway

My sister Vix is at the wheel as usual. She cuts through some back streets and empties the vehicle onto Route 3, then takes the onramp for the Garden State Parkway, coming to a near stop almost immediately. Typical.

The original plan was to head down to our beach house early tomorrow morning in order to avoid the Parkway clusterfuck. On a weekend, the traffic going to the beach is bad enough. But on a holiday weekend? It would be quicker to *crawl*. I've spent enough hours on this road to know that by now.

The problem is that my sister got a bug in her brain about hitting *The Tradewinds* to check out a band, and we had to hit the road a day earlier than we'd originally intended. Vix is my polar opposite when it comes to hooking up with random rock stars, but she does enjoy hearing their music. So do I, normally, and The Tradewinds is a really cool rock club. But I was out pretty late with Tess last night, and because I had to put in a full day's work only a few short hours later, I'm not sure I have it in me.

I have a job I really like, but I don't know yet if it's going to be my *career*. I love taking pictures, so the work itself is okay, but my boss pretty much sucks ass most of the time. If it weren't for her, the actual job would be pretty cool. Even still, I don't really love being stuck inside a windowless studio all day long, trying to get all those cranky kids to smile pretty for the camera. Taking family portraits for a living isn't necessarily the most inspiring venture, as one could hardly call the finished products *art*. My creativity isn't being sparked under such oppressive circumstances.

8

That's why I take every opportunity to bring my camera out into the real world as much as possible. I'm no photojournalist and TIME Magazine won't be beating down my door anytime soon, but I find I'm most inspired when I can take pictures of the things that, well, inspire me.

Inspiration is important.

I have this great Minolta Maxxum 400 with interchangeable lenses that I use for work, but I was forced to bring a more compact 35 mm to the concert last night. The cheapo-cam is a far cry nicer than the pink Le Clic I had in high school, but not the ideal device for taking the most optimal shots. It was, however, the only thing I was able to smuggle past the security guards. I'm pretty sure I managed to get some good photos, and am just dying to see what I ended up with. Fridays at *The Studio* are normally our "darkroom days," and I originally thought I'd be able to spend a little more private time with the members of Dark Forest while I developed the pix this morning. But Shana had other ideas, and instead, I spent my entire day cleaning out the storeroom until I eventually dragged myself home, exhausted.

I'd initially been looking forward to a date with my bed and then maybe one later on with my "boyfriend," but when Mitch didn't call, I figured I'd suck it up and salvage my Friday.

Because I'm riding shotgun, I assume the required DJ duties, flipping through random stations until I come across an "Eighties Weekend" on WPLJ. Vix shoots me a knowing look when Madonna's "Lucky Star" comes on. I immediately break into as much of a dance routine as I can manage in the passenger seat, then we both start laughing.

Vix says, "I can't believe you still remember our dance to this song."

I fire back with, "We were such idiots."

The two of us are subjected to an onslaught of awesome, cheesy, retro tunes as we make our way down to Sea Bright. It makes our slow pace easier to bear.

When we hit the second toll booth, Vix throws a handful of uncounted pennies into the basket. She takes off before the "go" light turns green, in the midst of the *chinkachinkachink* sound of the change counter maddeningly trying to calculate what has to be forty coins. The "didn't pay" buzzer sounds and Vix drops a hand low out the window to give the finger.

"What was that for?" I ask.

"It's for when I get that picture of the back of my car sent to us with the fine. I want to see if you can see me doing it."

That cracks me up.

"Besides, they deserve the bird for being wrong. I mean, I *paid*, didn't I?"

I shake my head. "Yeah... with pennies, you freak."

"Shut up."

The logjam of cars breaks up after the toll—thank God—and we pick up a bit of speed. We drive along, singing or chatting until Vix finally states the obvious. "See? We're already having fun. Isn't this better than waiting on Fonzie?"

I can't suppress a snicker at my sister's latest slam on Mitch. Vix has referred to him as everything from Easy Rider to Evel Knievel in the three months since I started dating him. Yes, he has a motorcycle. It's a pale yellow Harley and he looks fricking hot on the thing.

"Fonzie. That's a new one."

Vix laughs. "Yeah, but it's a good one. And you know it." She punctuates her statement with a self-congratulatory pat on the back before adding, "Besides, would you rather I go back to calling him 'Jackass'?"

I haven't heard from the guy since Tuesday, but thought for sure that he'd want to see me over the weekend. He always waits until the last possible minute to call with weekend plans, which is a little unsettling. It always manages to make me feel like he's waiting for something better to come up. I can't help feeling sometimes like I'm his consolation prize for bigger plans gone awry.

I don't normally put up with such crap from a guy, but it's just that he is *so damned good-looking.* He's been trying to break into acting the past few years, and let me tell you, this guy has the goods to make that happen.

And yet, after three months, I still have no idea where we are.

Nor do I care.

Basically, I suck at dating.

Not that Mitch is super relationship material, but he's a guy from my *real* life. Let's just say a pizza delivery guy with thespian aspirations doesn't get my panties in a twist (or around my ankles) in quite the same way a musician does.

Sex isn't why he's been sticking around anyway. If I had to guess, I'd say it's because he likes all those free headshots I've been supplying him with.

I know that it's not the greatest relationship, but he's the only prospect at the present moment and he's not really a bad guy. Well, he's a little bad. But I liken it to the Eating-Too-Much-Halloween-Candy variety of bad, not the Crying-On-Oprah's-Couch kind of bad.

After all, it's not like I'm head over heels in love with the guy or anything. We're just having a little fun.

On the days that he actually makes plans to see me.

Which are becoming increasingly infrequent as of late.

"Subtle, Vix. I'd appreciate it if you could refrain from calling my boyfriend a jackass." I stick my hand out of the car and let it surf along a wave of air as I concede, "Even though he is one."

Looking out at the speedblur of pines parading past my window at sixty-five miles an hour, I'm thinking about the turn of events over the past few weeks. "I'm pretty sure it's over between me and Mitch anyway."

Fonzie has jumped the shark.

Vix doesn't offer any commentary, and I'm sort of relieved about it.

I pause long enough to grab the Bic off the dashboard and light a cigarette. I'm expecting my sister to ream me out for smoking in our brand new Sebring but she wiggles two fingers at me, so I light one for her, too.

She takes a long pull and asks, "Have you talked to Mom or Dad at all? I haven't heard from them since last week."

Our parents are off on another excursion. Dad's band will roadtrip to play at rock festivals pretty regularly throughout the fall and spring, but once summer hits, they're gone *all* the time.

I guess some people would refer to my father as a struggling musician. But when you've been struggling for over thirty years, I don't know that that term is the best way to assess his lifestyle.

Music always played a huge role in our lives. Mom is a dancer—ballerina, not pole—and she teaches classes to the local kids in the basement of our house. She'd converted the space into a respectable studio a million years ago, and has a decent business going.

Between my father's music, my mother's dancing, and my photography, we're a pretty artistic bunch. The three of us have no idea where Vix came from. She's a personal assistant for D'Artagnan Maybury, CEO of *Manhattan Media*. Real white-collar, blueblood kind of shit. The people at her company would have a fricking conniption if they knew about any of the hippie nonsense she's been surrounded with since birth.

"Yeah," I answer Vix, playing with the frayed edge of my CBGB cami. "I talked to Mom for a couple minutes yesterday. They're in Vermont, I think, but they're coming back home because Dad's got a Brownstone wedding this weekend. They want us to come over for dinner on Monday."

"Fabulous."

"Well, if Mom's doing the cooking, it just might be."

Vix doesn't miss a beat as she slams a fist into my arm and shouts, "Punchbuggy!"

"Oww!" I yelp, and then even though there are no other VWs in our vicinity, I punch her back.

"Cheater!"

"You started it."

"I saw a Beetle! Those are the rules." She twists her right arm and peeks down her shoulder for an impromptu inspection. "If you gave me a bruise, I'm gonna kill you."

Vix is the furthest thing from a bad-ass, so I know her well enough to recognize when she's only barking.

And man, does she like to bark.

CHAPTER 3

Friday, May 26, 1995
9:43 PM

The Tradewinds
Sea Bright

We pull into the lot at The Tradewinds and do a quick mirror-check before heading for the door. Bypassing the long line out front, Vix gives me a wink as we head right for Clipboard Guy at the front of the line.

"What are you doing?" I ask, trying to ignore the grumbles from the awaiting club-goers we're presently trying to cut in front of.

"You'll see," is all she offers before turning to Clipboard Guy. "Chadwick? We're on the list."

Clipboard Guy is on a power trip, because he makes a big show of scanning down the list of names in his hand before granting access with an authoritative and entirely-too-serious nod of his head.

We file into the blue glow of the club and head for the bar as I ask, "Was he kidding?"

Vix lets out a snort and answers, "I hope so."

The place is packed as usual and my God, it's loud as hell already. We have to fight for every step as we inch our way to the bar. The Tradewinds is a *huge* club. High, curved ceilings and insulated for sound by the long bars that line the perimeter.

Vix reaches behind her and grabs a belt-loop of my jeans, ensuring we won't lose each other in the sea of people. The room is so crowded and the main band isn't even supposed to go on for another hour. But all the locals—mostly women—have already turned out in full force to catch a glimpse of the almost-famous Jersey boys.

As I squeeze past a rowdy group of surfer guys, I yell to Vix, "How the heck are we on The List? I thought you said we were coming to see Thunderjug."

I hadn't originally wanted to get out of bed tonight, but once Vix mentioned who the band was going to be, I jumped all over it. Thunderjug is a name I actually know. They're a newish band on the scene—local guys from up near home if I'm not mistaken—that currently have a hit song playing on the New York stations. It's always exciting to catch a band on their way up. Even if "Backyard" turns out to be a one-hit-wonder, it's still one hell of a song and will be enough to hold my interest through the night, waiting to hear it.

"Ronnie is friends with one of the guitarists."

"Ronnie? He knows these guys? No way. How cool is that?"

Our friend Ron Somers used to work at *The Sharper Image* a few stores down from me at *The Studio.* He and I hit it off pretty early on and used to do lunch together every now and then. He's gorgeous in an All-American kind of way: Colossal bod, straw-blond hair, and a misleading, apple-pie smile that could charm the skirt off a choir girl.

A total player in every sense of the word.

Vix is trying to carve out a space at the crowded bar. She manages to wedge in the middle of a group of girls who are all drinking Zima. I bypass the eyeroll and ask, "How does he know them? He never told me that!"

"Apparently, he grew up with the guy."

"So, Monty and Tom know him, too?" Monty and Tom are other childhood friends of Ron's from his hometown of Norman. We've known those guys for a few years now. It's not like we hang out together every other minute, but we know that crowd pretty well. "Don't you think it's weird that we haven't met this mysterious musical friend of theirs yet?"

"Maybe because they know you'd jump him the second you met him?" she shoots back.

"That is not necessarily a given. I've only ever heard one of their songs."

"Yeah, but if this Jack character is chummy with Ron, you know damn well he's probably hot."

That is undeniable information. Ron has some good-looking buddies. I've watched that Norman Crew turn a few heads over the years. All the better to pick up women, I suppose, which is Ron's most impressive talent. If he and I hadn't friend-zoned so early on, Tess wouldn't have had the chance to sleep with him before I could. He still tries to talk her into bed whenever they meet, and sometimes, she'll actually relent. But it's mostly treated as a joke between them. I find it a little disturbing, although with my ridiculous track record, I'm not exactly the best person to offer criticism.

Ron is officially off-limits for life now, because for all the guys she and I have both been with, we *never* do the overlapping hookup thing. It doesn't stop him from hitting on me like the world-class flirt that he is, however.

And lookee here. Speak of the devil and he appears.

"Ladies! How are you two gorgeous gals this evening?"

Ron throws his arms around the both of us as we wait for our drinks. "What's up, Somers," I greet him, giving him a kiss on his cheek. He grabs my ass and I give him a shove.

Vix goes to kiss him hello, first warning him, "Hands to yourself, Somers. You touch me, you die."

He laughs, that charming grin belying the cad attached to it. "You got that wrong, baby. I touch you, and *you'll* die."

"I probably would. Most likely from gonorrhea."

"Ouch!" He puts a hand to his chest and feigns a broken heart, which just makes us laugh. Our drinks are delivered, and Ron holds his bottle of Corona out to clink our vodka cranberries.

Just then, I spot Tom on the other side of the bar and give him a wave—he's in the process of chatting up a redhead, but pauses in his quest to wave back—before I catch a glimpse of Monty standing next to him, looking bored. Tom gives him a nudge to alert him to our presence, and when he turns in our direction, his posture takes on a relieved vibe. He immediately wends his way through the crowd toward us.

15

"Hello, ladies! Thank God you're here. If I had to play wingman to another Fat Friend, Tommy would owe me more than this weak drink he tried to bribe me with." Monty gives a scan to our surrounding area and asks, "Flying solo tonight, Liv? No Brando?"

I'm just surrounded by comedians.

In spite of the lame jab, I laugh and kiss him hello. "No. No Brando tonight." I don't add that there'll probably be no Mitch any *other* night in the future, either. "No Walter tonight?"

Walter is Monty's boyfriend. It's almost blasphemous for me to ask about him in the same sentence as Mitch, because those two are pretty serious. Mitch and I most definitely are not. Walter is a caterer, so he usually works nights—sometimes during the week, but almost always on the weekends. We normally only get to see the two of them together during our daytime visits.

"No," Monty deflates. "No Walter yet again. But he'd love to see you two. Why don't you spend the night at the cottage and I'll have him cook you some breakfast in the morning?"

Monty's "cottage" is actually a humongous stone mansion complete with wraparound porch that sits on a solid acre of prime, beach-block property. I have to admit, the idea of crashing at Monty's gorgeous house sounds pretty damned good to me. Vix and I will have an entire summer to spend crammed into the same bed down at our little Manasquan hovel. Tonight, we can kick off the summer in style.

I look to Vix for her opinion on the matter, and she simply offers a wide-eyed shrug. *Why not?* "Sure, Mont. That sounds great. Thanks!"

Ron tears his eyes from my sister's cleavage and adds, "Perfect. You two can share my bed."

Vix gives him the finger, but I've long since given up on trying to engage in battle with the guy. I turn my attentions back to my drink, and as I raise the glass to my lips, Monty's eyes go buggy. "Holy shit. Just what is the deal with your fingernails tonight, girlfriend?"

I completely forgot about my new nail polish, and splay my free hand between us to display my almost-black painted digits.

"You like? It's called 'Vamp.' There's a lipstick to match, but I thought that would be a little much." I overstress an eyelash flutter. "Apparently, it's all the rage in *Hollywood, dahling.*"

"I think you should've gone with the matching lipstick," Ron cuts in. "Show off that gorgeous Barrymore mouth of yours."

Ever since Drew Barrymore dyed her hair brown for "The Amy Fisher Story," the comparisons have been coming rapid-fire. I see the resemblance, but I don't think it's *that* close. At least he doesn't call me "Blowjob Mouth" anymore.

I wave him off, taking note of the color for myself. "It's really dark, though, huh?"

Monty grabs my hand for a closer inspection. "Well, I guess it's *supposed* to be, Vampira. Vix, did you authorize this?"

Everyone knows that Vix is twelve minutes older than me chronologically. This fact always makes for hilarious commentary on my maturity level. Not.

Vix takes a quick gander at my hands and shakes her head. "Do you think for one minute that I would have let her out of the house with that color on her fingers had I seen it ahead of time? Liv, that polish is hideous."

Great. I know she's only busting my chops, but I strike back anyway. "Well, gee Vix, thanks a lot. It's not all *that* bad, is it?"

Ron's lip curls into a smirk. "Not at all. In fact, I think those fingertips would look fantastic wrapped around my cock."

By the time Tommy finally decides to join us, we're ready for another drink, so he takes the honors while I take the opportunity to eye up my three friends. I wonder what they put in the water up there in Norman, because almost every guy I know from there is *huge.*

It's pretty weird that we didn't know these guys back in our high school days. I mean, we went to St. Nicetius, which is in their hometown. But the rivalry between the private school kids versus the public school kids created a turf war of *Warriors* proportions. We simply just *did not* mingle with the townies. I'm sure the locals all thought we were snobs, because a lot of the kids we went to school with came from some crazy money. Not me and Vix, though.

17

We hang around shooting the breeze for a while until the DJ signs off, and we know showtime is mere seconds away.

Tommy comes back with a full round, prompting Ron to ask, "Whadja hit the lottery?" as everyone raises their glasses and bottles to clink out a toast.

Finally, some ponytail guy comes onstage and announces, "Girls and boys... Thunderjug."

The lights flash. The crowd cheers. The music starts.

And that's when I get my first look at Jack.

Zowee.

CHAPTER 4

Friday, May 26, 1995
11:04 PM

The Tradewinds
Sea Bright

There are four guys onstage, but Jack is an immediate standout. Tall, but not lanky. Almost-black mane cut just right, hanging a little in front of his face, revealing only a fantastic smile of pure white teeth. His black T-shirt is grazing across a sculpted chest; his long white sleeves are hugging a set of powerful arms. He takes his right hand off the strings for a quick second to brush the hair out of his eyes... and I mouth a silent "Wow" to no one in particular.

Vix catches my reaction and raises her eyebrows questioningly.

I let out a huge exhale, turn toward her, and say, "I am going to ride that man like he was Secretariat."

My sister shakes her head and laughs out, "I knew it! I told you!"

I laugh back, "You *knew*? Who are you, Dionne Warwick?" before turning my attention toward the music once more.

Thunderjug is totally owning "Higher Ground" right now. They're playing the Chili Peppers version, although Stevie's is just as awesome. My heart is pumping right along with the kicking bass line, and I'm actually feeling a little dizzy looking at the guy who's belting it out. I want to floss my teeth with the threads from his ripped jeans. I want him to use the leather cuffs from around his wrists to bind me to his bed. I want to feel the chunky silver rings on his fingers knotting into my hair.

I haven't had this much of a physical reaction to a guy's appearance since the first time Jordan Catalano leaned against a locker... only this is much, much worse.

19

That is one talented band up there, and Jack is ripping the hell out of his groove. His fingers move in a frantic blur along the strings; his pelvis is thrusting against the back of his axe in time with the beat. I've never wanted to be a guitar more in my life.

I am sooo *going to let him do me doggy style.*

Thunderjug plays a wide range of songs, covering a three-decade catalog of music from classic rock to modern alternative. They look like they're having a great time and the crowd soon catches their contagious mood. People begin dancing and singing along. Over the next ten songs, the throng's enthusiasm builds into a fevered pitch.

And this is the best thing about music. The heart-pumping frenzy of hundreds—or even thousands—of people all sharing the same rush. The way you can feel it coursing through your blood, under your skin, straight into your brain, either recalling or creating a memory.

When they play "Shambala," I'm reminded of the time Dad's car got that flat tire on the Parkway, and instead of spending the day at the beach like we had planned, we spent it playing charades at the service station. When they play "Peace, Love, and Understanding," it brings back images of Vix and me on our seventeenth birthday, cruising around in our shared POS Camry, free at last. And when they play "No Rain," Jack is on backup vocals, and his voice shoots through me like I've been tasered. I know Bee Girl is being replaced in my mind with the very new visual of Jack moaning into the mic.

But then, before I know it, the band is taking its first break, the DJ is blasting out some filler music, and here's Jack, heading right for us with those damned *teeth.*

He says hello to the guys as Monty hands him a drink, directing him over to Vix first, then me.

He takes one step in my direction, narrowing the small space between us, and holy shit if the guy isn't the sexiest thing I've ever laid eyes on.

Sooo hot. Want to touch the hiney.

His skin is glistening in a silvery sheen, his hairline damp with sweat. He gives a swipe across his face with a towel before taking a swig from his water bottle with that talented mouth of his. His eyes finally meet mine as his eyebrows rise, his lip twitching into a perfect smirk. It's the kind of crooked smile that practically oozes *Let's fuck.*

He doesn't need to ask me twice.

Or at all, for that matter.

My brain is running in a constant loop of *do me do me do me do me*, but my mouth pulls it together enough to say—or rather, *yell*, "Hey, you guys sound really great up there!"

"Thanks," he says in the same deep timbre of his singing voice.

"I would have gone with 'Interstate Love Song' over 'Vasoline' for my STP pick, though. 'Big Empty' is my favorite off of *Purple*, but I know it wouldn't mesh with the whole bar vibe thing."

That throws him. I guess he wasn't expecting a rundown of Stone Temple Pilots' latest album. Or his set list, for that matter.

He lowers an eyebrow and says, "Everyone's a critic. What, are you in a band or something?"

"Nope. I just know music."

I watch Jack's baffled expression and assess that he is even better looking up close than I'd first thought when he was on stage. My stomach does this weird squidgy thing, watching as his smooth jaw tightens on a repressed smile.

Damn. Great eyes. Blue? Green?

The smirk is still on his face as he asks, "Hey... Did Monty say your name is *Vampira?*"

I didn't realize that Monty had said that. What a dork.

"Um... It's actually Livia. Or Liv, most of the time."

He takes another swig of his water and adds, "He also said you were a twin."

That immediately gets my feathers up. If he turns out to be one of those sicko perverts who tries to work an angle to get Vix and me *both* into bed, I'm going to gently remove his head from his neck. You can't believe the bullshit we have to put up with on a daily basis; when most guys hear *twins*, it automatically translates in their twisted minds as *threesome.*

21

But instead of putting the moves on, he asks, "So which one of you is the evil one?"

I'm relieved that he's not a freak, but my God. There're only so many times I can be asked the same questions in my life. My eyes roll as I shoot back, "Never heard that one before. For the record, we're both evil."

He totally cracks up. "I'll bet."

I start to ask him about his second set when some random girl with Susan Powter hair appears between us.

"Hi Jack," she purrs into his face, slipping a hand around the back of his neck. "You guys were great tonight."

Jack politely removes her arm from around his person. "Thanks."

"Hey, where are you going after this? We were going to hit the beach at Fifty-Third Street."

"Yeah, maybe I'll meet you over there or something."

Crap. There goes my night of debauchery.

He doesn't say anything more to her after that, so Hotsie Twatsie takes the hint and slithers back into the crowd. Jack leans in toward me and offers in a low tattle out the corner of his mouth, "I'm not meeting her over there."

That makes me laugh.

I'm not much one for conversation prior to hooking up, but I'm kind of obligated to make a bit of small talk with Jack, seeing as the guy is a friend of my friends. That isn't ever the case with my other rock conquests. Most of the time, I just want them to shut up, look pretty, and get down to business. But I figure there isn't any harm in getting to know the guy before I jump his bones. It's not like we can slip away until after his show is over anyway.

Therefore, I entertain his question when he asks, "So what have you got against our set list?"

"I don't," I answer. "I thought it was great so far. I'll have to see what you do during Round Two before I make my final decision."

He gives a chuckle and asks, "Well, what are you hoping to hear?"

22

"I don't know. You've got a good mix going on right now. Maybe some more older stuff? You do any Zeppelin?"

"From time to time."

"Beatles?"

"Maybe."

"Clapton?"

"*I* do. Thunderjug doesn't."

"No 'After Midnight'?"

"Nope."

"No 'Bell-Bottom Blues'?"

Out of nowhere, Ronnie spins around and pipes in with, "Dude. I love that song! You should add it to your set list."

I want to shoot back with, *Dude. You shouldn't eavesdrop on other people's conversations*, but Jack answers him before I can. "It's a tough one to play."

"Yeah, but it's killer," Ron says. "Clapton must have fucked up royally to write that thing. Have you ever heard anything more excruciating in your entire life?"

I stare at my friend in awe. "Ron, I never took you for the romantic type."

"Are you kidding?" He drops his head and shakes it. "Rips my heart out every time I hear it."

"I didn't know you had one," I snark.

That makes the both of them laugh.

"Jack writes one hell of an awesome song himself. He wrote 'Backyard,' you know," Ron offers with an eyebrow wiggle.

Jack seems uncomfortable with the spilling of such news, but I can't help but be impressed. "Your band's one hit song was all your doing?"

Before he can answer, Ron gives Jack a nudge. "Told ya chicks dig that shit," he supplies helpfully before pulling an Irish Goodbye.

Jack and I are left shaking our heads at our retreating friend. *Smooth, Ron.*

"So, it's true?" I ask, not letting the subject drop.

"About chicks digging musicians? What do *you* think?"

"Wiseass."

23

He chuckles, gives a shrug, and tries to sound humble, *"I scribbled all night rocking and rolling over lofty incantations which in the yellow morning were stanzas of gibberish..."*

My hippie parents had influenced a Beat-phase in my teen years, so I know every word of the poem he just cited. I find myself gawking at him, open-mouthed, completely blown away. "Are you quoting *Howl* at me?"

He doesn't answer, and instead, just... *looks* at me. There's a quick pause where he's no longer smiling and I'm just... waiting. For what, I have no idea.

He leans in slowly with a roguish look on his face which is so fucking hot and dirty, it makes me want to tear him to pieces without a second thought. Jack's sudden nearness is unexpected, and my goddamn pulse is actually skyrocketing as his face comes closer to mine.

But instead of kissing me, he doesn't stop his advance until his chest is against my shoulder and his mouth is an inch from my ear, his nose stealing an inhale.

His breath ruffles against my hair as he lets out a snicker and whispers, *"You've got one hell of a mouth on you, you know that?"*

"What?" I'm only taken aback because I'm pretty sure he's talking about my actual mouth, not the dirty words normally spewing out of it.

He pulls back to stare down at me with an incredibly hot, lazy grin, and I'm struck dumb because of it. The heated shift to our encounter has come out of nowhere and it's not often that someone gets the jump on *me* with something shock-worthy.

He must misinterpret my stunned expression, because he's still smiling that crooked smile at me when he says, "There's more going on between these ears than a pretty face, Lips."

I catch a quick wink from him as he turns and weaves his way over to the guys again, leaving me completely stunned and flustered. He's talking animatedly with his friends about the first set while I'm feeling like I've just been fucked and left for dead right here on the dance floor.

I finally shake myself out of the stupor and sidle up to Vix as I watch some chick in a skintight, leopard-print dress try to file her way through the crowd toward us. She has a blinders-on focus aimed at Jack and a come-hither attitude in her eyes.

I know that look. Hell, I *invented* it. That chick has "trouble" written all over her.

Jack detects the girl beelining his way when he suddenly excuses himself to head back on stage for the second set. Leopard Girl looks crushed for a moment before Ronnie notices her and moves in. Lord only knows what he's saying to her because she's giving him an evil little grin as he ushers her over to the bar to buy her a drink.

Tommy sees the exchange, too. "I guess that's the last of Ronnie for the night."

And the last of Leopard Girl.

Thank you, Ronnie.

CHAPTER 5

Friday, Saturday, May 27, 1995
12:15 AM

The Tradewinds
Sea Bright

Thunderjug reopens with Van Halen's "Unchained" which throws the crowd back into an excited frenzy. They bring the mood down a notch with Radiohead's "Creep" and then explode into "Machinehead" by Bush. They play a dozen more songs borrowed from bands like The Beatles, Squeeze, and Green Day before beautifully executing an electric, upbeat rendition of Bob Dylan's "Don't Think Twice" which I absolutely fall in love with.

They play a few original songs before launching into "Backyard"... and that's when the place goes nuts. It doesn't take me long to realize why.

Jack has been singing backup for most of the songs all night. But for "Backyard," he's on lead vocals. I snicker to myself while noticing that most of the ruckus is being caused by the *women* in the audience.

I think it's almost a shame that all these people seemed to be waiting all night to hear one little song when everything the band played has been great. Hell. I came here tonight with that same motivation, but they'd won me over long before they got around to playing their hit. Even still, as they belt out their signature song with unyielding energy, I find myself fighting the urge to rush the stage, too. Instead, I try not to notice how good Jack looks, all sweaty and jumping around up there.

Yum.

I only briefly consider how our hooking up might cause a problem. I've never been confronted with a musician that had any ties to my real life. But I quickly shake off my reservations,

26

realizing that it isn't going to stop me. This guy is pure catnip for a rock chick like me.

The song ends, and the place erupts in applause as Thunderjug closes with a funky version of the theme song from "The Banana Splits." It's very funny and unexpected and the crowd goes even more wild when it's over. With a quick "Thank you," the band leaves the stage. A few guys run out to help break down the equipment as the DJ sets up to play for the remainder of the night.

Jack comes back over to Monty, Tom, Vix, and me looking exhausted and out of breath, save for an elated smile and gleaming eyes. He has a towel wrapped around his neck as he motions to the bartender for a drink of water and downs it quickly. The bartender must be familiar with this routine, because when Jack returns his empty water bottle to the bar, a beer is waiting for him. He takes a sizable swig before turning his attentions to me.

"So, do we suck or what?"

I assume he's kidding, so I play along. "You blew."

He swipes his face with the towel and gives a shake to his head. "I can't believe I broke a string in the middle of 'Monkey Man'."

I realize he actually has no idea that nobody even noticed, and that everyone in the place seemed to love the performance. Especially the female members of the multitude who, at present, are slowly closing around our little clan like a silent, calculating, menacing horde.

If Jack notices the peculiar overabundance of women in our vicinity, he doesn't show it. He's still busy berating himself for the minor mishap he'd had on stage, and inspecting the welt where the string had snapped against his forearm.

I ask, "What, are you kidding? You guys are *good*." Taking notice of his red arm I add, "Are you okay?"

I watch as his knit brow relaxes before his eyes spark with gratitude.

They're gray. Holy shit, he has gray eyes.

27

"Oh, yeah. This is nothing. It happens from time to time," he says, freeing me from my concern before acknowledging the compliment, "And... thanks, Liv."

There is nothing quite like the flippy feeling you get in your belly the first time a hot new guy says your name out loud.

Jack mistakes the look on my face for confusion. "What, am I supposed to call you *Vampira*? Not likely."

I raise an eyebrow and smile out, "And *Thunderjug* makes sense?"

He laughs and shoots back, "Touché."

I'm about to ask him just exactly what a thunderjug is anyway, when he announces he needs to use the bathroom. I figure it's as good a time as any to call down to the girls and let them know we won't be making it there until tomorrow. "I'll go with you."

CHAPTER 6

Saturday, May 27, 1995
1:46 AM

The Tradewinds
Sea Bright

We have to cross over the crowded dance floor in order to shortcut to the other side of the large club. Jack is trying to carve out a path for us both when I see him inexplicably reach his hand behind him and blindly grab for mine. I just as inexplicably put my hand in his, and have the oddest feeling as we weave our way through the crowd.

It's kind of... *electric* in a weird sort of way. Our palms are flattened against one another's, our fingers intertwined... It's as though we've performed this act naturally a million times over, not just for the first time one minute ago. The thought has me baffled, but fascinated nonetheless.

Before I know it, he's led me over to the payphones situated near the restrooms. He gives my hand a quick squeeze before releasing his hold and ducking into the men's room.

When Jack lets go, I'm surprised at the loss that washes over me. *What the hell was that?* I don't even know the guy and he has me sweating from simply holding his hand? I can't even imagine what holding his dick will be like. I'll probably pass out.

I spend like an hour digging through the ton of junk in my purse to find the number for the beach house, but it finally appears and I make the call. Even though I'm not in the main part of the club, it's still loud, and I burrow into the alcove as much as I can while covering my free ear with my hand in order to hear.

Samantha answers.

"Hey, Sammy! What are you doing there? I thought you were sick."

29

"I was. But I slammed down a few Sudafed and managed to catch the girls before they left. Where are you?"

"Tradewinds," I shoot back. "Came to see a band."

"Any good?"

"Yeah, actually. They're fantastic."

I glance up to find Jack leaning against the wall having a cigarette, waiting for me. Fuck. He heard that.

"So, I'm going to assume you'll be spending the night elsewhere?" Sam chuckles at her dig, but it's not like I can take offense. My girls know me too well.

"Well, yeah, but not because... We ran into Monty. We're crashing there tonight."

I thought Jack would've headed back to our friends, but instead, he's just standing there watching me as I talk to Sam. His eyes are squinted as he blows smoke through those delectable lips, practically begging me to suck on them for the next twelve hours or so. Give or take.

"Lucky bitch. Tell him we said hi."

"I will."

Before I can get another word out, I suddenly feel the length of Jack's body pressed against my back. *What the hell?* It catches me by surprise, to say the least.

He chuckles against my hair as he swipes it away and lowers his lips to the back of my neck, my skin shivering at the touch. The whole time, I'm trying to have a human conversation with Sam, no easy feat while this dark prince is ravaging me from behind. I guess he isn't planning on wasting any time before getting this party started, and that is just fine by me. I'm more than game.

I snap back to the real world when I hear Sammy taunt, "Well, have fuuun!"

As if that isn't the understatement of the night. How can a hot rock star against my body be anything but fun? I offer a quick "I'm about to," before giving Sam a rather abrupt goodbye and hanging up, bracing my hand on the wall above the phone to press my backside against him.

At that, he gives out a snicker and whispers against my ear, "*Oh, so you wanna play, do you?*"

Oh, hell yeah I do.

There's an electric current running through my body as he turns me in his arms. He has his hands at my waist, running slowly up and down my sides, and a *just-kidding* smile playing at his lips.

He might be kidding around, but I most certainly am not.

I take a quick look down the hall before backing him against the wall, sliding a hand up his chest and meeting his eyes. I can see the surprise in his, because he has no idea who he's dealing with yet.

"Do I want to play? I thought you'd never ask," I fire back, watching a sly smile eek across his lips. Lips that I'm about to devour.

I bring my palms around behind his neck, grab a handful of that dark hair in my fist, and pull. He's taken aback by the aggressiveness, but I don't wait for him to figure anything out before rising on my tiptoes and meeting his mouth with mine.

His body stiffens at that, obviously caught off guard, but it doesn't take him long to warm to my advance. Our lips are perfectly matched, our bodies fitting effortlessly against one another's. I feel his muscles relax as he returns my kiss, and soon enough, everything goes insane.

His hands slide around my waist as he pulls me closer against his body, and well, what do we have here? It seems Mr. Happy has decided to join us.

Jack turns us around to slam *my* back against the wall, and holy shit, I think I'm going to die. Our lips meet again and there's a pounding in my ears beyond the blaring music, making me dizzy. His mouth opens, and I can taste his salty, minty flavor, smell the smoky, shaving-cream scent of him, invading my senses, causing me to grip the shirt at his chest and hang on for the ride.

Or maybe I need to take him on one.

I push off the wall and back him through the nearest doorway... which turns out to be a storage closet. But there's a lock on the handle, so I take advantage of that before kissing him again. The

31

smell of bleach and stale beer is permeating my senses as we touch and taste one another, the heat escalating off the charts.

Just as my hand slips down to cop a feel, he asks, "Hey, whoa. Liv. What are you doing?"

The dark is pretty blinding, but I still manage to meet his face, a scowl on mine. "What do you *think* I'm doing?"

He grabs my wrist and places my hand at his waist. Trying to cover for my pounding heart, I slide my palms around to the small of his back, up his spine, across his shoulder blades, and go back in for another kiss. His hair is brushing against my cheek as his tongue invades my mouth, and before I can stop myself, a slight moan escapes from my throat.

I've been with lots of guys before, but something is different with him and I can't quite figure out what it is just yet. He's hot as hell, which is normally my only prerequisite for hooking up with somebody. But this guy has totally upped the ante. He isn't just a rock star. He is a rock GOD. And from the first second I saw him on stage tonight, I knew I was going to wind up here at some point. Well, not here in a freaking closet for godsakes, but here in this guy's naked grasp doing the horizontal happy dance.

Or, I guess, vertical, in this case. TMI?

My hands go back to his jeans, ripping at Jack's fly, but before I can even get the first button undone, he braces his hands at my shoulders and nudges me away. "Whoa, whoa. Take it back some."

Still in a daze, I ask, "What?"

"This isn't happening. Not here."

Since when does a rock star give a shit where I do him? "I locked the damn door. No one's coming in here."

"You got that right. No one's coming *in here*. We can do better than this."

Is he serious? He started this whole thing, and now he's trying to put the brakes on? I'm suddenly struck with the absurd thought that he was only joking when he attacked me at the pay phones. No freaking way is that possible. Is it?

I cross my arms as my sight adjusts to the dim light, eyeing him up and down. "Is this the part where you try to convince me you're a gentleman? Trying to pretend that you want this to be 'special for me'? Because trust me, Jack, I'm not looking for 'special.' I'm not asking you to work that hard. You can drop the wooing bit."

"*Every* girl is looking for special."

"Not this girl."

He crosses his arms, mocking my pose. "Then what are you looking for?"

"Fun," I shoot back without hesitation. He eyes me in disbelief, so I add, "Do you have a problem with that?"

"Maybe I'm done with fun."

What is with *this guy?* "What's your game, player?"

"No game. Why?"

"You come on like gangbusters, but then the second you find out I'm into it, *bam!* Light switch off."

That makes him chuckle. "Oh, you're a real maneater, aren't you? My mother warned me about girls like you."

"You've never met a girl like me, pal."

"Wanna bet?"

We're staring each other down, and I'm trying not to let him see how humiliated I feel. Here I am, practically throwing myself at his feet, and he's *turning me down.*

Rejection can suck a bag of dicks.

He lowers an eyebrow and sighs, "Look, Liv. I've done this too many times to know that nothing good ever comes out of a situation like this."

"Out of what? A one-night stand? Who says I'm looking for anything more than that to come out of this?"

"Who says I'm *not?*" He lets out an exasperated breath and runs a hand through his hair. "Look. I like you. Can't we just, you know, get to know each other? Do *you* have a problem with *that?*"

Yes. He's messing with my whole M.O. I don't do the 'getting to know you' thing with rock stars. I have mind-blowing sex with them and then go on my merry way. Why is he making this so difficult? "I don't date musicians."

"And I don't fuck groupies."

We stare each other down, caught in a heated standoff. Who the hell does he think he is?

"First of all, I'm not a *groupie*. I'm a music-loving girl with a healthy sexual appetite who knows how to say 'thank you' properly."

"Thank you for what?"

"For being talented as hell, you idiot!"

That brings an unreadable smirk to his lips. I don't have the patience right at the moment to try and explain anything more than that to him, so I continue with my rant. "Secondly, you're not fooling anyone with this chivalry bit. You're a red-blooded male with a working cock that rose to the occasion the second my lips hit yours."

Why the hell is he just standing there smiling at me?

I shake off his smarmy face and line up the kill shot. "Thirdly... Since you don't fuck 'groupies,' feel free to go fuck *yourself.*"

At that, I storm out, leaving him standing there gawking at my retreating form.

When I get back to our group, Vix asks, "Where have you *been?*" with an expectant look that she's about to get some good gossip.

I'm still feeling the sting from Jack's rejection and don't know what to say, so I go the evasive route. "What are you talking about? I made a phone call and he used the bathroom."

"Yeah, but he's really cute and you were gone a really long time. Nothing happened?"

I don't normally keep my escapades a secret, but I have no idea what the hell that just was with Jack. I can't really describe the kissing incident as 'nothing,' but as far as I'm concerned, it may as well be. "A whole *lot* of nothing happened."

I catch a glimpse of him up on the stage, breaking down the equipment with the rest of his band. I immediately avert my gaze and down the last of my drink. Monty's babbling something about Jack meeting us back at the house with his van and how he and Tommy will be hitching a ride with Vix and me.

By the time the four of us make our way outside, it's late and it's cold and I'm ready for bed. But Monty makes us stop at a local bar for package goods and then Vix has to make another stop at Wawa for cigarettes. By the time we pull the car into the driveway, it's close to three o'clock and we all drag ourselves in the front door, exhausted.

Jack beat us home apparently, because there he is, sprawled out on the sectional couch in the family room, playing a sweet melody on an acoustic guitar. I don't recognize it, but instantly decide that for all the songs he's played tonight, this one is my favorite. The fact that I'm currently pissed at him gets forgotten as I lose myself in the pretty tune.

"That was nice," I say automatically when he's through, and Jack lifts his head to meet my gaze.

His eyes spark as he says, "There you are. What took you so long?"

I dismiss my elation that he'd actually been looking forward to my return and curse the involuntary flip in my belly.

Tom must not realize that the question was directed to me, because he answers, "Getting the beers, brother," as he proceeds to hand the cans out to everyone.

When he offers one to me, I decide I'm ready to turn in instead. It's kind of awkward being in the same room with Jack right now, and I'd rather be anywhere but here. Vix and I grab our bags from the foyer and head for The Pink Room. We use the adjoining bathroom to brush our teeth, then change into PJs and collapse onto the king-size bed.

Just as I feel myself drifting off to sleep, Vix says, "Jack's digging you."

I manage a drowsy, "Whatever," and then begin to dream.

CHAPTER 7

Saturday, May 27, 1995
9:07 AM

Monty's House
Spring Lake

The plan is to slip out early this morning. Gathering up our things, Vix and I and tip-toe downstairs, intending to leave a thank-you note for Monty before we sneak out the door. But there he is, already at the kitchen island reading the newspaper. Tommy's grabbing some juice out of the fridge, but Jack is nowhere to be found. Still sleeping, I guess.

Phew.

"Morning," I offer to our host. "Wow. I can't believe you're already awake."

Monty doesn't even look up from his paper. "Walter snores."

I giggle as I ask Tommy, "And what's your story?"

Tommy slams the fridge door closed. "*Walter snores.* Seriously, dude. How do you put up with it? I could hear him from the next room!"

Monty lowers the paper and removes his glasses. "I wear ear plugs. They're very effective at blocking out his snoring. What they *don't* do is block out the sound of maniacs banging down my bedroom door, *yelling* about the snoring."

Tom lets out with a growl before slumping onto a stool.

Monty gives a shrug and goes back to his paper. "Coffee's on, girls. Help yourselves."

Vix and I start to explain that we're getting ready to cut out, but just then, Ronnie bursts through the door. He has an opened beer in one hand and a brown paper bag in the other as he shouts, "Good morning! Anyone get laid last night or was it only me?"

"Oh My God," Vix and I reply as I add, "You've got issues."

36

"No, I've got *breakfast,*" he shoots back, unloading the bag from under his arm and tossing it onto the island. "You're welcome, assholes," he throws in as everybody pounces on the Taylor ham, egg, and cheese sandwiches.

Ron takes a swig of his beer as Vix huffs through a mouthful of food, "I can't believe you're already drinking."

"What do you mean, *already*? I never stopped," he answers back.

Like I said: issues.

* * *

As it turns out, our beach house is cuter than I had expected, with flower boxes at the green-shuttered windows detracting from the few spots of peeling, white paint.

I really hope that the girls got a good jump on the clean-up last night. Me and Vix kind of bailed on that task this year, but God willing, the three of them were able to bring the house nearer to hygienic without us.

The owners of the place had actually agreed to let us get in there a day ahead of season so that we could clean it up in advance. What did they care? Free maid service trumps all.

While none of us ever looks forward to donning a pair of yellow rubber gloves and brandishing a scrub brush, some things just need to be done. I don't know what kind of people just pack up and leave a house looking like the inside of a garbage pail, but we always seem to wind up with quarters previously vacated by filthy renters. Let the muck sit through the winter and it made for one hell of a chore at the beginning of summer.

No joke: In our house last year, I spent no less than *two hours* doing nothing but *scrubbing down the shower stall.*

Yeah. Ewww.

A few weeks later, we actually met the guys that had rented the place the year before. They were coming off the beach one day and saw Tess, Vix, and me sitting on the porch. They stopped to chat and just offered the incriminating information up. Vix completely lambasted them about what dirtbags they were, leaving us to clean up their disgusting mess. I mean, you should have seen this shower! And I won't even get started on the kitchen.

One of the guys actually had the balls to ask Tess where we were going that night and would we like to meet up with them. Vix sent them on their way and they trudged down the road to their current rental, probably intending to trash that place, too.

Shame, though. Vix thought the one with the Earth tattoo on his shoulder was kinda cute.

Vix and I have thankfully been pardoned from cleaning duties this year. We're both only in for a half-share on the house, apparently since we're the only two that will still have jobs over the summer and know we'll only make it down on the weekends. Tess isn't convinced. She doesn't understand why we would give up on a single day at the beach when summer is so short. We told her that most of the adult general population of our planet is expected to *work* for a living.

Tess has the luxury of a very rich father who believes his daughter should "have fun while she's young." I'm not kidding. Those were his exact words. And while I tend to agree with the theory behind such a statement, it doesn't really translate into real life. Not *my* life anyway. But Tess has elevated the premise of having fun to a new art form. God bless her; the girl is a *trip*.

She's actually capable of holding a random job from time to time, if only to stave off boredom. Her thinking on this is that there's no one to hang out with during the day anyway. Yes, I tell her, because WE ARE AT WORK. Nice, right? Whenever a boss gets a little grab-assy or if she just merely becomes bored with a job, she'll quit and walk out. That is, until she gets bored at home again, in which case she goes out and gets herself a new job. Oh, it's a vicious cycle, I know.

Hence her plan is to simply quit her latest job, figuring she'll grab a few bucks waitressing at *Jenkinson's* or *Martell's* or something enough to cover booze and food for the next three months, just in case she uses up her allowance too quickly. Her father's rich, but he's no chump.

Sam is an artist, like, *fine arts* kind of artist. She's got this great studio apartment right near Vix's and mine in Clifton, and the thing is the coolest place I've ever seen. There's barely enough room for her bed, because the place is crammed with her various creations: Countless drawings stacked up on her drafting tables, canvas paintings leaning along every wall, a few sculptures taking over a bit of floor space. She supplements her salary between gallery showings by painting murals on people's walls, and even those "sellout pieces" (her words, not mine) are really, really amazing. She's so talented, it makes me puke.

Rounding out the honor roll is Isla. She's fun, she's bubbly, she's sweet... and holy hell is she lacking basic common sense. Saddest thing is, she's a first grade teacher. When people worry over the state of public education in this country, Isla is the reason why. But she's got a beautiful heart and I totally love the girl, so it's hard to hold any of her faults against her. Because who doesn't have faults? We've all got 'em, right?

The five of us have been friends since high school and we've rented a beach house together every year since graduating. We've already stayed in Point Pleasant, Ortley, Belmar, and this year, the location is Manasquan.

I've already decided that this is going to be the best summer yet.

39

CHAPTER 8

Sunday, May 28, 1995
11:09 AM

Monty's House
Spring Lake

We get to Monty's early so we can help set up for his Memorial Day Weekend bash. He and Walter throw the party every year in order to kick off the summer with a bang. If it wasn't such a favorite event, and if Monty wasn't such a good friend, I would have just blown the whole thing off.

I'm still embarrassed to think about having to face Jack after our abandoned encounter the other night. After some minor sleuthing, I found out he'll be leaving the party early to play a gig, though, so I figure I'll be able to avoid him for the few hours he'll actually be here.

Tess, Isla, and Sam offer to take all our bags upstairs, so I grab my Minolta before following Vix to the back patio. I'll be better able to deal with being in the same vicinity as Jack if there's a camera between us.

I spot him right off, sprawled across a chaise lounge next to the pool with the rest of the guys. They're fully clothed, which leads me to believe he, Monty, and Tom are more likely fighting off hangovers rather than attempting to sun themselves.

Ronnie, however, is lounged out on a raft—also fully clothed—in the middle of the pool.

Must've been a rough one last night.

Ron is the first one to spot us. "Hello, twins. Where's the rest of your entourage?"

"Right behind us," Vix answers before jerking her head toward him. "Nice bathing suit."

Ron ignores her and instead turns his attentions to me. "Hey Liv! Better get that camera ready. I'm gonna do a dead-on impersonation of a humpback whale. You ready?"

"As I'll ever be."

I snap a few "before" shots as he rolls off the raft and into the pool. One second later, his naked ass breaks the surface of the water.

We all crack right the hell up.

"Ah, a face only a mother could love," Tess says as she makes her way out to the backyard. She's followed by a giggling Sam and a horrified Isla.

Jack isn't laughing. He seems almost annoyed as he spits out the first words he's spoken since we got here. "How many of you *are* there?"

I don't know who he's talking to, but I assume it isn't me, considering the *last* words he spoke in my presence had me storming off two nights ago.

Tess turns her head toward Jack, then slowly back to me. She slithers, "Who's the new meat?" and then heads over near the pool.

She removes her sunglasses and saunters to the end of Jack's chaise before bending over to extend her hand, practically spilling out of her halter top.

Jack smirks and surmises, "You *must* be Tess."

She shoots a look at Ronnie, who shrugs his shoulders in mock innocence. He grabs her ankle and she screams, hopping on one foot as she tries to twist out of his grasp, eventually falling into the pool.

There's a huge splash, and then her head breaks the surface. "Dick!" she yells, propelling a wave of water at her assailant as we all die laughing at the sight.

Ronnie goes to kiss her hello, but she dodges and shoves his head under instead. She paddles her way to the edge, throws her arms over the side and says, "Hey Liv! Where's Zuko this weekend?"

See? Comedians everywhere.

There is no godly reason for her to ask me that. I'd already told her that Mitch and I are through, however unofficially. Obviously, Vix must've spilled the beans that Jack had gotten under my skin on Friday, and Tess is screwing around, stoking the fire.

It works, because Jack abruptly announces that he's going to finally take a shower as he proceeds to get up and leave.

Tess looks at me, curling a wicked lip as she asks, "Did I miss something the other night?"

I'm feeling exposed and embarrassed and more than a little pissed off. "Hey Tess, why don't you shut your dick hole?" I answer, my eyes narrowing.

"Oh, it was a joke. Not a cock. Don't take it so hard."

Before we can say anything more, Monty hauls himself off the lounge chair and puts a hand under my elbow. He practically drags me with him into the kitchen, saying, "Hope you don't mind that I'm kidnapping you, but I need some help with all this food."

I scan my eyes over the sentinel of shopping bags on the island as I shoot back, "*Pfft.* You were just trying to save Tess from being murdered."

"True, but I really do need help. Do you mind?"

My anger deflates at that. Of course I don't mind. "No, of course not. Where should we start?"

Along with the ton of groceries, Walter left a list of detailed instructions for how we should prepare them until he can come home from his event and take over.

Monty and I are side by side at his counter, slicing up some peppers and onions when he throws out, "Sooo, I'm surprised you haven't asked me about Jack yet."

I keep my focus on the cutting board, trying to seem completely unaffected by his choice of subject matter. Hell, I'm doing everything short of whistling Dixie in my attempt to come across as uninterested. "Jack? Why would I ask about him?" I return as casually as possible.

I catch his smirk in my peripheral vision. "No reason."

We both go back to our slicing. "Seether" is playing on the sound system—appropriately enough—and I try to concentrate on that rather than the miniature Jean Claude Van Damme kicking the shit out of my stomach.

When I can't take the awkward silence any longer, I decide that the jig is up.

"Fine!" I say at last, putting down the knife and turning toward him. Monty keeps slicing away, but a smile is tugging at the corner of his lips.

Jerk.

I cross my arms over my chest and just let out with it. "Yes, okay, I'm curious. Alright? Happy?"

"Very."

"But," I go on, "*only* because I find it weird that we've never met him before now. I mean, I've known you for years and you've known him for even longer. Where have you been hiding him?"

That brings a chuckle from Monty. "*I* haven't been hiding him anywhere. His girlfriend has."

Girlfriend? Oh crap! I know I should be feeling crazy-guilty, but instead, all I can feel is my heart reluctantly sinking.

"Girlfriend?" I ask, hoping I don't sound too pathetic.

"Uh-huh. Sadie. I haven't seen her since they first started dating, but yikes. What a bitch."

It's surprising to hear such a negative opinion coming from a guy who normally likes everyone. I'm suddenly intrigued, and this time, I don't bother trying to hide it. My eyebrows rise as he continues his criticism.

"None of us ever liked her. She always came off a little snooty, like Jack's friends were beneath her somehow. I never understood why he even started dating her. I mean, her daddy was his *boss*, for godsakes. He'd been dangling this great construction job over Jack's head forever. It's the only reason he hung in there as long as he did."

Past tense. Okay. *Phew.*

I ask, a little too eagerly, "*Did?*"

43

"Yes. Did. They broke up a couple months ago. Or so we think. He doesn't really talk about it. He was MIA for years, but then all of a sudden, there he is, calling us out of the blue to hang out. By that time, surprise! One of his songs is playing on the radio. I knew he played guitar, but shit, I never realized he was serious about it; last I'd heard, he was planning on building houses for a living."

"It would be kind of hard to turn his back on the music thing now, though, right?"

"Yeah. He got lucky, but I know that even this little taste of fame has got him rattled. It's a lot to deal with." My memory flashes to the way all those girls were trying to get close to him Friday night in the club. *I* was claustrophobic just watching it. I can't imagine what that must've felt like for Jack. "It's weird, though. Even with everything he's on the verge of achieving, the sick thing is, I think he'd rather succeed as a contractor."

"Enough to get back with Sadie?" I ask, a little too quickly.

Monty replies, "Livi, nobody's *that* sick."

I suppress a giggle as I try to picture Jack with someone "snooty" like Monty assessed. Why would he have invested years in a bad relationship with someone like that? Even if that someone's daddy *was* holding the keys to some dream job. It doesn't add up.

But considering the convoluted lowlights of my dating history, who am I to judge?

While thinking, I get back to work beside Monty, preparing food for the party. He asks me to go fetch some Sterno pans from the hall closet, so I dry my hands on a dish towel before heading up the stairs.

I open the closet door... just as Jack emerges from the bathroom.

He's clad only in a thin, white towel; his hair is still wet, and his hands are slicking it back from his chiseled face. His arms and chest are roped muscle, practically shimmering in the afternoon light. I can see a tattoo at his left shoulder blade, and another on his right bicep, but I'm too stunned at the sight of his almost-naked body to make them out in any great detail.

44

Yeah, I know I already hooked up with the guy and all, but we were fully clothed in a dark closet, and this is the first look I'm getting of his incredible body.

And. Oh. My. God.

My stomach immediately does an uncontrolled somersault. To cover for the fact that he may or may not have just seen my jaw hit the floor, I execute a quick wolf whistle.

He turns, surprised to see me there, but offers a cool, "Good thing I didn't decide to air dry."

I laugh as he moseys into the Blue Room and shuts the door. Exactly one second later, the door opens and his hand shoots out, dropping the towel to the floor.

That has me barking out a laugh.

I retrieve the aluminum pans and start to head back to the kitchen. But before I can reach the stairs, Jack comes bounding out of the bedroom, wearing nothing but a pair of dark green track shorts. "Hey, Liv. What's your hurry?"

"I'm helping Monty and Walter get the food ready."

I'm still feeling awkward toward Jack, but if I'm going to be stuck in the same house with him for the next twenty-four hours, I can't very well give him the cold shoulder all day. He's a friend of my friends, and that means he deserves a smidge of common courtesy at the very least.

So he's not interested in me. So what.

I'm aiming for "unaffected," but my voice comes out sounding overly bored when I say, "Why? What do you want?"

His lips purse together, as if he is literally trying to bite his tongue. Instead, his eyelids lower to half-mast as he says, "You're not so tough, you know. You try to put up this big front, but your act is pretty transparent."

I put a hand to my hip. "What the hell is that supposed to mean? I'm not putting on an act."

"Sure you are. This whole groupie thing you've got going on. I'm not buying it."

"I wasn't trying to sell it."

45

At that, he cracks a small smile, and it makes me feel more vulnerable than had I been standing there completely naked. You know, kind of like how *he* almost is.

The thing is, I almost don't mind being called out by him, since most guys don't bother to scratch beyond the surface. It's flattering to think that Jack is intrigued enough to try. Because honestly? I was full of it when I said I wasn't acting. I'm sort of impressed that he was able to figure me out so soon. Hell. *I* haven't even figured me out yet.

Twenty-something is hard. Trying to discover who you are and who you're going to be. Some people figure it out early, have it all together. And some people go a little off the deep end and wind up with multiple sex partners, trying to shut out the crushing trauma of trying to find their place in the world.

That's why his assessment isn't necessarily a relief. No one likes having their walls torn down, having their shitty reality thrown in their face. I'm sure the unease is playing out on my face as I bite my lip during our awkward silence.

Right now, all I want is to make my escape. "I should bring these down to Monty. He's going to wonder what's taking me so long."

He gives me a long, hard look at that, his lip curling into a dangerous smirk.

"He can wait. I can't."

Before I know it, I'm dropping the pans to the floor as he backs me against the wall, his lips crashing down on mine. I want to shove him away, but hot damn. He's fucking way too good at making me fall to pieces. I kiss him back, because really, what the hell else can I be expected to do?

I smooth my hands up his torso, feeling the muscles of his chest jumping under my palms. I slip my fingers into his hair and part my lips against his, sweeping my tongue inside—his cool, minty taste invading my senses. His insistent lips slant across my own as his hands pull me closer against his length. Despite my wishes to the contrary, my heart starts beating out of my goddamned chest. It triples in pace when I realize Jack's is racing, too.

He pulls back to take a much needed breath, shooting those mysterious gray eyes into mine. He runs a finger across my bottom lip, lightly brushing it back and forth. "Your mouth," his aching voice scratches out. "I could lose myself against these lips."

My brain tumbles over itself as he comes back in for another kiss, wondering if this means he's changed his mind about letting me do all sorts of crazy stuff to his peen.

Because I totally will.

Just as soon as he lets me.

I test the waters, skimming a hand between us and sliding my palm against the front of his shorts.

He doesn't push me away.

Instead, he groans against my mouth and drives his hips into my hand, gripping my ass closer to his body. It's a fairly impressive piece of equipment he's working with over there, and I am more than thrilled to have it writhing against my palm.

Just as I tuck my thumbs into the waistband of his shorts, he tears his mouth from mine in a frustrated grunt, his hands braced against my shoulders.

He can't even meet my eyes as he says, "I'm sorry. I shouldn't have, uh..."

Goddammit. This horseshit again? I can't take it anymore.

"What the hell, Jack? Why don't you want to have sex with me?"

I'm trying very hard not to let any hurt show. But hurt I am.

He runs a hand through his hair and growls, "It's not that I don't want to. Believe me, I want to very much."

"So, what are you? Some sort of straight-edger or something?"

Jack chuckles to himself and answers, "No."

"Closeted gay?"

"No."

"A *virgin*?"

"No. Not at all. Trust me, in the old days, there was never anything virtuous about me. But I'm done being that guy."

"Well, then you seriously misread this situation. Because *I'm* not done being *that girl*."

47

He crosses his arms over his chest and stares me down. "You don't really mean that."

"*You* don't know me well enough to make such an assessment."

"I know you've had boyfriends. It's not *always* party time for you."

Huh. Looks as though someone has been doing his recon. I put my hands on my hips and give a huff. "So... what? You want to be my *boyfriend?*"

A sly grin cracks his face at that. He steps too close, and I catch a whiff of his smoky, shaving-cream scent as he lowers his head and nudges his lips against my ear. "Are you asking?"

The comment flusters me so badly that I actually stammer when I say, "That's not... You know what I meant."

He doesn't step away, and just continues running his nose along my jaw. "Hey, Lips? I don't even think *you* know what you meant."

"Will you stop that, please?" I ask feebly.

Jack halts his nuzzling to meet my eyes. "Stop what?"

"*Playing* me."

"Is that what you think I'm doing?"

"Well, how else can I explain your behavior? You're either the worst kind of tease or you're schizophrenic."

He lets out a snicker at that. "I'm neither. It's just that... I've been here before. I'm done with that life. I'm trying something new."

"I'm not some goddamned experiment, you know."

"That's not what I meant." He runs a hand over his face and lets out a heavy breath. "I just don't want to do this anymore. I'm tired of hopping into bed with women I don't care about. And I think I could care about you." He cups my jaw in his palm, running his thumb across my cheek, forcing me to meet his eyes. "Aren't you tired of it yet? Aren't you tired of all the meaningless sex?"

Sometimes. But I'm too wound up at the moment to admit that to him. Besides, the revelation has caught me off guard. I feel like a chink in my armor has been exposed. "You didn't seem to be tired of it a minute ago."

48

"I know. I got a little… distracted. I'm not doing a very good job of proving my point here."

"What point is that?"

He's still brushing his thumb against my skin as he aims those gorgeous granite eyes into mine. "That you're so much more."

His touch is obliterating my brain cells, and I'm feeling way too dizzy and confused to do anything other than stand here and take it. My voice comes out in a shaky cadence as I counter, "You don't even know me."

"I know enough."

My gray matter starts to regenerate as anger and frustration coils in my belly. I don't give a crap about his "reasoning." The fact of the matter is that this is now the *second* time the guy has left me hanging. I'm getting pretty sick of the way he's toying with me. Just who in the hell does he think he is?

Looks like it's *my* turn to push *him* away.

"You don't know shit."

CHAPTER 9

Sunday, May 28, 1995
4:09 PM

Monty's Backyard
Spring Lake

I spend the day as far away from Jack as humanly possible. Not such an easy feat, considering we're residing in the same backyard.

But I've pretty much decided that I'm done with the guy. Who cares that he's able to reduce me to a glop of mush within a few seconds of sustained lip contact? Who cares that he's gorgeous? Who cares that he's talented as fuck?

Not me. That's for sure.

I'm occupying my time with my girls, making a good-sized dent in the pitcher of Malibu Bay Breezes Walter has just delivered. The late-afternoon sun is beating down upon our heads as we lounge around the edge of the pool, wading our feet in the deep end. The current topic of discussion is Juliette Lewis's cornrows at the Oscars. We're laughing our asses off about it when…

…Jack's shadow cuts across my lap and into the water at my feet.

"Mind if I sit down?" his voice asks behind me as I down the last of my drink.

I catch Tess's eye for a quick second, just long enough for her to give me a wide-eyed *well, what are you waiting for?* glare. I turn to look up at Jack—he's even taller and more imposing from my seated position—and have to hold a hand against my forehead in order to shield my eyes from the halo of glaring white light that surrounds him.

Yeah. The guy's a real angel.

I'm not exactly happy to see him, and just before the words *Mind if you go scratch your ass?* can slip from my lips, he adds, "I'd like a chance to apologize, Liv."

"I'm hungry! Anyone else hungry?" Vix asks as she stands up and bolts for the patio. Every last one of my so-called friends leaps to their feet to file away behind her.

Traitors.

I think they're acting ridiculously, since I had, not one hour ago, confided in them about my victorious inner battle of Common Sense Vs. The Rock Star. I also think that I could simply make the decision to go with them and leave Jack in the dust. But the truth is, I'm curious to hear what he has to say.

I don't let their little coup affect me as Jack settles down at my side and drops his feet into the water before turning to me and smiling.

Yep. Still got a Colgate commercial going on in there.

While I'm still reeling from that, he launches into a lengthy diatribe. "I really do want to apologize, Liv. I'm sorry for running hot and cold with you, I really am. I want you to know that that's all on me. I'm the one who's going through some changes right now, and I just need you to know that my actions have nothing to do with you. You're great. And you're incredibly sexy and fun, and that's why I can't keep my hands off you. But you deserve better than some asshole pawing at you every chance he gets. And I'm going to do a better job from now on to treat you with the respect you're worthy of. Okay?"

My mouth gapes open at his words. No one has ever said anything like that to me in my entire life. My head moves on its own as I give him a dazed nod in answer, unable to speak a single syllable.

Without another word, he puts his hands on the concrete, closes his eyes, and tips his face toward the sky. We sit in a quiet, comfortable silence as I try to sort out all the internal musings pinging around my brain. I suppose the guy didn't have to apologize. I mean, it's not like he's trying to work his way into my bikini bottoms or anything, so his ulterior motive was only to… what? Make me feel better?

I guess he at least deserves respect for *that*.

Squinting an eye in his direction, I can see that he hasn't yet broken his pose, and I take the opportunity to steal a glance at his torso, partially exposed through his unbuttoned shirt.

Bad idea.

Trying to cover for sneaking a peek at his incredible abs, I senselessly blurt out, "I'm the asshole."

He cracks one eye open as he asks, "What?"

I take a deep breath and offer through my exhale, "I'm sorry, too."

He doesn't ask why I'm apologizing, but I figure I'd better cough up the explanation anyway. "The truth is that you kind of called me out for something I wasn't ready to acknowledge. But you're right. Sometimes, I get tired of all the..."

"Emptiness?" Jack finishes for me.

I haven't ever viewed my life as empty, but crap. He's right. "Yeah."

I'm pretty impressed that he doesn't twist the knife, and simply nods his head in acceptance. I'm grateful for that. It was hard enough admitting that I'd been exposed—which, come on, I happen to think deserves at least a *little* credit—I don't need him to be smug about it on top of it.

Truce attained. Change of subject needed.

"So... Monty tells me that your real job is in construction."

Jack looks taken aback. "Uh, yeah. Sort of. Well, not so much anymore..."

"Because you're a musician now?"

"Yeah, I guess so." His surprised look hasn't abated, and I'm sure it's because he expected me to have said 'rock star' instead. I'm glad I didn't. "The music's really going well right now. We're making money; we're having fun. But I haven't swung my last hammer yet, if you know what I mean."

"You want to get back to building."

"God yeah. Once *all this* dies down." He swoops his hand in a wide arc as he modestly refers to his overnight stardom simply as "all this." I think it's ironic. Some people would kill for the kind of celebrity Jack was achieving. And yet, he seems almost annoyed by it. There's something sort of cool about that, though. "Once I've sucked enough cash out of the music thing, I'm going back to building houses. But on *my* terms this time. Entire neighborhoods with signs out front saying, *Jackson Tanner Contracting.*"

"Wow. That would be something. But you need to work on the name. How about *I Built This City on Rock and Roll*, inspired by and named for what has to be the greatest song of all time."

"Ouch. Yet strangely appropriate." The lame joke earns me a fabulous grin before he comes back with, "Maybe I could go international: *El Projecto de Juan.*"

"Sí. How about *Yet another Home by Jackson Tanner*? It conveys a sense that you're already everywhere."

"Or—Hey, wait. I like that."

I give myself a pat on the back and then ask, "Did you ever consider a government contract? Big money there."

"What do you mean, like a professional assassin or something?"

"Yes, like a professional assassin." He starts laughing as I roll my eyes. "No, Stupid. I mean doing construction for a city project."

Jack absorbs the information. "Yeah, maybe something to think about. It's worth a shot, right?" A smile is playing at his lips as he asks, "You think they'd still give me a gun?"

The adorable boyishness with which he delivers that line has me smiling in spite of myself. The guy really is insanely gorgeous, but even more than that, he's... *genuinely nice.* I've never been attracted to a genuinely nice guy before, and now I'm wondering why that is.

Fear of commitment? Flat-out rebelliousness? Masochism?

Who the hell knows.

He's looking directly at me, and in this bright light, and maybe because we're sitting near a pool, his eyes are more blue than gray. I've never met anyone whose eyes could change color like that. I mean, mine are green. A little brownish, but you'd never mistake them for anything other than green. Jacks' were *kind of* greenish, mostly gray, and now they're straight-up blue.

53

The dude is a chameleon in every sense, apparently.

"Would you really just throw a music career down the tubes?"

He shrugs. "I don't look at it as throwing it away. It's just another Thing. You know... do something, explore it, find something new, and move on. Right now, I'm exploring this. But when my run is up, I'll go back to doing what I do best."

"Your construction skills are better than your music? I find that hard to believe."

He shrugs again. "I like to build things."

The words themselves are fairly innocent. But the vulnerability with which he says them takes over a small piece of real estate in my cold, dead heart.

He seems almost embarrassed by his statement, and tries to cover with a change of subject. "Quick. Name the first band that comes to your mind."

I'm not prepared for the question, and for whatever reason, the only thing to pop into my head is, "Bon Jovi!"

Jack's face takes on a scowl. "Bon Jovi? Seriously?"

"What? I liked them!"

He shakes his head in disbelief as he shoots back, "You liked *my* band, too! What does that say for Thunderjug? Jesus."

"Dude. I was a teenage girl in the eighties. Liking them was kinda the law. Are you actually gonna sit here and tell me you don't dig the pure awesomeness that is Bon Effing Jovi?"

"I'm a guy. Of *course* I don't like them." He gives a scratch to his chin as he adds, "I'll give them 'Wanted Dead or Alive,' though. And only because Richie strums a pretty kickass riff during it. But that's it."

Blasphemy. How can he not dig one of our state's most beloved native sons? Surely, he's full of it. "What about 'Living on a Prayer'?"

"Nope."

"Bed of Roses."

"Hell no."

"Runaway."

"No. Well, wait. Okay... *maybe* that one doesn't suck."

"Good. See? Now we don't have to kick you out of Jersey."

"Who's 'we'?"

"Collective 'we.' As in, everyone who lives here."

He swirls his hand through the surface of the water, flicking his wet fingers in my direction. "Lips, I'd hardly put some band at the top of my list because of two redeeming songs. And I can't be kicked out due to brand disloyalty. I grew up listening to Sinatra. And Frankie Valli. And I just happen to be a huge Springsteen fan. We've got a show lined up at The Stone Pony in a few weeks, and I can't fucking wait." He hesitates for a pause before adding, "I saw him there once, you know. Not on stage. Just hanging out at the bar."

"Springsteen? Oh my God!" Springsteen is practically royalty, local or not. And if he's the king of our garden state, then The Stone Pony is his castle. "How did you deal with that? I'd probably pass out if I ever found myself face-to-face with him."

"Yeah, no kidding. Last year, my guitarist Freddie and I stopped in for a few beers and he just *shows up*. Freddie elbows me in the side and when I look up, there he is, standing right there at the bar next to me. The Boss himself. I totally lost my cool."

"Lost it how?"

His lips are trying to contain a smile as he answers, "No. I haven't known you long enough to tell you that story. You'll lose all respect for me."

"I never had any to begin with. Come on. Tell me."

"No."

"Pleeease?"

That makes him chuckle. "Well, let me ask you... If you ran into Springsteen, what would *you* have said to him?"

"Hmmm," I offer, giving myself a moment to think. "I guess I'd probably tell him how much I love 'Born in the USA.'"

Our friendly banter is halted as Jack pauses in a dead stare. "Livia. It's widely accepted that 'Born in the USA' is *not* Bruce's best album. By far. Overproduced, synthesized..."

I give a dismissive wave of my hand. "I don't care about any of that technical, behind-the-scenes stuff. All I care about is that

55

flippy feeling I get in my stomach whenever I hear 'Dancing in the Dark'."

Jack looks like he's ready to pass out. "Yeah. That might be the worst song on there."

"Monica Geller and I would heartily disagree."

"It's pop!"

"I don't care. It's awesome," I defend.

"Casey Kasem can take his Top Forty countdown and shove it right up his poo-hole."

I snicker, "You know, you should really express yourself more. It's not good to keep your opinions and emotions all bottled up like that."

"Yeah? Well *you* need to get some better taste in music!"

"Well, I thought *your* band was great. Obviously, I don't know shit!"

We stop arguing and just look at each other for a long, heated pause… and then we both lose it.

We're still laughing as Jack hauls himself to his feet and strips off his shirt.

I stop laughing.

I only get a brief glance at his naked torso before he dives into the water, and it's just as beautiful as I remember from upstairs in the hallway. When his head and shoulders break the surface, I'm able to take a better look at him, now that I'm not either stunned by the sight of him in a towel, or brain dead from making out with him.

But even still, I feel like *I'm* the one treading water right now.

"So, what's that?" I ask, pointing to the tat on his left shoulder blade. He twists it toward me and looks over his shoulder, as if he needs to view it in order to remember. I can finally make out that it's a cratered full moon with a gnarly tree growing out the top. And when I look *really* close, I can see what looks like a small fox curled up underneath it. There are words ribboned around the entire design, but I can't get a read on them.

When Jack sees my squinted eyes, he takes mercy on me. "*Tu deviens responsable pour toujours de ce que tu as apprivoisé.*"

56

I think I just felt my ovaries explode. Holy crap did he sound hot speaking French. It's a physical feat to avoid leaping into the pool and licking every inch of him, and instead I ask as casually as possible, "Nice. But what does it mean?"

He gives a shrug and explains, "It's a quote from 'The Little Prince.' I'm French on my father's side... the youngest kid in the family..."

"Yeah, so?" I ask, having no idea what I'm supposed to glean from his "explanation." When I can tell he's not going to elaborate, I move onto the scrutiny of his right arm. "Fine. Okay. So, what's that one?"

Jack twists his shoulder and looks down his arm. "A rose."

"I see that, wiseass. What's the significance?"

"It's a replica of Paul Stanley's. He's got the same one in the same spot."

I can't believe what I'm hearing. "Paul Stanley? From *KISS*? They're horrible!"

"That's rich coming from a girl who just referenced "Bed of Roses" and "Dancing in the Dark" as being great songs. KISS is awesome," he fires back, shoving some water in my direction.

Snickering from his assault, I swipe the droplets off my legs. "Hey, my taste is eclectic, I'll grant you that. But I didn't go running out to get a Superman tattoo to be just like Jon Bon Jovi."

"I was eighteen."

As seriously as I can muster, I ask, "Oh, so you like to rock and roll all night and party every day?"

"*EV*-er-y day."

Oh holy crap that breaks me. I can't contain my giggles. "You. The biggest music snob in the universe and you're sporting a KISS tattoo? In other words, fifty percent of your ink has been devoted to a cheesy band!"

"Thirty-three percent."

I'm holding my sides and cackling, so his words don't register right away. "What?"

He gives a quick clench to his teeth before explaining, "I have *three* tattoos. But I don't know you well enough yet to show you that last one."

The smirk he shoots me stops my laughter and starts my mind racing: What is it? *Where* is it? I've already been thrown off my game by his comment... but now here he is hauling himself out of the water.

Christ.

I watch the muscles in his arms strain against his glistening skin as he pulls himself up and sits down on the edge of the pool with me again. He shakes out his hair and the water flicks onto my skin, breaking me out of my trance.

"Hey," I say, checking my vintage Swatch and finally taking note of the time. "It's Memorial Day Weekend for godsakes. Don't you have a gig tonight?"

Jack grabs my wrist and turns it to check for himself, the small touch shooting an electric current along my skin. "I do, actually. And it looks like I'll have to get out of here soon if I'm going to make it down to *Used To Be's* in time."

"Mantoloking?"

"Yep."

"Careful. That's a pretty rough neighborhood."

The comment catches him off guard and he sputters out a laugh. Mantoloking is hardly a "rough neighborhood." Spring Lake may be old money, but Mantoloking is most certainly *new* money. But who the hell cares? Money is money. You either have it or you don't... and Mantoloking has it. The town is populated by Wall Street CEOs, entertainment moguls, and plastic surgeons, amongst others. Driving by the ostentatious beachfront properties along Route 35 is pretty goddamn sickening. So much wealth on one stretch of road. Crazy.

"Keep your eye out for a smallish pink Victorian with a white porch on your way down," I suggest.

"Why's that?"

I shrug and answer, "I drew up some floor plans based on that house once. It's my favorite one." Jack is looking at me, clearly impressed. "It's no big deal. Just a hobby of my mother's and mine."

My mother and I have this little game where I'll sketch up a bunch of rooms and then she'll draw the exterior based on my designs. We've come up with some pretty wacky concepts over the years, but a few of the houses we've collaborated on are absolutely gorgeous. Not your average mother/daughter activity, but it's always been one of our favorite things to do, and a good way to play pen-pal over the weeks she's away with Dad for his gigs.

Artsy family, remember?

I don't add that the genesis of our little hobby is due to the fact that we used to be poor as dirt. I grew up knowing that those drawings would be the only mansions I'd ever own.

Just FYI- I really don't want you to get the impression that I'm bitter about that. Growing up poor builds character, and it sure as hell is the reason why I've always been such a dreamer. And truly, I really like that part about myself. But if I'm going to be honest, I'll admit that life was never easy when you didn't have two nickels to rub together.

We both sit quietly pondering the water at our feet when out of nowhere, Jack says, "So let me take you out sometime."

That jogs me out of my daze. "What?"

"We're having a good time. Let's not wait until we bump into each other to do it again."

"Like... a *date*?" I can't believe I'm actually listening to this, much less considering it.

"Yes."

I don't say anything.

"C'mon. You know you want to say yes. Let me show you what dating a man like me feels like."

"I've already felt your 'manliness,' thanks. Too bad you won't let me show you what dating *me* is really like. If you only knew what you were missing out on..."

"Oh, I don't doubt it," he laughs out. "Fact is, I'm already dying to sleep with you. But I told you already, I'm trying something new, here." He shoots me a grin before adding, "The thing is, when I finally take you to bed, I want it to be for more than just kicks."

I stare him down, trying to read his words. I mean, what's the point of getting it on if you went into it expecting to be *bored?* My head tips to the side skeptically as I ask through a snicker, "What do you want it to be, then?"

He crooks a finger under my chin, aiming those mysterious slate-blue eyes into mine. "Unforgettable."

Cue melty kneecaps.

I try to keep my cool so he won't see just exactly how much that one little word has affected me. "Hey, it's no skin off my back. I was just looking for a little fun."

"Oh, it'll be fun, Lips. You can count on it."

His mouth quirks into a mischievous grin, daring me to doubt him.

Seeing that smoldering look on his face and feeling the way those captivating eyes are turning my insides to mush... there's no way I can.

CHAPTER 10

Monday, May 29, 1995
2:10 AM

Monty's House
Spring Lake

It's just after two in the morning by the time Jack gets back to the house.

Not like I've been waiting for him or anything.

But because I've been drinking steadily all evening, and because he greets me with the biggest smile I've ever seen on a human, I realize that I'm more than a little happy to see him. We immediately find a private post in a darkened corner of the backyard to carve out a few minutes of alone-time.

"How'd it go tonight?" I ask.

"Good! Well, great show. Shitty audience."

"They didn't appreciate the musical stylings of Thunderjug?"

"Nah, it wasn't that. It's just that there was hardly anyone there." He pauses before adding out the corner of his mouth, "*The Nerds* were playing at Tycoon's. I guess everyone went there instead."

The Nerds are the premiere act in the entire state of New Jersey. They've been playing together for years and have built up quite the following. God help any bands trying to pull people into their gig if The Nerds are anywhere in the general vicinity. I know as well as Jack that it's a lost cause, and that there's nothing I can really say about it that he doesn't already know.

I skip the sympathy and instead scan the party scene. I'm looking for a change of subject when I see Monty on the patio, flipping burgers at the grill. Never one to do anything halfway, he's dressed in a chef's hat, oven mitt, and long apron over his bathing suit. He turns around, allowing me to make out the words on his apron: "Hot Meat Coming: Watch Your Back."

I cackle aloud, prompting Jack to ask what's so funny. Laughing too hard to repeat it, I point in Monty's direction. Jack squints in order to see from the dim light of the grill's fire, reads it for himself, and just shakes his head.

I giggle out, "He has no pride."

Without missing a beat, Jack looks me right in the eyes and says, "Yeah, but he's got really cute friends."

As much as the comment floors me, I make a concerted effort to take it with a grain of salt. He's already made it perfectly clear that he won't be down for anything more R-rated than a conversation.

It's pretty bad timing for him to choose this moment to press our abandoned subject from earlier. "So, have you made up your mind yet?"

"About what?" I ask, unconvincingly. We both know what he's asking me, here.

He humors me anyway. "About letting me take you out."

"I hadn't really thought about it."

Jack's lip quirks before he says, "I'll bet."

I don't like being caught in a lie, and now I'm feeling overly self-conscious. "Why can't you just drop it?"

"Why can't *you* just drop *the act?*"

His mocking tone makes me hyper-aware of my defensive stance. I've got my hands on my hips and my head cocked to one side... and I suddenly feel very, very stupid.

I turn to him and snip out, "I'd rather just drop this conversation."

And then I storm off.

Only once all night do I actually attempt to see if he's even still at the party. It's not until hours have gone by that my eyes scan the crowd... and land directly on his.

He's standing near the hot tub, leaning against its wall. And damn him if he doesn't look as though he's been standing there watching me all along. In the quick second it takes to break my gaze and pretend that I don't see him, a sly grin decorates his face.

Vix must see my eyes narrowing into slits, because she asks, "Hey, Liv. You okay?"

On a shaky exhale, I answer, "It's just really late and I'm tired. I'm going up to bed."

I throw out my cup on the way into the house and step over some sleeping bodies on my trek through the family room.

Making my way upstairs and into the bedroom, I change into PJs and climb into bed. I realize I forgot to brush my teeth and am almost drunk enough not to care. But when my head starts pounding, I figure it's just as well. I throw off the covers with a frustrated grunt and go into the bathroom.

I brush, down two Tylenol, sink back into bed, and will sleep to come. My last conscious thought is a wish to never see Jack again... then the realization that I'm lying.

* * *

I awake to the crush of my sister, climbing over me on her way to the bathroom. After a few groggy moments, I quietly slide out from under the covers, too. I'm trying not to disturb Sam, who's still sleeping in the big bed the three of us have apparently shared. I'm surprised that I slept so soundly, not taking notice of the fact that the two other bodies crept in while I dozed. Checking the time, I can't believe it's almost noon.

I step around Isla who's passed out on the bare floor and snicker when there's no sign of Tess. I crumple into a sitting position outside the bathroom door, still half-asleep and waiting on Vix's exit. When I glance up... I'm greeted with the sight of Isla's naked ass.

I guess she must've stripped off her shorts to pass out in only the shirt and thong she'd been wearing all night. But the sheet that covered her must have tangled away when she turned on her side, exposing her bare butt to the breeze. And now it's smiling directly at me.

My face buries into my elbow as I try to contain my laughter. My entire body is convulsing silently as Vix comes out of the bathroom. She crouches down next to me and puts a consoling hand to my back, obviously under the mistaken impression that I'm crying. "Oh my God. Liv. What happened? Are you okay?"

"No. I'm scarred for life."

I raise a finger to point in Isla's direction, and Vix can finally see my upturned mouth. She looks for herself and chokes on her own breath, joining me in the impossible task of trying to keep quiet. We have our hands over our mouths and tears are streaming down our faces, but it's no use. A slow crescendo of guffaws breaks from our throats as we start rolling around on the floor, laughing uncontrollably.

The commotion wakes both girls and I shout, "Put that thing away, Isla!"

Isla rises up on an elbow and looks at us over her shoulder, trying to figure out what the hell is going on. She's still half asleep, and her hair is tangled and matted to one side of her head as she tries to focus on us through her slitted eyelids. Her dazed expression, her crazy hair, and the fact that her ass is *still* staring us in the face has us howling even louder. I think I'm going to pass out, I swear to God.

Once Sam joins in with our snickering, Isla finally registers what's so funny. She sits up and pulls the sheet across her bare legs, and her cheeks—the ones on her face—turn red as she blasts, "Grow up!"

She's trying not to crack a smile as she grabs the closest thing within reach of her hand, and before I can blink, a chunky, black, Steve Madden sandal whizzes past my head and thuds against the wall.

I'm still laughing hysterically as I drag to my feet and go into the bathroom.

Vix calls from the other side of the door, "Don't be too long! We have to get on the road soon if we want to make dinner at Mom and Dad's!"

I shower quickly, and by the time I pack up my things, Vix is ready to go. We say goodbye to our friends and head downstairs.

The house is still pretty dead, which is to be expected after the late one we all put in last night. We have to find Monty to say goodbye, so we follow the sound of voices coming from the yard. As we exit through the open doors, I hope that Jack isn't awake yet.

Thankfully, he must still be asleep, because the only people outside are Monty, Ron, and Tess, a circumstance that has me breathing a sigh of relief.

"Slept in the cabana again, didn't you?" Vix taunts.

Tess makes a *durr-hurr* face in response, but Ronnie is looking fairly pleased with himself. The two of them had gone MIA shortly after midnight, and it didn't take a brain surgeon to figure out why.

Instead of sticking around for all the gory details that Ron is sure to impart, we all exchange pecks on the cheek and then get on our way.

Once in the car, Vix doesn't ask too many questions about Jack—she mostly inquires about my opinion of his band. Save for a few sly comments here and there, she pretty much lays off for once.

Despite the fact that she barely even mentions Jack's name, I'm thinking of little else on the ride home.

CHAPTER 11

Monday, May 29, 1995
2:11 PM

Mom and Dad's House
Shermer Heights

Even though my father has spent the majority of his adult life earning a living as a musician, he never advanced to The Big Time. He was close to The Dream back in the seventies when his band *Persuasion* was almost signed by Columbia Records. But then his drummer OD'd right before their showcase concert, and Columbia wasn't willing to wait around for Persuasion to regroup.

But regroup they did, only to find that they'd missed their window. These days, Dad's band tours the wedding circuit, and even then, they don't get regular bookings. Persuasion is currently the house band at *The Brownstone*, a reception hall a few towns over. He still loves performing, though, even if he's only playing covers, and even when "Celebration" is requested for the hundredth time.

I get it.

Fact is, his love of music has been passed down to his daughters, especially his "youngest" one. Too bad I didn't inherit any of my mother's grace. I can't dance for shit.

Growing up in such an unconventional household was pretty cool. While most of my friends spent their weekends at family barbecues and birthday parties, Dad would be dragging us all along on trips to his music festivals or rock concerts. Most of our outings were to watch Dad perform, but even then, he was normally on the bill with some other bands we'd actually heard of. Hell. I saw Black Sabbath at the age of five, and how many kids can say that?

Though if I'm going to be honest here, I have to say that there were definitely times when I just wanted to be a regular girl. I wanted to watch Saturday morning cartoons and join the cheerleading squad and go to the mall with my friends. Sometimes, it felt like I was forced to live his life instead of my own, and there was definitely a little resentment present because of it. Don't get me wrong—I never begrudged my father's dream. It was a good dream, so I was happy for him that he was pursuing it.

But you can't pay the mortgage with dreams.

Once Vix and I were old enough to take care of ourselves, we normally chose to skip the road trips and stay home with our friends. But doing so meant that we'd spend weeks at a time without seeing Dad while he was off playing some gig. Now that I'm in my twenties, I love having my own life, but there's a part of me that kinda misses hanging out with him the way I did as a kid.

Yeah, yeah. You want to get all psychologisty with me and say that I'm trying to deal with my daddy issues by sleeping with musicians? Go right ahead. But you'd be wrong. Fact is, I enjoy sex and I love music. End of story.

Before we can even knock, the front door swings open to reveal my Dad, smiling his goofy grin at the two of us. "Livia Moon!" he says to Vix, bringing her in for a hug. "And hello to you too, Victoria Star!"

Pretending to get the twins mixed up is one of the worst running jokes in our family. Trust me, people can tell us apart, no problem. Vix and I both have dark, reddish-brown hair and green eyes, but that's pretty much where the similarities end.

And oh yeah. The middle names. I'm just going to pretend you didn't hear that, okay?

"Ha ha, Dad," I offer through his squeeze. "New one."

He laughs and releases his boa-constrictor hold on me. "How was your weekend?" he asks, leading us into the den.

There's a platter set out with cheese and crackers, so I grab a slice of cheddar, nibbling on it as I answer, "Epic as usual. How was Vermont?"

Dad plants himself in his ratty, leather recliner. "Oh, there's not a bad season in Vermont. It was beautiful. They constructed an entire stage on this open field for the festival, and we were on the bill along with about twenty other bands. The thing went on for two whole days! It was just like Woodstock."

Yep. My parents were at Woodstock. It's where they met, actually, and they never miss an opportunity to bring the conversation around to their hedonistic weekend back in 1969. I won't bore you with the story here, but suffice it to say, the details have changed about a million times over the years anyway. Vix and I are pretty sure Mom and Dad were completely stoned the entire time, and have simply filled in the blanks for our benefit. So much so that my father swears he's in the picture on the album cover. Well, not the actual *album*, but in the original, expanded picture of it—the one he has framed on the wall of the very room we're sitting in—he's insistent that the guy in the upper right-hand corner wearing a red shirt is *him*.

Dad flips open the carved wooden box on the side table to roll a cigarette. It would be easier if he just bought a goddamn pack of Marlboros instead, but the hand-rolled ciggies have always provided him with a cover.

He rolls the cig quickly, licks the paper to seal it off, and lights it. As if we couldn't smell the difference, the fact that he's smoking inside tips us off that this is a straight cig. He always goes outside to smoke his pot.

Mom joins us, wiping her hands on the dish towel tucked into her belt loop as she kisses us hello. "Hi Girls!" Sitting on the arm of Dad's chair, she pinches the cig from his fingers. "Dinner's almost ready. Chicken Rollantine," she adds on a wink before taking a drag.

"So how was your wedding?" Vix asks.

Dad reclaims his cig, and taking a long pull, he answers on an exhale. "Pretty good. Well, at least up until the father of the groom got drunk and made a toast."

Oh God. We love these stories. Dad has absolutely seen it all. Vix and I are practically busting out of our skin when we ask, "Why? What happened?"

68

He smiles just to prolong the agony. "Dad!" I yell at him. "Spill it!"

"Okay, okay," he laughs out. "Well, the F-O-G staggers up to us in the middle of "Disco Inferno" and keeps pestering Phil for the mic. We finally wind the song down and hand it over, and he slurs out this totally creepy rant about how hot his new daughter-in-law looks in her low-cut gown."

"Ewww!"

"Yeah, well, I grabbed the mic before he could go into detail. But get this one: The F-O-B was so grateful to me for cutting him off that he tipped us an extra grand."

"Get out of here!"

"Yep." He snuffs out his cig and says, "I've had my eye on this sweet Fender Strat forever. I'm picking it up tomorrow."

I want to tell him to use the surprise two-fifty to pay the goddamn overdue phone bill, but instead, I shut up and try to look appropriately thrilled for him. Thankfully, Vix speaks up before I can lose my cool. "Were you there for that, Mom?"

My mother shakes her head and says, "Nooo. I skipped that one, thank God. I booked a few classes instead."

The doorbell rings, and we all stop and stare at one another. You'd think we never heard a doorbell before, because Mom is the only person who thinks to get up and answer it.

Do you ever have those moments when you're just going about your life and everything is normal, but then out of nowhere, you see something completely out of place? Like a guy in front of some fast food place in a chicken costume or something. And your brain takes an extra second to register it, like, what is *that* doing there?

Yeah.

That's kind of how I feel right now, watching my mother escort Jack into the room.

I jump up so abruptly that my knee catches the edge of the coffee table, and the plate of cheese and crackers goes sliding to the floor.

"What are you doing here?" I ask, perfectly astounded.

69

Jack plasters a crooked smile on his face to explain, "Monty gave me the address. Sorry. I didn't realize it was your parents' house."

"But why are you looking for me?"

"You forgot this." He holds up my camera case by its strap, the black canvas bag swinging from his fingertips. "I figured it was important, and your house was on the way home."

Crap. I can't believe I forgot my camera! But instead of dwelling on my boneheaded move, I remark, "Shermer Heights isn't on *anyone's* way home."

"It is on mine. I live here."

Jack Fucking Tanner lives in the same town as my parents?

Before Mom and Dad can start asking questions, I drop to my knees to clean up my mess. Jack crouches down to help.

While we're picking up cheese and crackers off the shag, he asks, "It's okay that I'm here, right?"

No. No, it most certainly is *not* okay. But instead of telling him that, I just give him a nod of my head and say, "Mm hmm."

When we stand up, I can see my parents looking at us curiously. I forgot that there were other people in the room. "Oh, uh... Mom, Dad... this is Jack Tanner."

My mother gives a wave and asks, "Nice to meet you Jack. Welcome to our home. How do you know our Livia?"

Before I can stop him, he answers, "She came to see my band play The Tradewinds."

My father perks up. "Ohh, so you're a musician, too!"

"Yes sir."

Dad lowers an eyebrow at him. "Call me that again, and you'll find yourself out on the curb. The name's Russ, got it?"

Jack chuckles. "Yes, *Russ*. Understood." As they shake hands, Jack nods his head over my father's shoulder. "Nice collection."

My father has four entire bookcases filled with record albums. Jack's interest in them gives Dad all the excuse he needs to declare, "Oh, albums are the only way to go. There's a reason Pearl Jam still releases on vinyl."

He walks our new houseguest over to the wall of music, and the two of them launch into a discussion, debating the merits of all the various titles.

I'm still trying to register the surreal sight when Mom asks, "Will you be joining us for dinner, Jack?"

I could cheerfully strangle her. How the hell am I supposed to get out of this one?

Jack is crouched down in front of the bookshelves, and I catch the unspoken question in his eyes as he silently seeks my approval. I'm quite sure the look on my face is *not* welcoming.

His lip quirks as he stands up. "Thank you, but I've got rehearsals in about an hour."

Thank God.

"I'll walk you out," I offer.

As we reach the front door, I start to feel badly about how I'm acting. Jack made a special trip over here just to save my ass, and here I am, treating him like an AIDS monkey. "Hey, um, thanks for bringing my camera back. It would've sucked if I had to use a backup all week."

"No problem," he answers, grinning at me. "It's not the only reason I came here, though."

I snicker out, "Yeah. No one should miss the opportunity to meet Russ and Linda."

"No," he says, seriously enough for me to take notice. "I wanted to tell you something."

He steps closer, sliding his hand up the side of my neck. I catch a whiff of his smoky, minty scent as his green-blue-gray eyes meet mine. "I don't want to be just another guy to you. I don't know why that should be important to me, but it is."

I'm frozen in place as he plants a soft kiss on the corner of my mouth.

And then he walks out the door.

* * *

71

After dinner, Vix goes upstairs to ransack the closet in our old room and Dad heads outside to the patio for a "cigarette."

Because of that, Mom and I have found a rare private moment alone as we wash the dishes at the kitchen sink.

I don't know why I suddenly feel the need to bring up one of our family's dicier subjects, but for whatever reason, right now I can't seem to think about anything else.

"Mom?" I ask. "How come you and Daddy stayed together?"

When Vix and I were little, our parents were separated for a short while. Even when dad moved back in, there was a good two-year stretch where he spent most nights on the couch. They never made a secret of the reason why, but we had never discussed it in any great detail.

"That's a silly question. We're married. We have two kids together."

"No," I correct her. "I mean... *after*."

The way I'm biting my lip serves as a dead giveaway for what I'm getting at. She takes a deep breath and exhales, her eyes focused out the window at the overgrown rose bushes in the backyard.

"I knew what I was getting into when I started dating him, Livia Moon," she admonishes in a voice that's supposed to come across as motherly. "But I couldn't stay away. It would seem falling for rock stars is in your blood, so I shouldn't have to explain the attraction," she teases, raising an eyebrow at me.

I don't want this conversation being turned around on me. I've never really asked about this and I don't want to just let it drop. So I evade her evasion by saying, "The problem is that I guess lots of *other* women find them attractive, too, huh."

She gives a shake to her head and goes back to the dishes. "Yes. But we were already married—already *parents*," she corrects on a smile. "He apologized. I believed him. What else could I do? I was crazy about the big jerk." She takes a peek outside to the big jerk in question. "Still am, as a matter of fact. I made my choices and I still stand by them, all these years later." On a sigh, she calls me out. "If you're looking for regret, honey, you won't find any here."

I find that statement to be completely impossible. Mom is making it sound as if all their issues stemmed from a onetime indiscretion, which I don't believe to be the case at all. Even now, my sister and I are pretty sure that nothing has changed; my father just got better at hiding it, is all. And if Vix and I know it, Mom sure as hell does. Maybe she's just learned to turn a blind eye.

I would never want to be in that position.

It's kind of why I don't allow myself to get serious about anyone, even going so far as to target musicians in my quest to control the situation. A rock star is the very type of guy that would put me most at risk for getting burned. If I don't feel anything more than attraction for them, if I can split before they get a chance to fuck me over… they can't hurt me.

I mean, there is *no way* I'd ever forgive a guy for doing something like that, whether we were married with kids or not. What kind of man is that? And what kind of trash bag would allow herself to be The Other Woman? For all my promiscuity, I *never* hook up with married guys. I'm trying to have some fun; I'm not looking to destroy a marriage. Because I can't see how any wife would put up with it.

My mother has to either be the most understanding or most desperate person on the planet.

The thing is, though, I'm *glad* they found a way to stay together. If they hadn't, I would have grown up in a broken home. But I can't imagine what they went through in order to give us a stable childhood.

I thought the conversation was over, but Mom waves a dismissive hand in the air as she adds, "And anyway, that's in the past. He's not that same person anymore." I get the impression she's trying to convince herself of that more than she is me. She turns off the water and dries her hands on a dish towel. "But I guess I wouldn't be doing my duty as your mother if I told you my choices were *all* sound. Have your fun. But don't…"

She shakes her head as she trails off, prompting me to ask, "Don't what?"

Mom turns toward me and swipes a piece of hair behind my ear. "Just don't sell yourself short. Attraction isn't everything. Got it?"

Loud and clear, Mom. Loud. And. Clear.

CHAPTER 12

Friday, June 2, 1995
10:02 AM

The Studio
Ridgewood

I drag myself through the doors of The Studio and fix a cup of coffee before slumping onto the black, leather couch on the far side of the showroom. I officially broke up with Mitch last night and the conversation has left me spent, even though our separation had taken all of ten minutes. I was only half surprised that he hadn't really protested the idea of ending our relationship.

Because of his aloof attitude, I was able to pound the last nail in that coffin without regret. I received all the confirmation I needed to walk away and not look back. After that conversation with my mother this past weekend, it helped me to see what I've been missing out on. Mitch was hot, but he had the personality of a mildewy sponge.

Why shouldn't I expect better?

He came to my apartment unannounced last night with some Chinese food and a bottle of wine. But before he could get too comfortable, I dropped the bomb, right there at the dining room table. "We need to talk."

Those four words set off a brief, emotionless dissolution of our dating status, and moments later, I watched him drive off on his Harley for the last time.

Vix got home from work shortly after, and she and I spent the rest of the evening polishing off the leftover Chinese, chain-smoking cigarettes, and downing a few cocktails in celebration. Once I finally 'fessed up about hooking up with Jack, she insisted on a few *more* cocktails in celebration.

Even though I got to sleep at a decent hour, I woke up with a slight hangover, and now I'm finding it difficult to get my gears turning.

Letting out a cleansing breath, I squint at Shana, peering over the glasses at her nose, clearly sizing up the sorry state of her employee. "Drinking on a school night? Tsk, tsk."

I roll my head to the side and am able to open my right eye. "Shut up, Shane. I am in no condition to kick your ass this morning."

Shana laughs and rummages around in her desk. She comes up with some Advil. "Here." She tosses the bottle to me and I fumble to catch it. "Take two of these and meet me in the darkroom."

Ahhh. A dark room.

Thank God Shana still insists on the ancient art of hand-developing her photos. Most places just shop that task out, but this is one area where I'm glad she's a perfectionist.

Everywhere else, her obsessions can get pretty grating.

Shana and I actually went to high school at St. Nicetius together, but she graduated a year ahead of me—a fact she likes to exploit often, as if it gives her the right to lord over my days, simply because she's eight months older.

We were in the same art and photography classes her senior year and just kind of hit it off. My group of girlfriends never clicked with her, though, and Vix went so far as to say, almost daily, that Shana is a pain in the ass.

I get it.

Before we started working together, Shana could sometimes drive me crazy with her self-centeredness. Now that she's my boss, that annoying little trait of hers has multiplied tenfold. As grateful as I am that she's given me a job, there's a part of me that feels she only did it to officially retake the role of my superior, picking up where we left off in high school. If her parents hadn't set the precedent by spoiling her her entire life, she wouldn't have been able to pressure them so easily into buying her this storefront in the first place.

This storefront that serves as my windowless prison.

76

With Shana as acting warden.

But what Vix can never understand is that Shana isn't *all* bad. We definitely share the same sense of humor, so working with her can sometimes be a lot of fun. And, like I said, she signs my paycheck every week, so I can't complain too badly. Even when she was interviewing new photographers last year, one guy showed up with an impressive resume. Shana still kept me in the full-time position and hired Manuel for part-time.

So, if she was a complete bitch, there's no way I'd still be working for her after three whole years. And I've learned so much in the time I've been here, not just about photography, but the ins and outs of running a business. Not so much from Shana—her mother is the one that does all the gruntwork to keep the place going—but I learned it all the same.

Within the hour, I'm on auto-pilot. I forget my hangover and dive into my work. One day a week is normally set aside to develop film, print photos, and confirm appointments. The only other humans we see on most Fridays are the rare walk-ins, since most of our clients are scheduled weeks in advance.

The day flies by.

* * *

I woke up early this morning—despite the hangover—to pack our bags for the beach. The plan was to leave for the weekend right from The Studio and then pick up Vix at the train station so we could head straight down.

So, it's still a gorgeous, sunny day as we cruise down the road en route to the beach.

We have the windows down as The Raritan Bridge comes into view. It's New Jersey's very own Mason-Dixon line, the point that, at least for me, always delineated the north from the south.

"Magic" by Pilot comes on the radio, and my mind is transported to a time so, so very long ago when my sister and I would ride down with our parents in Dad's convertible Cadillac—no seatbelts—the summer sun shining on our skin, sunburned before we even made it to the beach. The car would be crammed with beach chairs and pails and shovels and duffel bags. We'd sing along to 8-tracks of The Beach Boys and Chicago, The Four Seasons and Neil Sedaka, Blondie and ELO and Wings.

And when we hit the bridge, we knew fun was mere minutes away.

It was the spot where I could get my first whiff of the bay and its briny, fishy aroma, which was only pleasing because of the promise it held: Sandcastles and body surfing, cold drinks smuggled onto the beach in a mini cooler, and Dad's transistor radio blasting out AM gold while we baked in the sun on a scratchy, wool blanket.

No beach day would have been complete without a trip to the boardwalk, where somehow, Dad always found the cash for us to load up on pizza, play a few wheels, and hit some rides at the Funtown Pier.

My love of music was ingrained in me since birth, but was solidified in Dad's convertible and that stupid little transistor radio out on the beach.

In the middle of this all-consuming burst of heart-swelling nostalgia, Hall and Oates' "Rich Girl" comes blaring out of the speakers, creating the perfect soundtrack for my walk down Memory Lane. How many times have I been down this same stretch of the Parkway? Every summer weekend of my youth has started with this same road, traveling to the promised land of sand and surf.

Even though these days, a trip to the beach is for nothing more than a great night out with my friends, it is still there where I find myself most at home.

All the other seasons pale in comparison to the excitement and freedom of summer. It's the one time of year when I can cut loose and feel like a kid again. Before the responsibilities, before the soul-crushing pressure of trying to figure out my future. I can forget about my crappy job; I can forget about my even crappier love life.

Summer is my superpower.

CHAPTER 13

Friday, June 2, 1995
9:13 PM

The Beach House
Manasquan

"Where's my other brown sandal?"

Sammy's voice interrupts my hair ritual. I put the flatiron down on my dresser and ask, "Which pair?"

She's all huffy as she clarifies, "The ones with the cork heel that you borrowed last weekend?"

I check under the bed and come up with the missing shoe. "Sorry," I offer, handing it over.

"Bitch."

I finish straightening my hair and then go out into the living room to wait for everyone else to get ready. I got first dibs on the shower, so now I have some time to kill.

Isla joins me soon enough. Her hair is still wet, but she has to wait for Vix to finish blow-drying before she can. We learned during the first weekend that running two blow dryers simultaneously would not only knock out the power in this place, but cause a rip in the space/time continuum. The wiring in this ancient old cottage isn't equipped to handle more power than it would take to burn a piece of toast.

As Isla slips into her sandals, I notice that she's got on a pair of white jean shorts covered in a splatter-paint design.

I take one look at her and snicker, "Are you really wearing those out tonight? You look like Punky Fucking Brewster."

She doesn't even wait a beat before busting into a Running Man move, singing, "*In my opinionation... the sun is gonna truly shine...*"

"That's 'Blossom,' you turd." She laughs as I add, "Same wardrobe, though. I never thought about that. Huh. Bravo."

80

We both exchange our best *whoa* before I realize that the stupid theme song is now lodged in my head. "Crap. We need some real music."

I throw on the boombox, and "Smells Like Teen Spirit" comes blaring out of the speakers.

As excited as I always am to hear some Nirvana, the elation is always closely followed by heartbreak. Cobain offed himself last year, and I still haven't gotten over it. Dad and I were stuck in such a funk in the weeks following the news. We were glued to the TV, just soaking up every smidge of the story, trying to figure out how someone so talented could have been so haunted.

So wrong on so many levels.

I'm jogged out of my melancholy once I hear Tess screaming the lyrics from the bathroom. Isla and I soon join in, and before we know it, the walls are shaking as all five of us take part in the sing-along.

I feel stupid! And contagious!
Here we are now! Entertain us!

As the song is ending, Tess comes out of the bathroom wrapped in a fluffy towel, dancing around as she spritzes all of us with her Bath and Body Works glitter spray "just for some extra glow" as Vix starts futzing with my outfit again. She's been treating me like a goddamn Barbie doll all night, offering "helpful" suggestions about what I should wear, and it's starting to get on my nerves.

I slap her hand away from my skirt and snip, "Vix! Enough already. What the hell?"

She stops her adjustments and eyes me thoughtfully. "At least lose the Doc Martens. Here. You can wear my heels." She pulls the black platform shit-kickers off her own feet and thrusts them in my direction. I would fight her on it, but she knows I love those shoes. Plus, if it will get her to lay off, I'm down for anything.

* * *

81

Vix doesn't feel like drinking tonight, so she volunteered to play Designated Driver in order to avoid paying for a cab. It's only Week Two at the beach, but we've pretty much been drinking nonstop every moment we've been down here. I totally get why she wants to take a break.

We pull into the lot at The Parker House, and thank God, there isn't a huge line to get in the door. I guess that's because the whole world is already inside. We file our way to the bar without losing one another which is no easy feat; the place is packed and the music is already blaring. If the DJ is playing this loud, I can't even imagine the damage to my eardrums once the band hits the stage.

Years ago, we taught ourselves some basic sign language just so we could communicate in these situations, so Sam wedges out a space at the bar and uses her hands to ask us what we all want. I spell out *B-U-D* and add the sign for *lightbulb* to convey my order, then share a ciggie with Vix while we wait for one of the damned bartenders to make their way down to our end.

The DJ winds down, but it's still unbearably loud in here. I just know my ears will be buzzing all day tomorrow.

Tinnitus. The bane of every twenty-something's existence.

Our drinks are delivered in the nick of time, because I was about to die of thirst. I take a swig from my Bud Light as we commandeer a spot nearer to the stage just as the band starts in for their set. My back is turned, but as I hear the opening notes of "Higher Ground" kick in, I find myself whirling around for visual confirmation.

Jack is fucking playing.

My initial shock at the sight of him is immediately followed by the sinking suspicion that I've been set up.

I raise an eyebrow at my sister who is failing miserably in her attempt to look surprised. She gives a shrug, but her lips are twitching, and I give her a dirty look before turning my attention back to the stage.

In spite of my anger, it's impossible not to get sucked into Thunderjug's energy. Into *Jack's*. I take a moment to really watch him onstage, to appreciate the pure, unadulterated power he's selling. He's owning the music. He's owning the crowd. Shit, he's owning *me*.

He spots me in the middle of "When I Come Around," shooting me a dazzling grin and a wink from behind his mic. He's enjoying himself up there, and it's hard to do anything but smile back.

At the break, Jack weaves his way through the crowd toward us. I pretend not to notice his transaction with the rose girl, and act pleasantly surprised when he holds up the single, red bloom between us. "I'm glad you made it."

I used to find bar-bought roses kind of cheesy, but my opinion is suddenly changing on the matter. "Thank you," I say, accepting it. "But to be honest, I didn't realize I was coming to see Thunderjug tonight."

He smiles at that, then asks if I'd like to meet the guys.

I agree, and we wend our way to the side of the stage where the other three members of Thunderjug are surrounded by a group of people. *Women* people.

A few of the girls notice that Jack is nearby, and he's forced to make nice—kissing a few cheeks, accepting a few hugs—as we cut our way into the center of the circle.

He claps a hand on the shoulder of the tall, decently handsome guy with longish, dark hair, almost yelling the introduction. "Freddie! This is Livia. Liv, you may have noticed by now that Freddie and I trade off lead guitar and bass."

I shake his hand as Jack points to his drummer. "And that's Jimmy. Yo, Jimmy! Say hello to Livia."

Jimmy breaks away from the pretty blonde draped over his every word to turn toward us. He's got fantastic sandy-colored hair and insanely gorgeous blue eyes that are both wasted on an unremarkable face. "Lizzie?" he asks.

"Livia!" I correct him as I shake his hand. He aims a grin at Jack, which lets me know he's only busting my chops. It puts me under the impression that Jack has maybe mentioned something about me a time or two.

Jimmy grabs the guy next to him and pulls him into our conversation. "Did you meet Booey yet?"

83

"Booey?" I ask, sure that I misheard his name.

"Short for Ba-Ba-Booey," Jack laughs out.

"Like Gary from the Howard Stern show?"

"Exactly. He's kind of our unofficial manager, plus he's got that stupid moustache."

Booey gives Jack the finger, saying, "Nice, dickhead."

Jack ignores the slam and instead makes up for the insult. "Booey plays keyboards, harmonica, sax, rhythm and bass guitars."

"Wow!" I respond, clearly impressed.

"Yeah. The dude is pretty much a one-man band but he lets us hang around." He throws a wink at Booey just to rile him up.

It's nice to meet the guys, even though Jack makes a point to keep the conversation brief, almost as if he's trying to keep me all to himself. He directs their attention back to their adoring fans and suggests we go out to grab some air.

I'm feeling like a sardine crammed into this small area of the club anyway, so I'm relieved when Jack relocates us outside to the deck. It's hot as balls out here, but even the liquid heat being inhaled into my lungs is an improvement over the recirculated AC inside. At least I feel like I'm breathing my own air, instead of having to share the same oxygen with the rest of Generation X in there.

It's not quite so loud out here, but my ears are already ringing from the hours of assault. That's why I'm not quite sure I hear Jack correctly when he asks, "So, are you going to let me take you out or what?"

I roll my eyes, busting his chops when I answer, "Still pushing this?"

"Still avoiding the answer?"

"It's difficult to consider the question," I huff.

"Why's that?"

"Helloooo Captain Obvious. I like sex. And if I date you, I won't be having any."

Jack smiles through a sigh. "That's not what I said. I'm not planning to be celibate my whole life, for chrissakes."

"Just while you're dating me."

"Yes, but not the whole time."

I dismiss him with a wave of my hand. "Jackson, you wouldn't be able to hold out long enough to tell me no for even *one night.*"

"Wanna bet?"

"Wanna lose? Why? Whaddya got for me?"

His brows furrow as he thinks. "Okay. It's not really a bet. More like an arrangement." I eye him skeptically, watching as he tries to contain an evil grin. "Ten dates. That's all I ask. Ten dates is enough time for us to decide where we're going to go from there, if we like each other enough to take things further."

"Further. You mean have sex."

"Yes."

"And you want me to agree not to push the issue in the meantime."

"Yes."

I think on that for a minute. "Can we do other stuff?"

"Like what?"

"Like kissing and touching and stuff."

He scratches at the tuft of hair on his chin as he considers my question. Most guys look like dicks with chin pubes, but Jack is pulling it off without coming across as a soul-patched poser. "Kissing, yes. But let's just play the other stuff by ear."

"I don't know. You're not really being clear about the rules with this proposition, here," I fire back, eyeing him warily.

He takes a heavy breath. "Look, Lips. This is something new for me too, remember. We'll just have to make up the rules as we go along."

My eyes tighten as I assess the situation. I still don't understand this purity quest he's on, but what the hell. If some stupid bet is going to be all it takes to get this guy into bed, I'm game. It'll almost be a novelty, having to work that hard to get a guy to sleep with me. Men are so easy.

Well, normally, anyway.

"So, no sex for ten days," I assess. "I've done that before, no problem."

"Not ten days... Ten *dates.* It may be longer than a week and a half before we—"

"Whoa. Hold on." I haven't even agreed to this proposition and he's already throwing a wrench into the gears. What if he's planning to drag me through a *year* of this little "arrangement"? We need some ground rules.

"Okay," I say. "First amendment: All dates must take place by… the Fourth of July. That gives us an entire month."

"Deal." He's smiling as he adds his own term. "Second amendment: You don't date—or have sex with—anyone else in the meantime."

I hadn't really considered the monogamy aspect of our arrangement. But I suppose it's a reasonable request. "Deal."

"Wow, Lips," he says, crossing his arms and raising his brows. "I don't think I've ever seen you this agreeable before. Did you just take me up on my offer?"

I can't quite believe it myself, but holy shit, yeah, I guess I did. How did he manage to get me to do that?

I hold out my hand in answer. He shakes it, and I swear to God, there's an audible *clang!* as the chastity belt claps around my pelvis.

"Get ready for some fireworks, pal," I say through a playful grin.

"You first," he shoots back, digging around in his back pocket. "Here. I have something for you."

He replaces his handshake with a cassette tape, sandwiching it and my fingers between his palms.

"For me? How did you…?" My earlier suspicions come to light as I shoot him a sidelong smirk. "You knew I was coming tonight, didn't you?"

"A little birdie may have arranged our 'chance meeting'."

My money is on Vix. "You mean my own sister *sold me out.*"

His lip quirks at that, fighting the urge to smile. "Just give it a listen. I'll call you in the morning."

* * *

As soon as we're in the car, Tess lunges for the cassette. "Give it, Livia! I gotta hear what's on this thing!"

Before I can react, Tess wrestles the tape from its case and pops it into the dashboard's stereo. Isla, Sam, and I lean forward from the backseat as Vix puts the car in drive and Tess presses play. I haven't completely forgotten that my sister set up this whole evening just to throw me under the bus, but as I hear the first notes of Jack's guitar, I decide I'll let her live.

We're completely silent as Thunderjug begins to fill the car with music. It's a pretty song that doesn't take long to recognize, even though it's been sped up and layered with added instrumentals... it's the one Jack was playing that first night we met, back at Monty's house after The Tradewinds. Only now, there are words set to the tune as his low, gravelly voice sings along.

Between life and death I've lived alone
A darkness that I've always known
To live again, to live, to live:
This heart that beats is not my own...

I look down at the empty cassette case in my hands and then at the two girls in the front seat.

Tess sees the stunned look on my face and asks, "What? What's it say?"

My voice is barely audible as I manage to squeak out, "It's dated last Friday. The song's title is 'Vampire'."

87

CHAPTER 14

Date #1: Tuesday, June 6, 1995
8:14 PM

My Apartment
Clifton

Okay. Here I go. My first date with a rock star.
Damn. That sounds like the worst After School Special ever made, and will probably play out just as PG-rated. I can't believe I'm going to willingly date someone I'd rather be screwing instead.

Oh, who am I kidding? He's already seen through my bullshit. That fact should be a relief, but it's actually scary as all hell. Jack has made it pretty clear that he wants to get to know the real me, but the thing is, I'm not even sure who that is. I put some thought into it over the past week, and came to the conclusion that maybe it was high time I found out.

The morning after The Tape, I'd barely woken up before I was pressing play on the boombox I'd smuggled into my room the night before. I listened to my song the whole rest of the weekend, the entire way home, and then about a million times since.

Jack called as promised, and with the safety of some distance between us, I was able to enjoy our talk that day. And the one on the day after that. I finally caved yesterday, and we made plans to get together tonight.

Oh, God. Why did I even agree to this?
Because he's hot as hell, you idiot.
Well, yes, that's true. But come on. A fricking musician? There's cause to have guidelines against this sort of thing. I admittedly don't live my life based around some long list of rules, but the few that are in place are there for a reason.

My first rule is and always has been: *Thou shalt not loan money to my father.*

But, I guess I've broken that one a few times, too.

I mean, how am I supposed to say no? The guy raised us, spoiling the hell out of us whenever he could. Just because he can't seem to pull his shit together sometimes doesn't mean I should cut him off. He's my family. And you do what you can for your family.

Right there at Number Two on my commandments is: *Thou shalt not date musicians.*

Okay. I know how hypocritical that sounds. But there's a big difference between hooking up with some smoking hot guitarist for a night of fun, and entering into a relationship with the aforementioned man-whore. Life is too short to spend it worrying over some sex-stud's fidelity. That's the reason I don't date rock stars. I don't want to constantly wonder what some guy is up to when I'm not around. I mean, it's not that I can be instantly assured that a non-musician will guarantee faithfulness, but the chances are way better. I know all too well what sort of convoluted road my parents have traveled in order to get where they are now.

But since Jack's whole deal with wanting to date me is specifically to *not* have sex, I have to imagine his mindset extends to every other woman on the planet, too. Huh. Suddenly, a rock star has turned into my safest bet. How the hell did *that* happen?

I give a peek back outside and finally see Jack pulling into the driveway. 'Bout frigging time.

My stomach does a quick flip when he knocks, and I can't stop myself from sprinting for the door. I open it, busting his chops when I say, "You're late."

Jack is standing there, sporting a sheepish grin and looking delicious as usual. But suddenly, his smile fades. "What the hell are you wearing?"

He'd told me to dress casual, so I went with one of my standard uniforms: Black miniskirt, black tights, black Docs, and a lightweight flannel that I'm wearing unbuttoned over a tight-fitting concert tee. But his facial expression is suggesting I

89

missed the mark, and I look down at my chest, feeling tacky. Not that I'd ever let him know it.

"What, this?" I defend. "It's my Van Halen T-shirt."

"Livia," he sighs. "That is *not* a Van Halen T-shirt. That is a Van *Hagar* T-shirt. If anyone could make it look good, it would be you, but please, I'm begging you. Take it off."

Ah. The outfit isn't the problem, just my choice of band. His exasperation and complete music snobbery brings a smile to my face. Temperamental rock star. Yeesh.

"Right here?" I tease. "Because I should warn you, I'm wearing a matching Van Halen bra underneath this thing," I laugh as I head off to my bedroom to go change.

I get about five steps away before turning just enough to see his lip curl and his eyebrows rise. "Prove it."

Spinning slowly on my heel to face him, I fist my hands on my hips and meet his eyes. "Gladly."

That staggers Jack a bit, enough to make him realize what kind of game he's playing. He gives a snicker and runs a hand through his hair. "Hey, Liv? I'm sorry. Old habit. That sort of just slipped out. But you know I'm really trying to do the right thing, here, right? Can you do me a favor and not make it so hard?"

Oh, the comebacks I could fire at him for that. I'm about ready to back his delectable form onto my couch and show him just how hard I'm capable of making things between us. Instead, I take a look at the gorgeous man standing in my living room, warring with himself about taking the straight and narrow. The thing is, he's a *nice guy*. I'm not used to dating nice guys.

If I had any reservations about this dating thing prior to Jack's arrival, it was that moment that I felt them disappearing. If I am going to do this, I need to give it a fighting chance. I lose the chip on my shoulder and answer, "Okay. You're right. I'll be good."

I stand still for an extra second, waiting for another smarmy comeback, but it doesn't come. I decide that the way he's visibly biting his tongue from firing out a retort is good enough for me, and head off to my bedroom to go change.

* * *

His ride is a broken-down van which reminds me of that POS Camry Vix and I were forced to share when we first got our licenses. He does the gentlemanly thing and opens the door for me, and as I get in, I lean over to his side to make sure the lock is popped. I know Sonny made a huge deal about that move in *Bronx Tale*, but it's just common courtesy, right?

There are a few Styrofoam coffee cups on the floor and a stack of papers and notebooks crammed into the console between us. Great. I'm dating a slob. "You always make it a habit to give a girl such a stellar first impression by picking her up in this molester van?"

"Sorry. It was blocking my car and I was running late."

"Well, at least you keep it clean."

"Hey, *princess*," he offers through a laugh. "I told you, I was running late. And blame the mess on Freddie. He's normally the one riding shotgun in this thing."

We sit in silence as he pulls out of my street. I've never been much one for silence, and without any background music, the first-date jitters are amplified. In the ten minutes since he's walked through my door, I've already chastised him for being late, got defensive about my T-shirt, accused him of being a creeper, and insulted his hygiene. Not exactly the greatest start to our evening.

Told you I suck at dating.

The self-imposed tension in the car is more than I can take. "Hey. Mind if I turn on the radio?"

Jack taps his thumbs against the wheel. "Actually, yes. There's a Smiths tape stuck in the cassette player, and if I have to listen to it one more time, I may drive us off the road."

That makes me laugh. "Which one?"

"Best of."

"One or Two?"

"One."

"Mind if I take a chance?"

He sighs. "Yeah, go ahead."

I turn up the volume, and "How Soon is Now?" pours out of the speakers. I haven't listened to these guys in ages. I was never a humongous fan, but one time, I bought tickets to see Morrissey at the Garden. A week before the concert, he canceled the show, no excuses given. No refund either. I never forgave him for that, but I'm thinking that maybe I shouldn't have taken my anger out on The Smiths. This is a good freaking song. "I can deal with this."

"Me too. But it's going off again after this one, okay?"

"Deal."

After the song is over, "Hand in Glove" starts in, and Jack gives a groan, so I turn down the volume. I take a look at my date for the evening, trying to think of something to say, but I'm still mesmerized by his absolute gorgeousness, and after a while, I realize I've just been sitting here staring at him for way too long. *Awkwaaard.*

"How can you just ride around in silence?" I finally blurt out.

"I don't know. Silence is underrated. I do most of my song-writing in the car or the shower. That's easier to do without the distraction of someone else's music, you know? Inspiration doesn't come easily when it has to fight through noise."

I sit in the quiet, waiting for inspiration to strike, but it's hard to think about anything beyond the smoking hot rock star sitting next to me. I'm not used to this dating thing as it is, and am fighting the urge to slip into default-mode. I want to slide over to his side of the car and run a hand up his jean-clad legs. I want to tangle my fingers in the back of his hair and suck his face for the next couple of hours. I start to get all sweaty just thinking about it.

So instead, I ask, "You're not writing anything right now, are you?"

"Nope."

"Then do you care if I take a go at getting that cassette out of there so we can listen to some music?"

Jack shoots me a skeptical look. "There's a screwdriver in the glove compartment. Knock yourself out."

I rifle through the glove box and find it. Just as I jab it into the stereo, Jack says, "But I already tried to wedge that thing out a million times. It's pretty point—"

"Got it! Ha ha, sucker. I freaking got you!" I pull the cassette out, trailing a long ribbon of tangled tape behind it, and hold it up to show my stunned chauffer.

"How the hell did you *do that*?" he asks, perfectly astounded.

I wiggle the stuck ribbon out from the player, and wedge the screwdriver into the cassette holes to wind up the excess tape. "This night will go easier for you the sooner you realize I'm awesome."

I turn up the volume and start punching his presets, trying to find a decent station. When I come across Billy Joel's "My Life," I take a shot and leave it on. Sneaking a look over at Jack, I'm pleased to find him tapping a hand against the wheel, softly singing along, so I join him.

Maybe I got a little too into the duet, because I suddenly realize Jack is no longer singing. I have my head back against the seat and my eyes closed, but I snap them open to find him staring at me. "What?" I ask, completely self-conscious.

"You just sang 'victim of Son of Sam.'"

"So?"

"So, the lyrics are 'victim of circumstance.' Please tell me you were only joking."

I bite my lip and look at him sheepishly. "Umm, aside from being awesome, you should know that I'm also lyrically challenged."

That has him cracking up.

CHAPTER 15

Tuesday, June 6, 1995
8:45 PM

The Westlake Pub
Norman

The place Jack takes me is *The Westlake Pub*. It's the local bar in Norman, right on Lenape Lake. When I was in high school, I used to drive by it all the time. I always wondered what it was like inside.

I find out soon enough.

It's kind of a dive, but it has this great, homey feel to it. Lots of dark wood and scrungy old sports banners plastered all over the walls. Jack grabs us a couple beers and we head right for the pool room, chatting as we play a round of darts while waiting for our turn at the table.

"Thunderjug plays here sometimes," Jack says, just missing the bullseye. "It was the first place that ever hired us for a gig, actually. We play the beach all summer, but The Westlake is our home base the rest of the year."

"Just here?"

"Here first and foremost, but we play all the clubs in the area: Mother's, Rock the House, Shannon Rose, The Junkyard... wherever there's a stage, we go."

It's kind of weird that I've been to all those places that he just mentioned—numerous times—and never met him before now. I guess an argument for good timing could be made here.

Jack pulls his darts from the board, marks his points, and then hands them over. "How long have you been playing?" I ask.

He's leaning against the wall with his arms crossed over his chest. He looks so hot that I get distracted and miss my 15. "With these guys? About four years now. But I taught myself how to play guitar when I was twelve."

I take my third shot, then retrieve the darts for Jack. "I need to know: How did an unsigned band get a song on the radio?"

He takes the darts from me with a snicker and lands his final bullseye, ending the game. Dammit.

As he shakes my hand, he answers, "It just sort of happened. We recorded a few of our originals onto a CD a few months back—Booey thought it was a good idea to sell them at our shows along with the T-shirts—and one of the guys that bought one was a DJ at William Patterson's radio station." College radio. Yikes. It almost sucked me in a few years back, but there is really only so much Jimmy Buffet and Steve Miller a girl can take. I abandoned the WPU station almost as quickly as I had found it. "Anyway, I guess someone from the New York stations heard it and added 'Backyard' into the rotation. It kind of took off from there."

"Can they do that? Isn't that like stealing from you?"

"Are you kidding? Most bands flood radio stations with their CDs, just hoping that they'll get the chance to be heard. Before the bloodsucking business side took over, that's how it was done. It's just that nowadays, most bands don't get to break through without a little back-scratching from someone on the inside which is why anyone who's serious about their career will try to land an agent as early as possible."

"But not Thunderjug?"

"We just want to play music. Whether that's on a stage in a bar or arena makes no difference to us." The pool table has been vacated, so Jack throws his dollar in the box and racks up the balls before adding, "I'd be lying if I said it wasn't cool as hell to hear my song on the frigging radio, though."

While I'm laughing about that, Jack hands me a cue. "Ladies first."

I take a weak opening shot, then let Jack take his turn. "It's kind of crazy that you're planning to throw all this good fortune away."

He lines up his cue and asks, "Why's that?"

"Well, it would seem that music's been a whole lot nicer to you than construction ever has."

He almost chokes as he flubs his shot, then stands up to face me with a raised brow. "Looks like someone's been doing her homework."

Oops! I didn't mean to let on that I knew all about the drama with his ex. It takes quite a bit to get me to blush, but I know my face is probably flaming red right now.

"*Construction* wasn't the problem," he explains. "My girlfriend was. But I'm guessing you already know that."

I bite my lip and admit, "Monty may have mentioned something along those lines."

"Things weren't always awful between us, but I suppose we were doomed from the start. I mean, I only met her because her father was my boss. He liked me. Had some big connections in Contractor World. I guess I ended up sticking around way too long for all the wrong reasons." When I don't say anything, Jack asks, "Do you really want to hear this? Am I that guy who's going to spend the first date talking about his ex?"

"No, I want to know. Really. What went wrong?"

He gives a shrug and answers, "Lots of things. She hated my music, hated whenever I had to work late. She kept pressuring me to get married, and we were *so* not there yet. I kept trying to make it work, but she had really changed over the years, and I just couldn't stay in it anymore. Once I bailed, her daddy cut me off. My contracting career was dead."

I suddenly feel like I've been eavesdropping. "I'm sorry."

"Don't be. Trust me. I'm just glad the music thing took off when it did."

"There's just one thing I need to know about all this," I say, fighting to keep a straight face. Jack stills, readying himself for the Spanish Inquisition. "What the hell is a thunderjug?"

He laughs as he tosses his cue onto the table, temporarily abandoning our game. "You sure you want to know?"

I eye him skeptically. "I don't know. Do I?"

"Well, the short answer is that it's a container to store liquid."

"Liquid," I repeat.

"Uh huh."

"Okay…"

The smile is still playing at his lips as he elaborates clinically, "Well, there's a time in every man's life when he finds himself on a boat or stuck in traffic, basically in the middle of nowhere." When I show no sign of understanding, he goes on, "In such circumstances, sometimes it becomes necessary to ah, shall we say, *relieve* oneself, if you will."

"Isn't the whole world a man's toilet?" I ask, which makes him laugh.

"Yes, but not when you're in a car in the middle of a highway."

"Yeah, and?"

Jack raises an eyebrow to continue. "Empty milk containers, you know, the plastic, gallon-size? They're very useful in such a situation."

A dawning of clarity comes over me as I understand where he is leading. "Ewww! But why do you call it—"

"Because when you piss in them, it sounds like thunder! Hence…"

"The thunderjug," I finish for him, completely grossed out and cracking the hell up. "Why did you name your band after *that*?"

"Because it's funny."

I give an exaggerated shiver just as one of the bartenders comes into the room, wiping down the hightops.

Jack winks at me and nods in the direction of the man. "Hey, Liv. Rack 'em up. Care to make it interesting this time?"

The bartender turns toward us with a huge grin. He's an older guy; salt-and-pepper hair, really handsome, great smile. "Not a chance, Tanner. See the box?"

He points to the wooden box mounted on the wall. There's a sign over it that says: *NO GAMBLING. $1 donation required to play.*

I'd already watched Jack stuff some money into it prior to our game, but he plays dumb to bust the guy's chops. "Donation to what?"

"I haven't decided yet. OJ's defense fund?"

That has Jack sputtering out a cackle as he makes the introductions. "Livia, I'd like you to meet the owner of this shithole, Rudy McAllister. Rudy, Livia Chadwick."

97

"New girlfriend?" Rudy asks as he shakes my hand.

Jack snickers, "First date, Rudy."

Rudy gives a huff before admonishing, "First date and you bring her here? What's the matter with you, Tanner?"

I laugh at the way one carefully aimed jab is able to turn a successful, twenty-eight-year-old musician/contractor into a chastened, prepubescent boy.

"Hey Rudy," I say. "I actually think this place is awesome."

"Well, in that case, you'll have to let me buy you a drink."

"Sold!"

As Rudy leaves the room, Jack yells at his back, "Tell those good-for-nothing sons of yours I said hello!"

He waves without ever turning around. "You got it."

We finish our game and then finagle a couple of stools at the long bar, looking out the windows to the lake. The place may be a true dive, but it has a spectacular view and a great energy. People of all ages are crammed along the bar, and the jukebox has been playing such a mishmash of songs because of it—everything from Etta James to Soul Asylum.

As soon as we're settled with our drinks—compliments of Rudy McAllister himself—XTC's "Senses Working Overtime" comes on, and I am more than excited to hear it. "This is like the coolest place ever!"

Jack smiles. "I'm glad you like it. I guess you pass."

"Wait. Was this a test? I don't appreciate being tested unknowingly."

"Calm down. It wasn't really a test. I just always get a good idea of what I'm getting into whenever I bring a girl here."

"*Whenever you bring a girl here?* How many have there been?"

Jack meets my eyes guiltily, realizing what a tacky conversation we're having. "I'm sorry. If it makes you feel any better, it's been a long time since I brought anyone here. Like I already told you, I'm not that guy anymore."

As if on cue, a pretty young girl comes up behind him and mimes a silent shush at me before wrapping her hands over his eyes. "Guess who?"

She's beautiful, but I'm assuming she's just a friend by the way she's trying to share the sneaky giggle with me.

Jack's white grin is the only part of his face that's visible as he laughs out, "Suzi Quattro."

That makes her laugh and remove her hands.

When she does, Jack turns his head and she leans in to kiss him hello. He gives a rub up her arm and says, "Hey, baby. What are you doing here? Shouldn't you be in the city?"

The girl nods her head, and I register that she looks vaguely familiar. "Yes, but sometimes I like to visit my father, you dork. But yikes. If I don't get a job soon, I may not be living the city life much longer. God, can you imagine if I have to move back in with him?" She turns toward me and gives a wave. "Since my rude cousin doesn't look like he's going to get around to an introduction, hi. I'm Layla."

"I was working up to it, you brat!" Jack protests.

"Livia," I answer back, suddenly recognizing her name. "We went to school together, right? St. Nicetius?"

"Oh yeah! You were a year ahead of me. Class of ninety, yes?"

"Yep."

"Twin sister, Victoria? Hung out with Tess Valletti?"

"Still do."

"No way! Small world. How'd you end up here with this ugly loser?" At that, she punches Jack in the arm, so he maneuvers her into a headlock. I laugh while watching her try to break free.

Once she finally does, she gives Jack—and me—a kiss on the cheek, explaining that she's on her way out.

"Nice to see you again," I offer.

"You too. Tell the girls I said hello."

After she splits, Jack explains, "Rudy is Layla's next door neighbor; that's how I know him. I kind of grew up with his sons. He's got four—just like us—and we're all around the same age."

"No wonder this was the first place to be the guinea pig for Thunderjug. Nepotism has its priveleges, huh?" I ask.

"It's all in who you know, baby."

It's late by the time Jack pulls the van in front of my house and cuts the engine. The air is damp outside my window, seeping into the now-stilled car. I take a deep inhale; a mixture of early dew and humidity.

And maybe a little sweat.

Why am I so nervous?

Jack turns sideways in his seat. "This was fun. Are you glad you came?"

A million pithy rejoinders spring into my brain as I consider his question. Too easy. "I did. Thank you."

It's crazy, trying to reconcile my mind into this new way of thinking. Rock stars always equaled sex. Normal guys always equaled "boyfriend." But Jack is a rock star I'm *dating*, not screwing. And he's a *talented* rock star at that. I don't know how to thank him for his music, for this evening, without using my body.

Jack makes the decision for us as his mouth meets mine in a soft kiss. It's much less urgent than the first couple times we had locked lips, and I'm surprised that such a sweet kiss can be so... *nice*. I find myself sighing at the gentle pressure of his mouth, the feather-soft caress of his fingers against my jaw. It's turning me on almost as much as our hungry stolen kisses from the first weekend we'd met.

I kiss him back, only pushing it a little bit.

And then I let him drive away.

CHAPTER 16

Date #2: Friday, June 9, 1995
After 7:00 PM

My Apartment
Clifton

Jack is late. Again.

I'm waiting alone at the living room window, ducking out of sight whenever I spot a car's headlights coming up the street.

Vix and I share the rent on the bottom half of a two-family house in Clifton which is ten minutes from my parents, fifteen minutes from my work, and a one-block walk to the NJ transit so Vix can get to her job in the city.

Our "apartment" is nothing to write home about, but we each have our own bedroom, access to half of the large basement, and a kickass view of the New York City skyline out the picture window in our kitchen.

My roomie has already headed down to the Manasquan house for the weekend, offering a big hug and good luck for a fun time at the party. I am definitely going to need it. The party is happening at Jack's *parents'* house, which is freaking me out just the slightest bit on a lot of different levels. His reasoning is that since he's already met my parents, it's only fair that I meet his— despite the fact that he's the one who arranged *that* meeting, too.

I wished Vix was around a couple hours ago when I was debating what to wear. I decided on my knee-length, blue-on-white floral sundress, figuring that it could look either casual or dressy. Normally, I'd throw on my biker jacket and a pair of Docs, but tonight, I'm trying to class it up a bit. I skipped the leather on my back and opted for a pair of sandals at my feet. Why didn't Jack tell me what kind of party this was?

At least my hair is cooperating with me tonight. I'm glad I spent the extra time on it.

101

Where is he?

He'd called just once all week, and then only to confirm that we were still on for tonight, seven o'clock. I check the VCR for what seems the tenth time in the past half-hour. It's 7:24.

Finally, the doorbell rings and I open it to find Jack, breathless and apologizing for his late arrival. "I'm sorry, Liv. I got tied up with Booey trying to work out our damn schedule, and by the time I—" He stops mid-sentence and lets out a huge breath. "*Jesus*, you look good."

He's standing there looking at me like he's a shipwrecked cartoon character and I'm the hapless fellow castaway, transforming into a drool-worthy meal before his very eyes.

Trying to hide my unease at feeling like a hallucinated steak, I respond, "Thank you."

His arms slip around my middle, pulling me in as he brushes a sweet, soft kiss against my temple. His words are a seductive whisper against my skin. "It almost makes me want to blow off this party and stay home with you instead."

His touch is sending shockwaves through me as I feel the length of his body pressing against my own. His lips at my hairline are giving me chills, and I slide my hands up his back to pull him closer. "That can be arranged. Just say the word, Jack."

Before he can respond, his pager goes off. He gives out a sigh as he steps out of my grasp, brushes a hand through his hair, and asks to borrow my phone. About thirty seconds into the call, I hear him say, "Oh, shit."

"Is everything all right?" I ask, our almost-encounter now dutifully abandoned.

He escorts me out the door, saying, "Yes. But I've got to apologize again, Liv. Seems I forgot something. We'll have to swing by my place on the way."

"That's okay. As long as your parents don't get mad."

I take a look at the Mustang parked at the curb and my jaw drops. After he'd picked me up in that molester van for our first date, I wasn't expecting his car to be any nicer. But now this is more like it. The vintage sportscar is shiny and red and

102

practically begging Tawny Kitaen to writhe all over the hood. The thing is *sexy*, and suits Jack's personality to perfection.

He ushers me into the passenger seat before sliding into the driver's side. I'm not much into cars, but one look at Jack behind the wheel of this thing suddenly makes me realize I could become a Mustang *enthusiast*.

The rumble of the engine reverberates through my entire body as he starts the car, executes a K-turn, and pulls out of my street. Ten minutes later, Jack swerves into his townhome complex, bringing the Ford to a jarring stop in his driveway. I stay in the car while he leaps out the door and runs inside. I give the outside of his home a quick once-over and attempt a glimpse of his living room through the bay window. There's not much to see. Not a single picture on the wall, and no hint of furniture.

The townhomes are in their own small corner of Shermer Heights and are fairly new. I'd passed by curiously many times as they were being built, and wish we had more time to check out the inside tonight. But Jack is already bounding out the door holding a very poorly-wrapped present. He tosses it in the backseat, offering, "My brother's birthday," before pulling out of the driveway. "It's not for another week, but far be it for Sean to pass up the opportunity to be the center of attention at a party."

I giggle at the exaggerated grin on his face.

"Did you just move in?" I ask.

Jack scratches the back of his head, answering, "No. Well, yeah. A few months ago. Why?"

"Well, I couldn't really tell from the car, but the place looks pretty empty."

Jack shrugs and says, "I've got a TV, a fridge, and a bed. I don't need much more than that right now."

He shoots me a wink and I let the subject drop. So *transient*, this man. His career, his home... *Do something, explore it, find something new, and move on.* Is that why he set up this stupid bet? To keep himself *focused* on me?

We reach the gatehouse at the entrance to Norman Hills, a small community within the larger town of Norman. It's fairly exclusive, known for its elegant homes and wooded privacy. I

103

went to high school in this town, and I had friends who lived here, Tess among them. But even familiarity with the neighborhood doesn't begin to prepare me for what I see.

Jack pulls past the numerous cars parked along the winding drive which leads to the most beautiful house I've ever seen up close. The federal-styled saltbox home is two stories of period-authentic, olive green wooden clapboard with a deeply pitched roof sporting a large, arched dormer. The main house is flanked by a long wing on each side, each with three dormered windows of their own. For such a monstrous home, it is very tastefully done.

I ask, amazed, "You grew up here?"

Jack puts the car in park before admitting, "Yeah, that was my room, upstairs on the right." He points to the dormers almost directly in front of us. "It's a little much, wouldn't you say?"

I suddenly feel very underdressed.

"Just a little," I answer.

Jack takes the present from the backseat with his one hand and jots around to my side of the car to open my door with the other. He escorts me through the breezeway that separates the enormous house from the angled, four-car garage on the right and into the backyard. I notice how handsome he looks in his tan slacks and ivory, button-down shirt—a complete turnaround from the jean-clad rock star I'd initially met. Better, I think.

I tear my gaze from him in order to survey the yard, and actually gasp at the sight before me. The lush, green lawn rolls artfully downhill to a large plateau perched gracefully at the edge of a cliff and is surrounded by towering pines. Beyond the edge of the property, I can make out the scattered lights of houses far below and the shimmering stars making their first appearance in the sky above.

There are tents set up, their string lights illuminating the fifty-odd occupants who are already milling about with their cocktails and canapés.

We make our way down the torchlit path, past the stone-ensconced, in-ground pool on our left, past the guest house on our right, and lastly, between a pair of humorously carved topiaries in the shapes of an elephant and a giraffe, en route to the bar situated under one of the large tents.

"Drinks first," Jack says as he leads me to a long bar set with every possible liquor known to man. He puts his brother's present on an empty chair and fixes me a vodka cranberry before digging around in a metal, ice-filled tub, coming up with a Budweiser.

"I thought I left a few of these lying around here," he says triumphantly, as he twists off the cap and takes a swig.

Just then, I hear a deep voice yell, "Hey, Dickhead!" as a piece of shrimp goes flying past Jack's head, which would have hit him had he not bent quickly to the side.

The next thing I know, there's some huge, dark-haired guy maneuvering him into a headlock.

Jack squirms to break the hold and comes up with a fist aimed at the giant's stomach.

I take a step back to avoid the melee and bump into another huge form. When I turn around, I find myself looking up at yet another dark-haired monster, only this one has Jack's smile. He's beaming down at me in a way that lets me understand there's no immediate threat posed by the assumed attacker.

Jack laughs and runs a hand through his mussed hair. He points first to Gigantor Number Two, "Liv, the guy behind you, no doubt trying to hit on you, is Sean. And this little girl," he shoves a forearm into Gigantor Number One's chest, "is Stephen. They're my brothers."

I start to snicker as Stephen reaches out to shake my hand. "Funny thing, Pew, she's not even close to the mutant I was expecting."

Umm… thank you?

I raise my eyebrows at Jack. "*Pew?*"

"P-E-U means 'little' in French. It got kind of warped over the years to 'Pew'."

Our conversation at Monty's pool takes shape in my brain, and I realize he'd been trying to tell me his family nickname was *Little Prince*. Cute. Also interesting, because from the first second I laid eyes on him, I'd been thinking of him as my *dark* prince.

105

"Sorry about the shrimp. Did I get you?" Stephen asks.

I laugh and assure him that he did not.

Sean nudges his brother out of the way to take my hand, and— so help me God—the guy actually brings my fingers to his face to kiss the skin between my knuckles. The move would have been totally douchey if he wasn't so hot. Dude has some serious game.

Sean hasn't yet let go of my hand as he adds, "Please explain to me what a beautiful young girl like you is doing with an ugly bastard like Pew."

I chuckle as I suddenly notice an uncanny resemblance between Jack and his brothers. I answer, "Hey, I just met him. I'm only here for the free booze."

That makes Sean snicker as Jack responds, "Oh, really? That's it. You're cut off."

While we're laughing at that, a woman comes over with a tray of food. I know it has to be Mrs. Tanner; she looks just like her sons. She has black, shoulder-length hair cut in a stylish bob. She's very tall, but next to her enormous children, she seems miniscule.

Before she can even finish saying hello, Stephen and Sean mug some hors d'oeuvres before taking off into the crowd.

She shakes her head at their retreating forms and turns her attention toward me. "And who might this be?" she asks.

"This might be Livia Chadwick, Mom," Jack offers as he grabs a puffed whatever off her nearly-empty tray and pops it into his mouth, adding through his chewing, "And real smooth trying to pretend you didn't already know that."

She rolls her eyes and chastises him, "I was only trying to make your guest feel comfortable. Seriously, Jack. Who brings a girl home to meet the parents on a second date?"

I almost choke on my drink, and hold my hand over my mouth to try and stifle my laughter. The fact is, I've been wondering the same thing.

"No offense, Livia," she says to me. "It's actually very nice to meet you."

I decide this woman is my new favorite person on Earth. "Thank you. You, too."

106

"Jack tells me you're a photographer."

"Yes, I love it," I answer back. That's not a lie. I love taking pictures; I just hate my job.

Mrs. Tanner smiles. "Maybe you can take our family portrait this summer. It's been years since we've arranged to have one done."

I smile back. "I'd like that, thank you."

Mrs. Tanner excuses herself back to the party as Jack and I decide to load up on some food. We run into his Uncle Kenny on the buffet line, who joins us as we hunt for Jack's father. We find him standing near the bar with Jack's brother, Harrison.

It's a bit overwhelming trying to keep track of all the people in Jack's family.

"Ah. The infamous Miss Chadwick. Nice to meet you," Mr. Tanner says.

It's kind of cute that Jack has already told his family about me. I hope he spun the story of how we first met, though. I can't imagine his parents would be thrilled with the idea of their son dating someone like me.

The Tanner family is the freaking *Cosby Show*.

The Chadwicks are *Roseanne*.

Then again, everyone I've met tonight actually seems very, very cool. I shake off the chip on my shoulder and start acting like myself.

Harris offers a smile at our introduction, asking Jack, "Were you able to stop off for Sean's present?"

"Yes, and thank you for calling to remind me."

Harrison chuckles. "I knew you were going to forget." He directs his next comment to me. "I'm surprised he didn't forget to pick *you* up tonight. This guy would forget his head if it weren't attached to his neck."

I chuckle back. "Well... he was pretty late. Maybe he *did* forget to pick me up!"

Uncle Kenny almost doubles over laughing at his nephew. "Oh, this one knows how to dish it. Good for you, sweetheart. Don't take any of his garbage."

107

When I see the raised-brow look Jack is aiming at me, I add, "There's sure enough of it in that van of his."

Jack shakes his head. "Watch it, wiseass."

He's trying to look threatening, but his lip is twitching on a repressed smile.

"Actually," I offer, addressing our laughing group, "he may be a slob, and yeah, he's perpetually late… but it's kind of hard not to like him anyway."

Jack's face breaks into a genuine grin at that.

CHAPTER 17

Friday, June 9, 1995
10:17 PM

Jack's Parents' House
Norman Hills

We decide to take a breather, and Jack escorts me over to a more private corner of the estate, a small patio surrounded by hedges and lit with a dimmed lamppost. As he lights a cigarette, I take a seat on the concrete bench. We're separated from any party guests by a row of shrubs, but still in full view of anyone who chooses to peek in our direction.

Guess I won't be getting my hands on him just yet.

He props a foot next to me on the bench and crosses his arms over his knee before asking, "Are you having a good time?"

"I am," I answer, smoothing my dress over my legs. "Your family is a bunch of ball-busters, huh?"

"Yeah, but Stephen's the worst of them."

"I could tell. And wow. Your parents seem really... grounded." Coming from me, that's a compliment of the highest order. Jack chuckles, and I'm grateful that he understands where I'm coming from. He has, after all, already met my parents. "And Harris is pretty smart, huh?" I didn't get much chance to talk to him, but he reeked of 'intellectual.'

"First in his class at Syracuse."

"Wow!"

"Yep."

I'm still reeling from that bit of news as I add, "And Sean... Sean is so *incredibly charming*—"

Jack gives me a look of warning and cuts me off with, "You felt obligated to flirt with him?"

"No," I correct him, laughing at his jealousy. "I felt like it was my only duty to stand there trying to look pretty. It's like he

109

actually expects to be surrounded by gorgeous women twenty-four hours a day or something."

Jack bites his lip. "He does... and *is*."

"Oh."

I entertain a brief idea about setting Sean up with Tess. But I dismiss it immediately, realizing that they'd probably kill each other. Then me.

Jack holds his cig out between us, so I take a pull. "You know," I say, trying to change the subject, "I've been thinking about this rule you have."

"What rule?"

"Your No Fucking Groupies rule."

He reclaims his cigarette and takes a drag. "What about it?"

"Well, I think it's unrealistic."

"How so?"

"Lots of ways." I stand up and drape an arm around the lamppost. "I mean, first of all, you're constantly out playing. Aside from a bar, where else do you plan on meeting someone if it's not during a gig, someone who came to hear your music?"

Jack chucks the butt into the grass and answers, "Good point."

"Secondly, your classification system is all wrong."

He crosses his arms against his chest. "Pardon?"

"Your definition of 'groupie.' It's... *misogynistic*."

"Oh really?"

Grasping the lamppost in my hand, I lean my body away and swing toward him. "Yes. You think the mere fact that a girl has sex with musicians automatically lends a label. I mean, what about all those promiscuous cheerleaders who bang the whole football team? Or those girls who stalk famous actors into bed? There's no official name for them."

"Megaphone-Blowers and Starfuckers."

I know he's just trying to rile me up. "C'mon, Jack. You know what I'm saying. You label me as a groupie just because of my love of music."

"A groupie's most defining characteristic isn't her love of music."

The way he raises his eyebrow at that comment makes me think he's politely trying to avoid calling me a slut outright. "So that makes me a common whore? How many women have *you* slept with? No one goes around calling *you* a whore!"

"You'd be surprised."

"Surprised at your number or surprised how many times you've been called a whore?"

"Both. Now drop it."

"No. I just—"

"You just want to justify turning me into another one of your *conquests*. And while I appreciate the offer, I'm telling you flat-out that it's not going to happen. Not yet, anyway. I told you, I'm done being that guy."

I stop swaying around the lamp and meet his eyes. "What changed you?"

"You."

Ha! "Nice try. You were already on your celibacy crusade when I met you. I didn't have anything to do with that."

"Didn't you?" I look at him in confusion as my hand drops to my side, giving him my full attention. He lets out with an exaggerated sigh and runs a hand through his hair before explaining. "I never called you a whore, by the way. Nor would I. We obviously differ greatly in our definition of the word 'groupie.' I never said my problem was how much sex a groupie has had. That would be hypocritical of me, and I may be a lot of things, but I'm not a hypocrite. It's the clinginess that I object to. The claws-out, dig-their-heels-in way they try to claim a piece of me. Always hanging around the band, following us from place to place."

"Those are called fans, Jack."

"Fans I can deal with. What those girls are doing is entirely different. A one-night stand I can handle, the shaking them off I cannot." The revelation surprises me, but I'm even more stunned as he steps closer to deliver, "I finally got to the point where I *wanted* someone to stick around, but the problem was, I hadn't met her yet. But I knew who she was. I knew who she'd be." He runs a hand across my jaw, and I find myself melting more from

111

his words than his touch. "I was waiting for you before I even met you. And finally, one night, there you were. With your witchy green eyes and your perfect, pouty mouth."

"Why me?" I manage to squeak out.

"I don't know, Lips. From that first minute with you, it was…"

"Electric?" I offer. It's the word I always use whenever I think about the effect he had on me that first night.

"Yes. That's exactly it." His thumb is still rubbing gentle circles along my jaw as he adds, "But even more than that, it was what came after."

"Making out in a storage closet?"

He chuckles, shaking his head. "No. Talking to you that day at the pool. I realized I *liked* you, Liv. A *lot*." He smiles before adding playfully, "In spite of your awful taste in music."

I can feel myself softening, and I'm not sure I like it. My defenses, my *act*, had been put in place years before, and now suddenly, Jack is making me feel like all those years of "fun" have been incredibly pointless. But he's right: An empty life isn't any sort of life at all.

Jack figured that out before I did.

* * *

We make our way back to the party which has thinned out considerably in the time we've been gone.

Jack shakes a few hands of goodbye on our way to the pool area. He flops down to sit on one of the chaises and pulls me along to sit next to his legs.

Mr. and Mrs. Tanner materialize from the garden path, holding hands as they stop in front of our chair. Jack's mom rests her head on her husband's shoulder, saying, "I'm exhausted! But what a fun night. Livia, did you have a good time?"

I sit up and answer, "I did. This was an amazing party; everything was beautiful. Thank you so much."

"I'm sorry we didn't get much chance to talk, but I hope we'll get to see you again soon."

I catch Mr. Tanner sharing a smile with his son. I ignore it, though, and reply, "I hope so, too."

Mr. Tanner says, "Alright, Eleanor. Livia, it's been a pleasure. Jack, you alright to drive?" Jack assures him that yes, he's fine. "Okay, then. Good night, you two. Safe trip home."

Jack and I both say goodnight as Mr. and Mrs. Tanner head into the house.

The instant the door closes behind his parents, Jack grabs my hand, hoists me off the chaise, and runs me across the patio into the dark poolhouse in one swift motion. There's a *slam!* behind me, before he abruptly presses his body into the length of mine, backing me into the closed door.

"I've been waiting to get you alone all night," he whispers, before lowering his head and kissing me firmly.

It happens so quickly that I don't have time to think as I automatically return his kiss. My lips are pressed to his for all of three seconds when my heart starts hammering and my knees go weak. My hands move on their own, sliding up his muscular arms to wrap around his nape.

We'd been so hands-off all night that the sudden contact is more intense because of it. With such limited visibility, my other senses are heightened, and I'm reveling in the minty taste of his lips, the smoky, shaving-cream scent of his skin, the sound of his breath mingling with mine, the thumping of his heart against my chest. The quiet, dark room is an isolation chamber. Outside of Jack and me; the world ceases to exist.

When my fingers wind through his hair, the slightest moan creaks from his throat. He wraps his arms tighter around me and parts his lips.

The second my tongue meets his, his entire body hardens against me. It's a powerful feeling, to have him react so instantaneously to nothing more than my willingness to kiss him back. But hey, I'm having one hell of a reaction here, myself.

113

I expel a deep breath and Jack pulls back slightly, his sleepy eyes peering lazily down at me with a look of amusement.

Without asking, he leads me through the darkened room a few paces to the sofa and lays me down upon it. He slips off his shoes as he unbuttons the cuffs of his shirt, taking his time to roll the sleeves to his elbows, prolonging the agony. I'm left with no other choice but to lay here and wait. From the dim moonlight filtering in through the window, I'm able to make out his form, even if I can't see his face.

But I know that he's smiling.

So am I.

He finally lowers himself to the sofa and stretches out beside me, wrapping one leg across mine, tangling one of his strong hands around my waist and knotting the other one through my hair. Every motion is laced with authority, oozing pure sex from every pore in his body. My heart is racing like mad, a mixture of excitement and apprehension. Just how far is he willing to take things? *Is this the night that he'll finally cave?* He wanted to wait until he liked someone and didn't he just say he liked me?

To hell with our bet.

Sorry. Our *arrangement*.

I slide my fingertips up his spine and feel him shudder as his hips roll between my legs. I wrap them around his waist to push back, and from the tortured sound that rips from his chest, I know that he's already crossed over to the dark side. His hand slips up my thigh, under my dress, grabbing my ass and pulling me tighter against his body, his insistent hard-on grinding against the thin layers of fabric between us.

His breathing is choppy as he buries his face against my neck. "*Christ.* We have to stop."

"No. We don't," I immediately shoot back. I'm out of breath, my chest is heaving; his hips are still rocking against mine. I don't want this feeling to end. "C'mon, Jack. Don't you want to?"

I can hear a growl tear from his throat before he clenches his teeth and says, "What I *want* and *what's going to happen* are two entirely different things."

114

"*What's going to happen,*" I whisper, unbuttoning his shirt, "*is that you're going to take off those pants... and then you're going to pull down my panties... and then you're going to fuck me with that huge cock of yours... And you're going to do it* now."

His reserve cracks at that. The groan he lets out is tinged with pain, and there's no disguising the ache in his voice as he answers, "Oh, *fuck* yeah..."

He lowers his head to kiss me again when a voice interrupts his movement. "Don't mind me, Pew. I'm not even here."

A light clicks on in the corner, flooding the entire room. There's Sean, lounged out in a blue, upholstered chair.

I'm mortified. Shit. How much did he see? How much did he *hear?*

"Son of a *bitch!*" Jack spits out through clenched teeth. "What the fuck, Sean?"

Jack rolls more on top of me to cover my exposed skin as Sean stands up, gives a stretch, and laughs out, "In my defense, I *was* sleeping until about a minute ago."

Jack isn't in any state to stand up right at the moment, so he grabs his shoe off the floor and hurls it at his brother. "Get the hell out of here!"

Sean ducks as the shoe slams against the bookcase behind him. He turns his head to check out where it landed, then back to Jack as he raises his eyebrows and shoots him an impressed smirk. "Nice aim. Hey- you never gave me my birthday present."

"Jesus Christ," Jack curses, his voice rumbling against my chest. "It's on a chair near the bar. Now get the fuck out of here!"

"You know what, Jack?" Sean asks, his tone losing some of its playfulness. "You're being way too pissy about this whole thing. It's not like I was *trying* to spy on you two. Who the hell even knew where you and Livia both disappeared to? You made Mom and Dad have this party just so we could meet her, and you've been keeping her to yourself all night."

"Sean. Shut the fuck up!"

My mouth gapes open, shocked at Sean's words. Jack can't even look at me.

115

Sean must realize that he's said too much, because he gives an apologetic shrug as he walks out the door. "Sorry," he offers as he shuts it behind him.

Jack and I sit up on the couch, smoothing our hair and clothes back into place. I notice that my hands are shaking. "Is that true?"

He lets out with a heavy breath. "I could easily lie, here. You understand that, right?"

I bite my lip to keep from grinning. "But a gentleman like you, a man with such... *high moral values* would never do such a thing, right?"

"Wanna bet?" He grabs my hand and stares down at our intertwined fingers. "How 'bout I just plead the fifth on this one?"

My smile gets the best of me as I find myself chuckling at his words.

"Deal."

* * *

Jack pulls into the driveway of my house and I put a hand over my mouth, concealing a yawn. It's late and I'm thinking of the early morning drive to Manasquan tomorrow morning. I'll have to be on the road by eight if there's any hope of avoiding the in-season Parkway traffic on Saturdays.

He puts the car in park and drops an elbow over the back of my seat. I look at him as he runs the back of his fingers across my cheek. "It's late," he says quietly. "Don't invite me in."

"Don't be a tease," I fire back before leaning over and gently kissing him on his smiling mouth. "I had a great time. Thank you."

He gets out of the car and runs around to my side to help me out. I laugh when he tells me, "I'm not being chivalrous. The passenger door on this piece of junk only opens from the outside."

116

We reach my front door and Jack loops his arms around my waist, clamping his hands with mine behind my back. "Can I see you next week?"

I know he'll be spending the entire week down at Wildwood which is way further south than our normal beach towns. He won't be back until next Friday.

Suddenly, a week seems like a very long time.

"You know where to find me," I answer.

Jack kisses me softly, and I find it hard to tear my mouth from his. I can't quite believe it, but I'm starting to almost *like* the forced restraint. It's actually pretty sweet that he's so intent on making us wait—even if he did almost cave only an hour ago. Hell, we pretty much *both* reneged on our agreed-upon terms, but I'm going to write the incident off to temporary insanity on both our parts.

"Okay, you can come in," I joke, knowing full well what his answer will be.

"You don't play fair, Lips."

I slug him in the chest. "Fine. Goodnight, Jack!" I sing-song as I giggle my way in the door.

Through the peep hole, I watch him adjust the front of his pants as he makes his way back to the car.

CHAPTER 18

Saturday, June 10, 1995
9:38 AM

The Beach House
Manasquan

At nine-thirty-eight, I knock on the front door to our beach cottage. A groggy Sam opens the door and looks as though she immediately regrets that decision as she squints and turns away from the glaring, white sun invading the darkened room.

I laugh at her hungover state. "*Osprey* last night?" I ask, as I drop my overnight bag and camera case in the middle of the small living room.

Sam groans, "No, *Bar A*. And let's not talk about it. I'm going back to bed."

Chuckling at her slow trek toward the front bedroom, I plop down on the sheet-covered couch and turn on the TV. The adrenaline that has energized me for the past twenty four hours starts to recede as my muscles relax against the surprisingly comfortable sofa.

I must have dozed off, because the next sight I view is Vix standing over me.

"So, did you sleep with him?"

I'm still half-dead to the world. "What?"

"Did you go to bed with Jack?"

I adopt a look of frustration. "No!"

My sister shakes her head and says, "You lose, Tess. First round's on you tonight."

Tess pipes in from the kitchen, "*I* would have slept with him."

Rolling off the couch, I head to the fridge for some water. "I don't remember him asking *you*," I offer, tongue-in-cheek.

Tess throws a dish towel at me.

"Where are the rest of the girls?" I ask, putting the towel back on the counter.

Vix answers, "They're already on the beach. I suggest you get yourself into a bathing suit if you want to do the same. Tess and I have already waited an hour for your snoring ass to wake up before heading up there, so get moving already!"

I grab my bags and bring them to the back bedroom, squeezing myself into the one linear foot of floor space between the bed and surrounding walls. "I don't snore!" I snap as I shut the door in their laughing faces.

I put my bathing suit on under a pair of black shorts and an AC/DC baseball shirt, and we head up to the beach. It's a positively glorious day, and I tell you that with the understanding that I'm not the type of girl who goes around using words like "glorious" to describe stuff. But what else can I say? The sun is shining; the breeze is blowing. If the ocean was a decent temperature, the day would be perfect. But hey. Two out of three ain't bad.

Crap. Now I've got Meatloaf stuck in my head.

We find Isla and Sam fairly easily, even while they're doing their best sloth impersonations, lying face-down on a beach sheet. Vix is pretty big on beach sheets. She'd compiled a list of all the stuff each one of us was expected to bring down for the summer, and right there at the top was "Two SETS of queen sheets." Her thinking was that we'd of course use the fitted ones on the beds, but could use the flat ones to cover the gross couch in the living room, as a curtain across the exposed bay window, and of course, for laying out on the sand.

I've mentioned that Vix is an anal-retentive control freak, have I not?

Oh! And I don't think I mentioned this one yet, either: It turns out that Isla has become quite the Kissing Bandit over the past couple of weekends. She said she may as well take advantage of the fact that we're staying in MANasquan. So far, she's racked up five different guys from three different locations, and her goal is to hit *one hundred* by the end of the summer. With only fourteen weeks to go, I figure she better step up her weekly average if she wants to meet her quota. It's a lofty goal in any case.

She and Sam wake up from their face-down comas when they see us setting up next to them. Sammy turns her face toward me and groans out, "You have a nice time at your party, Livi-Girl?"

"I did!" I answer. I must have said it a bit too enthusiastically, however, because all four girls stop what they're doing to gape at me in a blank stare. "What?" I ask.

Tess is the first to pipe up. "You filthy liar! You totally slept with him!"

"I didn't. I swear."

"Bullshit. That's your just-got-laid voice."

I laugh, but assure her I'm just feeling happy.

"I don't know, Liv..." Vix busts. "I'm thinking you really like this one."

I stammer as I say, "Well, of course I like him. He's a great guy. And he's really talented. And funny. And hot."

Tess's mouth drops open. "You're totally buying into this thing! Jeez, girlfriend. You might be in over your head, here. You're not the type of person who can handle dating a eunuch."

"He's not a eunuch!" I laugh out. "And there's nothing to handle. It's just... I kind of get it now. I get that it'll be nice to wait." I have a sudden flash of Jack pressing himself to me the night before, whispering in my ear, *I've been waiting to get you alone all night...* and it makes me wonder if I'm equipped to handle *anything* sensibly in his presence. "It'll be better if I love him first."

The leading comment slips from my mouth, and I blink back a stunned expression at having actually spoken those words aloud. I couldn't have possibly meant what I said, could I? I definitely *did not* mean what I said. Right? Yes.

Tess isn't buying it. She's looking at me as if I've grown a second head as she asks, "Do you?"

I'm so caught up in my blunder that I don't register the question. "Do I what?"

"Do you love him?"

I think about Jack's lazy grin, the way his strong arms feel around me, and the way his lips feel *on* me, combined with the way he challenges me and laughs with me and busts my chops at every turn. He's incredibly handsome, extremely talented, and unbelievably funny. I can't think of anyone who's ever looked at me quite the way that he does, liquefying my insides when he aims those heavy-lidded, green-blue-gray eyes at me. More than that, he's the first guy to ever make me see I'm worth more than what I've previously allowed myself to believe. No other guy has ever done that before.

But the L-word? I wouldn't recognize such a Hallmark-card emotion if it jumped up and bit me on the ass. How would I know about something like that? It's hard to gauge a feeling I've never had before.

"It's too soon," I finally answer.

The girls let the subject drop after that and I'm relieved. I soak up the sun, enjoying the beautiful, breezy day on the beach. I'm guiltily happy that my friends are fighting off last night's boozing as they lay practically lifeless on the sand. I'm grateful for the silence and that they decided to leave me alone with my thoughts.

I have a lot to think about.

I try to be lulled by the sounds of the ocean rhythmically lapping its way onto shore, and I'm sure my body appears relaxed, but in actuality, my mind is positively racing. I dig my feet into the sand, forming two damp troughs, flicking the occasional shell fragments away with my toes.

Rolling the conversation around in my head, I try to make sense of what I had unwittingly revealed. I don't know what to make of it. Maybe Tess was right. Am I in over my head?

With every other guy I've ever been with, I tried to talk myself into what I automatically felt when I was with Jack. I made excuses for their behavior; I willingly joined in with their promiscuous lifestyle, lied to myself that I *wanted* to keep them at arms' length.

But Jack isn't having any of that noise. He won't allow me to pull my usual hit and run. He came up with this ridiculous bet in order to ensure that I can't run away.

121

Sorry. Our arrangement.

I'm still not sure how I'm supposed to feel about it.

Isla's muffled voice from under a towel breaks my train of thought. "*Leggett's* tonight, ladies?"

I respond, "Cool!" while the other three girls groan at yet another night of imposed alcoholism.

"Leggett's is a freaking sauna," Sam moans. "And I'm too hung-over to even think about it."

"Oh, a little hair o' the dog and you'll be fine," Isla counters before blurting eagerly, "Hey Tess! Can I borrow your purple top tonight?"

Tess grunts out, "You can *have* it if you shut up and let me go back to sleep."

CHAPTER 19

Date #3: Friday, June 16, 1995
11:19 AM

The Boardwalk
Seaside Heights

I played hooky from work and headed down to the Manasquan
house a day early. It was pretty cool to have the place all to
myself last night, even if I didn't take much advantage of that
situation beyond sprawling out on the sofa to watch a rerun of
Melrose Place with a box of Snackwells. Normally, we're forced
to enact a three-girl minimum, cramming our bodies onto the
lone couch in the living room.

The Studio is always closed on Mondays, so I'm really looking
forward to the extra-long weekend.

I need it.

Jack has a gig tonight at The Osprey, so he and I decide to kill
some time during the day at the boardwalk. He picks me up in the
Mustang with the top down, and we take off for Seaside Heights.

Somewhere on Route 35, I find myself staring at his profile as
he drives. He looks so adorably boyish with his sunglasses on, his
hand idly tapping the wheel to the beat of a Blues Traveler song
blasting out of the car's stereo. My heart speeds up as I watch his
lips pucker into a whistle and the smooth muscle flexing in his
forearm as he steers.

Once Popper hits the chorus, I decide to sing along. "*The
heaaart brings you baaack...*"

"Hook."

"Huh?"

"The hook brings you back," he says. "Not the heart."

"The hook? That's not romantic at all."

He practically snorts. "It's not supposed to be. Jesus, Livia! It's
the title of the goddamn song, for chrissakes. How is it that you

managed to sing the *title* wrong?" He's cracking himself up over there, and I can't do anything but laugh along with him. For someone who loves music as much as I do, it *is* pretty ridiculous that I always manage to fudge up the lyrics.

"You have to admit, 'heart' makes a lot more sense than 'hook.' I'm not taking all the blame on this one," I defend.

"Lips. The hook is the part of any song that sucks the listener in. The part that hooks, you. Get it? All the best songs have a strong one. Here, I'll give you an example: 'Sweet Caroline' by Neil Diamond. What's the most outstanding thing about it?"

I think on that for a minute. "The three trumpet notes after he sings 'Caroline'? The bum, bum, bum?"

"You got it. That's the hook. I mean, the slow start makes you take notice, but those three notes sell that song. All those idiot college kids yelling out those three notes are mangling what should just be the slow capitulation into the vibe of that song."

I know what he's talking about with all those idiots ruining the music. I'm getting pretty sick of hearing the way some classics have been contorted lately. All that accentuated 'unca-chucka' during the Ally McBeal version of "Hooked on a Feeling" or the way "Oh What a Night" has recently been remixed into a techno song. If it wasn't for the Seattle surge a few years back, listening to New York radio would be a near-impossibility.

Jack's voice snaps me out of my stewing. "I'll give you another one: How 'bout Weezer's 'Buddy Holly'?"

"No problem. Ooh-whee-ooh. Footnote: It's a killer video."

"Yep. 'Under Pressure.'"

"That's easy. Those opening notes suck me in every time."

"They suck in everyone else, too. There's a reason Vanilla Ice stole it."

I think about that and say, "Oh yeah, you're right! For 'Ice Ice Baby!' It's the same bass line!"

He turns up the volume on the radio so we can hear "Hook" again. "Really listen to the lyrics. They're all about a song's formula. It has nothing to do with love at all, but the way Popper sings it, if you don't listen too closely, that's exactly what he makes the listener believe. *That's* the hook."

It certainly hooks me. I listen to John Popper's rambling voice churning out its high-speed jumble of nonsense words, and find myself taking a much-needed breath along with him as he breaks back into the chorus.

"Well, maybe it *is* a love song," I finally reason. "It's about the love of music."

Jack aims a dazzling grin at me. "Well, yeah, sure, there's *that*."

We park in the lot at the south end of the boardwalk around lunchtime, and stop in at *The Sawmill* for some pizza and beers.

The Yankee game is on and Jack is yelling at the TV along with the other male patrons at the bar. O'Neill just popped out, leaving two men on base.

"What the hell, O'Neill?" Jack screams at the TV before absently sharing his thoughts with the guy at the stool next to his, "He could've tied us up just now! Overeager. Wait for your pitch, Paul!"

Jack is so loud, Paul can probably hear him all the way over in Yankee Stadium. I watch O'Neill throw a fit in the dugout, punching a container of Gatorade and kicking at the discarded paper cups on the ground.

The Yanks and their fans are pretty serious about their baseball. Case in point, the season has barely begun, and this particular game is only in the second inning.

I take a bite out of my humongous slice as Jack orders another beer. His face is still reddened with anger and a muscle is clenching in his jaw.

"Jeez, Jack. I don't think O'Neill popped up specifically to piss you off."

Jack spits back, "I'm not so sure about that."

The absurdity of that comment instantly defuses his anger and his face calms as he focuses his eyes on me. He smiles and shakes his head. "You think I'm bad now? Wait until playoff season."

His hand covers mine and squeezes. "We should go to a game sometime. My father has season tickets. Box seats right on the third base line. Would you want to go?"

125

I am completely uncoordinated when it comes to organized sports, but I've always enjoyed watching other people play. "That would be great! I haven't been to a game in years. My father took Vix and me a couple of times when we were little but I think he gave up when he saw that we were more interested in the snacks and souvenirs than watching the game. I always thought my father needed to have sons instead of daughters. He's like, obsessed with sports."

"That's insane."

I tip my head to the side. "Well, maybe *obsessed* is the wrong word..."

"No" Jack clarifies. "That you think your father would've rather had sons. Who needs boys? We're loud. We fight all the time. There's like a whole seven year stretch where we smell really bad."

That has me chuckling before I find myself caught in a pensive stare.

Jack sees me ogling him and asks, "What are you thinking?"

"I was just picturing what your daughter would look like. I'm seeing an adorable little terror with gray eyes and a mop of black hair."

"I'm actually picturing her with *green* eyes." He looks unmistakably at me as he picks up my hand and brushes a soft kiss across my knuckles. "And *brown* hair." He must see the look of panic on my face, because he quickly adds, "But I'm sure she'd still be a terror, though."

That makes me laugh. "No doubt about it."

Jack leaves a few dollars on the bar and slides the rest of the bills into his pocket. "All right then. Ready to hit the log flume?"

We chug down the rest of our drinks and cross over to the water rides. Thankfully, we have our own boat, so we don't get too soaked on the thing. Usually, there's at least one wiseguy who just loves to lean over the side for a handful of water to splash at the rest of the log occupants. Barring that nuisance, the flume is more of a floating roller coaster and less of a bathtub.

After the ride, we stop at the carousel house and Jack gets a cup of fries with vinegar. I only pick at a couple on our walk down to

Midway. The huge slice at the bar is still sitting in my stomach and I know I have to find room for a cheesesteak. You just don't come all the way down to the boardwalk and *not* get a cheesesteak from Midway.

Jack finishes his fries by the time we make it to the big green and yellow stand in the middle of the walkway. I watch the gargantuan yellow lemon slowly spinning on top of the structure as Jack orders up two sandwiches and lemonades. I grab a stack of napkins from the dispenser and we find a spot on one of the benches looking out toward the ocean. I have to stuff the pile under my leg while we eat to keep them from blowing away. It's a beautiful, warm, sunny day, but there's no escaping the strong breeze this close to the water. Thank God I brought a scrunchy to keep my hair out of my face while I eat. Cheez Whiz in the tresses isn't really the coolest look.

"Hey Jack. Say 'scrunchy'."

"What? Why?"

"Because I love hearing guys say stuff that they were never intended to say."

You know, like *Barbies* or *curling iron.*

"Scrunchy." He says it like he's angry at the word, and it makes me snicker. Jack looks at me like I'm nuts.

"Now say 'ballet slippers'."

"No."

"How about 'Jordache jeans'?"

"No."

By this point, I'm just about ready to lose it. "Okay, just say 'Nellie Oleson' and I'll leave you alone."

A wicked grin spreads across his face seconds before he hurls his sandwich wrapper into the garbage and comes at me in one quick motion. I jump up from the bench so abruptly that the movement manages to sploodge the contents of my cheesesteak almost completely out of the bread. Jack finds this predicament not only hysterical, but highly gratifying. I give him the stink eye as he sinks back down onto the bench.

I grab the scattered stack of napkins off the ground and swipe the food off the boards before the seagulls can attack and get everyone near us pissed off. Plus, I have to clean my forearm which is covered in grease, cheese, and bits of onion that had dripped out of the last of my sandwich during his attack. Attractive.

He kisses some cheese off the corner of my mouth. "Hey, finish that thing already. I want to hit The Zipper."

Satisfied that I've cleaned myself off as well as possible, I take a last bite and throw the remaining heel of bread into the trash along with all our crap.

Jack holds my hand as we walk down to the Casino Pier. I love the smell of the boardwalk on a sunny, breezy day. It's a mixture of rotting wood, salt air, and fried zeppole dough, which I promise you, smells a lot more appealing than it sounds.

When we get to the pier, the line at The Zipper isn't too bad.

The ride itself is.

Let's just say that after two beers, a slice of pizza, a couple fries, large lemonade, and a loaded cheesesteak, the last place you'd want to find yourself is upside-down and spinning. The ride doesn't seem to bother Jack, but it's all I can do not to lose the contents of my stomach over the longest three minutes of my life.

When the ride is over, Jack holds out his hand to me. "Hey Liv? You're looking a little pale."

"That's funny, I would have sworn that I was green."

Jack laughs. "Are you alright? Want some water?"

"Water would be great."

Only actually puking would be more embarrassing. Who wants to date a girl who can't handle a bumpy ride? I make a mental note to take Jack down to Great Adventure someday so I could prove my thrill-ride bravery. Rolling Thunder alone would accomplish my goal. The last time I was on that thing, I thought for sure the ancient wooden structure was going to fall down at any second taking Vix and me along with it. Instead, we'd walked away with our lives, albeit bruised and beaten because the rough ride had thrown us around like a couple of rag dolls. How that coaster hasn't been condemned by now is beyond me.

As Jack leads me over to the nearest concession stand I say, "I've never had a problem on The Zipper before. I love that ride. It must have been all that food. How come *you're* not sick?"

Jack pats his belly. "You gotta build up immunity to this sort of thing, baby." He throws his arm around me in sympathy and asks the girl behind the counter for a bottle of water. And a chocolate chip cookie. And a double-sized, vanilla-orange soft swirl cone. *Ugh.*

Jack eats his dessert on our walk back down to the car and I start to feel less ill. We play a few wheels along our route whenever something interesting catches our eye. Thus far, we have amassed two CDs, a box of Snickers, and a stuffed, three-legged dog which Jack promptly named Grendel. We pit-stop at the arcade, play some Skeeball, and then step into the photo booth. Four minutes and a few stolen kisses later, I'm admiring the black and white strip of pictures at the entranceway to the confectionary while Jack buys a box of peanut brittle inside.

From a few yards away, I watch a group of girls nudge each other and nod in his direction as they walk by. By the time they near me, I can hear their muffled voices as they comment on 'what a hottie' Jack is.

I'm thinking I should probably be jealous, but actually what I'm feeling is proud. Jack barely registered the girls' giggling, even though I know he had to have known what was going on. His non-reaction makes it clear that he's here with *me* today, and that's all that seems to matter to him at the moment.

I stand watching him from behind, seeing his tall form leaning against the counter and think that those girls have absolutely no idea how 'hot' he truly is. He's not only beautiful, but charming and thoughtful, funny and intelligent. He's the complete package. He's everything a girl could want in a man. He's everything *I* could want in a man.

An unfamiliar ache makes its way into my heart, a longing to put my arms around him and never let him go. I've never fallen in love before, but I'm starting to wonder if this is what it feels like. I've never had a stroke, either, but I imagine the symptoms are the same.

In any case, it's scary as hell.

My heart starts hammering in my chest as I realize I am somewhere between simple attraction and the high that would come from freebasing ground unicorn hooves. Why isn't there a word for that? That limbo stage between *like* and... *something more*? Whatever the unnamed emotion is, it's what I'm feeling as I gaze at Jack.

And then he turns around and sees it practically written all over my face.

I don't care. I don't try to hide it. And instead of screaming and running away from me, I watch as a slow, satisfied smile spreads across his handsome features.

Back in the car, as Jack pulls out of the lot, we're both uncharacteristically silent. I'm thinking about our fun day and how crazy I am about the man sitting next to me. After only three weeks, there's no way I'm going to be crazy enough to actually say it out loud to him, however. Besides, I figure the expression he caught on my face a few minutes before is enough drama for one day.

Turns out, I couldn't be more wrong about that.

CHAPTER 20

Friday night, June 16, 1995
11:00ish PM

The Osprey
Manasquan

Jack's gig is happening right around the corner from our beach house. I brought my camera so I could take some shots of Thunderjug strutting their stuff onstage, so I've been separated from the girls for most of the time we've been here.

I had introduced them to the guys as they were setting up hours ago, and Isla didn't waste any time adding Freddie, Booey, *and* Jim to her kissing tally. They were only trying to help.

But now Freddie is really playing it up, down on his knees at the edge of the stage, swinging his shoulder-length hair in Isla's face. I can tell she's trying not to crack up as I view her through my lens, and good sport that she is, grabs at his jean-clad legs to play along.

I snap a few more shots of Jimmy at his kit before swinging the camera over to Jack. He's acting a little strangely, clearly trying *not* to give attention to something on the far end of the room.

Then I notice why.

I look across the club and see a beautiful, dark-haired girl shooting daggers at me from the bar. I'm trying to pretend I'm unaware of her staring, but her dirty looks are making me feel pretty uncomfortable. Jack too, apparently. I know I won't even bother to ask him who it is, because I already know it has to be Sadie.

The band breaks soon after, and Jack doesn't waste any time coming to my side. I hand him his water bottle and swing my camera over my shoulder, using the opportunity to sneak a peek at Sadie, still staring me down with those stiletto eyes.

131

She leans into her friend and says something that makes them both laugh. Crooking her mouth into an evil grin, she makes her way over to Jack and me. I try to look oblivious about it, wishing Vix or Tess or anyone was there next to me for this instead of on the dance floor.

Sadie taps Jack on the shoulder, but I turn toward her the same time he does. She doesn't even bother to look at me as she purrs, "Hey babe! I didn't expect to see you here. My God, I can't believe it's been *days* since I talked to you!"

Days?

Jack offers an emotionless, "What's up."

She gives me the once-over before silently dismissing me and turning toward Jack, her back almost fully in my face. "So, listen. You know how I have that subscription to the Shubert on Broadway. They finally sent those tickets for us to see 'Chicago' next week. I was going to call you and see if we were still on."

Jack takes a sip from his drink, his bored eyes never meeting hers as he answers, "No thanks, I've made other plans." At that, he gives me a showy wink, purely for Sadie's benefit.

Right on, baby.

Sadie huffs at that and answers casually, "Well, maybe next time."

Again with the look.

"Oh- and you left your Soundgarden CD in my Miata the other night. It's right outside if you want to come get it."

I can't help the snicker that escapes from my throat. This chick is something else.

She plants a hand on her hip at the sound, turns directly toward me, and asks, "Excuse me, but who are *you*?"

I can feel my hands clenching at my sides. I swear, if we were both guys, she would have gotten a faceful of my knuckles by now. I'm ready to inflict more pain on this chick than a clone army of Tonya Hardings in a baseball bat factory.

Instead, as the well-bred young lady that I am, I've learned to utilize a bit more tact when dealing with such situations. I manage a cool smile, slide a hand along Jack's ass, and say, "I'm his *official photographer.*"

That brings a scathing glare from Sadie which is cut off abruptly when Jack's hand wraps around her upper arm. He hands me his water bottle and says through clenched teeth, "Actually, I think I'd better get that CD back. Livia, could you please excuse us for a minute?"

He then proceeds to usher a pissed-off Sadie through the crowd.

I smile to myself as I watch her try to wrestle out of Jack's grasp while he gives her an earful on their way out the door.

A few minutes later, Jack is back at my side. He reclaims his drink and takes a long swig. I don't see Sadie's friend at the bar and figure they must have taken off after Jack's tirade. He sees me scanning the room for them both and says, "They're gone. Can we please forget that even happened and try to enjoy the rest of our night?"

I'm actually dying to know what he said to her outside and what she meant by some of her comments. I'm definitely feeling a little pang of jealousy—I mean, Sadie is really pretty. But she's also a spoiled brat with bad manners. No wonder they broke up.

I think I'd feel better if he cleared the air about some of my unanswered questions, but then decide it doesn't matter. She is, after all, Jack's *ex*-girlfriend.

And I'm… well, hell. I guess I'm his new one.

CHAPTER 21

Date #4: Monday, June 19, 1995
9:42 PM

The Beach House
Manasquan

Just as I'm packing up my car to leave, Jack shows up at the beach house. I'm surprised to see him, and can't quite believe I'm watching his Mustang pulling into the driveway.

"Oh my God!"

Once he gets out of the car, I practically leap at his beautiful form to hug him hello. When I pull back, the first thing I notice is his newly-cultivated goatee. I give a pinch to his chin and ask, "What's this? You're like your own evil twin."

He has his arms wrapped around my waist and he's grinning as he answers, "I prefer 'alter ego'."

"Sure thing, Johnny Bravo. Oops. I mean, *Tanner Jaxx*."

He groans, "That sounds like the most made-up name in the history of rock."

"More made up than the feminine hygiene symbol that 'The Artist Formerly Known as Prince' changed over to?"

"Shit. You're right. That one's worse."

We're both just smiling into each other's faces like a couple of idiots until I finally ask, "What are you doing here?"

"I wanted to see you. That okay, isn't it?"

"Yeah it's okay!" He had his Osprey gig on Friday, two more up north Saturday and yesterday, and then he came all the way back here tonight just to see me? "But it's already ten o'clock. You drove all the way down here without even calling first? What if I'd already left?" I wasn't planning to leave so late, but I'd gotten caught up watching a "Real World" marathon on Mtv.

"Lips, you forget. I've got spies everywhere."

I roll my eyes. "You talked to Vix?"

134

"Yep," he laughs out before adding, "I wanted to bring you somewhere."

"Oh yeah? Where we going?"

His sly smile is raising my suspicions. "I thought we could hit Atlantic City."

"What? Now? It's so late!"

"Who cares? You don't have anywhere to be until work tomorrow morning. It's not like it's past our bedtime or anything. Don't try and tell me you've never pulled an all-nighter."

I should probably play the responsible working gal, here, but the truth is, I'm excited about checking out a new place. "I've never been there."

"I know."

I shoot him a dirty look at that. I'm starting to think his 'little birdie' is feeding him way too much info about me. "Well, it sounds like fun, but I mean, I don't even know if I'll know how to gamble."

His lips curl into a dastardly smirk and his head tips to the side as he fires back, "Something tells me you know *exactly* how to gamble."

Cute. I make one last attempt at a rationalization. "We wouldn't even get there until after midnight."

"So, what's the problem? You planning on turning into a pumpkin?"

I think about it for a minute. There's really no reason why we can't just take off. I look over at Jack, eyebrows raised, huge grin on his face, waiting on my answer. "Screw it. You're right. Let's do it!"

* * *

We're sitting in the Emperor's Club at Caesar's, inconspicuously trying to add up our winnings. We'd played slots and roulette all night, and the gambling gods had smiled upon us. Well, they'd smiled upon *me*. Jack didn't get so lucky.

"I can't believe you hit on double-zeroes. I never bet the zeroes!" he says in disbelief.

"Well, maybe you should start." I pull one of my twenty-five-dollar chips out of my purse and waggle it in front of his face. "There's plenty more where this came from."

"Beginner's luck."

"Skill, baby. And don't you forget it."

That makes him laugh. It's all I can do not to dump out all my chips and add them up right here. I don't have any idea how much I won, but I know it's a lot. I suppose we should've hit the teller before coming into the bar, however. The only actual money we have left on us is the cup of coins from the slots. Our bartender doesn't seem too thrilled about being paid in quarters.

Jack grabs our container of change off the bar, takes a final swig from his drink, and says, "Time for a new location."

"I get to pick the next place. After all, I'll be the one paying for our drinks out of my many winnings."

Jack throws an arm around me. "Say no more, mon amour; your wish is my command. Lead the way."

So I do.

After we cash out at the teller, we wander around the hotel in search of a place to hang out. I stop when we get to *The Libretto Bar*, and Jack lets out with a groan. "Awww. C'mon, Lips. Karaoke? Really?"

"My choice, remember? Besides, it'll be fun. We'll throw back a couple shots and laugh at everyone."

That seems to bring him around. "Fine. But I get to pick the shots."

"Deal."

Four drinks and over a dozen bad singers later, Jack and I are laughing so hard we're almost under the table. On the stage at the present moment, there's an overweight guy in a Hawaiian shirt belting out "Strangers in the Night." Once he starts in with the doobie-doobie-doos, it's about all I can take.

Jack has since switched to soda, and as the waitress delivers our drinks, she tells us the tables are for people who are going to sing karaoke. "If you want to stay, you're gonna have to play."

I aim a grin at Jack and suggest, "Why don't you get up there and show them how it's done, baby."

"Yeah right," he shoots back. "Why don't we just go somewhere else instead. This place is too crowded."

"I'm serious! Please. I love that we got a table and I don't want to give up this spot just to go stand around in some other just-as-crowded bar. Just get up there and sing something pretty for me."

Jack takes a sip of his Coke and eyes me curiously. "Why don't *you* get up there instead?"

I practically snort. "Oh, okay. That might be a better plan, seeing as how I'll clear the bar with my awful voice."

"I've heard you singing along with the radio. You've got a great voice. And you won't be able to mangle the lyrics, because they'll all be right there on the monitor."

"Very funny, but no dice. I've also got stage fright."

"Stage fright doesn't exist. It's a myth."

"Tell that to my stomach."

He scratches at his stubbly chin. "I'll tell you what, Miss Beginner's Luck. Why don't we bet on it?"

My lids tighten on a glare. "What, like, loser has to get up there and sing? I don't gamble what I'm not willing to lose."

"There's no money involved, here."

"My pride, Jack. Having to get up there would make me lose my pride."

He leans back in his chair and grants me a flash of those perfect pearly whites. "Since you seem to be on a winning streak tonight, this should hardly be a risk for you."

I eye him up cautiously, my curiosity getting the better of me. "Okay, tough guy. What's the bet?"

"Hmmm," he replies, scanning his eyes around the bar. "How about whoever gets someone to buy them a drink first wins."

Is he serious? I'm a girl. I have a way huge advantage over him. "Oh, you are so on, motherfucker."

He aims a smirk at me, and we both sit there for an extra few seconds, shooting daggers into each other's eyes. As if on cue, we both bolt from our seats and race each other to the bar.

I shove him into a table, and while he's busy trying to regain his footing, I scope out my potential victim. Old guy... Two guidos... *Bachelor party.*

BINGO.

I walk up to them casually—well, at least I think it's casually. My gait is hovering somewhere between "stumbling" and "staggering."

"Hi guys!"

The group of five turn at my greeting as I prop an elbow on their hightop table. How do I play this? Sly and sexy? Ever since I started dating Jack, I haven't had much opportunity to work my charms. At least on anyone new. I'm already feeling out of practice.

I arch my back a little bit, shoving the girls out front and center. I'm not very blessed in the boobie department, but I'm wearing a Wonderbra and a low-cut shirt. I can work with this. I'll have to, because there's no way I'm getting on that stage. I flash a *come hither* grin at the drooling men, and steal a look at Jack, trying to work over a pair of middle-aged women on the other side of the room.

Oh, man. I've got this in the fricking bag.

* * *

I wend my way across the room toward Jack as he's busily trying to charm the pants off the two women he'd targeted at the bar. The poor broads look to be half in the bag, an observation that is reinforced when I hear one of them slur, "Oh, you are just adorable! Donna, isn't he the cutest thing?"

Torn between letting the train wreck play out for my sole entertainment and wanting to save him from it, I opt for the latter as I nudge his back with my elbow.

"Hi, baby. I got you a drink."

I know my face is sporting a shameless shit-eating grin, but I can't help it. Not only did I manage to weasel a drink out of those drunken idiots, but I even got them to buy one for *Jack*.

His eyes tighten as he begrudgingly accepts the drink from my offered hand. His lip quirks as he introduces me to his new friends, a steady glare trained on my face. "Donna, Barbara... this is Livia. If you'll please excuse me, I owe her a song."

I'm finding it hard not to break out into a full-on giggling fit as he ushers me back to our table, grabbing the song-list binder from the emcee as we pass. He won't even let me look at the thing, so I have to content myself with sipping my vodka tonic as I wait patiently for him to make his selection. Once I see the smirk decorate his face, I know that he has. He brings the book back to the emcee's table and adds his name to the queue.

I'm drawing little imaginary circles on the tabletop with the tip of my finger as he slumps back down in his chair. I'm feeling sort of guilty about something, and figure I better 'fess up before things go any further. Jack must've picked up on my shame, because he asks, "What's the matter, Liv?"

Once I'm finally able to meet his eyes, I confess. "I cheated."

His eyes narrow into slits as he snarls, *"What did you just say?"*

"With the drinks. I thought I saw one of those ladies going for her purse and I panicked."

He doesn't respond, but his expression softens as he lets out a heavy breath. I can't understand why he seems *relieved* to find out I'm a dirty cheat, but I swear, he's almost smiling.

I bite my lip and scrunch up my nose to add, "I *may* have blurted out that I'd flash them for a drink."

"Livia! Jesus!" My admission surprises him, but thankfully, he can't seem to do anything other than laugh.

I'm laughing, too. "I guess they were impressed. They bought me *two* drinks!"

While we're cracking up over that, the emcee announces, "All right! Up next, we've got *Tanner Jaxx*. Come on up, Tanner!"

I stifle a snicker as he raises his eyebrows at me, then throws back the last of his drink before hopping up onto the stage.

I recognize his selected song from the first note.

"You" is Candlebox's on-the-road lament song. It's their Seger's "Turn the Page." Their Jackson Browne's "Load-Out." Hell, it's their Bon Jovi's "Wanted Dead or Alive." But if you don't listen to the lyrics too closely, it's simply a tortured love song.

Appropriate, because Jack is simply torturing me.

He groans the lyrics into the mic, and my heart cracks as I watch him. I can't help but smile into his face as he sings; not only is he a mesmerizing performer, but he's belting out every word directly at me. It's as if he isn't even aware there are other people in the room.

And so help me God... the look on his face while he screams out the chorus

And I'll cry for you, yes I'll die for you
Pain in my heart it is real
And I'll tell you know how I feel inside
Feel in my heart it's for you

makes me think he's dying inside just as much as I am. I swear, if I was capable of falling for someone, I would fall *undeniably* at this moment.

And it's pretty fricking incredible to watch him fall, too.

Jack punctuates the song with its final, haunting note, and the room goes completely silent. I can hear nothing in the brief pause but the distant dinging of slot machines until—finally—the place erupts in applause.

Damn. Stunned them into silence. Nice.

He gives a nod in acknowledgement to the crowd as he hops down off the stage. He's wearing that elated grin, that post-performance, just-kicked-ass, sexy-as-all-hell smile as he makes his way back toward me.

I get up from my seat to throw my arms around him in a proud hug. "That was insane! Jack! Oh my God!"

"Karaoke's for pikers," he says against my hair.

140

I pull back to look him in the eyes when I counter, "Maybe. But *you* turned it into *art*."

He kisses me for that as the applause dies down and we take our seats. The poor girl on stage trying to follow up his act with a nervous rendition of "I Will Survive" is all but ignored as Jack reaches across the table to take my hand, caught up in our own little bubble. His eyes are sparked with euphoria, and I can tell that *he* feels his little performance was a pretty big deal between us, too.

While we're smiling into each other's eyes like a couple of sappy dorks, some suit comes over to our table.

"Hello, you two. Looks like you're having a good time. My name's Lutz Hamburg."

Lutz puts a hand on my boyfriend's shoulder as if they're old pals, and instead of shaking it off and telling the guy to take a hike, Jack decides to take some liberties with the introductions. "Nice to meet you, Lutz. I'm Johnny Bravo and this here's Phoebe Cates."

That sends me into a fit of giggles, but Jack somehow manages to keep a straight face.

"Well, *Johnny*, that was pretty impressive what you did up there."

"Thanks."

"I'm the Events Manager of the hotel. I'm going to go ahead and assume that you're fairly comfortable up on stage?"

The jig is up. Jack gives a shrug and offers, "Yeah, actually. My real name's Jack Tanner. Nice to meet you again, Lutz." He shakes the man's offered hand and adds, "I'm in a band called Thunderjug. That's okay, right? I mean, it's not like I broke some casino law by entering an amateur Karaoke competition, right?"

I can't even breathe, trying as hard as I am not to pass out from holding in my laughter, my hands clamped over my mouth.

Lutz isn't fazed. "It's more than okay. In fact, I'd like to invite Thunderjug to come play my venue."

Jack's brows draw together as he replies, "The disco? Thanks, but we're more of a rock band."

141

"I know exactly who you are and what you play. I recognized your voice and realized I'd seen you before. Caught one of your shows at *The Ketch* down in LBI a few weeks back. Yes, *Dusk* is a dance club. But I'm talking about the Circus."

"The Circus Maximus? The *arena*?"

Jack's eyes meet mine in a disbelieving pause. I don't have any words that will help him make sense of this crazy conversation. I don't have any words *at all*.

Luckily, Lutz does. "We host a lot of local talent, but we've had our fair share of big names, too."

"Like who?" Jack asks.

"Oh, I don't know. Ever hear of Bruce Springsteen? Elton John? Paul McCartney?"

"No shit?"

"No shit."

Jack looks at me wide-eyed, his face mirroring exactly what I'm feeling.

Lutz starts in again. "I've got Stevie Wonder headlining here Fourth of July weekend. My opening act just cancelled and I don't really need a replacement, but I'd like one."

What kind of numbskulls would cancel on Stevie Fucking Wonder?

And wait. Is this guy actually asking what I think he's asking? Jack must be wondering the same thing, because he attempts to clarify the offer. "Sooo, you want Thunderjug to play. Here. At Caesar's."

"Five thousand seats are going to be filled, and like I said, I'd like an opening act."

"An opening act for Stevie Wonder. Are you serious?"

"Sure am."

"You know we're just a cover band, right? I mean, we've got originals, but—"

"*Backyard.* I've heard it. It's good. Any others?"

"About ten or so."

"Can you mix them in with a few covers, enough to fill an hour?"

"Yeah. Definitely."

"Well, good. Then do that."

I've been watching this exchange like it's a tennis match, my head darting back and forth between the both of them as Jack lets out with a sound that's half sigh and half whistle. "I've got to check with the guys, but I don't think it's going to be a problem. You have a card or something for me to get in touch with you tomorrow?"

Lutz procures a business card from his breast pocket, which Jack takes casually, trying to look as though playing a huge venue like a five-thousand-seat arena is no big deal. Good for him and all, keeping his cool, but *I'm* sort of panicking on his behalf. A lot.

"Hey, uh, Mr. Hamburg," he says. "I'm not trying to talk myself out of a cherry gig here, but you always make it a habit to book unknown bands to play on your stage?"

Lutz gives him a knowing smile. "All the time. I know good when I hear it. That's what they pay me for." He shoots us a wink and drops a hundred on the table, motioning a 'nother-round finger to the waitress. "Have a good night, you two."

I can't do anything but remain speechless while watching him walk away, but then I look over at Jack, sitting there with a stunned smile on his gorgeous mug.

"Jesus," he says at last. "That was so smooth! That cat might be the coolest dude I've ever met!" He swipes a hand down his face and asks, "But holy shit. What in the hell just happened?"

I'd been a mute throughout the entire exchange, but my voice finally finds me as I answer, "I think you've just been *discovered.*"

We sit staring at each other in silent disbelief for a minute when I add, "I also think you owe my boobs a huge debt of gratitude. If it weren't for them, I'd have been the one on that stage. And trust me, Lutzy What's-his-face would not be asking *my* band to perform at his club."

143

CHAPTER 22

Saturday, June 24, 1995
4:04 PM

Monty's House
Spring Lake

Monty is lounging on a raft chaise in his pool with a plastic hurricane glass when we saunter into the backyard. He lifts his sunglasses in fraudulent admiration for the parade of women filing across the patio.

We say hello, and then I ask, "Hey Mont. How is it possible that you've found the time to lollygag around the pool only one hour before showtime?"

He takes a sip of his blue beverage before answering, "Look around, Livi Girl. Walter sent *the staff* today. My stove-slaving days are over."

I snicker at his comment, because I've never seen Monty 'slave' over anything in his life. When he opted to entertain for friends, it was always a lavish production just for the pure enjoyment of it. For his larger parties, he often hired outside help. He must be expecting a huge crowd today.

Walter had sent a tuxedoed wait staff of twenty to precede his arrival. They set up dozens of long tables adorned with linen tablecloths, chafing dishes, and a rainbow of scattered orchids. One table is designated purely as a carving station, complete with a whole turkey and a roasted pig donning sunglasses.

In the driveway sits two, humongous, white trucks. One is basically a kitchen on wheels, allowing the previously prepared food to be warmed in any of the six ovens on board. Workers stream in and out of that one carrying fruit displays from the refrigerators, ice sculptures from the freezers, and trays upon trays of hors d'oeuvres to be passed butler-style. Even more workers are busily hauling in the booze for the three bartenders

144

who are arranging a million liquor bottles along the rented tiki-hut bar, and filling the bathtub-sized bins next to it with beer.

The other monstrous truck is "The Pee-Pee Mobile," as Monty likes to call it. Eight full bathroom stalls and sinks in all, accessible by either of two sets of steps: Men's or Ladies'.

By the time Walter pulls up in his white minivan, the girls and I are clear of our initial astonishment enough to help him lug in the huge boxes of flower leis, grass hula skirts, and Hawaiian shirts. He urges the girls and me to go upstairs and change into bathing suits, adding, "Report back poolside, seventeen-hundred-hours for cocktails!"

When we come back downstairs, a DJ is setting up near the cabana as Walter's assistant puts the finishing touches to the décor. Pineapple-shaped string lights drape over the architectural landscaping and roof eaves while two-dozen tiki torches are placed sporadically around the perimeter of the yard.

Monty has absolutely outdone even himself with this party.

I break from the pack to take over the spare bathroom downstairs, deciding to blow my hair out straight in order to look a little more luau-y. In the time it takes me to do so, the girls have ransacked the box containing the shirts, most likely fighting over the coolest designs. I rifle through what's left, then run upstairs to change into a top covered in a pattern of "Welcome to Hawaii" postcards. I leave the buttons undone and instead tie the tails below my bikini top, exposing my newly-tanned midriff. A black A-line miniskirt, straw sandals, and a flower tucked behind my ear complete the look.

The party is already well underway as I leave the Pink Room and head downstairs. From the backyard, Bruddah Iz's "Somewhere Over the Rainbow" is filtering in through the family room sliders as I make my way through the abandoned house.

But as I pass the kitchen, I stop dead in my tracks when I hear the sound of a deep voice slithering, "Well, Aloha..."

I turn slowly toward Jack, and the smile that he's extending makes my heart slam into my stomach.

145

"Aloha," I say back before busting up at the sight of him. "Where in the world were you able to find a T-shirt with a picture of *Don Ho*?"

He smiles proudly and offers, "It's all in who you know, baby."

I giggle, partly because Jack is making me laugh, and partly just because I'm happy to see him. We hadn't gotten together all week, and because he has a gig tonight, we didn't have plans to do so until tomorrow. This is a surprise visit.

I go over to kiss him hello, saying, "I knew you couldn't resist checking this spectacle out."

"Wrong," he shoots back. "I just wanted to see you."

At that, his hands go to my waist, lifting me to sit on the counter facing him. He runs his nose along my jaw and breathes in, as if he's trying to get his fix. I like the idea that he's addicted to any part of me, even if it's just my *ck one* perfume.

"That flower is on the wrong side," he murmurs before removing the thing and placing it behind my left ear. "*Un*attached young ladies wear a flower on the right."

I feel the brush of his fingertips against my cheek and my senses are awakened with the brief contact.

"And...?" I ask, leading him on.

Jack steps between my legs and runs his hands along the outside of my thighs. He touches his lips to the side of my neck and whispers, "And... you're *mine*."

The staked claim combined with the possessive way he's holding me disintegrates my gray matter completely. A million witty comebacks would have strewn from my mouth had Jack's touch against my legs not absolved my brain of all function. I seem to lose the ability to think or reason whenever he's in such close proximity, which makes keeping up my end of our arrangement especially challenging.

I am sooo counting this as Date Number Five.

I cross my ankles against the small of his back and draw his face to mine for a kiss. His hands slide further up my legs, under my skirt, pulling me into direct contact with his hardening body.

He presses himself against me *right in that perfect spot*, and my throat lets out an involuntary groan. Jack is doing some groaning of his own as he slides his hands around to my backside and grabs my ass. He drags me toward him and rolls his hips into me as I pull his hair and open my mouth against his. His tongue sweeps inside, the taste of him smoky and minty and one-hundred-percent *Jack*.

He sticks a finger down my cleavage and pulls at the knot in my shirt until the tails come undone and hang loose at my sides. His hand roams over my bikini top and massages my breast, his thumb rubbing over its tip until it hardens against the thin spandex of my bathing suit.

Then he pulls the fabric to the side and pinches me, sending a shock straight between my legs.

Oh God.

I arch my back toward him and he buries his face in my chest. His tongue is tasting at the space between my breasts, his hips are *still* grinding against me, he is so goddamn hard and it feels so goddamn good… and oh shit… I'm almost ready to…

No!

No, no, no, no, no.

I am *not* going to come with Jack for the first time in the middle of a party, for chrissakes.

Before I can completely lose all control, I tear my mouth away from his temple. "Jesus, what are we doing? We're in the *kitchen*, Jack!"

He continues to run his lips up and down the cord of my neck. "Yeah, so?"

I try to squirm out of his grasp, but there's nothing doing. "*So*, if things keep up like this, any wandering party guests are gonna get one hell of a free show."

Jack's tongue dips into the hollow of my throat as his voice vibrates against my skin. "Let 'em watch."

His hands are still buried under my skirt, so he grabs at my string bikini bottoms and starts to pull them down my hips. I'm almost lulled back into a deep enough daze to let him, but it looks as though it's my turn to be the rational one. I grab his face between my hands and force him to meet my eyes. "We have to stop, Jack."

147

His exasperated growl shakes the damn walls. He moves out from between my legs and slumps across the counter next to me, his forehead banging against the granite on every word, "We. Can't. Keep. Doing. This."

I hop off the counter and put myself back together, giggling as he stands and pulls one of the butter knives out of the drawer, pointing it at his chest. His eyes are pleading as he says, "Just one swift roundhouse kick to this thing, and you can end the torture. Please, baby. Just put me out of my misery."

"You started it, Celibacy Boy," I shoot back as I bound toward the sliding door. I look back to see Jack still manning his post behind the counter. "Aren't you coming?"

"Yeah. In a minute."

I furrow my brows in confusion, and he smirks out, "Hey, I love a luau as much as the next guy. It's just that I can't really go out there like *this*."

I clamp a hand over my laughing mouth.

It was so easy for my mind to be rational about Jack whenever I was away from him. I think I must have some involuntary shut-off switch on my brain, cutting off all reason within a few seconds of his touch. I'm astounded at how he can make me feel exhilarated and scared both at the same time. He can go from resolute seriousness to lighthearted joking to bold sensuality inside of a minute; the philosopher, the comedian, and the lover all rolled up into one irresistible human body.

And you're mine, I think to myself.

* * *

148

I find myself bolting upright in bed, an uneasy echo of noise still ringing in my ears.

I must have had a nightmare.

At first, I'm not even sure where I am, but as my eyes adjust to the dark, I remember that I'm at Monty's.

Checking the clock on the nightstand I can see that it's close to four in the morning.

Great.

I'm about to slink back under the covers when I hear Jack's voice singing one floor below me, and jump out of bed before he can wake the whole house. I scamper down the stairs to find him slumped on the floor in a corner of the foyer. *What are you doing?* I whisper-shout over him.

"Sitting," he offers with full attitude, as if I'm the crazy one.

"You're drunk."

"Nope!" he says way too loud, so I mime a shush to try and get him to lower his voice. When I have no other words for him, he can tell that I'm annoyed. "Babe. So I had a drink'r two on the way over."

"You had more than 'a drink or two'."

"No, I swear. I had like three drinks and then Freddie dropped me off."

"Uh huh."

"Whass that look? Four drinks and you're givin' me the stink eye?"

I should be angry, but instead, I'm doing everything in my power to keep from cracking up. Sad fact is, Jack has obviously had more than a handful of drinks, but goddamn if he doesn't make a very cute drunk. "Okay, rock star. Let's get you to bed."

"Whose bed? Yours?"

I purse my lips to keep from laughing and answer, "Normally, I'd take you up on the offer, but I don't make it a habit to take advantage of someone who's had too much to drink."

"I tol' you, I'm not drink!"

Shaking my head in exasperation, I crouch down and throw his arm around my shoulders. I get a grip on the belt loops of his jeans, trying to ignore the bumpy hardness of his abs. "I can't do this by myself. You're going to have to help me out, here. Come on. I've got you. Ready?"

I count to three, and Jack manages to get his feet under him as I help haul him upright. It's a scary trek up the stairs, and I have to keep reminding him to hold the handrail. One wrong move and this pile of Jell-O is going to tumble backwards and break his fool neck.

By the grace of God, I manage to get him into the Blue Room in one piece. I deposit him on the bed, where his body lands diagonally, his feet still planted on the floor. Short of waking up someone else to assist me, this is the best I can do.

"Sleep wi' me," he asks. "Naked."

I snicker at his request and answer, "Not a chance, pal," but I don't think he can hear me. He's already half-asleep and mumbling to himself, so I take one, last, lingering look at his beautiful form before turning to leave the room. "Goodnight, Jack," I whisper from the doorway.

"Okay. G'night. Love ya."

I stop dead in my tracks as my jaw gapes open. *"Whaaat?"*

"What, *what*?" he slurs.

"What did you just say?"

"I said 'good night, Livia.' Why? What d' you think I said?"

I'm not touching that with a ten foot pole.

"Nothing." I brush a hand over my hair and pull myself together. "See you in the morning."

150

CHAPTER 23

Date #6: Sunday, June 25, 1995
1:23 PM

The Stone Pony
Asbury Park

I am more excited than Jessie Spano on a caffeine pill bender as we walk through the doors of The Stone Pony. And if *I* am this excited, I can't imagine what Jack must be going through.

I'm surprised that the place isn't humongous. It's big enough, but its legendary status had me expecting it to be the size of a stadium. Instead, it consists of a decent-sized square bar adjacent to a raised platform of a stage which is so ordinary, it's almost boring. It sits on the edge of an adequate open area, where I'm sure I'll be dancing and sweating with the rest of Thunderjug's fans before this day is through. The whole room is painted black, the only splashes of color provided by the dozens of guitars mounted on the wall and the numerous band posters wallpapered on every surface. Names like Southside Johnny. The Smithereens. Patti Smith. Joe Jackson. Nick Lowe. Bruce.

And now Thunderjug will be added to the long list of iconic performers that have graced this famous stage.

I can't quite fucking believe it.

Jack is busy with his setup and sound check, so I sidle up to the bar and order a beer. It's totally a beer kind of day. The place is pretty empty, and I'm hoping it will fill up soon enough. Playing The Pony is exciting enough on its own, but I know Jack's band will have a better chance of being asked back if there's a good turnout for their show. It's the kind of place that can make or break a band's reputation, and Thunderjug is just figuring out what theirs will be.

* * *

Sometime after three, Jack joins me at the bar. The room has filled up considerably in the past hour, and people are still streaming in through the door. Good.

He orders a bottle of water and points to the plastic bag on the bar next to my purse. "What's that?" he asks, before downing half his drink. It's hot out there today, and The Pony doesn't have air conditioning. I'm kind of excited, thinking about what a sweaty mess he's going to be onstage later on.

"I caved. I bought a T-shirt," I answer sheepishly.

"Bennie," he shoots back like a colossal wiseass.

"I know, right? I felt like a total tourist buying it, but come on. We're at The Pony!"

He laughs, then admonishes, "Babe. Quit reminding me. I'm nervous enough as it is."

He downs the rest of his water, gives me a kiss, and then hops back up on stage. There are the usual twangs and adjustments as the guitars are tuned and tested, the usual squeaks in the mic as the final balance is found.

For all the pent-up anxiety the guys must be feeling, the venue is a casual one. I have to imagine it's making for an easier time of it up there.

The large speakers flanking the stage vibrate in anticipation as Freddie takes the honors. "Hey everybody. I'm Freddie. That's Jack. That's Booey, and that's Jimmy. We... are Thunderjug. Welcome to the show!"

And with that, Jack's guitar starts in with a scratchy, soul-shredding lick as he launches in with Van Halen's "Ain't Talkin Bout Love."

They've been rehearsing like crazy all week and it shows. This is a new song in their repertoire, but they're belting it out so seamlessly, I can't imagine anyone in here is able to tell.

152

Not that it matters. A bunch of people have already abandoned their seats at the bar in order to stand in front of the stage. Good sign.

Over the next ten songs, the room has filled up considerably. The Stone Pony is located right on the main drag of Asbury Park, and with the doors wide open, the music has lulled any pedestrians off the street and Pied-Pipered them into the building to check out the band. Before I know it, the dance floor is packed and the bar is three people deep.

By the time Thunderjug dives into "Backyard," the energy has reached a fevered high. I'm right in the middle of it all, jumping and dancing along, sweating my ass off, having a blast. Jack almost flubs the lyrics when he chuckles, watching me out on the dance floor boogying away like a maniac. I don't care that my moves are only slightly better than Elaine Benes's at a company party. I'm having *fun*.

They segue into Led Zep's "Moby Dick"—also new—and there's only the slightest bit of panic when I think about Jimmy having to tackle that fricking drum solo.

But not enough to leave this spot.

I'm sweating bullets. I'm out of breath. I'm suddenly being pushed through the crowd.

What the hell? I turn to see that it's Jack's hands on my shoulders, walking me over to the side of the stage. Without a word, he slips into the sliver of space between the wall and the humongous stack of Marshalls, pulling me inside the black hollow of its housing.

And then he crushes our mouths together.

As Jimmy's drumming rips against my ears, Jack's kiss tears across my lips. He's sweatier than I am and we're both out of breath, but oxygen isn't our biggest concern right now.

He pulls back just enough to scratch out, *"We've got eleven minutes. Twelve if Jimmy's really feeling it."*

I bite my lip, barely able to contain my excitement. "We can do a lot of damage in that time."

"That's what I'm counting on."

153

He slips a hand under my knee to hitch my leg over his hip, and I follow suit with the other one. I've got my feet braced against one wall of the wooden box and my back plastered against the other as Jack rams his hips against me, shoving his tongue down my throat.

I grab the back of his wet hair in my fist and pull—hard—and he returns the attack by shoving a slick hand up my shirt and squeezing my breast. I bite his lip for that. He rips my bra to the side. I scratch my nails down his back. He slams his hard-on against my shorts...

...I almost pass out.

He's got one hand on my breast as the other slides down my side, around to the small of my back, slipping his fingers under the waistband of my shorts, palming my ass. Skin to skin, he grasps a cheek in his hand and pulls me tighter against his body, rolling his hips against me and groaning into my mouth.

I think I'm going to die. My heart is about to explode—along with every other atom in my body—as this dark prince ravages me behind a goddamn speaker, for chrissakes.

Oh my God he is so hot.

Hot enough that I can overlook our less-than-romantic setting and get lost in this moment, because I know O-Town is only a short trip away.

Checking my watch, I see that we still have eight minutes left. Maybe nine.

He lifts my damp shirt up to my neck and lowers his mouth to my exposed breast. He tongues it hungrily before closing his teeth over my skin—lightly, but hard enough to send an electrical charge racing through my nervous system. When I bite his ear, he removes his hands from under my ass, grabs both my tits in his hands and shoves my back against the wall.

Reaching above my head, I find a metal bar to grasp onto, and between my grip on that and my feet pressed into the opposite wall, I'm able to maintain our position. Every time I slacken my hold, I sink down against his hardened length, crashing into me along with the beat as he sucks and licks and drives me insane. The man is a machine. *Ohmygod yes. Keep going.*

154

Jack's fingers dig into my front, my back, clamping my body to his as he slams me repeatedly against the wall. I'm appreciative of the narrow space, giving me some added leverage. Jack's about six foot four (and full of muscles—ha!), but even this fine specimen can't possibly possess the superhuman strength necessary to hold me aloft long enough to get the deed done.

Judging by his penile stamina, you wouldn't know that, however.

"Jesus, Liv," he growls, *"I'm fucking dying for you."*

His lips smash against my mouth once again as I lower my feet to the floor and palm the front of his jeans. He's hard as a rock as I run my hand along his length, moaning into his mouth, trying not to scream.

I check my watch. Six minutes. Maybe seven.

I tear at the buttons of his shirt, allowing myself exactly one minute to run my hands along his slick chest, down to his abs, feeling his wet, bumpy hardness under my palms. My heart is beating along with the thumpetathumpetathumpthumpthump of Jimmy's drums as I get the buttons of his jeans undone, and holy hell, I can't believe he's not stopping me.

Out of nowhere, Jack tears his mouth from mine, his eyes wide. "Oh shit!"

"What?" I ask, still caught in our trance.

"The fucking song!" he says, and he doesn't need to say anything more. I listen for about half a second, long enough to realize that Jimmy's solo is winding down way ahead of schedule and Jack is about to miss his entrance cue.

Goddammit!

We pull ourselves together as best we can; Jack only allows himself enough time to button his fly before he slips out of the speaker, grabs his guitar, and hops back on stage mid-chord.

He is noticeably late, and between the evil grin on his face and his state of undress, it's obvious to every person in this room what he's been up to. His shirt is unbuttoned down to his waist, his hair is a tangled mess, and he's got sweat dripping from every pore. He *looks* like he's just been fucked, and the audience

155

responds accordingly, raising their drinks amidst hoots and howls, toasting their god.

His snarl is liquid sex as he leers at me from the stage. I'm fairly certain the look he's aiming at me has just melted my clothes clean off. I actually take a quick scan down my body, expecting to see my shirt and shorts reduced to a puddle on the floor.

But nope. I'm still fully dressed.

Dammit.

CHAPTER 24

Date #7: Friday, June 30, 1995
5:24 PM

Pacific Ave.
Atlantic City

I know Jack was hoping to grab a quick nap before the sound check tonight, but it doesn't look like we're going to be working with that kind of time. He had to wait for me to get out of work—Shana refused to close her doors any earlier than two o'clock for the holiday weekend—and we got caught in Parkway traffic. I hope we can find the damn hotel already and check in, but I'm starting to think that Jack won't be left with much more time than it will take to haul ass over to *Caesar's* and set up for the show. You'd think a room at the venue itself would've been comped for the talent, but I guess Thunderjug doesn't carry that kind of weight yet. We're currently cruising the main drag of Atlantic City, searching for the Days Inn.

Where the hell is this place?

Sure enough, the sign appears in my vision.

"It's a Burger Barn, Gilbert!" I shout as I point at our destination.

We drive past the building and Jack swings the van into the south lot. I hop out and give a good stretch before throwing my purse over my shoulder and leaping onto Jack's back. He wraps his arms under my legs and piggybacks me across the parking lot into the lobby.

The place is not exactly what I was expecting.

Kinda dirty. Small. Really, really seedy. There's an overweight guy at the front desk wearing a wife-beater, his comb-over blowing in the breeze from a dirty metal fan, his feet propped up on the counter reading a magazine—I don't want to know which one.

Yikes. What a dive.

The "concierge" doesn't even raise his head when Jack greets him with, "We've got reservations?" As if *that* isn't the understatement of the day. "Under John Cocktoaston?"

I snicker to myself, well aware that Freddie was the one to arrange our accommodations. I'll have to remember to congratulate him for his name choice.

At first, the guy looks at Jack like he's speaking another language. But suddenly, he closes the magazine, straightens up, and starts organizing the papers strewn across the counter, as if he just this second realizes we're paying customers. "You made a reservation? Do you remember who you talked to?"

"No, man. My buddy set it up."

"Well, did we quote you a price?"

What the hell is this? Doesn't he know how much his own hotel charges?

"Yeah. Seventy dollars for the night. Some special or something," Jack answers, losing patience by the minute.

Wife Beater digs under the counter and pulls out a form for him to sign while I wander around the tiny lobby, scoping the space out. I'm trying very hard not to touch anything.

One can hardly blame me.

Jack signs the form, pays in cash, and is handed a key. "Room two-oh-one. "Outside, up the stairwell, first room at the top of the stairs."

"Thanks," Jack says. "Hey Liv. We're all set."

The two of us head back out to the parking lot so Jack can grab his guitars out of the van and lock up the rest of the equipment, explaining, "I don't trust this place."

We make our way up the stairs... and pass an actual fucking hooker on her way down.

What the what?

After she's out of earshot, I ask, "What the hell kind of place is this? You'd think a national chain would be a little..."

"Less disgusting?"

"Took the words right out of my mouth."

There's a guy at the other end of the balcony, screaming something angry in a foreign language to the hooker, now down in the parking lot. Jack puts the key in the doorknob as he speaks the very words I'm thinking. "Where *are* we?"

He opens the door and I realize we have our answer.

"Hell. I think we're in Hell."

CHAPTER 25

Friday, June 30, 1995
5:45 PM

The Devil's Asshole
Atlantic City

It's hot outside today, but my God. It's practically an *oven* inside the room. The heated dank greets us from the first swing of the door, and doesn't let up even when Jack manages to punch the air conditioner into submission.

I haven't moved beyond the doorway, however. I flip on the light switch, then immediately turn it back off. I don't think I want to see the place in any great detail.

The first thing I notice is the bed. Huge four-poster with an ugly, lacquer canopy, the mattress covered in a dingy floral bedspread and accented with four, flat pillows in mismatched cases. Two dark brown nightstands frame the shiny, black headboard, and a painted green dresser occupies the wall across from it. Rotting wallpaper—two different patterns—peels away from the walls at every seam, and the dim light shining through the window highlights what I assume was once a sheer white curtain. A scrungy bookcase holds a television (with a tin foil antennae) and an opened mini fridge (which is defrosting the layer of snow within, melting into a puddle of dark maroon on the carpet beneath it).

I am speechless.

Jack turns from the air conditioner and laughs when he sees my stunned expression. "Stick with me, baby. Look at the life of luxury I can provide."

I tell him that I'm afraid to look in the bathroom, so he accompanies me to check it out. Avocado toilet, pink tub, white sink… I've never seen anything like it in my life.

160

"I can't," I offer, feeling dizzy and unable to finish my sentence. "This is worse than a Rutgers frat house. I need to lie down."

I pinch the comforter between the tips of two fingers and pull it off the bed—not only is it nine thousand degrees in here, but there is no way I'm letting that disgusting thing touch my body even if it were freezing—and am pleasantly surprised to find some clean white sheets underneath. I strip off my Citizen Dick T-shirt and jean shorts but leave on my bra and undies, trying to cool off in any way possible until the air kicks in.

I see Jack staring at me, but I don't have the patience to deal with him right at the moment. "Deal with it," I offer, before kicking off my Dr. Scholl's. "God. I hope it cools off before I have to take a shower. There's no way I'll be able to blow dry my hair in this heat. Tell me again why Caesar's didn't comp us a room?"

"Speaking of rooms, I'd better try and track down which ones the rest of the guys are in. You gonna be okay by yourself for a little bit?"

I start to tell him, "Of course," as I flop down onto the lumpy bed, but wind up cracking up instead.

Jack pokes his head under the canopy to check out what's so funny. All I can do is point above me and laugh. He looks up and almost chokes. "*Mirrors*? Seriously? Where the hell are we?"

"I think we've already established that we're in Hell."

He climbs onto the bed and lays down next to me, the both of us laughing at our reflections in the ceiling mirror. "Please remind me to check for dead bodies under the mattress before we go to sleep tonight."

"Like I'd forget that."

He rolls over on his side and picks up the phone to call the rest of the band, find out where their rooms are, coordinate a time to meet up for the sound check. I'm trying not to move, just waiting on the AC to kick in, sweating my ass off in the process.

"*Martinique Motel*? What the hell?" Jack spits out.

I turn to see him with a confused look on his face, his eyebrows scrunched. I'm pretty confused myself.

161

His fingers go white as he grips the handset, practically snarling through his teeth, "You mean Days Inn, right?" He listens for an extra second, slams the phone onto the cradle, and announces, "Get your stuff. We're outta here."

"What? What's going on?"

"We're in the wrong hotel! The Days Inn is next door!"

"Ewwww!"

I can't get out of the bed fast enough. I throw on my clothes and try to shake the cooties off my skin. God only knows what perversions took place on that mattress. "You know what this is? This is a flop house! It's a fucking hooker house, Jack!"

I put my shoes on, but I know I'll have to burn them eventually, and we go back down to the lobby to talk to Wife Beater. He's still sitting there reading and sweating, his hairy chest sprouting over the neckline of his undershirt, looking like a character from a cheesy movie.

Jack walks right up to him and rests a fist on the counter. "Obviously, there's been a misunderstanding here. We'd like a refund."

Wife Beater doesn't even bother to put down his magazine as he asks, "Did you *use* the room?"

Eww. Is he asking us if we've just had a quickie? What a scuzbag! As pissed as I am, it looks like Jack is getting ready to jump over the counter and liberate the guy's head from his neck. Instead, he takes a calming breath and answers, "No, we didn't *use* the room. We didn't even want to touch anything in there. Besides, we checked in under false pretenses."

"I'm sorry, but I'm going to have to charge you twenty-five dollars for a short stay."

Jack isn't having it. "Look, pal. You either give me back every penny I gave you or you can use it to pay your plastic surgeon. Your choice."

Wife Beater decides he's messing with the wrong guy.

We throw our stuff back in the van and zip around the corner to the Days Inn. You'd think we just checked into the Waldorf with the way we *oooh* and *ahhh* over the clean, air-conditioned room.

At this point, I guess it's not going to take much to make us happy.

Jack has to tend to his sound check, so I opt to grab a shower and then take that nap for him. I stretch out onto the clean, cool sheets and take a huge, refreshing breath.

Heaven.

CHAPTER 26

Friday, June 30, 1995
8:30ish PM

The Circus Maximus at Caesar's
Atlantic City

Jack looks so freaking hot right now.

That sweet little ass poured into a pair of black leather pants? ME-OW.

I've got an up-close-and-personal view from my post at the side of the stage. Jimmy's girlfriend Collette and I were thrown together earlier, and now we're both hiding behind a curtain, peeking over a speaker at our respective rock gods. Jack went with a Robert Plant look tonight; along with the leather pants, he's wearing an unbuttoned, short-sleeved shirt to show off those gorgeous abs of his. And holy hell. It's almost a shame when they're blocked by his guitar.

There are thousands of fans out there in the audience, and even though they all came here tonight to see Stevie, they sure as hell seem to be digging his opening act. It's a different vibe here at the arena than it is at the bars. Louder, for sure. But it's way more real. Thunderjug isn't just some bar band right now; they are a *powerhouse*. And they are owning this stage.

I've listened to their CD enough times to know that Jack sings lead on most of their originals, but actually watching him belt those same songs out in person is a different animal altogether.

And Jack is on the prowl.

The confidence. The strut. The *sex*. It's just dripping from him, sweaty and scorching like a hot, wet, summer rain.

He puts down his axe and grabs the mic from the stand, stalking across the stage in a lethal slither, drawing every female eye to his mesmerizing form. Inviting every single one of them to put a new lipstick-stain on that huge dick of his, taunting and teasing

164

from behind those leather pants as he arches his back, screaming the final lyrics of "Momentary Madness" into the mic.

He's haunting. He's *ravenous*. He's overwhelming.

Thunderjug slides into a kickass version of "Vampire" as Jack moves to the front of the stage. I wouldn't have thought it was possible to love my song any more than I already did, but hearing the perfected version is positively mind-blowing. The thrash of Freddie's guitar, the pounding of Jimmy's drums, the agony of Booey's bass, the heartbreak of Jack's voice.

I almost forget how to breathe.

It's time to let the common people worship at the feet of Rock God, so Jack shakes his wet head over his screaming disciples, blessing them with holy water. They're just eating it up, and he is loving every minute of it. He shoots me a quick wink before sprawling out on his back, his head and torso dipped over the edge of the stage.

Lain out. Offering himself. A sacrifice on the altar.

Every fan in the front row pays tribute as they reach out to touch him, running their hands down his bare chest, trying to absorb his presence through their fingertips.

He is bigger than Elvis and The Beatles and the fucking New Kids on the Block right now. He is dripping, raw, animalistic sin. He exudes arrogance; he oozes swagger. He. Is. Sex, and every girl in this audience wants to get their hands on him.

Including me.

It's just crazy to see him in full rockstar mode. It's as if the expansiveness of the arena is allowing him to truly break free, as if those rinky dink bars he's been playing all these years were too small to contain him. He's been a big fish in a small pond for too long, and now it's incredible to see his full potential busting out. You can just *feel* that he's destined for fame. I know it. Every person in this room knows it.

He'll be a big fish in a big ocean soon enough.

* * *

165

The energy is palpable in the dressing room after the concert. We stuck around to watch some of Stevie's set—*from the side of the stage holy shit*—until about midway through the show when we were asked very kindly to get the fuck out of the way.

The guys have already cracked open the complimentary champagne and are spraying it all over each other as if they've just won the World Series. Any minute now, someone will dump a vat of Gatorade over Jack's head.

He is the man of the hour, accepting his bandmates' claps on the back and unending words of praise. Fact is, this entire night has only been made possible because of his and my chance encounter with Lutz Hamburg, Events Manager Extraordinaire.

I'd asked my dad if he knew anything about the guy, and as it turns out, he'd not only heard of him, but worked with him at one point over the years. Evidently, Lutz is way connected in the music industry. For a schlubby guy who chose to make his living in the armpit of New Jersey, he sure knew enough important people in New York.

Booey had done some research of his own and come to the same conclusion. He and Jack let the guys know going into it that playing this show was not only freaking awesome, but a fantastic networking move as well.

How fantastic was revealed a bit later as Lutz joined us backstage.

He'd come into the room to offer his congratulations, but more to pat his own back for being brilliant enough to hire Thunderjug. "You boys are welcome back any time. *Any* time!"

The guys all thanked him as he added, "I know producers. Are you shopping for a label?"

We all stopped and stared at him. The entire night had been surreal enough on its own, but his question seemed even more unbelievable.

I'd talked to Jack about this possibility a few days ago, and he had dismissed the idea with a wave of his hand. "Nah. This is a one shot deal. Shit like that doesn't happen in real life, babe." But still, he'd said, it was fun to dream.

And now here was Lutz, actually uttering the magic words.

166

Jack's hand tightens around mine before he finds his voice. "We, uh... We never really discussed it, Lutz. We always just thought of ourselves as a bar band. But I mean..." he takes a look around the room as his bandmates mirror his own wide eyes. "We'd be stupid not to at least consider it."

I thought Lutz was going to offer them a record deal right then and there. But as it turns out, he is simply talking shop with them. He brings up some names of people I've never heard of, but whom the mere mention of has Booey practically foaming at the mouth.

Collette and I leave the boys to their business and park our exhausted asses at the table in the corner of the room. We each crack open our beers and clink them together as I ask, "So, how did you meet Jimmy?"

She gets a dreamy look on her face as she twirls a strand of burgundy hair around her fingers. "Oh, we've known each other from the beginning. When these guys were first starting out, I was their very first fan."

"That's so cute."

She gives a huff and answers, "Cute nothing. I waited around for three whole years before he finally asked me out. Going to every show, watching him leave every night with other girls..."

I immediately dismiss the vision of Jack doing the same. "But you've been together a year now? Obviously, you were meant to be together. What took him so long?"

"What took *me* so long, you mean."

"Huh?"

"This bod used to be a lot bigger."

I don't know Jimmy very well, but he doesn't strike me as a shallow asshole. I actually think he's a pretty cool guy. I can feel that opinion changing almost immediately as I ask incredulously, "He wouldn't go out with you because you were *fat?*"

Collette shakes her head and explains, "No, no, no, no." She chuckles at me for being so short-sighted. "He wouldn't go out with me because I was so *inhibited* about it. Once I came out of my shell, Jimmy came to heel just like that!" She gives a snap to her fingers at the end of her statement as I stifle a laugh.

167

"How about you two?" she asks through a giggle. "How did you manage to land *Jack?*"

I don't necessarily feel as though I've 'landed' anyone, but I can't help the smile that breaks through as I consider Collette's question. "Well, the truth is... he kind of reeled *me* in."

"Wow," she says. "Who knew he had it in him? He used to be such a whore back in the early days. Well, you know, before the *girlfriend*." Collette gives a roll to her eyes, and I have to fight the temptation to ask her for details. She must see the troubled look on my face, because she quickly amends her statement. "Oh, wait, hey. The groupies? The girlfriend? He fell into all that. He *chose* you."

I know she's trying to toss me a compliment, but her comment is only serving to remind me that I'm dating a chameleon. I'm kind of crazy about this guy, and it's scary to think of how easily he could slip up. Crossing such a thin line could tear us apart.

And yet, I'm the last person in the world who has any right to judge him for his past.

My mind is spinning and a fake smile is plastered to my face as Jack comes over to retrieve me. "Hey. We're thinking of hitting the casino for a little bit. You up for it?"

The guys are pulling themselves together, gathering up their things, and getting ready for a night out on the town. I'm still pondering Collette's words as we all leave the cramped room to do some gambling and get our drink on.

And that's when... right there in the hallway of The Circus Maximus in Atlantic City New Jersey... We run into Stevie Wonder.

Well, we actually run into his *entourage*, a group of about half a dozen people—bodyguards, assistants, whomever—but there's no mistaking the famous face in the middle of it.

"Mr. Wonder!" Jack lets out, as the rest of us just look on in awe.

One of Stevie's monsters leans down to whisper something in his ear, and that's when he says this: "Oh, hey, yeah. I caught most of your set. You boys were really great tonight. Really, really great."

I am rendered speechless as his surreal words sink in. Stevie Wonder thinks my boyfriend's band is *really great?*

Jack is wearing a goofy grin, but he manages an elated, "Thank you! That means a lot, Mr. Wonder. Thank you very much."

And then Stevie says this: "No problem, no problem. Nice to meet you boys. Enjoy your night."

I freak out as I listen to him talk with those velvety pipes; that same voice sings some of my favorite, most-beloved songs of all time. He has just as much smile in his tone when he is speaking.

I want to comment on it, maybe share a laugh with him about such a silly observation... I want to tell him how amazing I think he is, how I've grown up with his music, that it's part of the soundtrack to my youth... I want to tell him about that time when my father's van broke down on the way to a music festival in Philly back in 1980, when Persuasion was supposed to be on the bill as one of his opening acts. I want to tell him how we got there too late and Foreigner ended up extending their set, and how I cried the whole night because I'd missed his show.

Oh God, there are so many things I need to tell him. Why won't my mouth work?

Wake up, Livia! How many chances am I ever going to get in my life to meet one of my childhood idols?

The guys all speak up to say goodbye, but I'm still completely unable to make sound come out of my throat.

That is, until I see him start to walk away... and I panic.

"Stevie!OhmyGodSteviethatwasanamazingshowtonightandthank youforsharingyourstagewellit'snotreallyyourstagebutyouknowwh atImean.Oh!AndIknowSongsintheKeyofLifeisthealbumeveryonet alksaboutbutIlovedyourworkonInnerVisionsI'mnotevenkiddingth atalbumchangedmylife!"

I take a huge inhale in the seconds of silence, my mind still racing with all that I still want to say. I'm already out of breath from my ramble, and I'm gearing up for a second round of babble when...

Stevie *looks* at me.

So help me God, *Stevie Wonder looks at me.*

"Hey, that's great. Thank you, thank you," he says to me.

169

To me. Stevie Wonder said actual, coherent words to me. At least one of us was able to remember how to speak like a human.

His people shuffle him on his way, so he gives a wave and says, "You boys take care now. And you too, young lady."

The guys all yell random parting greetings: "Thanks, Stevie!" "Appreciate it, Mr. Wonder!"

"Thanks again!"

And then we watch him walk away.

I put my hands against my mouth and stare at Jack, wide-eyed. "Oh my God! We just met Stevie Wonder!"

"Yeahwedid."

I slide my hands over my eyes and groan. "And oh my God, I just totally lost my cool in front of him."

Jack chuckles, "Yeahyoudid. But it was adorable."

He wraps his arms around me, consoling my embarrassed ass. I am physically cringing from my outburst, and I know there is no way I'll ever be able to relive this amazing moment without dying a little inside each time.

"I'm a complete dork!" I say, as I bury my face in Jack's chest.

He finally comes up with some words of wisdom for me. "Don't feel too bad, babe. Remember when I ran into Springsteen? Yeah. That's pretty much how it went down."

CHAPTER 27

(Technically) Saturday, July 1, 1995
3:27 AM

The Days Inn
Atlantic City

I'm sprawled out on our huge bed in our thankfully clean, blessedly cool hotel room. I'm staring at the ceiling, trying to calm my mind enough to get some shuteye. But after the electric night we've just had, I'm finding it hard to come down.

Plus, I have Jack lying right next to me.

And he's already asleep.

Getting my forty winks seems like a far-off request while lying next to the body of this rock god. I turn my head on the pillow and sneak a look at my sleeping buddy. He's lying on his side, facing away from me. I take a moment to appraise the sight of his naked torso, the sheets tangled around his hips, the waistband of his cotton boxers riding just low enough that I can make out the dimples at the base of his spine. I strain to hear, but I can tell his breathing is soft and even, and I'm pretty sure he's out like a light.

How in the hell can he stand it?

I mean, let's forget for the moment that under normal circumstances, I'd be all over any random musician after the show I just witnessed. Thunderjug was phenomenal tonight, and normally, my elation over listening to such great music normally translated into my, um, *grateful enthusiasm* afterward.

But how is it that he's able to fight the urge against a little celebratory action right now? I saw that look on his face when he came offstage. He was practically flying. We were both pumped up from the concert, Lutz's news, meeting Stevie... and now here we are, alone, in our very own hotel room, actually spending the night together for the very first time. The only thing that could

171

make this circumstance even more perfect is if we were at some swanky place instead of the fricking Days Inn.

Yet there's Jack, determined to keep our bet.

His bet.

Sorry. Our *arrangement*.

Grrr.

I flop onto my side and run a light hand over his hair. Just because we're not going to be having sex tonight doesn't mean I can't touch him, right?

I expect him to grumble and go back to sleep. But instead, my dark prince breathes out a comatose sigh and turns his body to face mine. His eyes are still closed... but his hand lands across my waist.

Hmmm. Promising.

I nudge in closer, quietly, slowly, moving my face just inches from his. I watch his thick lashes resting against his cheeks, feel the heat from his steady breaths against mine.

He skootches a bit closer toward me in his slumber, tucking my head under his chin and wrapping his arm fully around my waist, bringing me in for a nuzzle.

Full-frontal spoon. Alright. Getting somewhere. Maybe I can turn this into a snugglefuck after all.

I give out a sigh, pretending to be asleep as I press my body in closer, burrowing my face into the crook of his neck, inhaling that smoky, shaving-cream scent of him. Jack grunts, and I get the impression that he's not as fully unconscious as I previously thought, because his hand starts a slow slide along the small of my back.

I have to go for it.

My lips part against his skin, and my tongue darts out softly to touch the hollow of his throat. I slip my hand down his side and wrap it around his hip, drawing him against me as I taste his skin, breathing against that perfect little spot at the base of his neck.

Jack groans, and I feel a third member join our party. Well, not a *third member.* There's only *one* "member" popping up between the two of us. Whatever. You know what I'm trying to say.

His dick is getting hard, okay?

I slide my hand around to his ass and pull him toward me, and that little nudge is all it takes for Jack to roll completely on top of my body and grind himself against my shorts.

Score.

I swipe a hand through his unruly hair and press back. Jack's eyes are still closed as his lips find mine, and before I know it, our mouths are a heated mosh of gnashed teeth and tangled tongue. I arch toward him, smashing my cami-covered tits into his bare chest as he slams against me, that sleepy semi now a full-fledged hard-on.

Please pardon this unscheduled break and let's take a moment to appreciate The Dry Hump, shall we? Now. I should preface this by reminding you that I do, in fact, enjoy sex. Like, I think it's the greatest invention ever. Two bodies joined in perfectly choreographed, sweaty, mindless debauchery? What's not to love?

But even still, I gotta give props to The Dry Hump. The *want* on full display, the *can't* ruling your desperate measures. The Dry Hump brings me back to my teenage years, before I was the uninhibited sex goddess I am today. It's always been an incredible turn-on to just make out with a guy, feeling how badly he wants me, his almost-bursting trouser meat pressed right up against my lady bits, separated by a few layers of chaste-inducing clothing. It's empowering, and sexy, and kills me in the very best possible way.

"Mmmm," I moan, as Jack grits a breath through his teeth and rolls his hips against me *right there oh my God don't stop.* I sigh back and wrap my legs around his waist as he rises up on his elbows and finally opens his eyes.

He's still half-asleep, but conscious enough to be aware of what's happening.

For the hundredth time, I ask myself why I agreed to this situation. I know holding off on the sex is the right thing, but he suggested it when the idea of our imposed celibacy was nothing more than an abstract idea. After spending all this time with him, it's become increasingly difficult to keep up my end of the bargain. I already figured out that I was crazy about him, and I know he's waiting to hear me say so, but I just can't seem to find the words.

He has himself settled between my legs, and his tongue buries inside my mouth again as his hand slides under my shirt. I let out with a small groan, and it makes him press himself against me harder, feeling the sweet friction the move causes as he unclasps my bra.

My mind is begging for him to keep going. I slip my hands around his neck as he pulls my shirt and bra off my body, giving him unfettered access to every inch of my exposed skin.

He grasps my breasts in his hands and wraps his lips around one, making me shiver and gasp against his ear. *Nothing can stop this.* He pinches one and sucks on the other, ramming himself against me, making me writhe underneath him, my contented sighs begging him to take me.

He tangles his hands in my hair, taking my mouth with his once again, my tongue searching for... I don't know what... something... some sort of sign.

Because I'm about to explode and I need him inside me. Like *now*.

"Jack," I whisper, the sound causing a buzzing inside my brain.

"Yeah?"

"Do you have anything?"

He curses under his breath, ignoring my question as he continues kissing me, and I think maybe there's a chance he either hasn't heard or simply misinterpreted my question. So, I make things a little clearer.

"*Do you want to fuck me?*" I whisper, grabbing his ass and pulling him tighter against my body. He starts grinding himself against me harder, faster, almost painfully as he lets out with an aching groan, and I slam my lips against him and smash my bare tits against his chest, moaning and panting and licking... and before I know it, his entire body tenses and...

"Ohhh.... Oh Liv, I.... *Ohhhhh!*"

His body shudders against me before he collapses, his breath coming out in an exasperated sigh through his teeth. He buries his face against my neck and punches the pillow next to my head.

174

We're silent for a minute, the only sounds between us that of his staggered breathing against my skin and the thumping of his racing heart.

"Jack?" I ask warily, my voice breaking through his daze. "Did you...?"

"No!" he answers back. Clearly lying. Clearly frustrated.

His embarrassed, emphatic denial has me giggling, my chest shaking as I crack up under the body of this twenty-eight year old, adolescent boy on top of me.

He raises his head and looks at me incredulously, torn between mortification and hysteria. But soon enough, his lip twitches into a small grin which he's fighting hard to contain. "Stop laughing! It's not funny!"

"It so is," I answer back, my giggles turning into a full-on cackle. "I can't believe you just came!"

He finally breaks and starts laughing too. "Jesus. That hasn't happened since I was sixteen. What the fuck did you do to me, Liv?"

"I'm flattered. I think it just comes down to wanting something so much more because you can't have it. That's all."

"Oh, is that all?"

"Mm Hmm." I smile wickedly at him as I add, "Doesn't change the fact that you left me hanging, though."

He doesn't wait to be asked twice. Without another word, he slides a hand inside my panties and plunges two fingers inside me. The unexpected movement has me letting out with a startled gasp. Jack can't seem to help the evil smirk that crosses his lips before he lowers his mouth to mine and brings his thumb into play. *Captain Fingerbang reporting for duty!*

He's good at this.

I'm writhing underneath him, and he bites my lip, gliding his fingers inside me in a steady rhythm, rubbing torturous, tiny circles against my most sensitive spot. Little moans keep escaping from my throat, and I feel him harden against my hip all over again.

Things have already gone too far between us tonight. Why can't they go a little further?

175

"*Please, Jack,*" I hear myself say.

His body tenses on top of mine, his heavy-lidded eyes shooting straight into my soul. "No, babe. Just let me do this."

Okay. Okay. I'm unraveling too fast to argue. My heart is racing, my breaths are choppy, my eyes are rolling into the back of my head. I'm about to lose my damn mind.

He lowers his face to my ear and asks on a gravelly whisper, "*You like to watch, Lips? You like to watch me come?*"

"*Yes,*" I let out on a breathy sigh.

He closes his mouth over my breast, lightly nipping at it, speeding the movement of his fingers inside me. My groans are coming fast and furious now, my hips rolling to slam myself against his palm. He raises his head and looks me right in the eyes to say, "You wish this were my cock inside you."

Oh Jesus.

"Yes." I close my eyes and arch my back, my fisted hands gripping the pillow on either side of my head.

"You want me to fuck you."

"*Yesss.*"

Oh God. Oh God I'm going to—

"You want to come with me deep inside your hot, wet—"

"Ohhhh! Oh God!" I shatter at that as I rock with tremors, my body convulsing against his hand, my head thrashing back and forth on the pillow. I can hear Jack's throaty laugh as he watches me fall apart.

There is nothing funny about the situation. He just killed me. I am dead.

But soon enough, I find myself snickering, too.

When my breathing returns to human levels, he kisses me through our smiles. He pulls back, his steely eyes tight on mine as he whispers, "You are *beautiful* when you let go, you know that?"

"Hmmm," I answer back, exhausted and already half asleep. "That was just the opening act. I can't wait until we get to the real show."

CHAPTER 28

Date #8: Saturday, July 1, 1995
10:38 PM

The Beach
Manasquan

"You're crazy!" I yell to Jack as I watch him lunge into the ocean.

It's a beautiful night, perfectly clear, and I'm sitting on our blanket under an umbrella of stars. I grab a handful of sand and let it sift through my fingers onto my feet as I watch Jack dive through another small wave before it crashes onto shore. The ocean isn't incredibly rough tonight, and that eases any fears I have of him being washed out to sea. Even with such a clear sky, the water is almost completely black, save for a sparkling strip on the surface where the moon is casting a pale glow.

It's only the first day of July, and the night air is already sticky with warmth but the water is still freezing cold. It's as if Mother Nature forgets to tell the ocean that it's summer until sometime in August.

When Jack suggested we come down to the beach for a night swim, I agreed, even though I knew there was no way he was going to get me in the water. Just standing at the edge of the surf gave my feet a headache. I've been content to sit on the sand instead, watching Jack's long, purposeful strokes as he sluices through the water.

There's a slight breeze blowing, but until now, even the wind was actually hot tonight. I take advantage of the current's change of direction and fan my shirt in an attempt to dry out the little pool of sweat that has formed inside my bra.

Neither the sticky night nor the freezing water can take the smile from my face this evening, however. There's some good news in the works.

177

Jack had spent the better part of the day having lunch with Lutz Hamburg. The man was still blown away by the show Thunderjug put on last night, and wanted to talk shop with the guys about the future of the band.

He arranged a meeting for Monday with one of his promoter buddies up in New York, and if all goes well with this Shug Sealy person, it could really lead to some big things. Supposedly, Shug has an in with Mayhem Studios, a pretty big deal indie label that has launched a bunch of chart-topping talent.

The plan was hatched that Jack would meet with Shug alone, speaking on behalf of the band. Booey wasn't too happy about his manager job being replaced, but then again, his position was never official. Everyone knows their best shot at a contract is to let their most charismatic bandmate work the proper magic.

Because if Shug likes Jack, he'll get them signed with Mayhem. And a signed contract will immediately translate into a multi-artist, cross-country tour already in progress, where Thunderjug would simply be added to the bill.

I'm devastated at the idea of Jack taking off for all those months, but he's dropped enough hints over the past hours to make me think he might actually ask me to go with him. I guess he's just waiting to find out for sure before asking me outright. I totally understand why he doesn't want to jinx anything by talking about it, but I really wish he'd let me in on his thought process.

I'm trying to envision a way to make that lifestyle work when he *does* ask. I know that he'll be earning good money from the tour, so it's not like I would need to work. But I also know I'll feel like a mooch living that way after not too long a while. I'm thinking there's a chance that I can pay back the guys by serving as their official photographer during the tour. Lord knows they'll need someone to document their rise to fame, and who better than someone who already knows them well enough to capture them properly?

The girls have generously given up a few days down here so that Jack and I can have a bit of alone-time. They're not coming down until Monday when he leaves for his meeting, and until

178

then, the beach house is all ours. I'm relishing the thought of having him all to myself, alone and uninterrupted for this short while.

I'm able to take all these vacation days after working my tail off last week. Since Jack wasn't around, it was easy for me to throw myself into my job. I even took over some of Shana's workload, so I don't feel too guilty about leaving her alone while I take a few days off. I can use the break.

Shana has been on my case even more than usual this past month, and I don't have to guess why. Ever since I started dating Jack, she's been crabby. I think she just hates the idea that I'm with someone when she isn't. It's not like I've been flaunting my relationship in her face or anything. I rarely even mention Jack's name around her, and even then, I tend to keep the rundown limited to highlights only. Shane never *gives* the patience she expects *from* me whenever there's a story to be told. Meanwhile, I can't begin to count the hours she's regaled me with *every infinitesimal detail* about the most inconsequential things. It's like she can't believe I have the audacity to be happy in her presence, so I try not to show it too much. When it comes to Shana, at times, it just makes my job easier that way.

On the other hand, I'm happy to report that my work itself has never been better. I recently incorporated a great idea into my daily routine at the studio, which has me excited about my job for the first time ever. I've started setting up appointments for more than just our run-of-the-mill, in-studio portraits. Lately, most of my schedule requires me to either go to a client's house for a shoot, or meet at a favorite location of their choosing. My subjects get their "portraits" taken candidly while baking cookies or bowling or flying kites at the park. Being able to shoot people in a comfortable setting has yielded amazing results. I've rarely taken better photos in my entire life.

That divine inspiration led to the shoot I have planned for the Tanners tomorrow. Jack's whole family is coming down so I can take their family portrait on the beach.

I'm thinking about some locations while swirling a stick of driftwood in the sand. I look down and see that I've drawn a heart without even realizing I've done it. How dorky am I? I quickly scratch it out as Jack emerges from the ocean, shaking off the water like a dog after a bath. He is so beautiful that it's almost painful to look at him sometimes. I still can't quite believe he's mine.

"Hey Liv... You really should get in there. The water feels great!"

Yeah, sure, if you're a polar bear.

"Not a chance, Shrinkydinks. It's freezing! How can you stand it?"

He growls like a lion and shakes his wet head over me. I scream from the pinpricks of icy droplets raining down onto my body, and hold up a towel to try and shield myself from the onslaught. He grabs it away and dives onto the blanket, taking me down with him. His wet body is angled across mine, soaking me through my tank top and shorts as he kisses me. His salty, cold lips are rough and insistent as the water drips from his hair and runs down my neck, making me shiver.

Though I suspect my trembling has more to do with the way Jack is kissing me than the temperature of the water.

He laughs as he rolls off me and watches as I attempt to dry off ineffectively with the towel. He flops onto his back and lets his cold, wet head land in my lap. I toss him the other towel and he blots absently at his body while I give up drying altogether. I throw on his sweatshirt and settle my legs more comfortably underneath him before running my fingers through the strands of hair at his temple. He loves when I do this.

He lies quietly, staring up at the beautiful sky above us. I know he's been just as lost as I was the past week, and just as grateful that we've been together all weekend after what felt like an eternity apart. How crazy that our lives have already become so intertwined after such a short amount of time.

Most of which has been spent constantly fighting the urge to jump him.

But what? Would I really have been okay with our first time happening in his parents' poolhouse? On a kitchen counter? In a *speaker*? In the old days, I wouldn't have thought twice about it.

But Jack treated sex as something more valuable than just a stolen moment wherever we could find one. He taught me to value *myself.*

And now, here we are down at the beach, which is an *idyllic* setting. With no one else around except the two of us. For two whole days. And not only am I okay with it, I'm ecstatic about it.

"Hey, Jack?" I ask.

"Hmmm?" His eyes are heavy and half-lidded, and I hope he's not falling asleep.

"You want your sweatshirt back? You're ice cold."

"Nah. I'm fine. Unless you want to warm me up yourself."

I smile at his quirked lips and bend down to press a light kiss on the tip of his nose.

He closes his eyes and folds his hands across his chest. I see goose bumps forming along his arm and lightly dust my hand down his bicep, loving the feel of his skin under my fingertips.

God, even his chicken skin is beautiful.

"You're so quiet. Are you writing a new song?"

His eyes are still closed as he answers, "I don't feel the need to explain my art to you, Warren."

I giggle as he mumbles through a yawn.

"Jackson Tanner, are you falling asleep on me? Out here on this sticky beach?"

He twists his body around to lie on his stomach, rests his head against my thigh, and wraps his arms around my waist like I'm a pillow. "Yes." He peeks up at me with raised eyebrows and a devilish grin. "Wanna join me?"

CHAPTER 29

Sunday, July 2, 1995
The Crack

The Beach
Manasquan

I wake up shivering, even though the sun has started to rise. Jack is curled up next to me on the towel, bundled in his sweatshirt and wrapped in the entire blanket. Somehow, I must have relinquished all three to him during the night. I'm in the bare sand, barely covered with the remaining towel, thoroughly coated like a shake and bake pork chop.

Good morning!

The scene is more humorous than anger-inducing, however. And with the first sight of a majestic, hazy-pink glow of dawn before me, it's hard to generate any true ire. I shake out my hair and brush the sand from my clothes and body, reclaim some real estate on Jack's oversized towel, and nudge him awake so he can catch the show.

"Hey, Sleepyhead. Hey." I smooth his hair from his face and kiss his temple. "Jack. Wake up."

He groans. "Mmph."

Didn't he say he was a morning person?

"Jack, come on. The sun is rising. You gotta see this."

He rolls over and throws an arm around my waist. His response is garbled into my leg. "Sleep."

I chafe at my arms, trying to warm them while brushing off more sand, and blow some hot air into my hands. "God, Jack, aren't you cold?"

He rolls onto his back and performs a yawning stretch. He sits up and rubs a hand across his eyes as my plight suddenly becomes clear to him. "Oh, man. Did I hog the covers all night?"

He chuckles, but looks apologetic as he strips off his sweatshirt and hands it to me. I promptly throw it on and curl my arms around my knees, absorbing the traces of warmth and scent from his body.

Jack pulls the blanket across both our laps before leaning over and kissing me softly on my neck. Thank God he didn't plant one on my mouth, because I probably have some serious morning breath going on.

He smoothes a hand over my knee and says, "Good morning."

Much better.

We sit and watch the sun rise without speaking, as if the magic of the brilliant moment will be broken by our clumsy appraisal. I've seen the sun rise before, but never like this. Never with Jack.

The rising sun adds to the warm glow I'm starting to feel, thinking about the amazing man sitting next to me.

God, has it really only been six weeks?

Only a little over a month ago, I was in a miserable relationship, dissatisfied with my job, and disillusioned about my future. It was still a good life; don't get me wrong. But until I met Jack, I didn't realize that it was an *incomplete* life. Not in the corny, you-complete-me-Jerry-Maguire kind of way, but in a way that took all the best I already had and made it better.

I take a huge breath which fills my lungs with a salty, clean glee, and exhale. I'm happy.

No. Much more than that.

I'm at peace.

Probably more so than I've been in my entire life.

The sun is a huge, orange ball low in the sky, having fully ascended from the ocean. Jack stands and shakes the sand from his body before offering me his outstretched hand. I take it and he hauls me to my feet.

He flicks some foreign beach thing from my hair. "Ready for a shower?" he teases.

His tone is not lost on me. "Am I ever."

We shake out the towels and blanket before rolling everything into a ball and sauntering up the beach. A fisherman coming down the walkway gives us a sly smile, but I barely register his intent.

Here's a bit of wisdom from an old pro: It's a lot easier to do the Walk of Shame when you've had your clothes on all night.

* * *

Back at the house, I lose any hope about the possibility of sharing a shower this morning. I am regrettably reminded that the stall is roughly the size of a refrigerator and only capable of spewing a single, weak stream of water from its rusty head.

Despite the meticulous, first-of-the-season scrubdown (which thankfully was *not* my job this year), the shower walls are still permanently pretty gross, and I barely feel cleaner than before I went in.

Jack takes over the bathroom while I get to work throwing a quick breakfast together.

I am no chef by far, but Jack doesn't seem to mind. He just loves the idea that I'm cooking at all, saying it makes him feel like Fred Flintstone to have his woman lay out a meal for him. For all his caveman sensibilities, his enjoyment gives me the confidence to get creative every now and then. I hope it gives me some skill, too, because I have a fantastic endeavor planned for dinner tonight.

And one for dessert, too.

Jack finally emerges from the bathroom and peeks over my shoulder to inspect the last batch of banana pancakes I'm frying at the tiny stove. He's fully dressed in his jeans and white T-shirt for the photo shoot and smells of Ivory soap and shaving cream. He plants a quick kiss on my cheek along with a smack on my unsuspecting ass, which makes me almost drop the pan on my route to the table.

"Hey! Watch it, pal. You almost made me lose your breakfast."

He laughs. "Wow. Have we been together so long that you can do that for me? Remind me to get plastered tonight!"

"Ha ha."

I add the pancakes to the stack in the middle of the table. "Eat up. I can't have you fainting in the middle of your photo session, Miss Macpherson."

Jack stabs at the pile, coming up with five pancakes. He slaps them on his plate and slathers them with butter and syrup. Jeez, that boy can eat. Where the hell does he put it?

Jack stops his chewing when he catches me with my chin in my hand, staring at him. Through a mouthful of food, he mumbles, "What?"

Damn, he's cute.

"I have something to show you."

I pull a large folder off the counter and slide it across the table.

Jack gives me a curious look, wipes his hands and mouth on his napkin, and opens it. Inside is my oversized graph paper notebook which has been flipped a few pages in, revealing the completed sketches of that pink house in Mantoloking I'd told him about.

"You finished it? No way."

He takes the time to really look my drawing over, running his fingers across the paper as if his hand were a miniature person walking through the rooms.

"Liv... This is really something. Look at the kitchen! Is this what you've been working on?"

I nod my head, more than a little proud. "Mmm hmm. I finally finished it and wanted you to see it."

"Wow. This is..." He shakes his head. "...this is incredible. Really, Livia, when you said you liked to draw houses, I didn't know what to think, but I wasn't expecting this. I had no idea. This must have taken forever."

"Well, I had a lot of time on my hands this past week."

Jack still doesn't take his eyes off the paper. "I love this room on the side with all the faux windows. My music room?"

"Try photo studio."

"Ah. Of course. Is that the master bathroom? It's huge!"

185

"Jacuzzi tub."

"Naturally." He winks. "Have you given any thought about how you're going to pay for this?"

No.

"Hit the lottery, maybe?"

Jack laughs at that. "Well, it's a beautiful house. When we hit that lottery, building it will be the first thing on the agenda."

We.

"Sounds good. It's a deal."

"Deal," he agrees, and then shakes my hand to seal the matter.

Right then, there's a knock at the door, so I jump up to greet the Tanners.

CHAPTER 30

Date #9: Sunday, July 2, 1995
1:30ish PM

The Jetty
Point Pleasant

"No throwing sand, Sean!"

Stephen has just tossed a glob of seaweed in the general direction of his family and I'm trying to stop Sean from retaliating so I can get some decent pictures taken. I want them to be themselves, but I'm hoping they'll avoid getting injured.

I've been on the beach with the Tanners for over an hour and only about twenty minutes of that time was even mildly productive. I thought the jetty at Point Pleasant would be a beautiful backdrop. Instead, it almost turned into an ugly trip to the hospital. I was barely able to sneak in a few group shots before Jack's brothers started threatening to throw each other into the ocean. Mrs. Tanner didn't seem overly worried, but suggested we move back down to the sand.

I decided to take her cue and just try to relax. This isn't my first experience with their antics, but Mrs. Tanner has been dealing with the four of them for over thirty years. I guess she'll know when it's time to truly panic.

The boys are goofing around at the water's edge, and despite how chaotic it seems, I'm actually getting some great pictures. Now that they're are off the dangerous rocks and I can lay off the disciplinarian role, I'm actually encouraging them to play it up. This is essentially what I was hoping they'd be like when I chose the beach for the shoot, I remind myself.

"How the heck did you do it, Mrs. T?" Jack's mother asked me to call her Eleanor but I still don't feel comfortable about it.

Mrs. Tanner looks over at her four rambunctious boys. "I haven't the slightest idea. Livia, do yourself a favor and just have daughters."

Mr. Tanner and I laugh.

It's a beautiful day at the beach. I'm grateful there's such a cool breeze down by the water, because I don't think the Tanners would be so receptive about getting their pictures taken in the sweltering, July heat.

I brought four super-soaker water guns down for the boys to use as props, and I didn't have to ask them twice to start using them. I had them roll up the cuffs of their jeans to mid-calf so I could get them at the edge of the water with the ocean in the background.

As the boys battle it out, knee-high in the waves, I snap a shot of Mr. and Mrs. Tanner arm in arm laughing at them.

At that point, Jack runs up the beach toward me, throws me over his shoulder like a sack of flour, and charges for the ocean. I squeal for him to put me down, shouting that I'll kill him if he ruins my camera. He dips me into his arms and proceeds to rock me over the waves.

"One..."

"You wouldn't dare."

"Two..."

"Jack! So help me—"

"THREE!"

Harmlessly, he lowers my feet into the wet sand before my scream is even complete. I turn and snap a quick shot of his brothers pointing and laughing. Jack still hasn't released his arms from around my waist and I kind of dig that he's doing the PDA thing in front of his family. Although, before we get too shmoopy, I give him a quick peck on his smiling mouth and send him back over by his brothers. They are relentless ballbusters, and my mind won't be able to conjure up pithy rejoinders while trying to concentrate on the job I still have ahead of me.

I take three whole rolls of film before we decide to call it a day. Without even seeing the finished product yet, I know the shoot has been a success. I can't wait to develop the pictures but that will have to wait until I'm back at work next week.

Jack's father mentions that he and Eleanor want to check out a piece of property in Belmar and suggests that we all go out to *The Boathouse* for a late lunch. As much as I don't want to refuse his family, tonight is Jack's and my last night alone before the girls come down. I feel slightly guilty but extraordinarily relieved when Jack explains, "Sorry, Dad. We'd love to, but Liv's planning a special dinner already. Can we take a rain check?"

"Yeah, sure," Mr. Tanner says. "We'll get together next week at home when you both get back, okay?"

Harrison decides to take his parents up on their offer while Stephen and Sean choose to hit *Jenkinson's* before heading home.

Lord help the unsuspecting females at Jenkinson's tonight.

Minus Stephen and Sean, we all head back up to the Manasquan house. After Jack's family does a quick cleanup and costume change, we say our goodbyes.

Finally alone, I close the front door and slump onto the sofa against Jack's side. "I'm exhausted! How about you?"

"Yep. But I'm more hungry than tired." Of course he is. The man is an eating *machine*. "Get on it, Wilma."

"Crud. I did promise you a big dinner tonight, huh?" I twist into his arm and nestle my lips against his neck.

A low chuckle finds its way out of Jack's throat. "Yep. And don't think you can get out of it now by distracting me. Kitchen, woman!"

I don't take my mouth from his skin and slide a hand around his waist instead. "Just let me sit here like this for five minutes and then I'll have the energy to move."

"Livia, if you intend to sit here *like this* for even five more *seconds*, I'll find the energy to keep you on this couch."

Normally, that would be fine by me, but Jack knows damn well that after waiting so long, I want our first time together to be perfect. That doesn't include the two of us nailing each other on the stupid couch.

As I take over the kitchen, Jack takes over the television. The Yanks are on. Terrific.

I throw together a cold roasted pepper salad with fresh mozzarella and artichoke hearts, figuring that will hold us over until dinner. I open a bottle of wine and pour two glasses, delivering one to Jack along with his salad.

"What do we have here? Mmm. I think I like being waited on." Jack gives me a grateful smile before diving into his plate. "Damn. I'm so hungry I could eat a sandwich from a gas station, but this looks much better."

"I'm so hungry, I could eat at Arby's," I shoot back.

"I'm so hungry, I could eat the ass out of a monkey."

"Eww."

"Roll over, ya monkey," he adds, cracking himself up.

I chuckle as I trim the chicken and prep some veggies, and once I have that going in the pot, I decide to take a shower.

I'm a little on edge at the moment and I make myself shake it off in order to enjoy what I hope will be a very romantic and special evening.

Because I know I'm going to sleep with Jack tonight.

I knew it was a foregone conclusion from our very first kiss, only I guess I never considered that it would take this long. There's something pretty special about the fact that we've waited, though.

I can't believe I'm about to admit this, but I'm actually happy we did.

* * *

I step out of the bathroom and check in with the dinner progression. Looking good.

Phil Rizzuto's excited voice informs me that Bernie Williams has just hit a two-run RBI, and when there's no outburst from the living room, I realize Jack has fallen asleep. Good. I'll be able to

190

take my time getting myself ready and tweak our dinner until it's perfect. I turn down the sound on the TV and get to work.

In between numerous trips from the kitchen to the bathroom to the bedroom, I manage to finish cooking, get my hair done, and squeeze myself into a strapless, black sundress.

By the time I put some makeup on my face and some music on the stereo, Jack is awake. I'm expecting him to make a comment about how nice I look or about the beautiful, candlelit table. But instead, his eyes don't stray from the muted TV as he asks, "What was the final score of the game?"

Is he kidding?

"Seven six. Brewers."

He exaggerates a yawn and strolls into the kitchen. "Damn. I fell as—Hey! What's all this?"

I had my hands on my hips, but now they're busy fussing with the vase of flowers in the centerpiece and smoothing away some nonexistent wrinkles on the tablecloth. "I told you I was attempting *coq au vin* tonight. It wasn't necessarily all that difficult. Kind of a fancypants name for chicken soup."

Jack takes the lid off the pot and peeks in. "Well, it smells delicious."

"Thanks."

He steps behind me and wraps his arms around my waist, swaying a bit to the music. "So do you."

"Thanks." I cross my arms over his and add, "I wish I could say the same for you, Aquaman."

"I guess I should probably take a shower, huh?"

"That would be nice."

He stops moving, as if a thought has suddenly occurred to him. "Should I... Do you want me to get dressed up or something, too?"

He's on to me.

I peek over my shoulder and see the leading, unspoken question in his eyes. I wanted tonight to be special, but I didn't want it to be so *obvious*. I guess if I felt like conveying a sense of nonchalance, maybe I shouldn't have decorated the ramshackle kitchen table as if it were being readied for a cover shoot with

191

Better Homes and Gardens. I can't suppress an embarrassed smile, which is intended to look casual—but instead comes across as guilty—and manage, "If you want to."

He turns me in his arms to face him and catches me biting my lip. He gives me a quick scrutiny, decides he has it all figured out and says, "Yeah. I think I do." A devilish grin preempts a swift kiss. "Meet you back here in half an hour?"

"I'll be ready."

"I certainly hope so."

CHAPTER 31

Date #10: Sunday, July 2, 1995
8:54 PM

The Beach House
Manasquan

Jack is leaning back in his chair, one leg crossed over the other, taking a breather from eating. He looks positively lethal in his black pants and vee-neck knit shirt. It never ceases to amaze me how he can look so comfortably at ease, so thoroughly *male* no matter what the setting. Whether he's in ripped jeans onstage or a tailored pair of slacks at a formal dinner table, Jack exudes an enviable confidence wherever he is.

Enviable because I, on the other hand, am nervous as hell. I know I've slept with guys before, but I've never felt this way about any of them. This is a whole new scene for me, and the gamble I'm about to take is making me a nervous wreck.

I fortify myself with another sip of liquid courage and Jack casually refills my glass.

"I think the photo shoot went well today. I can't wait to see how the pictures turn out," I offer, by way of conversation.

Jack rolls the stem of his wineglass between the tips of his fingers and nods noncommittally, never taking his eyes off mine.

"I think your family had fun, don't you?"

He curls his lip, still refusing to look away, and offers another nod.

"How about this food, huh? Does your woman take care of you or what?"

An unreadable smirk decorates his face. "That she does."

"The coq au vin was pretty easy, but I've never made asparagus before. I think it came out okay."

Livia Chadwick: Queen of Dazzling Smalltalk.

193

I don't know why I'm having such difficulty talking to Jack. Well, I mean, yes, of course I know why. I obviously can't seem to concentrate on appropriate dinner conversation when my mind is only on what we'll be doing *after* dinner. Plus, it's kind of hard to hold a discussion with someone who's wearing a shit-eating grin and barely offering any responses to my witty repartee. Through most of our meal, we'd both been preoccupied with eating, but now I'm babbling like an idiot, making inane smalltalk with my dinner guest. Jack seems content to simply sit and observe this phenomenon, for which I could cheerfully strangle him.

I unconsciously yoink the top of my dress up a little higher and see that Jack is eyeing me curiously.

"Stop fidgeting. You look gorgeous."

Now we're getting somewhere. Five whole words. But not a conversation does that make. I swallow a bite of my food. "It's the candlelight."

"It's you."

Okay, enough of this.

"No, it's *you!* You're making me nervous sitting over there with that grin on your face. I can't tell what you're thinking."

"Can't you?"

"No, I can't."

"Well, you should." He takes a leisurely drink from his glass. "All I'm doing is patiently waiting for you to finish eating."

"Well, thank you. That's awfully chivalrous of you. But it's hard to chew when you're staring me down like that."

"You didn't let me finish." He folds his napkin and puts it on the table. "I'm patiently waiting for you to finish because when you're done, I intend to reward your efforts in the kitchen tonight by taking you into that bedroom back there and showing you my, ah... *appreciation.*"

I bite my lip, not only to contain my smile, but to stop myself from yelling *WHOOHOO!* "You seem pretty sure of yourself. How do you know I haven't changed my mind?"

"Shouldn't I be? Isn't that what you intended to happen here with all this? Isn't that your big plan?"

194

Busted.

I can't help but laugh. "That obvious, huh?"

"Yes. But I will give you some credit. At least you didn't serve raw oysters."

"Well, it *is* Date Ten. I know we haven't really talked about it since you first proposed this bet—"

"Arrangement."

"Whatever. In any case, I've been keeping track."

"Me too," he says through a smirk. "Technically, it's only Date Nine, you know. More like Date Eight-and-a-half."

"I counted the luau. And I split today into two dates, which, you know, I figured was only fair."

"That's stretching it."

"Getting cold feet?"

"Nope. Not at all." He aims a wicked grin up and down my body before adding, "I'm going to strip that little dress off you just as soon as you give me the green light."

I shake my head and chuckle. "Oh, *now* I get to say when? Jesus, Jack. If I knew you were going to let me off on a technicality, I would've split *all* our dates in half!"

The Ruffino has started to take effect, and a calm warmth is spreading down my legs and flushing my face. I touch the back of my hands to my cheeks.

"You're blushing."

I take another sip and motion to my glass. "It's the wine."

"I'll bet."

"You're impossible."

That has Jack chuckling. "Oh yeah? Well *you're* busted. Come here."

I cross my arms over my chest and lean back in my chair. "Would you like me to clear the table first or were you planning on ravaging me right here on top of the dirty dishes?"

Jack puts his elbows on his knees as he bends over, shoulders shaking. He composes himself slightly before answering, "I thought we could dance first."

"Oh."

We're still laughing as we both stand and I walk into his arms. I rest my hand in his as he slides his right arm around my waist.

This is nice.

I can't remember the last time I slow-danced with someone, and to tell you the truth, I don't want to try. I'm not concerned about anyone in the past. I'm not concerned about anyone outside that front door. We're here, in this dilapidated old kitchen with its dark wood paneling, faded yellow cabinets, and crusty linoleum floor. And right here is the most beautiful place on Earth and the only place I want to be. Because I'm dancing in the arms of the most incredible man I've ever met in my life.

I lay my head against his chest and his arm tightens around my back. Slowly, his hand starts to slide up and down my spine as he presses his lips against my hair and kisses me above my ear.

No, wait. He's not kissing me... he's *singing to me*.

I've listened to countless hours of music. I've analyzed every note; I've loved every word. But now here is a song being performed just for me. Sung by my very own rock god purring against my ear.

You know she thrills me with all her charms...
when I'm wrapped up in my baby's arms...

The sensation of his soft breath near me has combined with the ringing of my ears and has rendered me deaf. *Great. I'm deaf now.* Something deep in the rational recesses of my brain tells me that that should probably bother me. But it doesn't.

Jack gives out a sigh. "Not exactly the ballroom at the Waldorf, is it?"

Okay, I guess I can hear after all.

"No," I reply softly. "But it feels like it."

"You know, I've got to say, I don't think I've ever been the target of a *seduction* before. I think I like it." His boyish grin has me sputtering out a giggle against his chest as he spins us around in a full circle.

At the end of the song, Jack's arm stiffens around me. He's quiet—tensely so—and I sense that he's grappling with something. I step back slightly to look at his face. His mouth is set in a grim line, looking like he's in turmoil over whether to speak or remain silent.

"What? What's that face?" I ask.

He'd been looking off at some point beyond my head, but my question brings him back to Earth. He slides a hand behind my neck, holding my gaze locked to his as he asks, "Are you sure?"

"Sure about... you mean am I sure about... us? As in tonight?"

"I need to know before this goes any further."

I almost burst out laughing. Here I've been a nervous wreck all evening while he's been playing it cool as a cucumber. Now that I'm finally letting go and actually enjoying myself, *he's* the one on guard.

Jack sees me fighting a smile and instead of catching my amusement, he continues in an almost annoyed tone, "I just want to make sure that we're on the same page here tonight. I'm not normally in the habit of waiting, and I've waited for you. *Because* it's you. Because I was afraid of what would happen if you allowed me—if I allowed *myself*—to have you."

We are no longer moving, just standing in our dancers' pose as I look at him in disbelief. "And what would happen... exactly... do you think?"

Jack steps free from my grasp and grabs his pack of cigarettes off the microwave. He lights one at the stove and leans against the counter, arms crossed. He takes a long drag, and his words expel along with the breath of smoke. "Look. I wasn't looking for this, you know? I was in a relationship for a long time with someone who..." He trails off when he catches the glare I'm aiming at him.

I cannot believe he is actually alluding to his ex-girlfriend at a moment like this. The annoyed scowl on my face nearly approaches infuriation when he starts to laugh.

"Holy shit, that's not what I'm saying. What a dicky thing to bring up. I'm sorry."

"What *are* you saying, Jack?"

He takes another drag off his cig and holds it out to me. "Here. You look like you could use this."

197

I reluctantly pinch the cigarette from his fingers and take a pull as he continues, "I'm trying to say, Livia, that I'm crazy about you. I might be going about it completely the wrong way, however, and for that I apologize. But the fact of the matter is, if you haven't already figured it out..."

"I'm listening," I say, prodding him on.

He takes the cig back, pulls on it one last time, and throws the butt into the sink. He steps toward me and takes my hands in his, lifting one to raise my chin so that I'm looking into his gray eyes. "What I'm trying to say is that I wasn't looking for you." He brushes a kiss across my fingertips. "But I'm incredibly glad— and lucky—to have found you."

Okay. Not *exactly* a declaration of undying love and devotion, but pretty damn close. Besides, I'm too afraid to hear him say it out loud. The look on his face is already saying it loudly enough.

I brush my cheek against his hand in mine, then turn it to kiss his open palm.

Apparently, that small touch is enough to crack his reserve. His arms wrap around me quickly as his mouth takes mine in a possessive, demanding kiss.

The urgency in his embrace makes my knees go weak, and I brace my hands against his hard chest, breathing heavily against his warm lips. When they slide up to bind in his hair, his arms tighten around me and his mouth opens impatiently on mine.

It's not until this moment when I become acutely aware that he's been slowly walking me backwards toward the bedroom.

CHAPTER 32

Sunday, July 2, 1995
Who Cares???

My Bedroom at the Beach House
Manasquan

Jack grasps my wrists in his hands and raises them above my head, flattening me against the bedroom door with the length of his body. He presses against me as his tongue finds its way between my lips once more. I raise one leg to wrap around him which causes his hands to release their hold on my wrists and grab me under my backside, lifting me against the door, jacking his hips between my legs. My ankles are crossed against his back, but the sheer strength of his will is what's keeping me aloft.

That and his superhard dick.

It's straining against the fabric of his pants, grinding into my panties, and oh holy hell I can hardly breathe. I'm having speaker flashbacks. I think I'm going to die.

We are devouring one another; all's fair in love and war, and I guess that this is both. He bites my neck. I pull his hair. He lets out with a growl. I answer him with a moan.

I can't believe this is finally happening.

He raises his face to mine, his lazy grin sending lightning bolts through my entire nervous system. His half-lidded eyes focus on my mouth for the briefest pause before he moves in to kiss me again.

It's hot and exciting to be held captive in his authoritative grasp, but this kiss is almost... tender. Submissive. Reverent.

My legs slip down his sides, and I plant my feet on the floor once more. Sliding my hands around his neck, my thumbs lightly caress the hair at his nape. His arms wrap around my waist, swaying with me in a heartbreaking slow dance as he opens the door and backs me through it.

199

We'd gone from animalistic to sweet in a matter of seconds, and I can't decide which I like more. My heart is still hammering, but for an entirely different reason than it was just a moment ago.

For the first time ever, I'm nervous about going to bed with a guy. Suddenly, sex is going to *mean* something, and I guess I'm pretty freaked out about it.

But excited. I'm really excited, too.

When I feel the back of my knees hit the bed, Jack breaks free and gives me a playful shove, sending me sprawling onto my back on top of the covers. I laugh as I prop myself up on my elbows, watching as he grabs the back of his shirt in his fist and pulls it over his head.

I'm not laughing anymore.

The sight of him without a shirt on is enough to force my silence as I gape at him in awe. It surprises me every time. EVer-y time. I mean, the man has a body a *statue* would envy. That chest. Those abs. Lord help me, he looks like a mythical god, and the view knocks the wind right out of me. I feel like I've just been hit.

In the vagina.

With a sledgehammer.

Swung by The Mighty Thor himself.

He crawls slowly over me, kissing my collarbone, neck, and chin on his way to my lips. The kiss is gentle, his soft lips brushing against mine slowly at first, but gaining momentum, building authority as he lowers the weight of his body on top of mine, sinking me into the pillows. He positions his legs between my knees, and I pull him closer, arching my back and pushing into his hardened length, fitting myself against him. I flatten my hands over his bare back and shoulders, loving the feel of his smooth skin over his contracting muscles.

His lips are at my throat, running heated kisses along the side of my neck.

"God, you taste *so sweet.*"

I grab the back of his hair in my fists, drawing his face to mine in answer.

His mouth slants fiercely across my own, deepening the kiss and overwhelming my senses. The taste of wine on his lips. His smoky scent. His low moan as he opens his mouth against mine and grinds himself against me harder.

That puts me in such a state that I barely notice Jack sliding the top of my dress down. His rough hands run over my breasts before he replaces them with his soft mouth, teasing, tormenting me with the wet warmth of his tongue. The result is nothing short of spectacular, his expert mouth and the insistent pressure from his hips sending shockwaves through my body.

Jack's arms wrap fully around me, holding me to him, imprisoning my mouth to his as he rolls us to our side. Our bare skin touching, I can feel the pounding of our hearts—wild, furious, losing control.

There is only a moment of hesitation before I slide my palm over the front of his slacks and up to his waist. My hands are shaking as I fumble with the button but have an easier time with the zipper. Jack stares down at me, his gray eyes dark, a wicked smile at his mouth. Pressing a kiss to his full lips, I strip him, using my foot to kick the pants completely off his legs. I start stroking a hand over the length of him, barely contained within his cotton boxers.

Great. An endless stretch of abstinence, and Conan the Barbarian here is going to be the guy to break my streak.

The touch tears a breath from Jack's throat and then a staggered laugh. "Nuh-uh. Me first."

He kisses me onto my back and before I know it, my dress and panties are lying in a heap on the floor. Jack rolls off the bed and I'm momentarily left to try and act blasé about the fact that I'm presently sprawled out naked on the sheets, so I attempt to strike a suitable centerfold pose.

He digs briefly through the pocket of his discarded pants before his thumbs go to his waistband, and some long-lost sense of decorum has me turning my head away. Like I have any right to play shy now, lying naked on the bed like Miss January.

"You have a condom?" I ask, incredulously. "What was all your talk about this being Date Eight-and-a-half?"

201

He shoots me a smirk and replies, "Lips, I almost caved on Date *Two*. I wasn't going to take any chances after that."

He slides back up the mattress again, surprising me when he gives a leisurely swipe of his tongue between my legs. It almost has me launching off the bed. He settles himself in and groans against me, teasing and tasting and licking and *oh God*.

His voice vibrates along my skin. "*Christ*. I can't hold out long enough to do this right. I'm dying for you, Liv."

"Oh God. Me too. Come here."

I can feel him *shaking* as he moves his mouth over to my hip, feathers his lips along my stomach, my breasts, my neck, working his knees inside mine again, pressing that steel rod right between my thighs. It strains against me as his mouth closes over mine; my hands tangle in his hair as his arms wind around my back. He holds me close, kissing me sweetly, then firmly, slipping his tongue between my lips lightly, then deeply. The effect is drugging my senses and making my heart hammer uncontrollably.

I become aware that he's taking his time, drawing out our last tormented moments before the main event, and the anticipation is almost unbearable. His hardened body is poised against me, holding out, waiting. I'm almost insane with wanting him and the anguished look on his strained features tells me he's having a hard time trying to maintain control, prolonging this sweet agony for my sake.

But I'm ready for him now. I want him *now*.

Without breaking our kiss, I slip my hand down his back, grabbing his ass to pull him closer.

Jack takes the hint and starts a leisurely slide inside me, taking his sweet old time. It's almost torture to move at this speed, every inch of him pushing inside in slow motion, my body stretching to take him in. I can feel *everything*.

For him.

Oh God. I do. I feel everything for this man.

Jesus. There's a lump in my throat.

Jack smooths a hand over my hair as his low, rough voice scratches out, "Do you have any idea what I've been whispering over your lips this entire time?"

I open my eyes and look at his hard features staring down at me. My heart is already beating furiously but I am sent into oblivion with the sound of his voice. I can't even begin to answer.

Jack shakes his head in defeat and confesses, "*I love you. I love you. I love y—*"

I cut off his words with my mouth against his, and he drives into me full-length, making us both shudder with the force of his movement.

There is no apprehension, there is no uncertainty, there is no going back. I am gone.

He puts a hand at the small of my back, lifting me to him, driving further into me with slow, deep, tender movements and it's more than I can stand. I clasp his shoulders tightly, digging my nails lightly into his skin, feeling the power of his insistent rocking. I wrap my legs around his waist, needing to feel him deeper, as close as we can get.

It's... beautiful. There's no other way to describe it. I've never felt anything so incredible in my entire life.

We've waited so long for this, though. We waited forever, and because of that, beautiful is not nearly enough. We have way too much pent-up agony to take things slowly right now. Bravo to him for even trying.

"Jack, this is amazing and all... it's so sweet... but God. I've been dying for this. Right now, I really need you to *fuck* me."

There's a quick shiver along his body, and his head drops as he scratches out, *"Christ."*

It's as if I've just granted him a reprieve. I know he needs this, too. We can do beautiful later.

Without further deliberation, his arm sweeps under my knee as he rests my leg in the crook of his elbow... and drives full-force into me. Deep.

Holy shit. I've unleashed the kraken.

He pulls out almost fully, then does it again. And again.

His thumbs dig into my hips as his fingers clamp onto my ass cheeks, securing my body to his as he slams me repeatedly, hard and fast and deep and holy hell I'm about to lose my damned mind.

Before I know it, my leg is perched over his shoulder, bent backwards at an obscene angle as his upper body hovers over mine, his hands in fists against the mattress on either side of me. "Kiss me, Lips."

His movement becomes rhythmic, purposeful, building speed, and I feel a stirring deep within me, taking shape. But I don't recognize the form until the small electric charges at my center start to progress into a pounding cadence, racing from my belly to my toes and back again. I'm almost afraid of the force building inside of me; I've never felt anything like this before. I slam my eyes shut and hold on for the ride as I hear myself cry out, every nerve within me threatening to detonate.

"*Kiss me*, Lips," Jack says again, so I comply. I grab hold of his hair and plant my lips on his, our mouths a heated tangle of tongues and groans and panting breaths. I've never had an out-of-body experience before, but this may be as close as I can ever hope to get.

Wait. Nope. Hold on...

"Ohh. Ohhh!" I moan, as Jack's hand slips around to my front, sliding his thumb against me *right there oh my God yes*, his satisfied smirk daring me to come first.

No problem.

I thrash against the pillow and my leg drops from his shoulder, my torso arching toward the ceiling as the most incredible earthquakes rattle my insides. I'm clenching around him tighter than any kegels could accomplish on their own, and that, combined with the sound of my howling is enough to take Jack over the edge, too. I am still racking with tremors as his thrusting becomes more powerful, his pace picks up, and it sounds like the groans are being ripped from his chest as he covers his mouth over mine and plunges inside of me, pulling me tightly to him, pounding away at my body, shaking, panting, growling, harder, harder, harder...

"You like this? You like it deep?" Jack hisses in between thrusts.

Well, his cock is ginormous and I'm pretty sure I can feel it smashing against my sternum. So, hell yeah, I like it. "Yes! I love your big huge cock. Do me with it!"

Okay, my dirty-talking skills could obviously use some work. But it's not my fault. I'm out of practice and I think Jack has fucked my brain cells into oblivion anyway. Not that I really care at this point.

"You like when I fuck you hard?"

"Yes..."

"You love my cock inside you."

"Yes..."

"You want to watch me come?"

Holy shit! He's so *bad*. He is such a dirty, dirty man between the sheets. I love everything about that. I feel the current charging through my veins, every inch of my skin buzzing. My hand is planted firmly on that sweet ass of his, pulling him toward me on every stroke, deeper, deeper, deeper...

Oh my God. I'm almost ready to come. Again.

Jack knows it, too. His breathing is animal in my ear— groaning, panting, cursing, "You're so wet... tight..."

He clenches his teeth, trying to hold himself together, a white-knuckle grip on the headboard, slamming into me, breathing heavily, faster, faster, faster...

"Oh God I have to... *Oh fuck, Liv... I can't...*"

He lashes out with one final, tortured roar as his body explodes in mine, quaking again and again and again.

Jack collapses on top of me, sweaty and spent, but makes no effort to separate us. We lay unspeaking, out of breath, lightly caressing one another in contented fatigue.

He finds the strength to lift his upper body from mine and look at me, the expression on his face euphoric with just the slightest dab of astonishment. "Wow."

My thoughts exactly.

I brush a strand of hair from his damp forehead. "Yeah. Wow."

He raises his eyebrows. "Well, that was certainly worth waiting for."

"You have no idea."

He slowly rolls to his side, his arms still wrapped around me, the both of us laughing.

I snuggle in closer, running my fingertips along his smooth chest. It may sound ridiculous, but I could almost cry right now. I don't know what I was expecting, but that was just... so much more than I bargained for. Hot and sweet and serious and fun all at once. I never knew sex could be like this.

I rest my head against his chest and listen to his still-rapid heart and swift breathing. After a few minutes, they both even out and relax. I start to sink alongside him, barely aware that I'm falling asleep.

Jack adjusts his body more comfortably next to mine which knocks me out of my almost-slumber and leaves me feeling a little more exposed than I'm used to. In more ways than one.

The covers had come undone during our debauchery, and I try to look laid-back as I grab a sheet from the disarray at the foot of the bed, pulling it over us both.

Jack finds this amusing.

"Really? After what we've just done? Livia, I would never have expected you to be shy at a moment like this."

"Sorry. I can't help it."

That brings a wicked gleam to Jack's eyes. He assumes a sinful grin as he slowly slips a hand under the sheet. "Neither can I."

CHAPTER 33

Monday, July 3, 1995
8:06 AM

My Bed
Heaven

I've been tired before.

One time, I visited Sammy at Rutgers during her rush weekend. That was a pretty grueling and nearly sleepless couple of days spent on the floor of her dorm room. Another time a few years back, I had to work a twelve hour day after being out all night, showing up to my job that morning straight from the party in the clothes I was wearing the night before. Last year, I babysat for Monty's crazy nieces, who sucked the very life out of me, requiring a four hour nap upon their departure.

But this morning, I am simply *exhausted*. After a horrible night's sleep on the beach, then a busy day with the Tanners, followed by a full night of unrelenting sex with Jack, I feel like I'm part of some sinister sleep deprivation experiment.

I only dozed in tiny spurts all night, Jack interrupting my much-needed sleep with more important needs of his own.

The boy is positively insatiable. I now know why he eats so much. He needs a lot of fuel because apparently, he does *everything* to the extreme. The man is indeed a machine. But an adorable one at that.

I have no idea how long he's been awake, but his shower roused me even from my dead slumber. This prewar house with its paper-thin walls has plumbing that may as well date back to the Stone Age. On a quiet morning, the sound of the water groaning through the pipes is *loud*.

As tired as I am, I make myself stay awake to watch Jack get dressed. There's a certain intimacy watching a man go through his morning routine. *Almost* more intimate than how we've spent the past ten hours. Besides, I'm planning on passing out hard once he leaves. I can keep my eyes open until then.

I watch as Jack tucks in his button-down shirt against his slim waist and zips his pants. When he ducks down to fix his hair in the wall mirror, he catches my eye in the reflection and gives me a wink.

"How long have you been up?" I ask.

He checks the clock. "I don't know... an hour, maybe? Why?"

I give him a little smirk. "Wow. A whole hour. And you haven't jumped my bones yet."

His hand stills, frozen in the middle of a finger-comb through his hair. He meets my gaze in the mirror and raises his eyebrows. "I can fix that, you know."

He hesitates for a moment, almost as if there are words caught at the tip of his tongue. He shakes it off, though, and slides back into bed, wrapping his arms around my waist, lightly resting his lips against my ear. Suddenly, I'm not so tired anymore. Spooning rocks.

"Hey, Lips?"

"Hmmm?"

"I've really got to go."

"Tease."

That wrenches a chuckle out of him, but he makes no move to leave. Instead, he snuggles against my side, slowly kissing the pulse points along my neck. He didn't shave this morning and his stubble feels rough against my skin. I guess he's cultivating a grunge look for the gig tonight.

I can't believe how sad I am that he has to go back up north. I know I'm being ridiculous because he's only going to be gone for one stupid day. But a sense of foreboding is already weighing down on me and he hasn't even left the house yet. He hasn't even left the *bed* yet, and judging by the direction his hands are taking under my PJs, he might never get out of here.

Just as I'm untucking his shirt, I catch the hesitant look on his face again and ask, "What?"

His teeth clench, but before he can answer, his pager starts beeping. He gives me an apologetic shrug as he checks it, then picks up the nightstand phone to make the call.

Anyone that knows Jack is aware that he works nights and therefore, might be sleeping late. Anyone that knows him *well* is aware that he's on vacation this week and might be sleeping *with me* right now. What psycho would call him at eight o'clock in the morning?

"Yo, Ronnie. What's up, kid?"

Well, there you go.

"No, it's okay. I was already awake. Yeah, Liv's right here. Why? What's going on?" Jack sits up at the edge of the bed and listens for a few seconds. Then his hand goes to his forehead as his jaw drops to the floor. "You did *what?!*"

Crap. Now Jack is going to have to swing by the jail, probably making him late for his meeting with Lutz's guy. What the hell did Ronnie get himself into now?

I grab Jack's wallet off the dresser and pull out a credit card before asking, "How much is bail?"

Jack's expression turns amused as he relays my question to Ron, "Livia wants to know how much your bail is."

My face becomes a mask of confusion as he starts to laugh. While holding the phone to his ear, he puts his free hand over mine and gives a squeeze, letting me know the situation isn't dire. "I know, I know, but you can't blame her... Okay, yes, I'll tell her."

"What's going on?" I ask impatiently.

Jack swings the mouthpiece away from his face. "Well, baby, I guess I'm glad you're already sitting down. Get this one: Ron just proposed to Tess."

"*WHAAAT?!*"

Jack speaks back into the phone, "What's that? ...Oh yeah, totally freaking out... Yes, definitely, put her on. I want to—Hey, Tess! Congratulations... Yes, absolutely shocked... You, too? Ha! Yeah, hold on, she's right here."

My mouth is still agape as Jack hands the phone to me. "Tess wants to talk to you."

I look at him wide-eyed as I take the phone from his hand. "Um, *hello?*"

"Oh my God, Livia! You thought Ronnie was in jail? That's so funny."

"Tess?" My head is spinning and I actually feel woozy enough to faint. "Forgive me for asking this, but just what the hell is going on?"

I hear her giggle on the other end of the line. "Ronnie *proposed!* Can you believe it?"

No. No, I can't.

"How- How did this happen?"

Jack sidles up behind me and I lean into him for balance so I won't reel over as Tess says, "He just did it last night. Got down on one knee and everything. I mean, we'd talked about it, but— oh, I don't know. Wait until you see my ring! I'll tell you all the details when I get down there later."

I have to admit, she sounds happy. Giddy, actually. My brain is still processing the news, but I manage to match her elated tone. "Yes, you certainly will. And oh God, Tess, congratulations! I'm sorry, this just took me by surprise, obviously. I can't wait to see you and hear all about it. Tell Ron congrats, too, okay?"

"I will. And Liv?"

"Yes?"

"I'm really happy. I want you to know that."

"I know. I can hear it in your voice. See you later, right?"

"Yep. Hey, don't call your sister yet. I want to drop the bomb on everyone myself once we're all there together. Then we can go out and celebrate. The girls and I will be down around one-thirtyish."

"Tess! You can't seriously expect me to keep this to myself for the next—" I check the clock and do some quick math, "five hours!"

She laughs. "Just don't make any calls and don't answer the phone. That oughtta help you keep your mouth shut."

"Just get down here as soon as you can, alright? This is huge."

"I know. Okay. See you later."

"Yeah, okay. See ya."

210

I hang up and expel a deep breath before turning to Jack. "Oh my God. *Oh my God!* Tess and Ron are getting *married*. Married, like, you know, *married*."

"Sure seems that way."

"Did you have any—"

"Nooo. Uh-uh. No way. Well, I knew Ron hasn't been seeing anyone else in a while, but no one could have seen this coming."

"What do you mean, 'hasn't been seeing anyone else in a while'? He just hooked up with some bimbo a few weeks ago! The night we met, remember?"

"Yeah, but no one since then."

"That was only six weeks ago! How does he go from Mr. Swinging Johnson all around town to *proposing* to my best friend in just six weeks?"

"I don't know, babe. Who's to say? Look at where *we* are after only six weeks."

I try to determine if there's a hidden meaning in his last comment. Not enough to go on. "And where exactly are we, Jack?"

He puts an arm over my shoulders and nestles us both back against the pillows. He takes his free hand and laces it with mine on my lap. "C'mon, Liv, you know what I'm talking about. Who could have seen *this* coming six weeks ago?"

No one. Least of all me.

He's right. Who am I to judge? In only six weeks, we've managed to become indispensable to one another's lives. Who knows what those two are feeling after *years* of being together, however erratically.

"I hope Tess knows what she's doing."

"Look, Ronnie's a good guy and they've been seeing each other on and off for like, what, three years now? Has Tess been with anyone else in that time?"

I try to remember if she has, but I can't come up with a single name. My friend could talk a good game, but I guess 'talk' is as far as it's gone for a while now.

Huh. Go figure.

"No, I don't think she has. For at least the past few months, anyhow. Do you really think they've been more to each other than just the occasional hookup all this time? She's my best friend. You'd think I would have been kept informed of something like that."

"Well, maybe some things are just too personal to talk about. I mean, are you really going to blab to all your girlfriends about the intimate details of *our* entire night last night?"

Yes. "No, of course not."

"And it's not like you went out of your way to alert them ahead of time about what you were planning to do once you got me down here all alone in this secluded old beach house, right?"

Wrong. "Right."

"And you certainly don't think you're actually getting away with bullshitting me right now, do you?"

Whoops. I bite my lip and scrunch my nose. "Hopefully?"

He shakes his head in the negative. "Nope. Now you owe me for lying." He checks the clock again and practically leaps off the bed. "Unfortunately, I'm going to have to collect on your debt later. I gotta go or I'm gonna be late."

"Well, good luck today and break a leg tonight."

"Ah, spoken like a true *fan*." He leans in and plants a lingering, full kiss on my lips. When I start to slide my hands up his arms, he breaks free, laughing. "Oh, no you don't. Baby, I really gotta *go*."

I pretend to be miffed. "Fine."

"I'll see you in twenty-four hours. And oooh, pick up those sausages I like from that place on Thirty-Five for the barbeque tomorrow, okay?"

"As you wish, my lord."

He gives me a quick kiss. "And also, if you can remember, get over to Grieco's and pick up a bottle of champagne for Ron and Tess. And what? Maybe a beer ball or something?"

"Aye, aye, Captain."

"I guess it doesn't have to be Grieco's, but I like their beef jerky. The kind on the counter, not the display."

"Anything else, dear?"

He finally picks up on my sarcastic tone. "Yes, *dear*, there is one last thing."

"Yes, Pooh-bear?"

He points to the empty spot next to me on the mattress. "Be in that bed waiting for me by the time I get back."

"You got it."

He puts a hand behind my neck as he leans down to press a goodbye kiss to my mouth. I watch his retreating form in admiration as he grabs his bag and sprints for the door.

And then I crash.

CHAPTER 34

Monday, July 3, 1995
1:34 PM

The Beach House
Manasquan

I wake up from my nap and throw my sheets in the washer just as the girls come barging through the door. Tess waits for all of two seconds before she takes the diamond ring from her purse, making a big show of sliding it onto her finger.

Everyone's mouths drop.

Sam asks, "Where'd you get that?"

Tess looks over the four of us before answering proudly, "Ronnie."

In the dead silence that ensues, I can actually see the steam escaping from Vix's and Sam's ears as their brains try to wrap around what Tess is telling them.

No steam from Isla. "Why'd he give you a ring? Your birthday's not until—"

"She's *engaged*, Sherlock," I cut in. "Ronnie gave her a ring when he *proposed*. Get it?"

Finally, she does get it. She asks incredulously, "You got engaged? *To Ronnie?*"

Isla has no filter.

I start to feel bad for Tess, standing there looking at us, waiting on a reaction that hasn't come. She sounds a little sheepish when she answers, "Yes."

I finally break the awkward silence. "Girls! Our friend just told us she's getting married." I scan the three dumbfounded faces. "*Tess* is getting *married!*"

They all crack at the same second, going in for hugs amid shouts of "Oh my God!" and "Congratulations!"

Sam actually has tears in her eyes which makes Tess's dam break as well.

Vix flops down onto the couch. Out of the corner of my eye, I can see her trying to get my attention and don't dare look at her for more than a split second. I can *feel* her silent question about Ron's hookup at the Tradewinds that night. Twin thing, I guess.

Tess catches the exchange and pulls her hand out of Sam's appraising grasp to put it on her hip. "Okay, you two. Let's just get this over with. I know what you're thinking."

Oh no you don't. But before I can speak, Vix offers, "Tess... we're just blown away right now, that's all."

Tess gives the both of us an indignant scowl. "Bullshit. I saw that look. You're just 'blown away' by the fact that Ron popped the question only weeks after screwing that bimbo at the Tradewinds."

Okay. I guess it's *not* just a twin thing.

I blurt out, unthinking, "You know about that?"

Apparently, I have no filter either.

Sam and Isla look like they're having trouble keeping up. Vix looks like she's ready to kill me.

To my surprise, Tess starts laughing. "Yes, Livia, I know about that."

Vix starts in a huff, "So, what, is that the kind of 'open marriage' you guys are planning on? You deserve better than that, Tess. I can't believe—"

"He didn't sleep with her."

Vix and I roll our eyes as Isla cuts in. "Wait a minute. What the heck are you guys talking about?"

Tess is still laughing when she explains, "Isla, the girls here think that Ron nailed a Thunderjug groupie a few weeks ago. The night *they* went to The Tradewinds and *we* cleaned this house, remember?"

Vix says, "He *did* nail her. We saw him leave with her and he said as much the next day."

"Yes, Ronnie did leave with that girl," Tess reiterates. "But by the time he got outside the club, he couldn't go through with it."

I ask, "Is that what he told you?"

215

"Yes," she says. "And I believe him. I wish you would, too."

When we don't speak, she goes on. "Liv. Remember that night we caught Pearl Jam at the Meadowlands? The night you blew Rider MacLaine?" I wince at her words. I don't even feel like that same person anymore, but I guess I still have a past to own. "After I dropped you off, I went over to Ron's. That's when he and I said 'I love you' for the first time. The next night, you guys all met up at The Tradewinds. He told me afterward that even though he knew how he felt about me, he still just freaked out a little. He had gotten me this ring that very day and thought that he was *expected* to have one last fling before proposing."

Vix counters, "But the next morning, he said—"

"I know what he told you guys. He was trying to save face. Come on. You know how proud he is of his man-whore reputation. Well... *was*. Truth is, he put the girl in a cab and then spent the night on the beach alone with a six-pack."

"Tess, you can't really believe—"

"Why can't I? You girls don't know everything about Ron and me." She runs her gaze over the four of us. When no one speaks, she continues. "Do you know that neither he nor I have been with anyone else except each other for the past six months? Do you know that almost every week for an entire *year*—while you guys are at work—I've been meeting him for lunch at his mother's house? Do you know that the night of Monty's party when we disappeared into the cabana all night that we didn't even sleep together? That we'd spent the whole night talking about getting married? He didn't propose then because he still felt so weird about almost going home with that girl two nights before. The girl he *told* me about that very night, crying to me to forgive him."

Tess is almost in tears and I feel like a humongous jerk. I had no idea. But how could I? Apparently, my best friend has been living a secret life for the better part of an entire year.

But our cluelessness isn't helping her to feel any better at the present moment.

"Tess, I'm so sorry." I steal a look at Vix's guilty face. "We both are. We just want you to be happy, really. Ron's awesome.

He's a great guy and he obviously loves you a lot, which is nothing less than you deserve."

After a pause, Vix sums it up facetiously with, "Does this mean we don't get to be in your wedding?"

Tess loses the gloomy expression and starts laughing. She looks at the four of us, her best friends in the entire world and answers, "Well, it's too much of a hassle to find anyone else. Bitches, will you be my bridesmaids?"

CHAPTER 35

Monday, July 3, 1995
10:35 PM

Jenkinson's Pavillion
Point Pleasant

"To Tess and Ronnie!"

The girls and I have been at Jenkinson's for all of ten minutes and we're already on our second round of shots.

We clink glasses and throw our heads back, downing every last, revolting drop of our tequila. *Blech.* I'm trying to suck every molecule out of my lemon wedge in an attempt to abolish the taste of the liquor from my mouth when I ask, "Whose bright idea was it to do tequila?"

Tess slams her shot glass upside down onto the bar with a *woohoo!* "Honey, I'm getting married. When you're getting married, *you do tequila.* C'mon, let's dance."

She grabs my hand and I grab Vix's, forming a human train on our way out to meet Isla and Sam on the dance floor. The Nerds are playing, which always makes for a good time. Their niche in the bar band scene is a set list comprised solely of eighties songs, and right now they're playing "Whip It."

Tess is in rare form. The girl is normally a bucket of energy, but tonight she's practically busting out of her skin. As apprehensive as I was about this engagement, I have to confess that I've never seen her happier. She's bouncing around, singing along, looking positively... radiant. Her elated glow is even outshining the huge, two carat rock on her finger.

The Nerds move out of "Whip It" and right into "Jessie's Girl," which makes Tess scream cheerfully and twirl madly around the dance floor. She's spinning around like a crazy woman when she crashes dead on into... Sean Tanner.

218

My eyes practically bug out of my head as I cross the dance floor to say hello. Sean has his hands under Tess's elbows, trying to haul her to her feet. Instead of being embarrassed about wiping out at the feet of some cute guy, I see my friend using the opportunity to make eyes at her captor. She is such a flirt.

I approach just as Stephen turns toward the scene being played out next to him. He sees me before Sean does. "Livia? Hey! What's happening, sister?"

Sean looks up, and Tess gives me a wide-eyed look as if to say, *You know these guys?*

I kiss them both hello and ask, "What are you guys still *doing* here? I thought you left last night."

I become aware that they're both still in their same clothes from yesterday's photo shoot. Even with their day-old scruff and artfully mussed hair, they make a pretty picture: Two tall, dark, handsome men in their matching jeans and button-down white shirts. The girls in this place probably don't know what hit them. Or hit *on* them, as the situation may more accurately be described.

Tess sure as hell looks as though *she's* been met with a speeding bus. She's still gazing up at Sean as he answers, "Nope. Too wasted to drive all the way home. We crashed on the beach."

I laugh. "And it didn't occur to you to go home *this morning?*"

Stephen explains, "I'm not on duty until tomorrow night. We were having a good time, so we decided to stay another day."

"In your same old grungy clothes from the beach yesterday."

"Hey, we *showered*," Sean protests. "We snuck into the locker room at Gold's Gym."

I shake my head at the two of them. "Why didn't you just come by the house? We could have found room for you."

Thinking about how Jack and I had spent our evening, I realize that last night would never have happened if these two galoots decided to crash our party. I'm actually thankful they didn't come by.

Tess gives me an impatient glare which makes me apologize for my oversight. "Oh, I'm sorry. Tess, these are Jack's brothers. Stephen, Sean... this is Tess."

Stephen gives her a charismatic nod, but Sean takes her hand, holding her fingers lightly in his as he pours on the charm. "Ah, this is Tess! I should have known. Nice to finally meet you. Livia told us you were beautiful... She wasn't lying."

"Save it, Sean. She's engaged."

Tess is actually blushing. I don't think I've ever seen that before. She's normally the one putting the color into other people's cheeks. She must realize that at the same second I do, because suddenly, her lips curl up like the Cheshire cat. Trademark Tess.

"Yes, I'm engaged. But not *married,*" she purrs.

I roll my eyes. "You are a shameless, shameless flirt, my friend."

The guys insist on buying us a round, so I introduce them to the rest of our group before Stephen hurdles off to the bar for shots. Kamikazes this time, at least.

They stick around most of the night, everyone trading off rounds of beers and the occasional shot. After a few hours of that, we're all feeling pretty loose.

Scratch that. We're all feeling *really* loose.

The Nerds break into "I Love Rock and Roll," and Tess lets out with a "WHOOHOO!"

Before I can register what's happening, she grabs my hand... and *drags me up on stage*.

With about ten drinks less in me, I may have shaken her off. But because my BAC is somewhere around eighty percent, I think it's a great idea.

I hear a cheer go up from the crowd as she throws an arm around my shoulders and leans us both into the mic.

The beat was goin' strong
Playin' my favorite so-ow-ow-ong...

The rest of the guys onstage are prodding us on encouragingly as we sing and dance along, while the girls are falling all over themselves laughing uncontrollably.

We are having a blast, laughing our way through the impromptu performance; the booze has abolished every hint of stage fright, and being up here is actually *fun*. I'm staring out at a sea of faces, and I gotta say, it's quite a rush. I get why Jack loves it so much. Is it my imagination or do we actually sound pretty good?

God, I must really be wasted. I don't even think my voice sounds good in the *shower*, and here I am belting away into a microphone in front of five hundred strangers. I am just buzzed enough to decide not to care. I'll never see any of these people ever again in my life.

The music starts winding down, so I give a silly curtsy and climb down from the stage.

Tess opts for a grander exit, however. She gives a yell and throws her arms over her head as the audience roars back…

…then stage dives into the crowd.

Holy shit! We all just about lose our minds cracking up. Actual tears are streaming down my face and I can't even catch my breath. Vix is leaning into me, hysterical. A night out with Tess is always a good time, but she reset the bar *unapproachably* higher tonight. How the heck are we going to top this for her bachelorette party?

As Tess finds her way back to our laughing group, I see that she isn't alone. Some blond guy is following closely behind and trying to get her attention. Even without the stage show, Tess is a girl who gets *noticed*. I can't recall a single night out when she hasn't been hit on. As a group, we're not too shabby or anything, but that chick has always had it all over the rest of us. Combined.

So I'm a little taken aback when Blondie brushes by Tess and introduces himself to Vix. It wasn't a rude maneuver, however, and since Tess is busy giving high-fives to her fans, I'm sure she hasn't even noticed.

No one in our circle seems to realize that our pack of seven has just become eight. I steal a look at the new guy and am convinced that he looks familiar. You don't see too many beach-blond crops of surfer hair on guys past their teens. Not to say that his look isn't working for him. He is definitely cute. In fact, judging by

Vix's response over there, I'm betting that she'd say he's *extremely* cute.

It's not until he goes to scratch his upper arm, sliding his short-sleeve up in the process, do I see the round, blue-and-green tattoo. A sudden recollection enters my mind.

A porch in Point Pleasant. Tess, Vix and me. Three surfer dudes coming off the beach and stopping to say hello. Their admission that they were the filthy prior tenants of our present rental. A disgusting shower stall, a science-experiment-in-the-making kitchen...

...and Vix lambasting them for trying to ask us out, even though she thought the one with the Earth tattoo was kinda cute.

I guess she either doesn't recognize him or she suddenly thinks that being messy isn't that big of a deal. I'm banking on the former. Vix is an absolute neat freak.

Stephen leans down to me and nods in her direction. "What's up with Spicoli over there?"

"I don't know," I answer. "I was just wondering the same thing."

"Think we should save her?"

I take stock of the situation, watching as Vix demurely takes a sip of her drink from her straw. Her eyes don't stray from his face as I see a smile tugging at the corners of her mouth.

"You know what? I don't think she needs saving. C'mon. Let's get everyone to the outside bar; I need air. Next round's on me."

CHAPTER 36

Tuesday, July 4, 1995
Way too early

My Bed (I think)
Hell

Somehow, I'm not dead.

My brain has imploded and my limbs are missing, but I am, in fact, alive.

I almost wish I weren't.

I wipe the crust from my eyes and raise my head from the pillow. Even slowly, this is a bad idea. I sink back down into my beach-damp sheets and take a huge breath.

Another mistake.

I start coughing spasmodically, my lungs heaving to overcome the too-many cigarettes I sucked down last night. The coughing just adds to my splitting headache. As the fit subsides, I lift my head again. Then my upper body. Then miraculously, I manage to swing my feet onto the floor.

I rake my eyes over my bed partner Vix, still sleeping. Even with the oscillating fan churning away, there's a stale beer smell permeating the room and I don't know whose breath is responsible. Smacking my tongue against the roof of my mouth, I realize it very likely could be me.

I don't need to peek beyond the slivers of light framing the pulled shade of the window in order to tell that it's a beautiful, bird-chirping morning out there.

It's a hellish, hangover morning in here.

Happy Fourth of July!

I stagger out of the bedroom—stumbling over my discarded platform heels on the floor in the process—with only the picture of a very large glass of water on my mind.

I almost trip again over Sean, passed out on the living room floor, and wonder how he's able to possibly sleep through his brother's snoring. Stephen must have won the coin toss, because he's dozing away, albeit noisily, in what looks like relative comfort on the couch. After spending the night on the floor, Sean is most likely going to wake up in more pain than me. If that's even possible.

Poor bastard.

I fill a red Solo cup with water straight from the faucet. I'm so thirsty that I only barely register that the taste is off. Tap water isn't ever so great to begin with, but at the beach? *Yargh.*

I shuffle into the bathroom and paw through the medicine cabinet in search of the Tylenol. I down four, then scrub the miniature socks off my teeth with my toothbrush. I throw my hair into a ponytail and wash my face with cold water. This is about as good as it's going to get for now.

I'm starting to feel more like myself by the time I sit down at the kitchen table with a Pop Tart and a Diet Coke: The Breakfast of Champions. The wooden chairs are hard and unpadded—not quite the ideal place for slumping—but Stephen is commandeering the only comfy seat in the room.

Peering across the table, I picture Jack as he looked two nights ago sitting in the now empty chair: One leg crossed over the other, his gray eyes silently staring me down. I chuckle to myself when I think of the way his lips had curled into a calculating smile as he told me what he planned to do to me.

And then the way he carried out the plan itself.

Checking the clock, I decide that it isn't too early to hit the stores and get the rest of our provisions for the barbeque today. The girls brought most of the food down with them yesterday, but I still haven't even started on Jack's little wish list. Plus, Isla forgot the ketchup. How in God's name do you forget to get ketchup for a barbeque?

I go back into my bedroom and dress quietly so as not to wake Vix. I scribble a note for the girls, leave it on the coffee table, then step over Sean again on my way out the door.

I check my watch for the millionth time. Jack isn't the most prompt person in the world, but it's already two o'clock and I expected him here hours ago. Even if he hit holiday traffic, he should have certainly been here by *now*.

He should have certainly at least *called* by now.

I know it's stupid, but I refuse to call him. If his meeting with Shug went well, he would have been ecstatic to spill the news. I'm starting to get the impression that things didn't go so great yesterday, and I don't want to be up his butt about it if he's not ready to discuss it. And he must not be ready to even face it, much less discuss it, because he's running pretty late.

Stephen and Sean have already split for home. They waited around until a little while ago to see Jack before heading out, but he didn't make it down in time.

I check my watch, *again*, and Vix catches me. "Will you just look at this," she starts in. "Livia just can't wait for her stud to get here."

I'd confirmed for the girls last night in a drunken haze that I had finally slept with Jack and more interestingly, how he said he loved me. Even though I thought I was being secretive when I mentioned it, my volume *was* set to 'Beer.' *In front of his brothers*. How embarrassing.

"What time was he supposed to be here, Liv?" Sam asks.

"I don't know. No set time, I guess. I just thought... you know... he'd be here earlier."

Tess stops scrubbing down the grill to chime in, "You just thought he wouldn't be able to get down fast enough for Round Two."

"Tess!"

"What? Oh please. Like you can actually keep your mind on anything else today. You little sex kitten, you."

She takes the plate of raw ground beef and holds it out to me. "Nice job on the burgers, by the way."

Vix, Sam, and Isla all stifle their giggles. I'm the only one who isn't in on the joke.

Until I take a look for myself.

On the dish Tess is jabbing in my direction, there's a pile of inconsistent, barely round burger blobs. One isn't even patted down flat. I start laughing when I see the lone meatball glob amongst the other pathetic patties.

Oooh. Note to self: Good name for an all-girl band: *The Pathetic Patties*.

"Fine." I say. "You caught me. But I'm just a little freaked out that he hasn't called yet. Do you think things could have gone that badly yesterday?"

Vix shrugs. "I don't know. I hope not. That meeting was a pretty big deal, huh?"

I nod. "Well, yeah. I mean, the money from this one contract alone could get Jack all set up with his own construction company someday. He really wants that." I get up to repair the hamburgers so Tess can throw them on the grill. "Do you think I should page him? I don't want to bug him if there's bad news, but I can't imagine what's keeping him."

Vix dismisses my worry with a wave of her hand. "It's probably just traffic. It *is* the Fourth of July, you know. Why don't you call his brothers? They're probably home by now and can tell you what the Southbound side looked like."

"Good idea. I'm right on top of that, Rose!"

I finish fixing the burgers and then go inside to wash my hands and use the phone.

Sean tells me that the roads were pretty clear.

Now I'm starting to worry.

I go back outside to relay the information to the girls, but before I can speak, Jack's convertible pulls into the driveway.

It's about time.

I go through the gate at the side of the house and meet him in the drive. "Hi, babe. Welcome back!"

He gets out of the car slowly, looking like a beaten man. Surely, this isn't just because of a late evening playing guitar all night. This is something more. The look on his face is forlorn, haggard. His shoulders are slouched, his eyes are red and he looks... completely dejected.

Crap. I guess the meeting didn't go so well. Still, I'm surprised by the severity of his reaction. He looks entirely *miserable.*

Dancing around the subject, I ask, "Bad day, yesterday?"

He's uncharacteristically apprehensive for a beat. Then he steps forward to wrap his arms around me—tightly—resting his head against my shoulder. "You have no idea."

"Oh, Jack," I say, my heart breaking for him. "I'm so sorry. This totally stinks. But everything's going to work out fine, I just know it."

"Will it?"

I pull back to look at his face. His eyes are hard, not meeting mine directly.

"Yes," I say. And more importantly, I believe it. "Come on in back. I'll get you a burger and a beer."

When I lead him into the yard, the girls are lounging around the lawn chairs and offer a united sing-song of a greeting, a la *Charlie's Angels.* "Hiii, Jack!"

That makes him smile in spite of himself. A sad smile, but at least it's a crack in his cheerless reserve.

I set him up with a beer as Tess flips a burger onto a bun for me. I fix it up just right and then deliver it to Jack, before settling myself at the end of his chaise, digging a stone out of my sandal. Our "yard" is nothing more than two-hundred square feet of sand covered in beach pebble. Even with my summer-tempered feet coming along nicely, walking around barefoot out here is not an option.

"Your *brothers* said to tell you 'hi'."

Jack pauses mid-chew. "What?"

I proceed to ramble on about our entire evening, telling him about Tess's crash-landing into Sean, Vix meeting her surfer dude, Chris, and of course, my performing debut. He simply refuses to believe that we truly sang onstage. The other girls back me up on my story, but it's not until I catalogue the sheer quantity of alcohol consumed prior to my Joan Jett impersonation that he actually believes me.

227

"You should have heard your brothers tearing me to shreds. Sean was all, 'I guess there's more than one rock star in the family.' It was so funny."

Jack has a polite smile pasted on his face that doesn't reach his eyes. Man, he's just a barrel of laughs today. Shug must have really done a number on him.

"Babe?" I ask.

"Yes?"

"You okay?"

Jack takes a sip from his beer and rests the back of his head against the cushion. "No." He glides a hand lightly across my knee. "But don't worry about it. I guess I'm just overthinking things today."

Don't worry about it? The guy looks as though he's ready to stick his head in the oven.

By his tone, it's almost like he's mad at me for something, but I don't remember saying or doing anything worth catching attitude for. It's not like him to dance around a subject if there was a problem, anyway.

I decide to just let him sulk. He'll open up when he feels ready, and I'll just make sure to be there for him when he does. As concerned as I am, there's really nothing else I can do. If *I* was in a mood, I wouldn't want anyone hovering all over *me*. Besides, I still have some salads to throw together before the guys get here. I excuse myself from Jack's side with a concerned smile and a pat on his leg.

CHAPTER 37

Tuesday, July 4, 1995
9:37 PM

The Beach
Manasquan

Once it gets dark, we decide to take the party up to the beach. It's amateur hour up here with all the budding pyro-technicians setting off their ill-gotten fireworks. Theoretically, it's illegal to set off explosives in New Jersey, but the beach patrol normally looks the other way on the Fourth. You can't even buy fireworks around here, so I know most of these people must have driven down to South of the Border to stockpile for the event. Every few dozen yards along the water's edge, there's a makeshift launchpad set up, surrounded by the silhouette of a few daring drunkards with lighters.

Our group is back far enough to avoid any potential injuries, our beach chairs arranged in a semicircle facing the ocean. With nearly every burst of color in the sky, someone, if not all of us, will respond with an "Oooh" or an "Ahhh." I know it's corny, but it's tradition.

Bucking tradition this year is Monty, who's in London for the holiday with Walter. Good place to be on America's birthday—out of the country. But thankfully, Ronnie and Tom showed up within a few minutes of Jack.

From the first second they walked into the backyard, we all made a big deal of congratulating Ronnie and busting his chops about the engagement. Now that their relationship is official, I can see that he and Tess really do make a great couple.

It's good that he and Tom got down when they did, because I was able to let them deal with Jack for the afternoon. I kept my distance because I didn't want to constantly be buzzing around him, annoyingly trying to cheer him up. Not that the guys had much luck on their end in that department, either.

Jack remained remote all day. Whenever I would ask him a question, he'd give me a one-word answer, if at all. I know he's upset, but he's never been *moody*. It's starting to get my feathers up. Even now, he isn't even sitting next to me to watch the fireworks. He's at the end of our semicircle, drinking a bottled water. At least he's not drowning his sorrows in alcohol.

I wish I could get a moment alone to talk with him. He hasn't even alluded to his meeting yesterday, but I think it will do us both good to discuss it. I'm sick of tiptoeing around the subject.

The fireworks are winding down, so everyone gathers up the chairs and coolers to go back to the house for dessert. Vix made this really cute cake with blueberries, strawberries, and whipped cream arranged on top like an American flag.

I'm lagging behind, trying to fold my uncooperative beach chair as Jack comes to the rescue. But instead of helping, he takes the chair from my hands and sets it back down in the sand.

I look up at him. "Do you want to talk?"

He nods in the affirmative, looking blankly at something over my left shoulder.

I jog a few steps to catch up with our group, letting them know we might be a while. Tess raises her eyebrows and offers, "Have fuuun."

I just roll my eyes. I can pretty much guarantee that there won't be any beach sexcapades tonight. But I don't bother to tell her that. It's probably beyond her comprehension.

I walk back to our chairs only to find that Jack isn't there. He's at the edge of the water, looking out at the ocean, his hands crammed into his pockets. I hate seeing him like this. From the back, even his posture makes him look completely despondent.

Walking up behind him, I slip my arms around his waist in a consoling hug. Before I can even complete the movement, he grabs my hands to stop me.

What the hell?

He turns to face me, and by the look in his eyes, I already know this is going to be bad.

I don't want to speak first and he looks like he can't speak at all, which makes for this heated, awkward silence between us. I'm just looking at him, waiting, and he won't even look me in the eye.

Finally, he breaks the silence. "There are some things we need to talk about."

Ya think?

"Like what?"

Jack runs a hand through his hair and then slides it down to massage his neck. "The meeting with Shug went really well." For such exciting news, he doesn't seem very happy about spilling it. "But that means we're leaving for this tour. Effective immediately. As in, first thing tomorrow morning."

"Well... wow! That's... Congratulations, Jack! This is exactly what we wanted. But why—"

"By 'we,' I mean me and the band. *I'm* leaving for this tour. Understand?"

Understand? My eyes narrow as his words—combined with his crappy mood all day—suddenly start to become clear. "Without me, you mean."

"I just can't see it happening."

There are more people in the band than just Jack Tanner. Chances are good that he has to take their wants under consideration along with his own, and I guess Collette and I didn't make the cut. I'm stunned and devastated, but what am I supposed to do? Beg him to take me with him? Pout until he does?

It's all a little too Yoko too consider.

Again, he runs a hand through his hair, looking like he's holding back from saying something more. I wish he would. Something along the lines of, *I don't want to go without you. Please come with me.*

But he doesn't say it.

And I can tell that he won't.

Instead, he says, "I mean, I'm not going to just float with you through these next months on tour. You need to give me something here."

Wait. *What?*

When all I do is stare at him in confusion, he takes a deep breath and asks, "Why couldn't you just say it back?"

His eyes are broken, staring into mine, waiting for me to understand his question. He's annoyed because... because I never told him I *loved* him? What the hell? "Is *that* was this is about?"

"Isn't that enough?"

I don't like the angle of this entire conversation. It came out of nowhere, and I'm not sure what he expects me to say. Everything I've felt for him has been terrifying, and I don't have much experience dealing with such foreign emotions. I'm not comfortable just blurting out something I've never said before.

While I'm trying to think of the right way to explain, Jack tips his head to the side and says, "You can't do it, can you?"

He's almost smug with the way he asks me, almost as if he knew this was exactly how I'd react. "What, do you want me to stand here and lie to you? Tell you something I don't really mean? I just don't know yet, okay? Why is that a problem?"

"The problem isn't that you can't say it. The problem is that you don't feel it."

"It's not that I don't, Jack. It's not that at all. I just..."

"Then tell me. Tell me what we're doing here."

My head is spinning. I don't *know* what we're doing. "Why are you pushing me on this? Why does it have to be defined all of a sudden? Everything was fine when you left yesterday. I thought things were going great."

"They *were.*"

Something about the way he says that makes me snap to attention. His eyes are unblinking and his mouth is set in a determined line, his resolute expression speaking as loudly as if he were screaming... and I can't quite believe what I'm hearing.

"Wait a minute. What's going on here? Are you *breaking up with me?*"

He puts a hand to his forehead and swipes it down his entire face, ending with a balled fist at his throat. He finally looks at me, and in the one second pause it takes to answer, his face becomes drawn and his shoulders go limp.

A zombie, he answers deadpan. "That depends on you."

"What?" I get the distinct impression that I'm being tested, and I really, really don't like it. "*Why?*"

"Please don't ask me to answer that again."

Is he fucking kidding me?

"Well, what *should* I ask you, Jack?" My heart starts to hammer as I feel my stomach drop clear out of my body. "Should I ask if the sex wasn't good enough?"

"No. That's not it and you know it."

"Should I ask if there's someone else?"

"No."

"'No' I shouldn't ask or 'no' there's no one else?"

"There was only you."

"*Was?*"

"That's not what I'm saying."

"Well, forgive me, but I don't know what the fuck you *are* saying, so I guess I'm just trying to clarify."

He clears his throat before answering. "I'm saying now what I've been saying for weeks. I'm done with fun. I need something more. I need something *real*. I thought you would have told me the other night, but when you didn't…"

What the hell is he talking about? This has been the most 'real' relationship I've ever been in. Or so I thought. "Oh, real nice timing, Jack. You wait until after we finally have sex to bring all this shit up? So you're just going to fuck me and leave me then, huh. You're no different than the rest of them."

His eyes turn to slits, and my blood runs cold from the look on his face. I may have gone too far. "Are you kidding me? You've been hiding behind sex and music for so long, you can't even see what's right in front of you. I've gone *above and beyond* to prove I'm different. Now I'm wondering why I bothered. You can't seem to tell any of us apart anyway. I guess we're all the same with the lights out."

Before I even realize it, I'm slapping him across the face. "Fuck you!"

Where the hell does he get off saying something like that to me? Haven't I proven to him over these past weeks that I'm not that same person anymore? If I didn't know any better, I'd think he was setting up for all the groupie tail he's sure to encounter out there on the road.

How long will he be gone? Two months? Six? A year? I have no idea.

I would wait for him if he wanted me to.

It's shocking that he can't seem to wait for me.

I thought it was a foregone conclusion. We aren't just Jack and Livia anymore. We're *us*. Even if it's only been six weeks, that doesn't matter. I thought we were perfect together.

And just because I can't tell him any of that *right this very second*, now he wants to leave me behind.

Jack barely flinched when I slapped him, but now he's running a tongue across his teeth. He gives a rub to his scruffy jaw, looking genuinely humbled. "I'm sorry, Liv."

His apology calms me down somewhat, but it doesn't make anything better. "Jack. How can you even question this? Don't you already know?"

"I thought I did."

"Yet here you are, cutting your losses."

"Don't say that."

"Why not? That's what this is. Own it."

"Look, I'm not trying to hurt you."

"Too late."

I can feel the heat of tears burning behind my eyes and I hate myself for it. *This isn't happening.* Why should I be fighting back tears over something that isn't even happening?

He takes my hands, and wimp that I am, I let him do it.

As if he were answering the unasked question in my brain, Jack says, "I didn't mean for this to happen. I didn't see things going down like this."

"What the hell is that supposed to mean? You *made* this happen." He's the one that wanted this, that wanted me to feel something for him. Well, I do. I feel *everything* for him. And now he's leaving.

He may as well take my heart with him when he goes, seeing as how he went through all that trouble to rip it out of my chest.

His brows are drawn together tightly as a muscle pulses in his jaw. "You asked me yesterday morning where we are, and here I am, telling you. We can't go on like this."

"Bullshit."

He looks about as tortured as I do, however, and I guess I never realized that along with singing and playing guitar, he's also a very talented actor. I'm under the delusion that that revelation is giving me strength when I hear him say, "Please don't."

Please don't what?

And then I realize the tears aren't lodged behind my eyes, they're actually streaming down my face. I can't believe he's doing this to me. I can't believe he's doing this to *us*.

I hate the pleading sound of my voice when I look up and ask, "Why are you doing this?"

His face becomes a twisted, tormented caricature as he grabs me behind my head and pulls me abruptly against his body, crushing my face to his chest. I feel his lips against my hair as his hand attempts a soothing caress up and down my spine. "Liv..."

The dam breaks.

I can't help it. I start bawling against him, my shoulders heaving with sobs, and I cannot, for the life of me, make it stop. We stand like that for an eternity, my tears unrelenting and my brain a swirling mess of questions. It doesn't help that I'm seeking solace in the arms of the very person who is causing me this pain. I want to push him away and tell him where he can shove his sympathy. I want to scratch his eyes out for making me feel cold-hearted and humiliated and unwanted.

It doesn't make sense. Nothing does. It doesn't make sense that he feels the need to toss out this ultimatum; it doesn't make sense that our plans are being shot all to hell because of it. It's not fair that he's expecting me to say something I'm not ready to say. I don't know how I'm supposed to handle any of it. So I stand here, letting him hold me, listening to his mantra of, "Baby, please don't" over and over again like some pathetic loser. Relishing the sound of anguish in his voice. Lying to myself that this is hurting him, too.

Just when I think things can't get any worse, I feel his hand under my chin, lifting my face to his. He bends down slowly, unsurely... and before I know what's happening, his lips are brushing across mine. I'm dazed and spent from crying and have no energy left to fight him off.

At least that's what I tell myself as I realize I'm kissing him back.

His thumbs brush against my cheeks, swiping away my tears as his lips slant firmly against my own, taking from me the last of what I have to give.

His arms pull at my waist, holding me tightly against his body as I feel him lower me to the ground. The sand is damp and cold against my back, but Jack's lips are warm and insistent against my skin, his body hard and demanding against mine. I'm still crying, but the illusion through my tears is that Jack's eyes are watering up as well.

Maybe I can show him what he'll be giving up. Maybe if I can let him *feel* how much I care about him, how good we are together...

I smooth my hands up his chest and mold my body to his, kissing him, holding onto him for dear life. I run my fingers along his strong, muscular arms. I grip his thick, beautiful hair in my palms. I touch my fingertips to his sculpted jaw, trying to imprint his features into my memory through touch.

He lets out with a groan, that earth-shattering reverberation of pleasure and pain that always tears right through my insides. I start to slip into that familiar daze, that trance he's always been able to put me under as I groan back, his heart pounding against mine, our breaths mingling in the night salt-air.

There's something different in the way he's kissing me, almost like he's trying to *possess* me. It's scary. And it's not him at all. When I feel his cool hand sliding under my shirt, the touch snaps me awake.

Whatever the hell is going on here is just too pitiable to fathom.

Somehow, I muster up enough pride to tear my mouth from his and put a halting hand against his chest.

"Stop."

236

His dark eyes look down at me in anguish, and if I didn't think he was such a jerk at this second, I would swear that he looks ashamed of himself.

He breaks out of the moment with a pained, "I'm sorry."

I can't even look at him as I rise to my feet and brush the sand from my clothes. I shake out my hair and finally turn back to him, all business. "So. What now?"

He's still sitting in the sand, legs drawn, elbows bent over his knees. "I don't know, Liv. Maybe one of us will be able to figure it out."

I can't believe we're caught in such a standoff, and that neither one of us is willing to back down. He wants more... and I just can't give it to him. And until one of us caves, we'll be stuck right here in limbo.

I'm still in denial as I go to say goodbye. So, instead of coming up with some zinger, some perfect sentence that will haunt his days and nights while we're apart, I offer flippantly, "Well, good luck. Or break a leg. Whatever it is I'm supposed to say, do that."

I give a quick salute and then turn on my heel, leaving Jack sitting there on the beach.

* * *

When I get back to the house, I discover that thankfully, everyone has already turned in for the night. The living room is dark and quiet as I tiptoe past Tom on the couch and make my way to my room. God bless Vix, she must be bunking in the middle room with Sam and Isla tonight, because I find that I have the bed to myself. Then I become aware it's because she obviously assumed I'd want this room for Jack and me. The realization starts the tears flowing again as I curl up into my bed—the bed I shared just yesterday morning with Jack—and will sleep to come.

237

It doesn't.

A few hours later, I hear Jack's car start. My body tenses at the sound; my heart wrenches all over again. It takes him an excruciatingly long time to put the car in gear, the engine idling low outside my window, almost daring me to take this last chance and go to him. Is he having second thoughts? Is he ready to acknowledge how completely wrong this is? Should I just suck it up and tell him what he wants to hear?

I fight the deplorable urge to run outside and beg him to change his mind. *Please, Jack. We don't have to do this. I just need a little more time. Just tell me you'll wait for me.*

But then finally, I hear the crunch of his tires pulling slowly over the gravelly driveway and onto the road, holding my breath until the sound fades into an oppressive, deafening quiet.

Do something, explore it, find something new...

...and move on.

CHAPTER 38

Tuesday, April 30, 1996
Who knows? Earlyish.

Lenape Lake
Norman

It's a cold, wet, miserable day outside.

Perfect.

I don't know what possessed me to decide to go for a run today, other than to burn off all this nervous energy. Unbridled anxiety has woken me up at dawn consistently for days now.

Checking my face in the side mirror of my car, I can see that the proof of my near-insomnia is evidenced in my eyes, which are shadowed with a deep, dark gray. My skin is pale and lifeless during the winter, but by April, it's simply screaming for some sunshine. I figure I'd better hit the tanning booth a few times before Tess's wedding, which gives me exactly twenty-six days to acquire a tan.

I'm parked in the lot between the post office and The Westlake Pub, sitting sideways out of the driver's seat, lacing up my sneakers. Lenape Lake has a pretty good running route, although I suppose I chose the location just for the added torture.

I'd be able to take advantage of the pretty views if it were a nicer morning than this, but no matter. Aside from a few diehards, I won't be passing too many other runners on such a gloomy day, and that is just fine with me.

I stand and stretch against my car, making it look as though I know what I'm doing. I execute a few lunges and then take off in a counter-clockwise trot around the lake.

Running in the cold serves to be only mildly distracting. Unavoidable is the fact that I am now alone with my thoughts. The memory of my first week without Jack is almost too difficult to bear. But as it happens so often lately, my consciousness is inevitably brought back to last summer and the worst night of my life.

When the girls woke up the next morning—I didn't sleep much at all the night before—they found me bloodshot and bleary-eyed. I was barely able to mumble out the reason why. They listened in sympathy, the looks on their faces stunned and sad, but even that outpouring of support wasn't enough to get me crying again.

I was done crying already.

Nevermind the fact that I was probably too dehydrated to muster up any more tears, the long and short of the situation was that after a sleepless night spent doing nothing but, I just refused to cry anymore. It was the principle of the matter. I rejected the attempt by my broken heart to turn me into a sniveling, depressed little weakling.

Been there, done that.

Despite my sister's protests, I decided it would be best if I just went home. I just couldn't do five more days down there in that house when my wounds were so fresh. I told the girls not to worry and told Ronnie and Tom thanks, but no thanks on the offer to kill Jack for me. I was sure they were only trying to cheer me up. He was their friend, too—their friend *first*, actually—after all.

I caved only once on my newly-instituted, anti-crying policy. It was that very morning on my way out the door. I had gathered up all of my things in my duffel bag and had my hand on the knob when I saw Grendel on the windowsill next to the door. I looked at the goofy face of the ridiculous stuffed dog Jack had won for me. My prize for a day on the boardwalk when I first realized he had worked his way into my heart.

My entire body froze, then started to shake uncontrollably as I reached out to grab it. My walls shattered, my defenses down, I felt the tears pouring down my face. I held the stupid dog to my chest as I sank to the floor, sobbing. Thankfully, everyone was out in the backyard and didn't witness my drama. I was able to pull myself together and was replacing him on the sill as I turned and saw Ronnie and Tess coming through the back door. I looked away quickly, hiding my face while I gathered my bag over my shoulder.

Tess sounded concerned. "I thought you'd gone already."

My voice was overbright when I answered, "Yep. Just cutting out now. I'll give you a call when I get home to let you know I got back safely."

"Liv?"

I still didn't turn around for fear of being caught with wet eyes and a red face. "Yeah?"

I had one foot out the door as Tess asked, "Aren't you going to take... that?"

"Burn it," I said, then stepped out into the sun.

I went directly home and opened a big bottle of wine. I sat my ass on the couch and spent the next eight hours watching a "Twilight Zone" marathon, before passing out right there in the living room.

The next morning, I woke up feeling so sick that I ran for the bathroom and puked my guts out. I just didn't have the stomach to make a very good drunk.

I guessed *alcoholism* was off the table.

I spent the whole weekend on that couch. When I got hungry, I ordered food, and when it would show up, I realized I couldn't eat more than a few bites. That little conundrum lended to the pile of Italian sandwich boxes and Chinese food containers mucking up my refrigerator.

So, I guessed *eating my feelings* was out, too.

The girls called every few hours, probably just to make sure I wasn't hanging from the showerhead by my terrycloth belt or anything.

Which brings me to The Robe.

I'd put it on shortly after getting home on Wednesday, and didn't take it off the whole weekend. I hadn't changed clothes or showered for four days. I hadn't even looked in the mirror, which is probably why the delivery guys would stare at me a little funny whenever I answered the door. I must have been a sight.

By Sunday afternoon, I'd had enough.

241

I surprised my parents when I called and told them I'd be there for dinner. I just needed something normal, something routine to get me through the day.

I finally dragged my sorry self into the shower and managed to put on clean, matching clothes. I practiced a happy face in the mirror and then headed over to Mom and Dad's.

Dad and I found ourselves alone in the den while Mom finished putting our meal together.

"Glad you decided to join us, Livia Moon. How's tricks?"

"Epic as always, Dad." I plucked an olive from the bowl and popped it into my mouth. I was trying to avoid getting into too much detail about the events over the past week.

"Work okay?"

"Whatever. S-O-C-K-S," I answered in the small bit of Spanish I knew. *Eso sí que es; it is what it is.* Thank you, late night infomercials. "Maybe Phil's daughters and I can start our own girl-band. Second generation of you guys. We'll call it '*Female Persuasion*'!"

"You don't want to end up like me."

I did a double-take at his resigned tone. My father was normally a cheerful kind of guy, and I just delivered a solid joke. He kind of threw me by turning our lighthearted subject into a serious discussion. "What are you talking about?"

He aimed a sad smile at me. "The rock and roll lifestyle takes no prisoners, Livia. Temptations from every angle. I made mistakes in those early days because of it. Mistakes I can't take back."

I didn't know if he was referring to the drugs or the women or what, but there was no way I could sit there and have a conversation about it. He was my father, for godsakes, and I didn't think I could bear hearing all the gory details straight from the dog's mouth, much less listen to his excuses about it.

But when I looked up, I saw the drawn look on his face. I could see that he wasn't trying to convince me of *anything*. He was just taking the opportunity to beat himself up over it.

And that's when it hit me.

In that one second, I became wholly convinced that his regret stemmed from the person he was in the *past*. He screwed up once—and he screwed up big—but he'd been a faithful husband and father in all the years since. The revelation surprised me, but I knew without a doubt that it was the truth. I suddenly felt guilty as all hell for the assumptions I made about him all those years.

He deserved better than that from his own daughter. Why was it so much easier for me to believe the worst about him? Why hadn't I ever told him how amazing I thought he was anyway?

I shot him a genuine smile and said, "Are you kidding? You're awesome. How many kids have dads who are still rocking out at your age?"

He sighed before sinking back into his chair. "That's exactly it, Livia. Where has it gotten me? Here I am, a 46-year-old bass player in a wedding band. It wasn't supposed to be this way. I never wanted to grow up and get a real job, and thirty years later, I'm still chasing the dream."

"You have a real job. You're a musician."

"In a wedding band that doesn't even get regular bookings. This wasn't the dream."

Just because my dreams were broken didn't mean everyone else's should be. "The dream can still happen."

"If dreams were meant to come true, we'd have a hell of a lot of princesses and astronauts out there in the world."

"And the world would be a better place for it."

The subject got dropped once Mom called us up to the table, but I took the opportunity to give him a big hug all the same.

All was going well, according to plan. Mom had made a pork roast with oven potatoes and fresh string beans. Once Dad heard I was coming over, he took a trip to Calandra's Bakery and got my favorite crusty bread and some cookies for dessert. It was enough to get my appetite back on track.

I was using a piece of the aforementioned bread to sop up some gravy when my dad gestured to the bottle of wine on the table. "Would you like some, Livia?"

Ugh. "No thanks, Dad. I'll stick with Diet Coke."

243

"So how was Fourth of July at the beach?" Mom asked in her usual, upbeat tone.

I cleared my throat. "Alright, I guess."

She continued, "Who came down?"

The dinner conversation was turning out to be harder to deal with than I'd imagined. "Uh, the usual. Vix, obviously. Tess, Sam, Isla."

"None of the boys?"

Yes. Ronnie and Tom. Stephen and Sean... Jack.

I hadn't heard from him since our encounter on the beach, and couldn't believe he hadn't come to his senses yet. I knew getting in touch with me from the road wouldn't be easy, but it wasn't impossible. Except that the past days of zero-contact made me think he was really digging his heels in about it. He wasn't going to come to me, and I'd started to realize it was going to be up to me to make the first move.

My head started to swim. I had to change the subject before I started blubbering. "Hey, did Vix tell you that Tess is engaged?"

My mother smiled and shook her head yes. "What a beautiful bride she'll be."

"I know, right? She asked us to be in the wedding."

"Well, of course she would. Did they make any plans yet?"

"No, not yet. She's thinking maybe Pleasantdale Chateau, but she hasn't made any phone calls or anything."

Okay, I could deal with talking about my friend and her wedding plans. Knowing my mother, I probably could have stretched that thread of conversation out through dessert.

But then my dad finally decided to pipe in. "Oh, you know who I ran into over at Guitar Center the other day?"

"Who's that, Dad?"

He took a sip of his water and said casually, "Your friend, Jack Taylor."

A lump of bread got stuck in my throat. I swallowed hard, trying to pass it. "Tanner."

"What's that?"

"His name," I said, my voice scratchier than I would have liked. My hand shook as I reached for my glass of soda. I took a sip and clarified, "His name is Jack *Tanner*."

"Oh, that's right. Don't worry, I didn't call him by his last name," he said, giving me a wink. "Well, anyway, I saw him on Friday."

Friday?

"Don't you mean Wednesday, Dad? He was only home on *Wednesday* before he took off for his tour." Right? Fourth of July was a Tuesday. Didn't Jack say that he was leaving first thing the next morning?

Dad wiped his mouth on his napkin and leaned back in his chair. "I think I know my days of the week, Livia. It was Friday. Trust me."

I almost spit out my soda. This was too much. The old man must've been mistaken.

My poor father didn't know why I looked about ready to jump out of my skin.

No effin way. NO EFFIN WAY was that possible.

A thought came to me just then and the revelation made my stomach churn. I put it out of my head long enough to stammer out an apology. I probably looked like I was about to lose my dinner right there at the table, however, so I guessed my parents weren't fooled by my attempt at nonchalance.

I had to get out of there.

I grabbed a few cookies for the road in a feeble attempt to be polite. I was eating and running, after all. I thanked my parents for a great meal and then lit out.

Once in the solace of my car, I explored my epiphany.

Jack had *lied*.

He lied to me about having to leave so soon. He lied because... why? To force my hand as soon as possible? Was he just using the tour as an excuse to do so? Was he even *going* on tour?

Maybe he was still home. Maybe there was still time to talk things out with him, make him understand. I could go to him, couldn't I? I could talk to him. I could tell him how miserable I've been without him. I could tell him what an idiot I've been.

245

I could tell him that I loved him.

As soon as the thought entered my brain, I knew it was the truth. My heart slammed around my ribcage as my knuckles went white on the steering wheel.

Holy shit, *I loved him.* I did. How come I couldn't see it before now? I was completely, undeniably, head over heels in love with Jack. I knew he was it for me from the first moment I saw him up on that stage, even though I tried to fight it. The days since had only confirmed it.

Whether I wanted to acknowledge it to myself or not, the fact was I knew it *now*.

I knew Jack loved me. I mean, the day we broke up, he was a brooding mute all afternoon and evening. Why else would he have been sulking around the whole day? Maybe he knew going into his big ultimatum that I wouldn't be able to tell him what he needed to hear, and it had been wreaking havoc on his emotions. And if he was so heartbroken about it then, maybe he was having second thoughts about it now?

When it came right down to it, though, no matter how many straws I grasped at, I couldn't avoid the one, rational, niggling argument: If he really *was* so torn up about leaving me behind, then why the hell did he do it?

My revelation opened up a whole new can of worms and kept me focused while I fixated on a plan of attack for two whole days.

But then Tuesday, the mail came.

CHAPTER 39

Tuesday, April 30, 1996
???

Lenape Lake
Norman

I stop jogging when I make it to the end of the dam, too overcome by the memory of that otherwise indistinct Tuesday when things turned from bad to worse. I put my hands on my knees and bend my body in half, but that just adds to my aggrieved brain. I start into a canter again, trying to clear my head.

And yet, I make myself think about it. I make myself remember the pretty cream envelope addressed to me in some imitation of calligraphy. Some scratchy, self-taught version of what was meant to look refined and elegant but fell short by a mile. I remember thinking that it must've been a note from one of Monty's nieces, trying to appear all grownup with her fancy writing. I ran my hands over the childlike printing with a smile on my face.

A smile that disappeared once I opened the envelope.

There, in my hands, was an ordinary-looking card embossed with an image of a dove. Upon opening it, I saw the engraved words I'd since committed to memory:

Mark your calanders!
Save the date for
Sadie and Jack's wedding!
July 4, 1996
Details to follow…

Sucker punch.

I read it over and then over again, not believing the words I was seeing in front of my very eyes.

Jack was getting married.

There was no air.

I fell onto the couch, the wind having been knocked right out of me. Suddenly, the pieces of the puzzle were fitting together.

There I'd been broken-hearted, grudgingly beginning to comprehend that the demise of our relationship was due to my failure to admit that I loved him.

But that wasn't all there was to it.

The fact was, he left me behind because there was another girl that he wanted more. I couldn't commit to him, so he went back to someone who would. How was he able to go from telling me he loved me one minute, to making plans to marry someone else in the next?

Holy shit. Was she in the picture the whole time? If he lied about the tour, didn't it stand to reason that he was lying about other things?

I thought about that night Jack and I ran into Sadie at The Osprey. She acted more like a jealous girlfriend than a spurned ex. I remembered how mad Jack was with her as he ushered her out the door, probably reaming her out over her fit of jealousy, consoling her with the knowledge that we were absolutely *not* having sex. It would make sense that he was able to hold off on sleeping with me if he was sleeping with someone else the entire time.

It hurt to know I'd been such a willing idiot, and stupid enough to have believed he cared only for me. I tried telling myself that if Jack was nothing but a two-timing asshole, then my heart couldn't be broken by someone like that. I shouldn't be so sad about losing him. I supposed I should have been grateful that I found out what kind of person he really was after only a few weeks: a lying, cheating, calculating snake.

I looked at the card again as the small shred of dignity I'd been holding onto slipped right through my grasp at that moment. As if I hadn't been humiliated enough. Jack strung me along and then dumped me for someone else. But then just to drive the point home, he sent me this.

Message received, Jack.

I envisioned Sadie at the stationers, pouring over the albums of card designs before settling on that perfect little embossed dove. I pictured her filling out the order form and choosing her font and misspelling the word 'calendar.' I pictured her sitting on the floor of Jack's townhouse, happily addressing the numerous envelopes to alert all their family and friends of the good news.

Then I thought about her having a good laugh as they addressed one just for me.

For all the devastation that little card in my mailbox caused, I was actually glad they sent it. I'd been living in confusion every minute of every day since our separation and at least I finally had some answers. Hell, he even told me flat-out that he needed something more. When I couldn't give it to him, he doubled down on the sure thing.

Jack was apparently an even better actor than I had given him credit for. When he showed up on the Fourth all miserable and beaten, it was just an act. All that moping and solitude. And I had spent the whole day worrying about him! How could I have predicted then that he was simply looking to hedge his bets?

Even through all of this unsettling information, there was the denial. The useless hope that it couldn't have *all* been an act. There were the memories that cracked through my defenses and kept me up at night: The look in Jack's slate-blue eyes when they'd rake over me in laughter or amazement or even simple appreciation. The way he kissed me; his arms wrapped around me so tight I'd find it hard to breathe. The way he whispered 'I love you' that one, beautiful, wretched night.

Maybe he never intended to let things get that far between us. Maybe he planned to break it off with me before sex could even enter the picture. I mean, the night we finally slept together— ahead of schedule, I might add—wasn't *I* the one that set up that whole evening? Why *wouldn't* he have just gone along with it and taken what I was offering? And for him to go so far as to say he loved me? Maybe he just got caught up in the moment enough, at least a little bit, to say it out loud.

* * *

Whenever I find myself making excuses for all the rotten things Jack did, I shake it off and try to remember the facts. Regardless of the feelings he had for me, it doesn't change the reality of the situation: He loved someone else more.

It doesn't help that in the past months, I've heard my song being played a few times on the radio. The New York stations have added "Vampire" into the rotation along with "Backyard," and it seems I can't go more than a few weeks without hearing one or the other. When I do, pathetic martyr that I am, I can't ever bring myself to turn the dial.

Especially with the acoustic version of "Vampire."

My song.

The thing is... I found the hook. It wasn't the thrashing bass line or the kicking backbeat. It was the words, that up until then had been forced to the background of one jamming song. But with Jack singing it alone, stripped down to nothing but his guitar and a microphone, it all became incredibly clear.

It wasn't a song about a vampire screaming to God to take back his curse... It was a song about how he'd been cursed by me. *I* was the vampire who'd led his heart astray.

Between life and death I've lived alone
A darkness that I've always known
To live again, to live, to Liv:
This heart that beats is not my own...

This face that I've been forced to hide
Can't be seen 'cept deep inside
To live again, to live, to Liv:
I promise you, it hasn't died...

250

Losing sleep, up all night
It's finally time to see the light
Vampire's heart
It's not so dark
After all

Told you I'm lyrically challenged.

As much as it always pains me to hear Jack's voice, I make myself suffer through it. Every time I make it to the end of one of his songs without breaking down, I feel marginally strengthened by my efforts. Besides, his music is the only thing I have left of him.

Well, that and a folder of photographs. But I already know I'm not strong enough to look at them yet. I pulled them out one day around Thanksgiving and felt my eyes getting hot almost immediately. And I've been sticking to my decision not to cry anymore come hell or high water.

I haven't cracked yet.

I've settled into a kind of blessed numbness which I've tempered to perfection. This state allows me to smile when I am supposed to and basically look appropriately happy on a daily basis without any suspicions being raised. In all honesty, I am a shell of the person I used to be. The person I was when I was with Jack. But I hide that little fact from everyone fairly well.

Well, everyone except Vix. But thankfully, she doesn't bug me too badly about it. And even though I'm sure she's tipped off the girls as well as my parents, *they* don't bug me about it *at all*.

Shana, on the other hand, barely even noticed.

A few days into my death sentence, I finally forced myself to develop and print the pictures from the Tanners' shoot. Seeing the smiling images of Jack and his family was nothing short of torture. I tried to detach myself from this task by pretending that it was just another assignment. I printed out some 5 x 7s of the best shots and made a contact sheet of the rest.

251

Normally, at that point, the client would come in to choose which photos they wanted. But obviously, there was no way I could face any of them so soon. When I explained my intention to mail the proofs to Mrs. Tanner, Shana told me that it was a completely unacceptable plan.

Gritting my teeth, I asked if Shana wouldn't mind taking over to finish the job, based on my unique circumstances with those particular clients.

Her response? "Oh, just suck it up and do it."

My response was to quit.

In spite of that, a few days later, I went back. The negative things that were happening in my life in regards to the whole Jack Chronicle were out of my hands. The bad blood with my friend wasn't beyond my control, however. I just wouldn't have ever felt right about how I'd left things and wanted to at least clear the air.

Shana looked up from her desk, caught off guard to see me there.

Before I could lose my nerve, I started in. "Shane, first of all, I'd like to apologize for storming out on you like a big baby. I just—"

"You just left me out in the cold with no full-time photographer!" she snapped. "Do you have any idea what I had to offer Manuel to take on all those extra hours?"

Well, I knew she wasn't going to make it easy. "Shane, like I was trying to say, I'm sorry. I wasn't trying to leave you in the lurch. My emotions have just been a little close to the surface these days." She didn't lash out again, so I continued babbling. "Look. You and I both know what working together is doing to our relationship. I don't know what's been happening lately between us and it makes me sad. We used to have so much *fun* together."

I plopped down onto the couch next to her desk. She took off her glasses and turned her chair to face me. After a huge sigh, she said, "Liv, I know you stayed here longer than you ever thought you would. I also know you did it because we're friends and because you knew I needed you. Truth is, I stayed here longer than *I* ever thought I would, too."

"What do you mean? You live for this place."

She shook her head down at the floor. "No. It was a weigh station for me, too. Kind of a way to kill time after college until I could get my *Mrs.* degree."

That actually made me smile. "Seriously?"

"Yep. Thing is, between you and my mother, this little time-killer did better than I ever imagined it could. But I don't see myself doing this forever." She picked up a pencil and jabbed it in my direction. "At least a few more years though, so if you're planning to strike out on your own, stay away from my turf."

That made us both laugh. It felt good to laugh with Shana again. Hell, it felt good to laugh *at anything* again. Strange that it should have been Shana of all people who was responsible.

I felt better about how I left things the second time I walked out of there. Shana sent me on my way with the Tanner portfolio, though. She explained that the pictures were more mine than hers anyway and that I could deal with them any way I chose.

So there I was, starting a new business with my very first clients: The family of my ex-boyfriend.

I did end up mailing the proofs to Mrs. Tanner, however. There was just no way around it. I enclosed a business card of a good photo printing service—one that Shana had always refused to shop any business out to—and figured the Tanners could order their own pictures. The reason would have been self-explanatory. If it wasn't, I didn't feel guilty about letting Jack handle the inevitable questions.

Sicko that I am, I admit that I kept a copy of the proofs for myself, just for those days when I might need a little extra torture. They're stored in a blue folder—along with our photo booth pictures from the boardwalk, my random shots of his gigs, a pressed red rose, and my cassette tape of 'Vampire'—in the "T" section of my filing cabinet.

In preparation for my new freelance photography business, I set up a makeshift office along one wall of the living room in my apartment. Along with the filing cabinet, I've amassed a

253

computer and a fax machine. They sit on top of my old desk which I reclaimed from my parents' garage. I finally broke down and got a mobile phone to use as a work line for *Real Life Portraits* and took out some ads in the local papers.

The business started off slowly, but once word of mouth got around, things picked up. I am currently a proud member of the Women's Small Business Association of Clifton, and just last month, Real Life was the subject of an article in the *Star-Ledger*. That little write-up has been responsible for a flood of new clients. I've been thinking of hiring another photographer to handle the overflow, but I won't have the time to devote to expanding my company until after Tess and Ronnie's wedding.

Four more weeks and then I can start thinking about it.

Only twenty-six more days until I have to face Jack again.

When Tess first told me that she had invited him, I was taken aback. When she told me last week that he'd sent back his response card checked 'yes,' I almost fell over.

She explained that they couldn't *not* invite him, but that she never thought he'd actually come. He was one of Ronnie's oldest friends, regardless of the fact that they hadn't spoken in close to a year.

It seems I'm not the only one who hasn't heard from Jack in the past ten months.

Sometimes during that span, we'd find ourselves down at Monty's for random weekend parties. Even though I knew Monty hadn't spoken to him, I always expected Jack to come walking through the door.

But he went completely MIA after our breakup last summer. The guys had all at one time or another put a few calls into him, but I guess he never bothered to check his messages while he was off bouncing around the country. After a while, they gave up. I suppose they thought he was just pulling another disappearing act on them again. It seemed to be his pattern when he was with Sadie.

And now... Well, now he's planning a wedding with the bitch.

I could just die when I think about it.

I slow to a walk by the second footbridge of the peninsula and peek over the railing to look down at the water below. The lake is almost black, the color of molasses, and moving just as slowly. Spring came late this year and from the looks of it, the water isn't sure whether it's supposed to stay solid or thaw out. The tiny waves lumber in slow-motion and lap against the still-frozen earth at the shoreline.

I blow some air into my hands and do a quick jog in place to stay warm while trying to enjoy the view. Even after only thirty minutes of being out in this weather, I'm wet and cold and ready to go home. The overcast, drizzly day has turned even uglier. It is now officially raining. My car is still a half-mile away, so I decide to make a break for it. Sprinting is supposed to be good, no?

I flip the hood up on my sweatshirt and set off at a respectable pace, trying to drown out my thoughts.

I inhale deeply, feeling the cold air enter my lungs. Thank God I don't smoke anymore; I'd be coughing up one of those lungs by now.

But then, right there on the road I am running on, I see something that makes it even harder to breathe than had I smoked a *carton* of cigarettes before coming out here today.

A few paces up is a brand new home on the lake, under construction, but nearing completion. I appraise the house, reluctantly admitting to myself that it's unbearably charming. I would be more accepting of the pleasant sight if it weren't for one, tiny, little detail:

A beautiful house, a perfect location...

...and the white and gold sign out front which reads: *"Yet another Home by Jackson Tanner."*

255

CHAPTER 40

Sunday, May 26, 1996
12:45 PM

Bridal Room at The Breakers
Spring Lake

"Crap."

My nerves are already at the breaking point and now apparently, so is my shoe. My refusal to stop applying makeup and use the bathroom—for the *millionth* time this morning—had me dancing around on my feet in front of the mirror. One wrong step and the damn heel has broken off of my lavender, store-dyed stiletto. Serves me right for buying cheap shoes.

As if this day isn't stressful enough already.

I've been suffering from schizophrenic emotions in regards to Tess and Ron's wedding. Mostly, I'm just excited for my friends. They're an amazing couple and I couldn't be happier for them.

But a huge, selfish part of me is in dread over the thought of having to face Jack again.

I'm not too proud of myself about that.

So, because of my stress over seeing Jack, I'm dealing with my guilt over being a self-centered friend *on top* of some general bridesmaid-anxiety.

I'm keeping those thoughts to myself, however. Externally, I am The World's Greatest Bridesmaid today. I woke up at the crack to pick up bagels for our bridal suite brunch. I spent two hours supervising Tess's stylist, making sure every hair on my friend's head was curled to perfection before I even got my own bod into the shower. I was the one who ran out to the store when we realized we didn't bring cups for our mimosas. Basically, I've been hovering over Tess and making sure the day goes as smoothly as possible. For her, at least. And actually, as long as I concentrate my focus on my friend, I'll be distracted from the terrifying prospect of being in the same room with Jack Tanner later.

It doesn't help that it's the anniversary of the day we met, one year ago today. Tess and Ron picked this date because it's kind of their anniversary, too. It was exactly one year ago that Ron told her he loved her for the first time. Twenty hours later, Ron was with me at The Tradewinds the first time I laid eyes on Jack.

They have also methodically chosen this reception hall in Spring Lake because it's right down the street from where they first met, at Monty's house.

They could have done worse for themselves.

The Breakers is a charming, oversized beach cottage with all the amenities of a fancy reception hall.

The bridal suite is basically an entire apartment located upstairs from the main ballroom. We've been here all morning getting ready for the wedding. The ceremony is going to take place across the street, right on the beach.

Tess picked this place specifically to have oceanside nuptials and I'd hate to see the festivities get relegated to the indoors due to inclement weather.

I thought it was a pretty bold decision to plan an outdoor ceremony during the month of May in New Jersey, what with the climate being so unpredictable and all. Although, Tess and Ron have thus far lucked out. It's a cloudy day, but not raining, and it looks as though the sun will win the battle by the afternoon. We've all been keeping our fingers crossed.

The girls are all in the back bedroom conducting some sort of witchcrafty, sun-inducing rite at this very moment. Once they broke out the cinnamon incense, I had to get out of there. They know I can't stand the smell of that stuff. So, I set up shop in the living area of the suite, keeping company with Tess's dad who hasn't sat still for more than a thirty second stretch all morning.

He sees me falter and leaps off of the leather club chair to come to my rescue.

"Livia, give me that shoe right now. Claude! CLAUDE!"

Tess's wedding coordinator practically drops the flower arrangement he's carrying down the hallway and rushes into the

257

bridal room to see what service he can render unto Louis Anthony "Big L.A." Valletti.

"Yes, Big Lavalletti?"

Big L.A. practically spits in Claude's face, "For the last time, it's either 'Big L.A.' *or* Mister Va-LET-tee. Lord knows I'm paying you people enough money for this wedding. The least you could do is get my name right."

Poor Claude glances at me and I give him an apologetic shrug. Mr. Valletti is loud and boastful, but he's not normally rude. In fact, he's probably one of the most sane and composed people I've ever met. But I guess even the best of us is feeling the pre-wedding jitters right now. Can't say that I blame him. After all, his daughter is getting married in two hours.

Two hours.

I still have two more hours of peace.

"Yes, sir. Yes, Monsieur Valletti. My apologies. It will not happen again. What can I do for you, sir?"

Mr. Valletti holds my shoe with its dangling heel out to the harried wedding coordinator. "See if there's anyone who can do anything about this." He must realize that even though he's stressed, it's no excuse to act like a jerk because he adds, "Please."

Claude takes my shoe and scurries off to places unknown, while I decide to take that bathroom break after all.

CHAPTER 41

Sunday, May 26, 1996
1:05 PM

Bridal Room at The Breakers
Spring Lake

My bag is near the bedroom door, which is only opened a sliver. While I'm rifling around, trying to find my other shoes, I can hear the energy coming from the rest of the bridal party as they perform their voodoo chanting.

I hear Tess light up a ciggie. "Hey guess what?"

Vix, Sam, and Isla stop their mantra. "What?"

Peeking through the crack in the door, I can see Tess lounged out on the king-size bed, arranging her crinoline underskirt around her legs. She tips her head back and blows out a perfect smoke ring before answering, "I'm getting married today!"

"You sure are, sister."

Tess lets out with a "*Whoohoo!*" and then asks, "Hey, Sammy, hand me my glass, will ya?"

Sam dutifully fetches her mimosa as Tess sits up and adjusts her strapless bra. "Thanks, BM."

I can hear the exasperation in Vix's voice as she says, "Tess, for godsakes, will you *pleeease* stop referring to us as poop."

That makes me chuckle to myself. I dig underneath my pile of clothes and come up with one of my slip-on sandals. Great. Now where the hell is the other one?

I'm still scrounging around in my bag as I hear Vix continue, "If I knew agreeing to be your bridesmaid was going to be this degrading, I would have told you to shove that unity candle right up your—"

"Okay! Jeez. Got it," Tess cuts in. "Don't be so uppity, girlfriend. No more BM references, okay?"

"Thank you."

"Even though you *are* my *NUMBER TWO.*"

I can *hear* Vix gritting her teeth as Tess giggles and resumes blowing her smoke rings. "Speaking of, where did Number Two Chadwick Sister disappear to?"

I stop digging around in my bag and go completely still. I haven't necessarily been trying to hide all this time, but I guess they have no idea I'm anywhere within earshot. Now that my name has been brought up, however, I find myself unabashedly eavesdropping.

Isla stops applying her mascara to answer, "She couldn't take the incense and went out to the living room to put on her makeup. She said to let her know if you needed anything. Do you? Should I go get her?"

Tess leaps off the bed and starts to adjust her undergarments in front of the mirror, and I flatten myself against the wall so I won't be seen. "Nope. Let her be." Then she asks Vix, "How's she been all week?"

Vix must be peeking over to make sure the door is still closed, because there's a distinct pause before she lets out with, "Oh, you know. A nervous wreck."

"Shit."

"I know. She's been on a cleaning rampage. The apartment has never looked better. And she's been absent-minded as hell, too. Yesterday, she spent a good hour packing a bag for this weekend. Good thing I checked it before we got down here, because she would have had to wear her bathing suit to your rehearsal dinner."

"She spent an hour packing and forgot clothes?"

"No... She packed clothes. But no underwear. And no toothbrush."

"You're kidding."

"Wish I were. Oh- and no shoes. None at all. She actually walked out to the car barefoot which is what made me check her bag."

"Oh my God."

Sam cuts in. "It's been a year, already. She can't still be thinking about Him, can she?"

260

No one ever says Jack's name out loud in front of me, and I appreciate the effort they all make. Even though I'm not in the room right now, avoiding the J word has become old habit.

"I don't think she sits around all day thinking about him," Vix replies. "It's just knowing she's going to *see* him today that's got her rattled. He destroyed her when he left, you all saw that. Now to have to face him... knowing he's going to be married..."

I've heard quite enough. Aside from the fact that their commentary is only serving to make me feel worse, I'm not too proud of the fact that I've been spying on their conversation. The jig is up.

I cough as I enter the room, trying to give them all a one second advance notice of my arrival. When four sets of wide, overly-innocent eyes greet me, I call them out. "Okay. What's going on?"

They all avert their guilty faces, but Tess fesses up. "Sorry. We were talking about you."

"I'm sure I can guess why."

Tess flops backwards on the bed, and as we all protest that she's going to ruin her hair, she lets out with, "I can't believe I let Ron talk me into inviting him! Who would have thought that swine would have actually said 'yes'? And he's bringing *her* with him!"

The girls stop dead, but I almost fall over. Tess sits bolt upright and bites her lip.

Sam is the first to speak. "What do you mean 'he's bringing her with him'? Not the girlfriend!"

Tess looks guilty as she snubs out her cigarette. "Okay, look. I didn't say anything about it because I thought it was bad enough that he was going to be here today at all." She aims a guilty look at me, then acknowledges Vix's gaping jaw. "Vix, you'd better shut that trap before the flies move in."

I can't do anything but stand here and shake my head, trying to rattle her words into some sort of sense. "I can't believe you didn't tell me about this!"

"I know, I know. It's just that you were so upset when I even mentioned that he was coming, I couldn't tell you the worst of it.

261

But he clearly marked down 'plus one' next to his name on the response card. I couldn't believe it either. The nerve, right? I meant to say something, but..." Tess trails off as we all try to absorb the newest bit of drama in an already complicated soap opera.

Vix slumps down onto the bed as she asks me, "You're going to freak out right now, aren't you."

I want to curl up into a ball and die. As if it wasn't bad enough having to face Jack today as it was, now I have to steel myself to face his fiancée, too?

I take a look at Tess who's sitting on the edge of the bed, tensely wringing her hands.

For crying out loud, it's the girl's wedding day.

With a deep breath, I grab her hands and say, "Look, Tess, it's ridiculous for you to spend your wedding day worrying about me, so let's just pretend you didn't say anything, okay? Truth is, I'll be fine. All I want is for your big day to go perfectly and as long as you're happy, I'll be happy, too. Can we please all just focus on the more important story playing out today?"

I meant what I said about the importance of Tess's big day. I was lying when I said I'd be fine, though. I must have put on a convincing performance, however, because Tess shakes off the sour puss and snaps immediately back into Bride Mode. "You're right. I'm getting married today! Come, maids. Hold my skirt so I can pee."

As the girls head into the bathroom, I snuff out the incense before bringing up the rear. When I open the door, Vix, Isla, and Sam are all in there, laughing while trying to hold Tess's crinoline out of the toilet. She's practically buried within her underskirt. Her body is contorted in such an awkward stance and she's surrounded by such an ocean of tulle that I can't help but laugh, too.

"Oh, Jesus. Why the hell didn't I do this before putting this stupid thing on? How are we gonna handle this when I'm wearing my *gown*?"

"I don't know," I shoot back. "But you'd better hurry it along, sister. Some of us are waiting to use the bathroom, too."

Tess looks up and catches my eye. "Don't tell me you need to go *again*."

I thought I'd been holding up pretty well all morning. My only tell was the frequent trek to the bathroom. Guess she noticed.

"Yeah. But obviously, I'll have to hold it until you're done. Are you even in there or are the girls just holding a hundred yards of tulle over the toilet? All I see is a mountain of white."

Vix snips, "Ballsy, no? Where does this slut get off wearing white?"

Tess's arm emerges from the fluffy mass in an attempt to backhand Vix. She misses. After she gets situated near drier land, I help her smooth the garment back into place. She cranes her neck to look down at my feet.

"Hate to break it to you, girlfriend, but you're wearing two different shoes."

I had only found the one before I was forced to stop my search and terminate my eavesdropping. "I am aware of that, thank you. My heel broke clean off, can you believe that? Your dad sent Claude to go fix it. I didn't want to get a run in my stockings, so I put this one on."

Tess moves over to the huge wall mirror, vying for space with her bridesmaids. "Is Big L.A. still out there? How's he holding up?"

I take the opportunity to utilize the vacant throne. "Seems okay, I guess. Definitely stressing."

"Great. That's all I need. Do you know he's referred to me as his 'little girl' no less than seven hundred times today? The poor sap."

"Aw, don't be too hard on him. His 'little girl' is getting married today. Even *my* father has been emotional about it."

"Really?"

"Oh yeah. He can't believe that 'Theresa's all grown up.' He keeps getting misty-eyed whenever we talk about the wedding, right, Vix? My mother said she was going to make sure to pack extra Kleenex in her purse for the old man because she's sure he's gonna lose it during the ceremony." I nudge my way to the sink, saying, "So make it good when you say your vows. Lots of emotion. Don't leave a dry eye in the crowd."

"Done."

I head into the bedroom and call over my shoulder, "Speaking of the wedding, we'd better hurry up and finish getting ready. Wanna put your dress on?" I start to unwrap Tess's gown from its plastic bag when there's a knock on the bedroom door.

Tess lets out with a sigh. "Liv, can you go distract my dad for a few minutes? Tell him I'll be out ASAP, just as soon as I'm dressed and can touch up my hair."

I tell her I have it covered and slip out the door. Mr. Valletti hands me my shoe.

"Thanks, Mr. V!"

"Oh, don't go thanking me. Claude is the one with the power tools."

I move into the living room and peek out the suite's door. Tess's wedding coordinator is in the hallway, looking very proud of himself. I inspect the two flathead screws at the bottom of my insole and direct my approval to Claude. "Wow. Good work, MacGyver. Jeez. Like you both don't have enough other things to do today."

"It was my pleasure, Mademoiselle."

I thank him again and he scurries off to attend to more pressing wedding matters.

Big L.A. assures me that he was grateful for the diversion. "I don't know if you've noticed, but my nerves..." He holds out his hand and exaggerates a shake. He assumes his post again, sitting in the leather club chair while I slide the repaired shoe back onto my foot and attempt to finish my makeup.

"I just can't believe my little girl is getting married."

"Yep. She sure is. To a *great* guy."

I've always thought Ron was a great guy, but over the past months he's proven that he'll be a great husband now, too.

Tess's husband. Wow, that sounds weird.

Big L.A. interrupts my thought. "The photographer wants to get started. That guy you recommended better be good. He sure charges enough. Is Theresa ready yet?"

Why is it that the people with the most money are always the ones to complain about the cost of everything?

"Um... I think so. Let me go check."

I head into the bedroom to find Vix helping Tess arrange her veil. She's standing in front of a large wall mirror and catches my reflection as I walk in. When she turns around I am blown away at the sight of my best friend, looking more beautiful than I have ever seen her, which is saying a lot.

Tess hadn't let any of us see her dress until today. She only let us peek at it as it hung in the suite this morning. From what I could make out, it looked lovely on the hangar, but on Tess? It is breathtakingly stunning.

I try to take it all in, the sight of her standing there like a page torn out of Vogue Bride. The gown has layers of cream fabric and tulle which drapes artfully from under the bustier bodice and elegantly to the floor. Her golden hair has been pulled off of her forehead with a crystal headpiece and the thick, round curls spill over her shoulders like a china doll's. The accompaning veil is whisper-thin and flowing down her back, almost to her knees.

A more beautiful bride there never was.

I put my hand to my heart. "Oh, Tess. You put Wedding Barbie to shame. You look *so gorgeous!*"

I can feel the tears welling in my eyes and I catch Vix swiping at her cheek. Who knew we'd turn into such cornballs? But I allow the both of us a little sentimental sniveling. *Our friend is getting married today.*

Tess says, a little worriedly, "I'm going for 'princess.' Do you think this is princess enough?"

Vix replies, "Tess, honey, I'd say you've skipped right past 'princess' and are headed for '*queen*'."

We all nod in agreement.

"Okay, good. Thanks." She fans herself with her hand. "I'm all sweaty already. It's hot in here, right?"

Sam offers, "It's just your nerves. There's a nice breeze blowing on the beach. You'll be fine once we get out there."

Tess gives us all a round of high-fives. "Alright, BMs. Let's do this!"

265

CHAPTER 42

Sunday, May 26, 1996
3:26 PM

The Beach
Spring Lake

Sam was right about the breeze. I'm hoping it's not windy enough to mess up my hair, but the other girls seem to be holding up well, so I take that as a good sign.

Despite the draft, my hands are clammy and I am mentally trying to keep my body from breaking out into a full-on, allover cold sweat as the string quartet breaks into "Canon in D."

Zero-hour.

I peek over Vix's head to watch Isla and Ron's cousin start the procession. Then Sam and another cousin. Then Vix and Tommy. I throw a nervous smile over my shoulder and wish Tess good luck before I take Ron's brother's arm and head down the aisle.

I'm worried about tripping on the white aisle runner, wondering how in the world my heels aren't going to sink into the sand on my route. But, thankfully, it turns out that there's some sort of platform under the runner and now all I have to concern myself with is not snagging my shoe on the fabric or landing a foot between the seams of the plywood pieces.

That and not breaking my heel again.

Or passing out from my nerves.

Or throwing up.

Other than all that, I'm fine.

I plaster a convincing smile on my face and hold onto Kevin's arm for dear life.

I don't have the courage to look at the crowd on my right, even though I know Monty and Walter are sitting on the Groom's side. I can't chance seeing Jack right at the moment.

Instead, I smile brightly and cast my eyes over the guests seated on my left, recognizing and acknowledging some of Tess's friends and relatives. My parents are seated in the third row and I can see the water works already underway on my father's face. I give a little wave and then focus my eyes on a beaming Ronnie, standing on top of the world.

I separate from Kevin and take my place in the lineup.

Phew. Made it.

The processional music winds down and there's a silent pause. Despite Tess's threat to have the quartet play "Another One Bites the Dust," they start in with "Here Comes the Bride," and the entire crowd stands at attention to do a one-eighty toward Tess and her father.

If I'm going to look for Jack, now is the time to do it. I quickly scan the crowd and spot him instantly.

He's the only one facing front.

Fuuuck!

My traitorous heart slams into my stomach as I immediately avert my eyes and proceed to concentrate on Tess coming down the aisle like a beauty queen... Ron's elated expression... every single one of the priest's words... the beautiful and tear-inducing exchange of vows... the thunderous applause from the audience... Kevin's arm... the white runner... crossing the street. I don't exhale until we reach the temporary haven of the reception hall.

I find a few seconds to breathe while I congratulate my newlywed friends and then get into position with the rest of the bridal party for the receiving line.

Tess's cousins. Ron's sister-in-law. Ron's friends. Tess's crazy Aunt Shirley. Big L.A.'s business associates. Vix's boyfriend, Chris. Monty and Walter. My parents.

I shake a million hands in introduction, grateful that the air conditioning is on, keeping my palms dry. I look back to check on the line and can see that it's almost through.

Tess's wheelchair-bound grandmother is holding things up as she chats with Isla. "Congratulations, dear. Are you the bride?"

Isla answers, "No, ma'am. I'm the bride's friend."

267

Tess's Aunt Paula leans down to explain that the bride is her granddaughter, Theresa, over there in the big white dress.

That's when I see Jack coming through the double doors.

Late as usual.

I thought I'd braced myself to speak to him, but Tess leans over and notes, *"You look pale as a ghost."* As Ron bends down to kiss her Grandma Carol, she addresses the entire bridal party. "We're pretty much done here, guys. Go on ahead. We'll meet you inside."

Temporary stay of execution.

I quickly whisper to Tess, *"Thank you, Wedding Barbie."*

"No problem, BM."

The girls and I shuffle straight into the Ladies' Room to touch up and use the facilities. Then we haul ass back outside for pictures. Then upstairs to the main level to join the cocktail hour already in progress on the wraparound deck.

"Here, eat this," Vix says as she shoves a mini quiche in my direction. "You didn't even touch the bagels in the bridal suite this morning. You should have had something then. You looked about ready to pass out during the ceremony."

"My stomach was in knots. I couldn't even think about eating. But I'm okay now."

Yeah right.

Vix gives me that look of hers that lets me know I'm not fooling her. She procures another miniature food item from a passing waiter and hands it to me. "Eat this, too. Just in case."

I chew and chew whatever flaky puffed thing Vix has just offered, only to have the entire mouthful wad into a collective mass in the back of my throat as I swallow. I pass the clump and manage through a cough, "I could use a drink."

"Yes, you could. Be right back."

Vix jaunts off to the bar as I try to shake off my anxiety. She comes back with two glasses of champagne and hands one to me.

I take a big sip and then another. And then I notice my hand is shaking. "Did you see Him?"

Vix lets out with a huff. "Sure did. Staring you down the whole ceremony. I couldn't believe he had the nerve to just stand there like a lost puppy and—Hey, you okay?"

What?

No. Can't be. She's obviously not on my same page. "Wait. Who are you talking about?"

Vix scans the porch and lowers her voice to a whisper. "*Jack*, stupid."

I must be looking at her like she's bonkers, because she blinks at me, surprised. "Didn't *you* see him? He was right behind Monty and Wal—"

"Yes, I saw him. But I spent the entire ceremony trying not to look at him." I bite my lip and look imploringly at my sister. "Was he really staring? At *me*? Are you sure it wasn't at Tess and Ron?"

Vix's eyes turn down as her lips purse together. Is that pity? Shit, I guess I must sound pathetic.

She indulges me anyway. "Yeah, Liv. He was really staring at you. I almost felt bad for the poor guy. Almost. Not that it matters, though, right?"

"Right. Not that it matters," I hear myself repeat.

"The worst is over! You saw him for the first time in a *year* and you didn't fall to pieces. This is the easy part where you get to concentrate on just having fun."

Vix is right. I can easily avoid Jack all night just by having a blast at my best friend's wedding. There's going to be dancing and eating and socializing... There will be a million diversions allowing me plenty of distance from Jack Tanner this evening.

I'm covered. Good to go. I'm finally looking forward to this wedding again for the first time in five whole weeks.

I smile my first genuine smile all day as I polish off my glass of champagne. "You're right. Let's go turn this mother out."

"You are such a nerd sometimes."

CHAPTER 43

Sunday, May 26, 1996
8:00? 9:00? Whatever.

Reception Hall at The Breakers
Spring Lake

"Hey Liv! Wanna reenact our stage show?"

The band is playing "I love Rock and Roll" at Vix's request, and Tess has just bolted across the room to grab my hands and twirl me around the dance floor.

"Not a chance in Hell, Mrs. Somers."

"Ack! *Mrs. Somers.* Doesn't that sound crazy?"

Yes. But it also sounds right.

"Livi Girl, are you having fun?"

I note the hesitant catch in her voice and am humbled that my friend can find the time to worry about me on her wedding day. There's a reason Tess and I have stayed so close all these years. It's the same reason that snapped me out of my anxiety attack over being in the same room with Jack: We both put each other's feelings ahead of our own. I haven't seen much of him tonight anyway and I haven't even seen Sadie at all. That's just fine with me.

"I'm having a *great* time. Look at your wedding! Doesn't everything look beautiful?"

Ronnie joins our dance party just then and wraps his arms around his wife's waist. "Some things more than others," he says, as Tess stares all googly-eyed back at him.

I decide The Happy Couple doesn't need a third wheel. "I'm going to the bar. Want anything?"

Tess shakes her head 'no' and Ronnie puts in an order for a beer.

I fan myself on my way out of the room. I've been dancing since we got in here and the sweatiness is only catching up with

270

me now that I stopped. I do a quick spot-check as I pass the wall mirror and decide that no one else would guess that I am melting. I turn toward the bar three paces away... just as Jack is turning from it.

Of course.

As much as I would like to, I can't very well run out of the room. So I hold my ground and paste a polite smile on my face. He's holding two glasses in his hands, which he almost drops upon the sight of me. "Livia! Hi."

"Hi Jack."

He's still gorgeous, dammit. Not even a nasty zit on that chiseled face where I can focus some disillusionment. He's dressed in black from neck to toe, coming across disturbingly like a hawk readying to swoop in for the kill.

There's an awkward pause where he looks as though he's not sure if he should kiss me hello, give a hug, or shake hands. In light of the drinks he's holding, he opts to start in for a kiss, then decides against it. Thank God.

The bartender breaks the moment. "What can I get for you?"

"Oh. I'll have a white wine and a Sam Adams, please."

There's the smirk.

"Double fisting tonight?" he asks.

I'm amazed that I'm able to casually lean against the bar and reply, "The beer isn't for me." I nod in the direction of his hands. "You?"

"Relegated to Waterboy myself, I'm ashamed to say."

A drink for the fiancée, naturally.

I resentfully take notice that he looks great in his suit; I've never seen him in one before. He looks a little thinner than I remember, though, a little tired, too. I guess the nightmare of being with Sadie makes for some sleepless nights.

"Freddie's been throwing these back all night."

What did he just say?

"Wait, what? Freddie? Freddie's here?"

Jack looks at me, puzzled. "Yeah... Didn't you see him yet?" I shake my head 'no' as he adds, "He shaved his head, so maybe you didn't recognize him. He's a pretty cheap date, I'll give him that much. What with the open bar and all."

We both chuckle, but my mind is positively racing. At least I won't have to worry anymore about bumping into Sadie tonight. I wonder why she's not here, but think maybe it's just too hard to get out of the house for a nuptial celebration while in the final weeks of planning her *own* wedding.

I retrieve my drinks from the bar and Jack walks with me the few steps to the reception room, where we turn to part ways.

"Hey listen, Livia?"

I turn back. "Yeah?"

"Save me a dance later?"

Like hell I will!

It's easier just to blow off the request. "Yeah, sure. Guess I'll see you later."

I deliver Ron's beer to him and then head right back out of the room and up to the bridal suite... where I bawl my eyes out for a good ten minutes.

Seeing Jack after all this time... it feels like my heart is breaking all over again.

I finally give a curse to my weakness, compose myself, fix my makeup and hair, and head back down to the party. I grab Ron's brother Kevin and drag him out onto the dance floor for two songs. Vix lets me borrow Chris for a third, then I rip it up with the girls before sitting down for dinner. Immediately following our meal, I dance with Walter, my dad, and then Tommy, in that order. Then I get a glass of wine and down it quickly while talking to Tess's crazy Aunt Shirley. Monty comes to save me and leads me out onto the dance floor.

And that's when Jack taps Monty on the shoulder.

"Mind if I cut in?"

I could kill Monty as he *smiles* and hands me off to the enemy. "She's all yours, er, well, *used* to be. You know, if you weren't such a horse's ass all those months ago."

I look at Monty wide-eyed. I am speechless. I am without speech.

Jack slides into place and starts moving me around the dance floor. With his arm around my waist and my hand in his, I'm instantly reminded of the last time we danced together. It feels like a million years has passed since that night in the crusty kitchen of the beach house. The night we made love. The night he told me he lov—

"This is familiar."

Is he flirting with me?

I look up at the sound of Jack's voice. I'm torn between my opposing desires to either run out of the room or stay and bash his face in. Does he actually think enough time has gone by that he can joke about that night?

He's looking down at me with that damned gleaming white smile, and instead of envisioning flicking out each and every one of his perfect teeth with a ball-peen hammer, I decide to play it cool.

Living well is the best revenge, right? Well, heck, then I'm living well. I'm going to let him see just exactly what he gave up. Just exactly what kind of girl he played and then kicked to the curb.

I'm a good person. Too good for him. Good enough to muster up a smile on my mug while out here on this dance floor with the spawn of Satan so as not to cause a scene during my friends' wedding. I am an up-and-coming photographer with my own successful business, dammit. I've been written up in newspapers and asked out on dates by hot models. Well, okay... *one* model— and I turned him down—but he *was* incredibly hot.

Jack, on the other hand, is a liar and a user and stuck at home with that brat for a wife for the next hundred years. No wonder he brought Freddie out tonight instead; it's probably the first chance he's had to escape.

Yeah, nice life, pal.

I can't wait for the song to end, but in the interim, I'm forced to display a pleasant composure which I do not feel in the least.

My cheeks actually ache from the fake smile on my face, but I assume his genial tone. "Tess and Ron lucked out with the weather today, huh?"

"Holy shit! You hate me!"

I guess my 'genial' ruse fell short of its mark and landed on 'venomous.'

I miss a step. "Hate? That's a little strong, don't you think?" *But true.*

Jack looks up at the ceiling and lets out a huge breath before his eyes land back on mine. "I was really looking forward to seeing you today but I guess I didn't count on you still being so angry with me. I was kind of hoping we'd be able to put all that bad stuff in the past and enjoy ourselves tonight."

Enjoy ourselves tonight? Is he out of his mind?

Yeah, sure, Jack. We're just a couple of buddies out here sharing a dance while reminiscing about the good ol' times. Let's just put all that "bad stuff" out of our minds and pretend that you didn't lie when you fucked me over like the snake that you are.

I, for one, am not going to let him forget it.

"How's the wedding planning going?"

Jack's expression turns confused. "Uh... great. Really great. All set for August tenth." His eyes spark as he adds, "You know about it?"

Know about it?! KNOW about it? My head starts to spin and I feel like I'm going to puke. How dare he stand here flirting with me while casually referring to his fucking wedding.

"Well, I didn't know the date had changed..." My eyelids involuntarily turn into slits. "I only received the *engagement* announcement."

"Katrina sent you an engagement announcement?"

I stop dancing. "Who's Katrina?"

Jack blinks twice and looks at me like I have a fork in my forehead. "Freddie's fiancée." He pulls me to him again and we resume dancing. "Isn't that what we're talking about here?"

I feel dizzy. "No. I was talking about... *your* wedding. With Sadie."

"*Sadie?* What the fuck are you talking about?"

"Are you kidding me right now?"

274

"Are *you*?" The song has ended, but Jack hasn't removed his arm from around my waist. "Livia, I don't know where this is coming from, but I think you've been misinformed."

Who does this guy think he is? Leaves his fiancée at home to try and 'enjoy his evening' with *me* tonight? Like she can just be swept under the rug for a few hours? Now I'm fuming.

"I got *the announcement* that you sent months ago, Jack. Did you forget about that? A few days after you *lied* about having to leave for the tour "effective immediately" and broke up with me? Remember *that*?"

I'm trying to keep my voice down so as not to turn any heads in the direction of our little drama. Jack is stunned into silence, so I can't help myself from rambling on with my barely leashed tirade. "I guess you were right when you said I hated you, because I do, Jack. I *hate* you. I hate everything about you from the way you're disrespecting your fiancée right now to the vile way you turned me into *the other woman* without my knowledge. At least you *tried* to stay faithful to her, I'll grant you that. No wonder you made that bet."

"Arrangement!"

"Whatever!" I push a stray curl off of my cheek and notice my parents watching us from the edge of the dance floor. I turn back toward him, lower my voice, and drop the bomb. "I don't know what you're trying to do here, but I'm *not* falling for it again."

At that, I turn on my heel and storm off.

CHAPTER 44

Sunday, May 26, 1996
Who the fuck knows what time it is? I need to get drunk.

My Brain
Confusion

I only get a few steps away when I feel the vice of Jack's hand around my wrist, pulling me out of the room. He scans the lobby bar quickly and changes course, jerking me into the more private parlor off the main lounge.

He points his free hand in the direction of the sofa. "Sit."

I wrench my hand free of his grasp and cross my arms.

Jack looks about ready to blow his top. He hisses through his teeth as he grabs me by my shoulders, backing me against the couch until my knees buckle and my ass hits the cushion. 'Sit!" he commands again, like I'm his disobedient dog.

I've never seen him like this before. His face is red, his teeth are clenched, and his steely eyes are wild with anger. He is simply furious. If I weren't frozen in my seat with fear, I would make a hasty exit out of the room immediately. But the look on his face doesn't even dare me to consider it.

He slams the door shut and just... *unleashes* on me. "Apparently, there's a few things we need to get straight here, Livia!"

His hand flings up between us as he loudly counts off the talking points on his fingers.

"*ONE*: I never cheated on you *or* my ex-girlfriend! She and I broke up *months* before you and I ever started dating. She called a few times and even went out of her way to "bump" into me on occasion, treating me like the guy I was when she and I first met, fucking anything that moved. But I wasn't that guy anymore. Everything about that life ended the night I met *you*. So, no, I'm not engaged, for chrissakes.

276

"TWO: I didn't 'lie' about leaving for the tour. When I went for that meeting with Shug, nothing was put down in writing. We showed up ready to hit the road the next day, and *that's* when we realized Mayhem's contract was *crap*. By the time we got everything hashed out, it was weeks before we got on that bus. I didn't come back to you during that time because…

"THREE: Nothing had changed! I kept waiting for you to call, to tell me you realized how you felt about me. But you didn't do it!"

He stops pacing and swipes his hand through his hair, slowly calming down and getting his breathing under control. He sees my crossed arms and the look of incredulity I'm wearing and sits down next to me on the sofa.

It's as if his little tantrum has taken the air right out of him as I watch him slump into his seat.

He puts his elbows on his knees and hangs his head in a defeated posture before saying softly, "I don't know if you even want to hear any of this. All I can do is ask that you let me explain."

He looks up at me with beautiful, wounded gray eyes.

Those beautiful, lying gray eyes.

I uncross my arms and wave a prodding hand toward him. "Oh, please continue. I'm finding this fascinating."

He drops his head again. "Livia, I don't want to fight with you right now. Not when I've been looking forward to seeing you for weeks. I didn't picture tonight going down like this. I thought—"
He reaches out to take my hand but thinks better of it before turning his head back toward me. "I thought that when I didn't see you here with that motorcycle guy, that maybe you and I... I don't know. I don't know what I thought."

Motorcycle guy? "Mitch? My ex-boyfriend? Is that who you're talking about?"

"So he's your 'ex' now, is he?"

I have no idea what Mitch has to do with anything. "Uh, yeah. He's been my 'ex' for about a year now. Why would you think that I would be here with him? I haven't even *thought* about him for like—"

"Monty told me you were back with him."

What the hell? "When did he tell you that?"

"Months ago. I called him to see how you were and he told me to forget about you and leave you alone because you were happily back with Mitch."

Monty. Monty of all people knew what a mess I was after Jack broke up with me. So much so that I couldn't ever bring myself to discuss it. I mean, why should I? They got save-the-date cards of their own, didn't they? I was sure they were quite able to draw their own conclusions regarding the circumstances surrounding our breakup.

By coming up with a cover story about my "happiness," Monty was obviously trying to protect me from getting hurt again; a misdirected deed from a very good friend. I can't believe he never told me. But then, I guess that was the point.

I was wrecked over those days but I'd been able to push all the sordid little details to the back of my mind. Now here was Jack, bringing them all back to the surface. "And what the hell gave you the impression I was engaged to Sadie?"

His tone is believable enough, but I'm sure he's just trying to save face about doing something so cruel as sending that vile little card.

"*You* told me. When you guys sent me that announcement card back in July."

"I never sent any announcement card."

"Uh, yeah you did." I try to find something in his features to confirm an untruth in his denial. I can't. "Well, maybe Sadie sent the card and you just didn't know about it. But trust me, I received a card."

"We are *not* engaged."

I almost bark out a bitter *Ha!* but I manage to keep my mouth shut and let him continue.

"That night at The Osprey? When I dragged her out of the bar? Yeah. That was the last time I ever saw her. She was hanging all over me, telling me she wanted to get back together." He sits up straighter on the couch, and this time, he does grab my hand. I try to pull it away, but he clasps me firmer and looks right into my eyes. "I told her there was no chance for that because I was already in love with *you*. She stomped off to her car, and I haven't seen her since."

Bullshit. Maybe they aren't together anymore, but he can't sit here and pretend like it never happened. "Then why did we break up? You still can't even be honest with me about why you did it. You made me think it was all because of me. Because I wasn't able to tell you something you *knew* I wouldn't be able to say. It's like you were intentionally setting me up to fail you."

"I know. I fucked up. I shouldn't have backed you into a corner like that."

"But you did it!"

"Because I was insane over you! Don't you get it? I was crazy about you from the first moment we met. I've never felt that way about *anyone*. Ever. Is it really so fucking awful that I wanted you to love me back?"

I wish I could believe him. I really do. It would be so much easier on my pride to suppose that Jack truly wasn't the monster I thought him to be. It would take the dejection off my heart to trust that he really did love me all those months ago. It could be so simple to believe him right now...

But I just can't.

I stand slowly and have trouble meeting his eyes. "I'm sorry, Jack. But too much time has gone by, too many things have happened between us for me to possibly believe you, to believe-"

He practically leaps off the couch. "You think I'm *lying* to you?"

The disgust in his eyes as he looks at me is almost too much to bear. Silly me, I thought I was past the point where he could have any pull on my sympathies anymore. But seeing his pained expression puts just the smallest, hairline-sized fracture into my heart.

Nobody could fake that look. Not even Jack Tanner. Hell, not even Jack *Nicholson*.

The observation keeps me silent. I am mute.

"I've shut my friends out for close to a year in order to let *you* have a life with them. I came here to face them—knowing they

279

thought I was a piece of shit for disappearing the way I did—in the hopes of seeing you tonight. And yet you can stand here, practically calling me a liar right to my face! You've been completely ignoring me all night and I've stuck around, enduring it, hoping to find a few minutes to talk to you. But I guess there's nothing left to talk about being that you've already decided to dismiss every word I say as a lie."

He walks over to the door and opens it, apparently intent on leaving me standing here with my mouth gaping open.

He takes one step out but then stops himself and turns back around. "No. You know what? I'm not leaving this room until you hear what I came here to tell you."

His eyes are tired and his shoulders are slumped, but his jaw is set with determination.

"Livia... it's not easy for me to stand here spilling my soul out to you, but there's something about this entire conversation that you're not hearing me say."

Shoving his hands into his side pockets, he leans against the door frame. "The thing is, I'm not only trying to make you understand that I loved you last year, but I'm trying to make it damn clear that I *still* love you now and I *have* loved you for every day that's passed in between."

He looks at me for a hesitant pause before he steps closer, and I am so frozen by what he's said and what he's doing that I don't think to move away.

His voice shakes as he goes on, "I've spent every day while we were apart trying to get over you." Inches from my body, he continues in the same, aching voice, "Seeing you today, I realize that I'm not even *close* to getting over you yet."

He leans his head down slowly, tentatively, bringing his face closer to mine. I'm standing still as a statue, not quite believing he's about to kiss me. I catch the scent of smoke and shaving cream a mere second before his lips are on mine.

This isn't real. It can't be.

His hands never leave his pockets, mine never leave my side. For such a soft kiss, I shouldn't be hearing my heart beating out of my chest... I shouldn't be going weak in the knees... I shouldn't be unable to keep my hands from shaking...

I shouldn't be kissing him back. But I am.

He pulls back slightly and I open my eyes, dazed and defeated.

I feel his warm breath against my lips as his rough voice whispers, *"Now tell me I'm lying."*

At that, he turns abruptly and walks out the door.

I sink back down onto the sofa before my weakened legs can bring me to the floor. I still have the minty taste of Jack's lips on my mouth and the scent of him is still lingering in the room. With that comes a flood of memories that knock the wind right out of me.

What if he's telling the truth?

CHAPTER 45

Sunday, May 26, 1996
Probably around 10:00 PM or something.

Reception Hall at The Breakers
Spring Lake

I march back into the ballroom and straight up to Monty, interrupting his conversation with Vix. "What were you *thinking?*" I demand. "How could you just hand me over to Jack with a *smile on your face?*"

Monty doesn't look taken aback to see me standing here seething. "Oh, so it's 'Jack' now, is it?"

"What?"

He casually directs his attentions to his tie, heedlessly scraping off some bits of invisible crud as he clarifies. "We're actually back to using his real name? As opposed to 'The Jerk,' 'That Snake,' or my personal favorite, 'The Colossal Shitbag'?"

Grrr. "Whatever, Mont. Just tell me why you did that to me."

Satisfied with the inspection of his tie, he splays it back down against his chest and finally looks up to meet my eyes. "I did it *for* you, my friend. And for him, too, if you want to know the truth."

When I only offer a skeptical look, Monty continues, "The fact is, tonight is the first time I've talked to Jack in months. He said some things that made me realize you two would be better off together than apart."

Traitor. "So you believe him."

Monty's shoulders rise in a careless shrug. "I have no reason not to. I have the benefit of being able to look at things objectively. *I'm* not as emotionally invested in the two of you as the two of you are. Aside from the fact that I like to see my friends happy, of course." He pauses for a beat before looking at

282

me, shamefaced. "And Livi Girl... truth is I'm trying to lessen my own guilt here. I told Jack way back in August—"

"I know what you told him. He mentioned what you said."

"He was getting ready to hit the road and you had already made it clear that he wasn't planning on bringing you with him. I thought it was best if I told him you were not only doing fine without him, but doing great. I mean, even if you two got back together, what would have been the point? He was just going to be leaving in a few days anyway. You guys were already broken up. Why put you through that all over again? I was trying to protect you."

I sigh and return, "I know. And I appreciate it, really."

"But it was a blatant lie."

"Yes, it was."

"And if I had just stayed out of it, who knows? Maybe you two could have hashed all this out months ago."

Maybe.

But I was such a heartbroken mess that I would have just taken him back in order to stop the pain. Our relationship would have consisted of me following him around the country, supporting his life without ever finding one for myself.

I would never have had the displaced anger to leave Shana and start my own business. I wouldn't have had the blinders-on focus that turned that venture into the success it is today.

I've created my own triumphs and boosted my own confidence for the first time without absorbing the deflected light of someone else's accomplishments. Back then, I was so caught up in being a fan, I'd forgotten to find a *life*. If I'd gotten back together with Jack before figuring that out, I wouldn't have realized that I was able to survive without a star to gaze at, be something on my own, find out what *I* wanted to be.

And I obviously wouldn't be standing here right now, warring with myself over whether I should bother giving Jack the time of day to speak to him or not.

Just then, the band leader winds down their song and announces, "At Tess and Ron's request, we'd like to invite their friend Jack up on the stage to join us for a song."

I almost have a heart attack, watching as Jack hops up on stage with his electric guitar in hand. How can I be expected to just stand here and listen to this? But I don't have much choice.

He plugs in, takes a seat, and adjusts the mic, his smooth voice explaining, "I haven't played this song in a long time, and I've never done it in public, but for Tess and Ron's sake, I'm going to try." He has a pick pinched between his fingers as he absently brushes some hair out of his eyes, and my heart cracks, remembering how I'd pretty much fallen for him the very first time I saw him pull that move exactly one year ago today. "You may be familiar with this one, so you'll be able to tell if I screw it up."

The guests all laugh, but I'm trying not to cry as I hear the opening strains of "Bell Bottom Blues."

Sonofabitch. He's going there.

Tess takes Ron onto the dance floor as he throws up the horns. It almost has me smiling.

Almost. You know, if I weren't so close to crying.

The night I first met Jack, Ron had said it was the most excruciating apology song he'd ever heard. I guess Ron had fucked up a time or two himself, and now he's recruited his buddy to play it for his new wife.

But even though Jack is playing this song on Ron's behalf, he's shooting a few surreptitious glances in my general direction, making it clear to me that he's singing every word purely for my benefit.

He sings with the agony of a broken man, a man with nothing left to lose.

He sings about us.

I know what's coming, so by the time Jack gets to the chorus, I'm already shaking. Most of the wedding guests are out on the dance floor by this time, and even though my eyes are blurring, I can see him singing only to me:

Do you want to see me crawl across the floor to you?
Do you want to hear me beg you to take me back?
I'd gladly do it...

284

Every note, every chord, every word rips through me, blocking the passage of blood through my veins.

He's killing me.

When he's through, I swipe the tears from my eyes as the rest of the guests give a round of applause. I take a deep breath and pull myself together before anyone can accuse me of having a nervous breakdown.

Vix utilizes her Supertwin powers to sense that I'm ready to crumble into a heap right here on the dance floor, and pipes in with, "You know, Liv, you probably should at least talk to him. I always thought he was a good guy. I mean, you could do worse."

"I *have* done worse."

That brings a laugh to our group before Vix continues. "Monty filled me in and I think there's a pretty good chance the poor guy isn't the evil jerk you imagined him to be."

"Poor guy! What about your poor sister?! *He* broke up with *me*, remember?"

Vix sighs heavily, letting me know she's bored with the direction of the conversation. "Of *course* I remember. Lord knows you've never let any of us forget it! He made a mistake, Liv. So did you. *Surprise*, he's not perfect. I think you're being too hard on him for falling off that pedestal you put him on a year ago. You've practically been... *vilifying* him for it every day since."

I let that sink in, fighting the small spark of hope that's stirring deep within me. She has a point, but I am scared to death right now. I really don't know if I'm strong enough to chance it again. I just can't imagine what I'd do if I lost him *twice*.

Vix sees me floundering and goes for the jugular. "The real question is: Are you going to dwell on his one mistake for the rest of your life and be miserable or are you going to get over it already and at least *try* to be happy?"

My sister's words are hitting home. If Jack really was telling the truth, then maybe he deserves a second chance. Maybe *I* deserve a second chance.

A sudden burst of elation fills my head and courses through my blood. What do I have to lose? I just hope I have some time to psych myself up for what I'm about to do.

I grab Monty's wrist and turn it to look at his watch. "Okay, fine. The reception will be over in twenty minutes. I'll go talk to him then."

Vix raises her brows at me. "Now."

I can see that Sammy and Isla are gathering up the last of the centerpieces, so I know I'm only making excuses when I counter, "Oh sure. Just leave my best friend's wedding in order to—"

Vix cuts me off. "Tess already knows and she told me to wish you good luck. So go. Now."

I take a last, beseeching look at Monty who only offers, "Go get 'em, Tiger."

CHAPTER 46

Sunday, May 26, 1996
10:56 PM

Outside The Breakers
Spring Lake

Jack and I don't say a word to each other on our walk outside to the parking lot. The valet brings his car around and not until we are seated, buckled and rolling out of the drive does he finally speak.

"I'm not taking you to Monty's."

Well, I could have figured as much. When I agreed to let Jack drive me home from the reception, the idea was to give us a chance to talk. With Monty's house mere blocks away, the short drive wouldn't have left much time for any sort of in-depth discussion.

The craziest thing is that I don't even know where to begin the dialogue. I've had a million questions swirling around my brain for months, and now, I can't think of what to ask about first.

Jack solves that problem when he asks, "So what changed your mind?"

"Changed my mind about talking to you?"

"Yeah."

"I'm not sure, really. Something Vix said about 'trying to be happy,' I guess."

Jack accepts that but starts fishing. "I think I was kind of hoping it was because you realized I wasn't lying to you."

It's never fun for me to admit when I am wrong. But if we're really going to do this—and do it honestly—Jack deserves at least that small concession from me.

"I wouldn't be here if I didn't believe you."

287

He nods his head in understanding. I watch a muscle clench in his jaw and my pulse speeds up a little faster in that maddening, involuntary way it always did whenever I was this close to him.

He'd ditched his sport coat by the time we reached the car, draping it sensibly over the back of my seat. He can't possibly realize that by doing so, he's forced me to be completely surrounded by the scent of him.

Looking at him isn't much easier. The cuffs of his black shirt are rolled back to his elbows, offering a view of his bare forearms. Even after all this time, I find myself fighting the urge to reach over and touch him. I'd almost forgotten what it was like to be near Jack—seeing him, smelling him—it's a full-on sensory overload. Christ.

I make a conscious effort to breathe through my mouth. "There are still a few things I'm not clear on."

Jack turns down the radio. "Go ahead and ask. That's what we're here for."

"Well, okay... Let's start with that night on the beach, when you broke up with me." Jack winces at the memory. "Why the sudden push to get me to tell you... you know..."

He lets out a deep breath and says, "The night before that? After my meeting with Shug, I had a gig at Mother's, remember?"

"Yeah?"

"Yeah, well, Lutz brought a few of the guys from the tour to come see us play. Kind of a preliminary introduction before being stuck together for the next three months. Anyway... one of the guys was *Rider MacLaine.*"

I don't know whether my face is bright red or pale white as he continues, "I'm sure you can understand why I had a chip on my shoulder when he was talking about the *last* time they were in Jersey, and how he had to look up the "brunette Drew Barrymore" who blew him after the show. *The very night before we met.*" He drums his fingers along the steering wheel, trying to pull himself together enough to continue. "It got in my head. We'd just slept together, and all of a sudden, I felt like another notch in your bedpost."

288

The hurt in his words humbles me, and my eyes drop to my dress as I become fixated on a stray thread. "You knew about my past. You always said it didn't bother you."

"It's one thing to know something, but it's an entirely different thing to have it thrown in my face." He raises an eyebrow as his lips purse together sheepishly. "I knew what we had together, but there I was, making love to you... and all you wanted to do was *fuck*."

I cringe, aware that his recounting is wholly accurate. Hell, he was looking right into my eyes and telling me that he loved me, and I went and turned that night into nothing more than a depraved sex-fest. He may have been a willing participant, but I was the one that changed the direction of that entire evening.

He clears his throat and says, "I had to know for sure. I had to know if I meant more to you than the rest of them. I knew I was going to ask you about it, and I knew you were going to evade the question. I was a fucking mess, because all I could think about was losing you. It wasn't until *after* when I realized how wrong I was to do that to you. I knew how you felt about me, even if you couldn't say so right when I wanted you to. I knew we could make it work and all I needed was to learn a little patience."

All I could think about was losing you.

I know the feeling. I lived through weeks—*months*—of misery because I couldn't get past that one single thought. It took me an eternity before I was able to return my life to some sort of normalcy. And now, here he is, trying to turn me inside-out all over again with his version of events.

"Okay... But when you realized all this, why didn't you try to tell me then?" I choose to leave out the words *if you loved me so much.*

"I already told you; I did try, back in August. Feebly, I admit, but I did try. By then, weeks had gone by. After leaving you like that, I had no idea how you would react to me just barging back into your life. I was going insane without you and thought maybe it wasn't too late to tell you I was wrong. I wimped out and gave Monty a call first. That's when he told me you were happily back with your ex. Do you have any idea what that was like for me? Thinking you were over me enough to already be 'happy' with somebody else?"

Oh, I think I have a good idea.

He shakes his head, reliving the memory. "It was hell, of course, but I truly believed that letting you be happy—even if it was with someone else besides me—was the best thing at the time. I looked at it like it was my penance for being stupid enough to let you go."

Always the gentleman.

I admit, "But I wasn't happy."

Jack adds, "Me either. I thought I was being noble and selfless, but the truth is, I was a miserable fucking mess every goddamn minute of every goddamn day."

"Me too."

We catch each other's eyes and almost laugh.

God, all that wasted time. I can't even blame Monty for his deception. He thought he was doing a good thing at the time, keeping Jack and me from destroying each other even more than we already had. By August, I had gotten pretty good at faking contentment and looking like a normal person. Monty must have interpreted that as genuine closure. Hell, I wanted him to. I wanted *everyone* to.

"So all this time, you thought I was back with Mitch?"

"Yep."

I thought about having to face Jack at the wedding, dying about having to see him there with Sadie. As a bridesmaid, I had no choice—I *had* to be there. Jack showed up voluntarily, thinking he was going to see me hanging all over another guy all night.

"And knowing that you were going to see me at the wedding, in love with some other guy, how were you planning on facing that?"

"Why do you think I brought Freddie?"

This time, we do laugh.

Then Jack says, "Ron ran into Freddie at The Westlake one night and threw a verbal invite his way. Once I heard that, I just RSVP'd for him on my response card as 'Guest.' Jeez, you should have seen the looks we got when we checked into the hotel together. I don't know how Monty does it."

"You're staying at the hotel?"

"I was kind of hoping I wouldn't have to. I only booked the room in case I crashed and burned with you tonight and decided to get completely wasted." He throws me a confident smile. "Looks like Freddie will be taking the shuttle bus there alone."

Dear God. I hope he's not planning on sleeping at Monty's. I'm not nearly ready to be under the same roof with him overnight. He breaks my thoughts on that when he asks, "Mind if I ask *you* a question now?"

"That's what we're here for."

"Okay... because I need to know. What in the world led you to believe I was *cheating* on you?" He says it as if the words are actually laced with a foul odor.

I give a shrug. "I didn't know *what* to believe, Jack. I just put the puzzle pieces together with what little information I had available to me at the time. We had our big stand-off on the beach, and then a week later you were engaged to someone else. I just thought you were using me for a last fling."

"How could you think that? After everything I said? Or did?"

"I was scared, Jack. I'd never felt that way about anyone before. I couldn't acknowledge how hard I'd fallen. But after we broke up, I started second-guessing myself like crazy, coming to the realization that of course I knew all along, but that I was just too stupid to see it. I couldn't *wait* to tell you; I was *busting* with it. I was working up the nerve to find you somehow, when I found out you hadn't even left at all. Two days later, I received that horrid little card in the mail."

"But I had nothing to do with that."

"I didn't know that at the time."

He gnaws on his lip for a minute. "But... I mean, why wouldn't you have just seen through that? Isn't it obvious that she just sent that thing to get you out of the picture?"

"It's obvious *now*."

"But why not then?"

"Three reasons." I take a breath and almost smile as I start counting off the talking points on *my* fingers. "One: The announcements were professionally printed! You can't just buy *one* of those things. She would have had to order a minimum of like fifty of them. Who would be that calculated?"

"My ex-girlfriend."

"I didn't know her as well as you did." He smirks—that trademarked upturn of his delectable lips—as I continue, "Two: It takes a couple *weeks* to get them done. A few more days for the mail to be delivered. At the time, I thought that meant you had to have been engaged while we were still together." I watch the muscle pulsing in his jaw as I add, "And three: If we were still speaking when I received it, I could have just asked you about it, we would have cleared everything up in about one minute, and then we would've shared a good laugh at her expense. But we were already separated when that thing landed in my mailbox. Pretty coincidental timing, don't you think?"

Jack runs a hand down his face. "Uh... There's nothing coincidental about it. She knew we were on the rocks."

"What? How?"

"I told her."

Before the seethe can set in, he explains. "When I said The Osprey was the last time I saw her, that was the truth. But she still called every now and again. I didn't spend more time talking to her than it took to get off the phone." He shakes his head and continues, "But that weekend after we broke up? I ran into your father. It was too much. I went on one hell of a bender after that. She called right in the middle of it, twisting the knife about my 'new girlfriend' this and my 'new girlfriend' that... I don't know, I just blurted out that we weren't together anymore."

"Oh Jesus."

"Yeah. Exactly. But how could I have predicted she'd do something like what she did to you?"

"You couldn't," I willingly concede.

"She really tried working me over after that. Called every few hours, for chrissakes. I couldn't even change my number because I was still hoping *you* would call." He shoots me a smirk before

292

continuing. "After about a week of that, I finally told her in no uncertain terms to stop calling, it's never going to happen, I was still in love with *you*. She just went ballistic, and that turned out to be the last time I ever spoke to her."

"But the announcement cards…"

"Her sister works at a printing place."

There's a pause between us as we try and make sense of all the new revelations.

I'll have to check with the guys, but I'm guessing I'm the only one who received the lovely little piece of mail. Unbelievable.

While I'm silently contemplating the right way to launch an apology, he asks, "You're not going to boil my bunny now, are you?"

The question is so unexpected that I find myself cracking right the hell up. Before I can pull myself together, he says, "Oh, hey! I saw your article in the *Ledger*! It was really, really great. About time the world recognized your talents."

"Ha! Thanks. It's going well. Getting more business every day."

"I gotta say, opening the paper that Sunday morning almost stopped my fucking heart. There I was, settling in for a nice cup of coffee, thumbing through the Lifestyle section, and *BAM!* There's your face smiling up at me. Nearly killed me, I swear."

"Nice to know I still have that effect on you."

Whoops! I guess I let down my guard.

One night with Jack and suddenly I've fallen right back into our flirtatious banter. I don't feel too weird about it, however. After a year of self-doubt and heartbreak, it's nice to accept that maybe being here with him isn't so dangerous anymore. It's a little scary, but mostly uplifting to allow myself some hope again. For the second time tonight, I start to believe that maybe this can really happen.

But there's one thing I just still can't get past.

"Jack?"

"Yes?"

"There's something that we're kinda brushing under the rug here." I steal a look at him and catch him gritting his teeth. He knows what's coming.

"The fact is, you did break up with me. If you loved me so much, how could you just let me go like that?"

Jack swallows every bit of what I throw on his plate. He pulls off the road and comes to a slow stop before putting the car in park and turning to me.

He takes my hand before answering, "Livia, my God. At the time, all I was thinking about was getting burned. I was really hoping you'd say it back. When you didn't, I thought I could *force* you to admit it." He runs a hand through his hair and continues. "I should have been more understanding, given you more time. But I was hurt and I was leaving and I didn't know what else to do. I just figured the tour was a good enough excuse to draw a line in the sand."

"I thought you were going to ask me to come along."

"I know you did. I was."

I want to ask him how the tour went, but it's not really the most pressing subject at the moment. "So, when you left without me...That must have been hard."

"It's not what I wanted, no. But I couldn't allow myself to think about it. Because it hurt too much to dwell on that."

The hopeful look on his face is tearing my insides to shreds as the freefall starts all over again.

We were both wrong. But maybe together, we can find a way to make it right.

I look down at our hands and find that I've been unconsciously stroking my thumbs against his fingers. One glance at the look on Jack's face tells me he is *very* conscious of what I've been doing.

"So what does Jack want?" I ask, already knowing the answer.

He lifts a hand to my neck, stroking my cheek with his thumb. "I want *you*." He leans in and plants a soft kiss on my lips before adding, "...to kick my lying ex-girlfriend's ass."

I'm still laughing as he kisses me again.

CHAPTER 47

Sunday, May 26, 1996
11:47 PM

Jack's Car
No idea. Belmar, maybe???

A new game springs up between us as Jack wends the car through some side streets, lost in our quest to find Route 35 again.

Me: "I'm sorry I said I hated you."

Jack: "I'm sorry I yelled in your face."

Me: "I'm sorry for hurting you so badly you felt you needed to."

Jack: "I'm sorry for hurting *you* so badly that *you* felt you needed to."

Me: "I'm sorry that Monty called you a horse's ass."

Jack: "I'm sorry for being one."

Me: "Okay, you win."

Jack laughs at that. It's great to hear the sound of his laughter again. It's great to feel great about *anything* again. But even through our friendly teasing, I know I'm only allowing myself to merely dip my toes in the water. I know Jack is telling me the truth, I know I'm still crazy about him, and yet I'm still a little hesitant to do a full-on cannonball just yet. My defenses took months to build. It's going to take more than a few hours to tear them down.

Alanis Morissette's "You Oughta Know" comes on the radio, and I start laughing hysterically.

Jack is looking at me like I'm nuts, probably wondering if I've lost my mind. "What's so funny?" he asks.

"This song. I must have blasted this thing nine hundred times over the course of the past months, and now here I am listening to it with you right next to me." He starts chuckling, so I add, "I know. Such a loser thing to do."

"It's not that," he explains. He points to himself and says out the corner of his mouth, "Aretha Franklin. 'Ain't No Way'."

I bite my lip to keep from cracking up, and divert the subject with a question. "Hey, buddy. Where the heck are we anyway?"

Jack doesn't say a word as I watch him try to hide a smile.

"We're not lost, are we."

He's still working the shit-eating grin. "Nope. There's something I want to show you. In fact, close your eyes, we're almost there."

"Close my eyes? Are you serious?"

"C'mon, Lips. Don't spoil this for me. I waited a long time to bring you here."

"Fine." I close my eyes and put my hands over them before he can accuse me of peeking. "But so help me, Jackson Tanner... If this little sidetrack brings me anywhere near a microphone... or a freezing ocean... you're gonna pay."

The car comes to a stop and Jack cuts the engine. "I think I've paid a heftier fee over this past year than any man should have to. Okay. Open your eyes."

I remove my hands to find that we're parked in the driveway of a beautiful, beachfront house. It's a large yellow Victorian with a huge front porch...

"Oh. My. *GOD!* That's my *house!* Remember? It's almost exactly like that pink Mantoloking house I told you about, right? How did you ever find this?"

Jack looks immensely proud of himself. "I didn't 'find' it. I built it."

I blink back my shock and finally find some words. "You *built* this? You built this... from my plans? How did you... Who would have—"

"I took all that money from the tour and used it to start my own construction business. This was the first project I was hired for as an indie. C'mon. Let's get out of the car so you can get a better look."

I'm still in shock as Jack comes around to let me out of the car. He takes my hand as I stand in the driveway and just stare at the living, breathing manifestation of my paper dreams. I am in awe. I don't even care that it isn't mine.

Everything clicks for me in the seconds I gape at the sight before me. He never forgot about me. Even over the months he thought I was with someone else, he did this. To make himself remember how much he loved me.

There's no defense against this.

I feel my walls fall away as my eyes scan over the roof eaves and the flower boxes at the warmly lit windows. I take in the side wing comprised almost completely out of glass. I notice the front porch and the paver-stoned driveway and the perfect landscaping and the lighted walkway. I can't believe I'm looking at *my house*—a house built by the man, let's face it, the man that I love.

Then I notice the man standing next to me, beaming down with unparalleled pride to see me so taken with his work.

"Jack. Wow. This is just so... *amazing*. It's more beautiful than I ever even dreamed it could be. Whose house is this?"

He smiles ear to ear as if I've just asked the million dollar question. "I happen to be very well acquainted with the people who hired me for this job. Wanna go inside?"

"Isn't it a little late to be dropping in for an unexpected visit?"

"Nah. What can I say? Nepotism has its privileges."

"I'll say."

We walk around to the back, which Jack informs me is really the 'front' when referring to a beachfront home, and I take a moment to marvel at the ocean view. Nepotism may have its privileges, but money sure buys the rest.

Jack slides the glass door aside and escorts me into the humongous great room. Even though it's close to midnight, the entire Tanner clan is sitting around the kitchen island playing cards.

Mrs. Tanner is the first to notice us standing there. She clasps her hands together and announces, "Oh, Jack! You did it!"

297

Mr. Tanner, Stephen, Harrison, and Sean all turn toward us. As Jack ushers me into the room to greet them hello, I see Stephen handing Sean a ten dollar bill.

He grins but says flatly, "Yeah, Pew. *Real great* to see you were able to talk Livia into coming back with you. Good job, brother." Before I have the chance to misinterpret his comment, Stephen turns to me and extends a warm smile. "Best ten bucks I ever lost, however."

God, I missed these guys.

I immediately wrap my arms around Stephen's huge neck and hug him. As I do, I notice a large, framed family portrait on the wall above the fireplace. It's the shot I liked best, the six of them on the jetty at Point Pleasant right before Sean tried to shove Harrison into the ocean.

Mrs. Tanner has artfully arranged four, smaller framed prints underneath the main photo; random shots of the boys goofing around at the water's edge.

"That was a good day," she offers as I swipe a tear from my cheek. How did *that* get there?

I think back to the day on the beach with this family and about the night alone with my favorite member of it. It seems like so long ago but only yesterday when Jack and I were in love.

"Yes," I consent. "That *was* a good day."

But today is shaping up to be even better.

* * *

Jack and I are holding hands, walking along the water. For now, there are no more words that need to pass between us, no more questions left unanswered. The damp sand is squishing between my toes and there's a cool breeze whipping my hair out of its bobby pins. I must look like hell but I feel fantastic.

I gaze at the man standing next to me, so handsome in his formalwear-turned-casual shirtsleeves and slacks. I think about how he's even attractive in a pair of ripped jeans or swimming trunks and realize he's beautiful not just because of how he looks but because of the person that he is. *It is only with the heart that one can see rightly; that which is essential is invisible to the eye.*

His gorgeous body doesn't really hurt the overall package, however.

I'm reminded of something I haven't yet told him. "I read 'The Little Prince,' you know."

Jack stops walking to look at me, an eyebrow lowering as he asks, "You did?"

"Yes. I was just trying to torture myself, I guess."

He smiles at that, asking, "The English version, I hope?"

"Yes."

"Well, what did you think?"

My lips purse for a moment before quoting my favorite part. "*You are responsible, forever, for what you have tamed.*" I didn't know a lick of French, but when I read that line, I knew they were the words from his tattoo. "The thing is though, I can't figure out whether you've tamed me or I've tamed you."

Jack aims a smile at me, proud that I was able to figure it out. He doesn't attempt to respond, and just lets the revelation float in the air between us. There's no right answer anyway.

I bite my lip, trying to hide a grin when I say, "At least it's better than the Bart Simpson tat on your ass."

Jack almost chokes on his laughter. "I was hoping you forgot about that."

He pulls himself together and points out an empty lot, a few houses down from his parents'. "That's my next project. I start on Wednesday."

He seems so proud of himself and that makes me proud *for* him. "What, no more Thunderjug?"

He laughs and explains, "There will *always* be a Thunderjug. But I'm not the only guy in the band to get a real job this past year. After three months on the road, *some* of us realized it wasn't the life for us. We still play together every now and then, so it's cool. It's like it was when we first started out, just having fun, you know?"

"Sounds like it."

He checks his watch. "Aw crap. I'm late."

I don't know what he's talking about, but respond, "You're *always* late."

"Not *too* late, I hope."

"Huh?"

He smirks and offers, "It's after midnight. I didn't get a chance to wish you happy anniversary. We met one year ago today—well, yesterday."

I stop walking and just look at him, amazed. "You remembered that? I was dying all day thinking about it."

"Of course I remember that. It was the day my life was changed forever. How could you think I'd forget about—"

His words are cut off by the crush of my mouth against his. Instantly, his arms enclose around me tightly, imprisoning my body in a combustible embrace. I press myself against the length of him, loving the feel of his body close to mine, wrapping my hands in his hair as his lips part, sending me into that familiar spiral of oblivion I've been living without for much, much too long.

Damn, the boy's still got it.

I pull away slightly and look into his darkened, gray eyes. My voice cracks as I whisper, "Happy *new* anniversary, Jack."

He looks even more taken aback than I feel.

"I love you, Livia. I never stopped."

I look over his shoulder at the beautiful house, wondering what he must have been thinking while building it. If he was as heartbroken as I was, it must have been excruciating for him to work on such a labor of love, building it for my eyes, not knowing if he was ever going to get the chance to show it to me. How agonizing it must have been for him to see it through.

But maybe everything in this world starts out a little rough around the edges and just needs someone to love it in order to make it truly beautiful. Maybe the most lasting things are so sturdy because they've been tested and restructured, tempered and reinforced.

Like us.

Maybe all that matters, at least for now, is that we still love each other.

"I love you too, Jack. I really, really mean it."

And I do.

There's a year of hurt feelings to overcome, the challenge of trying to forget how much pain we caused one another.

But right now, none of that seems to matter. I know we'll get past it and make each other happy. I know that things won't be perfect and that I shouldn't expect them to be. I know that this man—this gorgeous, incredible man—is holding me right now, smiling into my eyes, and telling me that he loves me. I can feel with every ounce of my being that it's the truth.

And for now, that's enough. It's a solid foundation to start with.

As for the rest?

Well... we can build from there.

THE END.

NOT.

EPILOGUE
JACK

Friday, May 26, 2000
8:10 PM

My Townhouse or Condo or whatever
Shermer Heights

"How 'bout these steaks, huh?" I ask Livia, putting down my knife and fork.

Liv eases back into her chair and folds her hands against her middle with a groan. "Mmm. So good, Jack."

I shift in my seat at that, and I see her trying not to smile.

She's doing this on purpose. She's been tormenting me all night with her little sounds and her subtle touches, letting her fingers drift across my skin every chance she gets…

And now she's giving me the fuck-me eyes along with a sexy moan.

Livia pulls this on me a lot, but she's really amping it up tonight, what with it being a special occasion and all. Fact is, it's the fifth anniversary of the day we met. And while we were separated for some of that time, we still treat it as a day worth celebrating.

It is.

So, I made dinner tonight. Liv normally does most of the cooking, but because I'm trying to be all romantic, I volunteered. Ever since she bought me that Weber grill for our *last* anniversary, I've become quite the barbecue master.

It's funny the way she's constantly buying "me" all these presents. Like the curtains in my living room or the throw rugs in my bedroom. She's managed to turn this empty condo into a real home, but I know she's just stockpiling all this decorative stuff for when she finally moves in someday.

If she moves in someday.

305

I've asked her about a million times over the past four years, practically since the first day we got back together. No luck, though. She said it was because she didn't want to leave her sister hanging, but how hard is it to find another roommate? Besides, Vix and Chris just got married last month. Now that they're in their own house, Livia's out of excuses.

I haven't bothered her about it in a while, but tonight's going to be as good a time as any.

I have a feeling she won't turn me down this time.

After I refill her wine glass, I raise mine in a toast. "To second chances," I say, just like I've done during every toast between us for the past four years.

"To second chances," she answers back.

I'll always be grateful that we figured our shit out. Better late than never, right?

As bad as it sucked while we were apart, I wouldn't have changed our reconciliation for the world. We spent those first weeks taking things *really* slowly. Livia set up an "arrangement" where we agreed to hold off on the sex until both of us were out of questions. We did a *lot* of talking over that time. It was torture, because after so much time apart, all I wanted was to get my hands on her.

But I respected what she was trying to do.

More importantly, we both learned to respect our *dynamic*. I've learned not to push her, and she's learned to tell me what I need to hear.

I took her back to The Westlake. And my parents' house. And the boardwalk... trying to relive every moment we'd spent together, trying to reignite the spark.

Turns out, it had never left.

We barely clink glasses and take a sip of our drinks before I'm bounding from the table. "Time for presents!" I announce, pulling a large box out of one of my kitchen cabinets. By the time I set it down at Livia's spot at the table, a small, flat box is waiting for me at mine.

"You first," she orders me with a smile.

306

When I tear off the paper, I find myself looking at a kickass silver watch.

Pulling it out, I wrap it around my wrist, saying, "Wow, Liv. This is really cool!" I take note of the fact that it has two faces on it, most likely so I can set it for two different time zones. I travel a bit for work, and I guess Livia's getting sick of me calling at odd hours. "Hint taken, babe."

She snickers into her hand, explaining, "I just wanted you to have a reminder that I'm counting every minute until your return." She bats her eyelashes, busting my chops, but I know there's a hint of truth in her statement.

"But mostly," she says, almost shyly, "After I met you, I started to realize time was something to be treasured." She's been drawing little imaginary circles on the tablecloth as she speaks, but she stops her doodling to meet my eyes. "Every moment with you has taken my breath away."

I smile, then lean across the table to kiss that sweet mouth of hers. "Well, I love it, babe. Thank you. Now you," I command, waving at the box next to her plate.

"I don't care what's in here. I'm more impressed that you cleaned the condo. Thank you for not being a slob for at least one day."

She's still giggling as she pulls off the paper, but her mouth drops when she sees the digital camera in her hands. I don't know much about this kind of stuff, so I just got her the best one I could find. She deserves it. Her business has been going great, so much so that she just added a fourth photographer to her employ. She's amazing, and I couldn't be more proud of her.

"Do you like it?" I ask. "Is that the right one?"

Livia is turning the box over in her hands as she answers, "This is way nicer than the ones I was looking at, Jack. My God. Thank you!" She doesn't waste any time opening the box and pulling the thing out of its plastic.

The camera cost a pretty penny, but I received another royalty check from Mayhem last month, just like I do at the end of every quarter. It's not enough to quit my day job—not that I'd ever be able to just sit around on my ass and do nothing all day anyway—but it always allows for the extras. Freddie and me will still get together and jam pretty regularly, but Booey and Jim formed a new band once I went with the construction full-time.

JT Contracting has been expanding steadily over the past five years. I brought my cousin Bruce on board a couple years back, and he's been a huge help to me. He likes to build things, too.

I miss the rock star thing sometimes, but I'm happy with my life now.

Besides, touring was a killer. I love playing music but the endless days on the road were brutal. I know it's not the career for me. I really don't know how Livia's father has been able to do it all these years. Russ is still hitting the festivals, but once all that travel got to be too much for Linda, he cut his roadtrips down by half. To make up for it, he and I started a little side gig where we give guitar lessons to some local kids. It's going well.

After some friendly pressure from Lutz, Thunderjug is gearing up for a reunion tour this summer. We're limiting it to Jersey, and we'll be revisiting some of our favorite places here up north as well as down the shore. Livia rented us a house in Manasquan just for old times' sake. This one's got plenty of room for all our friends, a huge bathroom, and—thank fuck—central air.

Finished with the inspection of her camera, Liv pops up to clear the table. I take the opportunity to throw a good music station on the TV and stretch out on the floor in front of the couch. I finally got some furniture in this place, but I still don't mind sitting on the carpet. It's comfortable.

Especially when Liv comes over and plunks herself down on my lap.

"I ate too much," she groans, straddling her knees on either side of me. "Do you mind if we hold off on dessert for a little while?"

"Yeah, of course. What are we having?"

"No-bake Éclair Cake. It was easy enough to put together, but I had to lay out about a million ingredients to do so. I figured I'd take advantage of all your awesome counter space. My kitchen is so small!"

"Well, you could take advantage of it all the time if you moved in."

308

She gives an exasperated sigh and moves off my lap. "Jack, we've been through this. Do you really want to see me sitting on the couch in my PJs, my hair in a ponytail because I haven't washed it in days, and Cheeto dust staining my fingers?"

"I've already seen that. Numerous times. And it's adorable."

"Yeah, sure, every once in a while. But when I don't have clients coming in, that's how I spend my life. You'd lose respect for me."

"I never had any to begin with."

"Ha ha. Besides, my apartment is where I have my studio set up. There's nowhere to do that here."

"We could find a new place and I'll build you a new studio."

She bites her bottom lip, and it makes me want to suck it between my own teeth. But I can tell she's holding back what she really wants to say. "What is it, Liv?"

Her gorgeous green eyes meet mine, and I swear, I still get surprised every time I see them.

"I've also been a little dishonest with you about my reasons for not moving in." She curls her legs underneath her and confesses, "This is going to sound so stupid, but I wasn't ever the most... *conservative* girl during my young adulthood." I can tell this is hard for her. I know she's not necessarily embarrassed about her past, and I've always done my best to convince her that it never bothered me, but I do know that she has some regrets. "Until I met you... I didn't realize what an empty life I'd been leading. Falling in love with you? It's been the single most amazing thing in my life. I just..." she twirls a strand of hair in her hand, watching as the ends kick out across her fingertips. "I just think that I'd like to do things a bit more... conventionally from here on out."

Ah. The old commitment conversation.

"Well, shit, Liv. We've been together for the better part of five years. I think it's safe to say I'm committed to this relationship."

That has the intended effect I was going for. She looks up from her hair and meets my eyes... and then loses it.

While she's laughing, I clear my throat and say, "Or you could just let me marry you."

Her laughter stops as astonishment drifts across her face. But then, she must think I'm only kidding, because her stunned expression breaks into a smile as she slaps my chest and chastises me. "Very funny, Jack."

I rub the spot she just smacked. It's a little sore.

"I'm serious." I reach my hand under the couch, pull out the small box I'd hidden hours ago, and crack it open. Liv's eyes go wider than I've ever seen them, wide enough to mimic the round, princess-cut emerald in my hand. "Marry me, Liv."

She puts a hand across her mouth as tears spring to her eyes. "You mean it?"

That makes me laugh. "Yes, baby. I'm sitting here with a ring and everything. Of course I mean it."

In spite of the fact that I'm excited and proud and whatever, I'm also a little sick to my stomach, too. Liv is just frozen in place, staring at the box in my hand, not offering me any clue as to what's going on in that brain of hers. I've never asked anyone to marry me before, but I didn't think I'd be waiting this long on an answer.

This isn't the reaction I was expecting.

"It's my birth stone," she finally says, reaching out toward the ring. But her hands stop just shy of actually touching it. "Is it... Isn't it bad luck for me to put it on myself or something?"

I swallow hard, because I know now that her answer is a yes. "Just tell me what I want to hear, and I'll take care of it."

"Oh God! I'm sorry! Yes! Of course, yes. Oh Jack. It's... You're beautiful. I love it. I love you! Yes, yes, yes." She grabs my face and pulls it toward her, and the ring gets forgotten for the moment while I kiss her back.

And then I toss the thing onto the couch and roll her onto the floor.

Some things are more important right now.

She grabs me by the lapels of my button-down shirt, pulling me toward her as our mouths part against one another's. I've got my arms wrapped around her middle as I drag her body underneath mine and settle myself between her legs, our tongues tangling together in a kiss so familiar, it feels like coming home.

Every time.

I rise up on my knees and shoot a leer down her obliging body, sprawled out on the floor before me. I unbutton my shirt, loving the way Livia watches me, biting her lip in anticipation.

But I love torturing her like this. I love drawing out our lovemaking as long as possible. She'll try to play cool about it sometimes, but I know she loves it, too.

Grabbing my T-shirt between my shoulder blades, I pull it over my head... and Livia's jaw drops. I'd like to think it's because she's so stunned by my awesome bod, but the truth is, I know what she's looking at. Her hand comes up to touch the skin around my heart, the part that isn't inked.

"You... You got my lips tattooed over your heart?" Her mouth puckers into a kiss as she points to her face, as if *I'm* the one who's not sure that these are her lips branded onto my chest. "Is that why you asked me to kiss that notecard the other day?"

I'm almost shy to admit it, but, "Yeah. That's why." I meet her eyes, and they're staring back at me, stunned.

"But that's... *permanent.*"

"So are we."

She's in tears by the time I slip the ring on her finger.

Liv holds her hand out to inspect it, her free hand covering her mouth. "I can't believe this is happening."

That makes me chuckle. "I'm glad you're surprised, Lips, but I didn't expect you to be *shocked.*"

Despite what I just said, the fact is, I can't believe this is finally happening either. I can't believe I made this woman mine.

Done with the inspection of her ring, my *fiancée* slides her hands around my neck, pulling me in for a kiss. "I am *so* in love with you, Jack. Nobody has ever loved anyone as much as I love you."

Lowering my face to hers, I kiss her back. Softly, slowly, I fit her body along the length of mine, loving every inch of this woman underneath me.

Slipping a hand up her shoulder to her face, I cup her jaw in my palm and fix my eyes on hers. "Wanna bet?"

NOW IT'S THE END.

As always, I'll ask that if you enjoyed this book,
to please leave a review, loan it out,
and talk about it every chance you get. :)

Indie authors are only able to bring you new stories when there's
an audience waiting for them, and we rely on word-of-mouth
above all else to make a living.

If you haven't already, please come join the fun on my
Facebook page!

Email me at: ttorrest@optonline.net

Or check out my webpage: www.ttorrest.com

THANK YOU!

COMING SOON!

BRIDESMAID FROM HELL

Read all about Jack and Livia's wedding from the perspective of the World's Bitchiest Bridesmaid, Shana Benedict.

Add it to your Goodreads TBR!

(And flip the page for a preview.)

BRIDESMAID FROM HELL
Excerpt from Chapter Three

I head to my bedroom via the hallway off the kitchen. The original design of our house intended this area to be the "Maid's Quarters," but years ago, my parents had converted the space into an apartment for my grandmother. When Gram had to move into the nursing home, it became mine.

It's not a bad setup. Lots of square footage and plenty of closet space. I only had to put up a small fight when my younger brother Cooper tried to lay claim to the room. But seeing as he was getting ready to head off to grad school at the time, there was hardly an argument.

My dog, Snowball, is on my bed waiting for me as usual. I pick him up and tuck him under my arm as I flop down onto the bed. I pick up the remote and try to watch TV, but my brain is still mulling over the conversation I had with Tommy in the car. He was acting a little weird and I can't make heads or tails of it.

I pick up the phone and call Livia for a second opinion.

"Hello?" she answers.

"Hey Liv!"

She whispers into the phone. "Shana? Are you alright? What time is it?"

Ooops. I quickly check the Piaget clock on my nightstand. One-thirty.

"Shoot, Liv, I didn't realize it was this late. I guess I figured you'd still be up. Can you talk? I'm kinda freaked out right now."

"Yeah, yeah. Hang on a sec, okay?"

I can hear her shuffling around, probably going into the other room so as not to wake Mr. Perfect.

319

"Shane, jeez, is everything okay?"

"God, Liv, don't be such a worry wart. Were you actually in bed already?"

"Well, yeah. It's one-thirty."

"On a Friday night!"

"Sorry. I didn't realize I was expected to leave my boogie shoes on. In any case, I'm awake now. What's up?"

Man. Ever since Livia got back together with Jack, she's been a wet blanket. In the old days, we wouldn't have thought twice about going *out* at this hour, yet here she is already asleep at one-thirty on a Friday night. I decide to lay off the ballbusting, however. After all, I called because I need to talk and I don't want to aggravate her to the point where she won't. I *did* wake her up out of a sound sleep, for godsakes.

"It's Tommy. He was acting a little weird tonight."

"How do you mean?"

I pause for effect, just so my friend knows how serious this is. I give Snowball a scratch under his chin and say, "Well, we were having a great time at dinner and I suggested that we head over to *Gentleman's* for dessert."

"Wait. *The Gentleman at Leisure*? The strip club? Tell me you didn't!"

"I did. But when I started to give him a lap dance—"

"Shana, shut up!"

I start cracking up. I knew Livia would find a recap of my evening entertaining. "No, *you* shut up and let me finish."

"I can't believe you gave Tommy a lap dance at Gentlemen's. What was it like?"

"The club or the lap dance?"

"Shane!"

"Oh, alright, alright. Lots of red velvet and candles. Very Poconos, very Mount Airy Lodge, only classier."

"Is that even possible?"

"I know, right? Anyway, this big, fat bouncer comes over and tells me I can't do that and threatens to kick us out if I don't stop, so we leave. So, I'm thinking after my little dance number that Tom's probably all worked up and all, but when we get back to my house, he wouldn't even come inside. Isn't that weird?"

"That's what you're so freaked out about?"

"Yes. Don't you think that's a little strange?"

I can hear Livia sighing on the other end of the line. I know this isn't the most pressing matter and it certainly isn't the first time I've asked her to play amateur psychologist with one of my boyfriends, but she seems a little less tolerant whenever we discuss Tommy. I guess she gets a little skittish whenever she thinks there might be a problem between us.

She wasn't crazy about the idea of me dating one of Jack's friends in the first place, probably because if things end badly, it could create a rip in the space/time continuum or something. Maybe she should have thought about that before she practically set us up! The way I see it, she's the *best* person to consult on the matter of Tommy. Who better to offer insight than someone who knows him so well?

"I don't know, Shane. Maybe he was just tired or something. Did he *tell* you why he didn't want to spend the night?"

"He said he had to get up early for work tomorrow." I didn't mention the part about my mother at the window, waiting up for us.

"Well, okay then, Captain Obvious. I may be going out on a limb here, but I'm going to have to go with A: *He has to get up early for work tomorrow.* Final answer."

"Gee, thanks a lot, Liv."

"Ha! Okay, look. I think you're just overthinking this. You *do* this, you know. Just chill out and roll with it, okay? Tom's a good guy, you're a hot, happening babe... Just play it cool, huh? I'm sure he'll call tomorrow and turn back into Prince Charming once he's got a few hours of sleep in him. *Capice?*"

"Yeah, I *'capice'* perfectly." I bite my lip nervously, anticipating the reaction to what I'm about to suggest. "But do you think that *maybe* you could ask your boyfriend to talk to him? Just to find out what his deal is?"

There's a big silence on Liv's end. Crap. I'm thinking I probably went too far with that one. I know she's been trying to keep her distance from the goings-on between Tom and me. So it catches me off guard when I hear her say, "Jack's not my boyfriend anymore."

Shit. Here I've been rambling on about my stupid crap and Livia's been dealing with losing her boyfriend of five years. Some friend I am. "Why didn't you call me?"

"I was planning on it. At a more decent hour tomorrow morning."

"But what happened?"

Liv pauses, unable to find the words. She takes a deep breath and then blurts out, "Well, he *proposed*, that's what happened! So he's not my boyfriend anymore. He's my *fiancé!*"

I can hear her busting a gut laughing over there in Shangri-La, while I'm still trying to digest what she just said. "Holy crap. So you're *engaged?*"

"I am engaged. I am *of the affianced!* We're getting married next year. No date set or anything yet. He just did it tonight and my head is still spinning."

I know the feeling.

All I can say is, "Wow..."

"I know, right? Hey, I'm sorry if I just dumped this on you. *You* called *me*. But I just couldn't wait to tell you. It's okay, right?"

I say, "Yeah, of course. Wow. How's the ring?"

"Gorgeous! I am marrying a man with exquisite taste. Wait 'till you see it. Do you have plans tomorrow night?"

I was kind of hoping to see Tommy tomorrow and make sure everything is still okay between us, but I answer, "No. Not really. Why?"

"Well, I really wanted to do this in person, but obviously, I'd like to ask you if you'd be a bridesmaid. So... will you?"

A bridesmaid. This from the girl who knows she will be Maid of Honor at my wedding someday. Although, I guess it's pretty obvious that her sister will be the one to take the lead role in this wedding.

So, even though I'm miffed, I answer, "Of course I'll be a bridesmaid. I'd be honored."

"Okay, great! Because I'd like to get my *wedding party* together tomorrow for a Girls' Night Out. You in?"

Without thinking, I ask, "Who's going?"

Livia laughs and says, "What are you, brain damaged? The *usual suspects* are going: Vix, Tess, Sam, Isla... and you, hopefully."

Of course. *Those Girls.*

What I try to forget on a daily basis is that Livia has this group of girlfriends that she hangs out with when she's not hanging out with *me*.

The problems go all the way back to high school. Livia and I had met when I was a senior and she and I took the same art and photography classes that year. She was a grade behind me and has been fighting to catch up ever since.

The girls in my grade never really formed a "clique," at least not one I was ever part of, but that junior class was as thick as thieves. Her little group consisted of girls who just did not like the idea of Liv befriending someone outside of the five of *them*:

(Trumpets, please...) Livia and Victoria Chadwick, Tess Valletti, Samantha Baker, and Isla St. Parque.

Vix is Liv's twin sister who has essentially despised me from Day One. I guess she felt threatened by how close Livia and I had become. But the girl is my best friend's sister, for godsakes, so I've had to put up with her.

Sam and Isla are basically lap dogs. They don't necessarily offend me, yet I've never really found the desire to get to know them extensively for any reason. At least I have the capability to stomach either of those two when I need to.

But Tess...

Tess Valletti has been in a class all her own since the day she came strutting through the doors of our high school her freshman year. What sucks most about her is that she is beyond beautiful. And believe me, I take no joy in admitting that. Back when we were teenagers, she even dated some guy who's now an actual Hollywood movie star. I'd tell you who he was on the off chance you've actually heard of him, but I'm not a name-dropper.

The point is, Tess is the kind of girl that things like that happen to.

Aside from that annoying little fact, she also happens to be an absolute hellraiser. She's never hidden her distaste for me and doesn't know how to keep her mouth shut about it. It's not like I've ever gone out of my way to be friends with her or anything, but at least I have enough class to be civil. That girl can barely contain herself when we're in the same room together, which thankfully, isn't *too* often. Not that she goes out of her way to push my buttons, but I try to steer clear of her whenever I'm in her vicinity, just to avoid giving her any opening for a confrontation.

I can't believe Tess has been married to Ronnie for like four years already. Ron is another friend of Jack's, like my Tommy, so I'm forced to be in her company slightly more lately, ever since he and I started dating. The way I see it though, is if *that* bitch can pull off a happy marriage with one of Jack's friends, then getting Tom to fall in love with *me* should be a cakewalk.

Key words there being: 'should be.' That's always the tricky part when it comes to guys—trying to predict what they're thinking in order to hang onto them.

Attracting them, at least, has never really been a problem for me.

Looking back now, it all seems rather incestual, but Livia and I have always had the same taste in men and we look alike, which naturally put us in the position of dating a lot of the same boys during our school years. Back then, we were so wrapped up in the microcosm of high school that picking the same guys out of that particular dating pool wasn't so taboo.

It was really weird once we grew up and were forced to deal with the rest of the world's time-honored policy: Another girl's boyfriend is off limits for life, even after a breakup.

Which is why I almost choked on my tongue the day her boyfriend Jack walked into *The Studio* for the first time. To borrow a phrase from my mother's dictionary, that boy is a world-class *hunk*. No wonder it took Livia five whole years to wrangle a proposal out of him. If he were with me, I would have closed the deal within a year, two tops. Unfortunately, I'll never get the opportunity to prove that theory.

Jack had broken up with Liv only a few months after they first started dating. Lord, what I wouldn't have given for the chance to sidle on in there. But I was honor-bound to our newly adopted Code of Dating Ethics. And besides, more importantly, Liv was heartbroken at the time. What kind of friend would I be if I made a move on her ex while she was trying to put the pieces of her life

325

back together? Sure enough, those two eventually patched things up anyway.

And now, here I am, listening to my friend impart the news of their engagement. Even worse, however, is the fact that now I have no choice but to spend a night celebrating the event with Those Girls tomorrow.

"Yeah. I'm in," I respond flatly.

I'm sure it will be *tons* of fun.

ALSO BY T. TORREST

The REMEMBER WHEN Trilogy
Starring Jack's cousin, Layla Warren.

Flash back to the '80s in this decades-long coming of age romantic comedy between a smoking hot, A-list Hollywood actor and his high school sweetheart.
It's hysterically funny, super steamy, rip-your-guts-out heartwrenching, and incredibly romantic.

#1 Teen Romance
#1 Highest-Rated New Adult
#2 Romantic Comedy (Thanks a lot, Janet Evanovich.)

Find all three books at all major bookseller sites worldwide.

ALSO BY T. TORREST

BREAKING THE ICE

Sidle up to the bar at The Westlake Pub.

A second-chance love story between a superhot ex-NHL-player-turned-bar-owner and the straitlaced event planner who comes barging back into his life.

Find all three books at all major bookseller sites worldwide.

Down the Shore
T. Torrest

Copyright ©2015

Made in the USA
Middletown, DE
31 July 2020